D0901703

BERSERKER

JACK LIVELY

GENERAL PROJECTS

1

THE ATTACK

ONE

ANKARA, Turkey. November 16, 2016.

TOM KEELER OPENED his eyes and saw Calcutti's weathered face looming over him like a desert cliff blocking sunlight. "You're up."

"For what?"

"Canada didn't respond to the ping, so I sent Karim up an hour ago. He says they've pulled the curtain."

Keeler got up on an elbow. *Canada* was the code name for a safe house up in the diplomatic district. "What's the move?"

"I'm switching Karim to overwatch. I want you to do the pass at Canada."

Keeler nodded and swung his feet off the narrow bed to the floor. Calcutti looked at him and walked out. Across the room, another man grunted and rolled onto his side to face the wall. Bratton was up next for a shift, which was why Calcutti had woken Keeler. He put on his boots and stood up, feeling the buzz as his joints cracked pleasantly.

Keeler strapped on a money belt and checked that he had

cash inside, plus the passport he'd used to enter Turkey. You never knew what would happen, so it was best to be prepared, even for a training mission.

Five of them were in the apartment, taking rotating four-hour shifts in the ready room. Three guys on duty, two guys in the back bedroom. Keeler had come off shift only two hours before.

He took his jacket from where it hung behind the door and walked into the front room of the apartment. Calcutti was on the sofa with a bag of spicy Turkish potato chips. The window was curtained with a batik sheet held in place by a couple of thumbtacks. The sunlight coming through was orange.

Calcutti pointed a red-powdered crinkle-cut chip at him. "You do your SDR and see if Karim can pick you up in Çankaya." He crunched a handful of chips between powerful jaws. "Mess him up, Keeler, test that kid. Make it hard."

The toilet flushed and Cheevers emerged, looking tired. Keeler noticed that he hadn't washed his hands.

Calcutti said, "Mr. Cheevers, issue Keeler a weapon, please, he's going for the pass at Canada."

Cheevers looked at Keeler, then back at Calcutti, deadpanning. "Just the nine or you want the operational pack too?"

"Just the weapon."

Cheevers shrugged, went to the kitchen, pulled open a panel on the tiled wall, and began rooting around in the cavity. He came up with a plastic-wrapped Yavuz 9mm, the Turkish version of a Beretta 92. Keeler removed the plastic wrap, balled it up, and tossed it in the can. He checked the pistol, inserted one of the magazines, and checked it again before slipping the weapon into his jacket pocket.

He was confused about the combination of training the new guy, name of Karim, and the fact that Canada had missed a ping. He said, "So what's the deal with Canada? Is that for real?"

Calcutti wiped potato chip residue on his jeans. "I don't know. If I did, I'd have told you. Just go up there and check it out. Probably bullshit. Use the opportunity to grind Karim a little."

Keeler said, "I'm asking if they actually missed the ping."

Calcutti nodded slowly and shrugged. "Affirmative."

The three men stood in the apartment's entrance. Keeler pushed earbuds into his ears. The buds looked identical to the civilian version, but were different on the inside. He paired them to an iPhone, also a heavily modded version of the civilian device. Calcutti thumbed a device into his left ear and spoke. "Feel me, bro?"

The voice came through into Keeler's ears, stereo and clear. "Roger that."

He tapped on the earbud and got the electronic click. Tapped twice and got two. Nodded at Calcutti.

Calcutti said, "Switching to channel five." Spoke into the air. "This is Sierra, Charlie, do you copy overwatch?"

Karim's voice came through. "Copy." Something about how the vowel met a consonant gave away Karim's Middle Eastern accent.

Calcutti looked at Cheevers while speaking to Karim on overwatch. "Kitty is leaving Brooklyn."

Keeler left the apartment, another safe house, this one code-named *Brooklyn*.

He rapidly descended three flights of stairs to the street, enjoying the movement. The November air felt clean and crisp, Ankara being a city at a high elevation, almost a thousand meters. Keeler started the steep walk up the hill to Çankaya, where all the embassies were located. The neighborhood quickly turned residential, the shops and restaurants thinning out.

He walked the Surveillance Detection Route, moving the way he'd been taught, unpredictably, switching back on himself and ducking into alleys and street food stalls and generally doing whatever he could to smoke out any mobile squad that might be on him.

The team was on a training mission and Ankara was a great place for it. The capital of Turkey was teeming with spooks, all of them looking out for surveillance, many of them hostile to Americans. If a new guy like Karim could make it in Ankara, everyone would feel a whole lot better about working with him when it wasn't a training mission.

Keeler went up to Çankaya the long way, down the other side and up again through Botanik Park. At the other side of the park he entered Atakule, a shopping mall in the shape of an enormous donut, and took the escalator down three levels to a Lacoste store. He tried on a sweater and flirted with the saleswoman, complimenting her on her English. He bought a latte.

Karim's hoarse voice croaked into Keeler's ears on his way out of the mall.

"This is overwatch. Blue skies." Karim, telling him that he was clean of surveillance and could proceed.

Keeler hadn't seen him and was mildly impressed he'd come in the back way. Keeler tapped twice on the right earbud, confirming receipt of the message. "Good. I didn't clock you." He waited for bravado but it didn't come, which is another reason people liked Karim. "What's the deal with Canada?"

The audio popped in his ear. Karim said, "I went up the back way and the curtain was pulled. I called it in."

"Okay. I'll finish the SDR and take a look. Just stay with me."

The street was pleasant, cafés set back from the road with

patios and outdoor heating. Couples sitting around drinking coffee. A group of friends playing cards. Karim was a local of Turkish and Persian descent who'd been recruited as a street operative able to blend into the environment. So far so good. It had been a while since any of them had managed to screw Karim up; he was coming along nicely.

TWO

KEELER JUMPED ON A BUS. Wondered how Karim would keep an eye on him. He checked in the crowd, but didn't see him. Maybe he was mobile—on a bike or a scooter? He jumped off the bus ten minutes later.

"Status?"

Karim's voice came through again. "You just came off the bus, and you're looking at the nut stand thinking about roasted cashews. Blue skies."

Proceed.

Canada was an apartment on the fourth floor of a building set back from the street behind another, larger building. It was accessed by a pretty path curving through a garden that the autumn foliage had turned to orange and brown.

What Keeler didn't like was the taxi parked across the street, the driver sitting still at the wheel, a newspaper spread in front of him. He clicked once on the earbud.

"I see it," Karim responded. "There's a store on the corner. Go in there and buy the nuts you've been craving."

Keeler walked past the taxi, ignoring it. He still hadn't seen

Karim. Maybe he was leading, keeping watch from the front, anticipating Keeler's movements.

He got to the corner and went into the little store and took his time buying a bag of roasted nuts.

Karim's voice: "You can enter the back way, it's clear. You'll be unsighted in the park."

Keeler crossed the street. The taxi was still parked in the middle of the block. Karim must have checked it out and decided the driver was just a driver. Keeler walked downhill a block. He turned left to cut into a small neighborhood park and sat on a bench eating the nuts.

Three other benches faced north. Two of them were occupied by men looking or talking into phones. One middle-aged, the other a young guy eating Burger King and watching a loud video. A mother ate the leftovers of a children's snack, her three kids cavorting around a sandpit with a climbing structure.

A third man entered the park from the north. He wore a brown leather jacket, jeans, and leather ankle boots. Midthirties with thinning hair greased and combed back over the visible pink of his skull. He glanced at Keeler and kept moving, out of the park the way Keeler had entered.

Keeler let the guy leave. He spoke into the earbuds. "You see that guy? Looked spicy to me."

"Just seeing him now. He's walking down to Tehran Street. I'm going to let him go."

Keeler gave it a couple of minutes before standing up and crossing to the north side. He took a little path through a wooden fence and ended up at the rear of the apartment building where the safe house was located. The building was unfinished and looked half abandoned. Six floors with the top two levels yet to be completed and open to the elements. Ropes and pulleys hung down from the sixth floor, snaking into open window cavities on the fifth.

From where Keeler stood, he could see one of the fourth-floor windows. The curtain was drawn all the way closed—the emergency signal.

He said, "Sierra, Charlie. Confirm red light."

Calcutti's voice came through. "Copy that, Kitty. Go in for a look but do not touch, repeat do not touch."

Keeler tapped the earbud twice instead of speaking. *Click, click.* He scanned the park and the surrounding buildings, before turning his attention back to the safe house. A staircase going up the back of the building looked pretty unsafe. Some of the structure showed steel reinforcing bars waiting for the poured concrete. The stairs themselves looked okay. He walked up, past the fourth floor, giving the empty corridor a good glance before continuing to five.

Karim's voice cut in. "I've got you covered on the stairs, but you'll be naked inside."

Keeler tapped twice on the earbud. No backup from here on out, which made this kind of work different. On a regular JSOC op, they'd never go in with one guy like this, even for a training run. Joint Special Operations Command ran four-man teams, minimum. Stealth drones and sniper overwatch too. But that wasn't how it worked with the clandestine service.

The fifth floor had walls but no windows and no doors. Keeler looked inside and saw construction equipment and pools of rainwater. Back by the staircase, he stood looking out over the park and finished the bag of nuts. Turkish nuts were good. Not as good as what he'd been getting in Syria, but pretty good anyway. Definitely better than American nuts.

He climbed to the sixth floor and stood at a gaping hole in the half-built wall, looking over the city. That part of Ankara was very quiet and residential and rich. The middle-aged guy in the park had looked like a Turkish government functionary. The younger guy had looked like a migrant from the south, Syria or

Iraq. But had he looked like a combatant or an asylum-seeking refugee? The taxi across the street was another interesting data point.

Keeler finished chewing. "Sierra, Charlie, I'm up on the sixth floor. Nothing visually off. I want to go down to four and touch base."

Calcutti's voice came through. "Overwatch?"

Karim said, "Blue skies from where I'm standing."

Keeler couldn't see where Karim was standing.

Calcutti said, "Overwatch, you keep back. Kitty, you're clear. Move in and keep the line open."

"Copy that."

Keeler went down to the fourth floor and entered the corridor. The building was relatively narrow, and each floor had only one apartment. The door was across from the elevator. The indicator above the elevator showed zero, which in Turkey was the ground floor. He knocked on the door and waited. No answer. Keeler could hear Calcutti breathing on the other side of the encrypted military satellite connection.

He pulled the sleeve of his sweater down over his right hand and grasped the knob. It turned and he pushed the door open. Immediately inside he saw a thick smear of dark blood on the tiled floor. The smear had been made by a boot. The owner of the boot lay face up with his throat cut. The wall next to him had been sprayed with arterial blood, now pooled below his corpse.

Keeler's first thought was that the simulation was pretty damned good. They'd set it up to look ultra-realistic. But the stench that hit his nostrils from inside the apartment blew that thought away. This was no simulation.

He took a step back from the open door and stood listening. Time to reorient.

Keeler didn't know if there were hostiles in the apartment.

Calcutti's voice came through the earbuds. "Give me a sit-rep, Kitty."

Keeler tapped his forefinger on the earbuds. *Click click click.* Three rapid hits in a row to signal that he couldn't talk. Two clicks came back. Message received.

He drew the pistol and snicked back the slide, putting a round into the chamber. To his left was a narrow window looking into the back of the building next door. Mild traffic noise came from a block away. A cat meowed and someone coughed, maybe from the second or third floor.

Keeler didn't wait any longer. He stepped into the apartment and shut the door behind him.

THREE

THE KILL LOOKED RELATIVELY fresh to Keeler's practiced eye. The stuff on the wall and the smear had begun coagulating, but the blood collecting below the body had more volume and hadn't started to thicken around the rim area. The dead man was approximately forty years old with a dark shock of straight hair. His light-brown eyes were open, looking into nothing.

Keeler stepped around the corpse.

The entrance gave onto a living room with an open-plan kitchen straight ahead and to the left. There was more blood splatter. The place was cluttered with takeout containers and empty water bottles. Whoever had been living there hadn't been big on cleaning up after themselves. Worse, the apartment was foul with the stench of excrement and the rusty odor of human blood.

A second corpse was curled in a fetal position by the coffee table, throat cut and blood from the carotid artery soaking into a Persian carpet. This one was female and maybe thirty-five years old. The dead woman's sweater had gotten rucked up so that her back was exposed above the bra strap. Keeler resisted the urge to pull the sweater down. The corpse's hair was blond but dyed. She had been a natural brunette.

A floor lamp had been turned over and now leaned against the couch by the wall. A camera tripod stood in the center of the room, well back from the windows. The tripod mount was raised high, maybe six feet up. A simple chair stood next to it. There was no camera attached to the tripod. Something caught his eye, and Keeler glanced to his left to see a hand extending on the floor tiles past the kitchen island.

The hand was connected to another body. Male and older, maybe fifty. Gray hair and a salt and pepper beard. This one had been shot in the chest once. The killers hadn't been satisfied with a bullet, they'd cut his throat and let him bleed out like the others. Keeler pictured the sucking bullet wound. The guy dropping, gasping in shock. A big kitchen knife lay on the floor near his outstretched hand. The knife had been used. The man had managed to stab one of his attackers.

There was a good quantity of blood on the tiled floor. Impossible to tell if some of it had once belonged to an attacker, at least not until someone ran a forensic analysis of the scene. Despite the takeout wrappers and disposable junk polluting the place, the counter area near the sink was clean. A French press gleamed next to a large bag of ground coffee, sealed with a black clip. A minimalist draining rack held plates, coffee cups, and a small quantity of cutlery.

Looked like a division of labor. Someone had taken command of a small area of the safe house and had insisted on a limited degree of order, which made no sense. The safe house was supposed to be cold, nonoperational. The clandestine service would have a skeleton crew to make sure it was maintained, but this wasn't just maintenance. It looked to Keeler like a full-on operation was being run out of the place.

Keeler pushed that out of his mind and went through the narrative.

Gray-haired guy makes it to the kitchen and gets his hands on the knife. He surprises one of the attackers and is able to draw blood before they put him down. The attackers aren't satisfied with a bullet. They cut his throat. Since that had been a needless act, it now assumed a symbolic aspect in Keeler's mind.

They were sending a message.

The apartment had two bedrooms, each equipped with twin beds. One of the bedrooms was a disgusting mess, the other was relatively clean. The cleaner bedroom faced south and had the white cotton curtains that Keeler had seen from below. There was a bathroom with tub and shower and an empty clothes-drying rack. The toilet was separate, in a room the size of a closet with a single small ventilation window facing the building next door. The window was open.

Once he'd cleared the apartment and was sure that no hostiles remained, he opened a living room window and stood by it, breathing in the fresh air. Looking out, he saw the clear blue sky and skeletal branches of the trees losing leaves.

Karim was out there waiting, as was Calcutti.

Keeler tapped the AirPod earbud once. *Click.* He said, "Canada is clear."

Calcutti's voice. "Overwatch?"

Karim said, "Blue skies."

Calcutti again. "What's the deal, Kitty?"

Keeler had checked the corpses and ransacked the entire apartment. Besides the clothing on the bodies, he found zero personal possessions, no identification documents and no phones. If there had been any spare clothes or personal effects, they'd been removed.

He said, "I've got real bodies here. Three dead people, throats cut. Relatively recently. The other thing is that this place is operational." He looked at the tripod, lonely without a camera. "Surveillance or maybe they were doing interrogations, not clear."

He heard Calcutti drawing breath. The older man's voice came through, pissed off but professional. "Copy that. Get out of there and get clean. You two stick to the routine and run a full SDR. Don't come back here until you get in touch for permission."

Keeler said, "Copy that."

Keeler's gaze fell to the tripod. He was over six feet tall and didn't need the chair. Someone shorter had been operating the camera. He got himself in-line with the tripod head. From that vantage point he had an east-facing observational view out the window to three neighboring apartment buildings. Not only was the camera missing, the mounting plate was gone. Someone had hastily taken the camera directly off the tripod, not taking the time to unscrew the mount.

He looked down at the woman on the Persian carpet, and it occurred to him that none of these dead people looked American. They looked Turkish, which was weird since Canada was a CIA safe house.

Not that you could tell a hundred percent. Both of the guys had what Keeler thought of as a Turkish haircut. The woman's hair dye wasn't proof either, but it added up to a feeling. All of which could be a manufactured performance, a way for clandestine American operatives to fit in to their surroundings, but he didn't think so. Keeler got down from the chair and went to the older dead guy in the kitchen. He pried open the man's jaws and saw a mass of dental fillings in the back of his mouth. He did the same for the other two corpses.

More fillings than an average American of their age would have. The Turkish government did zero water fluoridation, which meant Turkish nationals growing up in their home country would have an eighty percent greater chance of tooth decay than a comparable American.

Karim's voice came over the coms. "This is overwatch. Is there a problem, Kitty?"

Keeler said, "I'm coming."

He exited the apartment and closed the door behind him. The park was now completely empty. It was afternoon and the sun was getting low. Keeler walked the long way around and then up the hill and took a right on the street he'd originally taken. The taxi was gone.

TWO HOURS LATER, it was dark and Keeler entered a market, lit up and boisterous. He and Karim had worked their way deep into northeast Ankara, an area populated by asylum seekers and migrants. There had been no visual contact between them, but Karim had his back, watching over him for any hostile surveillance.

Sellers hawked spices and dried nuts and fruit, kitchen utensils and Tupperware, fish and coffee. Meat sizzled over burning embers and slid from steel skewers into freshly baked bread lathered with onions and chili sauce. The place was bustling with hungry people back from hard work, crowding around the hot coals, mesmerized by the blackened chunks of grilling meat.

Karim emerged out of the crowd. Keeler almost didn't recognize him.

He was a thin man in his early forties, the son of a Kurdish woman and an Iranian doctor. He'd grown up in Istanbul speaking fluent Farsi, Turkish, and Kurdish dialects. His dad had left Iran under duress and his grandparents had been killed by the Turkish military in one of the regular genocidal massacres.

Anti-regime didn't even begin to describe the hostility Karim had for authoritarian rule.

He called it a midlife crisis, approaching the Americans and offering his help. They'd put him through a year and a half of training. Now, Karim was at the end of the clandestine pipeline, learning from the best. Keeler figured Karim would be able to recruit more local operatives to work for the Americans. In time he'd become a real spook.

They exchanged looks. Keeler said, "Fully FUBAR."

Karim had learned what that meant. He nodded. "Let's eat."

They pushed through the crowd and acquired hot handfuls, retreating to a bench and sitting side by side. The kebab was good and warming. Keeler ate it hungrily. When they were done, Karim secured paper cups of coffee and a fistful of sweet baklava, loaded with honey.

Keeler took three sips of coffee to each bite of baklava. He looked at Karim. "I've figured out what was bothering me."

Karim gave him a look like, *What are you talking about?* No way he could have guessed with his mouth fully occupied. Some kind of grunt came out of it.

Keeler said, "Three corpses in the apartment, but four coffee cups on the draining rack in the kitchen." He slurped at the thick black brew. "I was trying to visualize it while we ran the SDR. I'm a hundred percent sure. Four cups and maybe four plates drying on the rack."

Karim wasn't slow. "Someone's missing, is what you're saying."

Keeler crushed the paper cup in his hand. "Yeah. I don't know. Maybe hiding or something. We have to go back."

Karim's wise face looked at him. "Aye aye, Captain."

But Calcutti wasn't having it.

His voice came hot and heavy over the encrypted connection. "While you two were dicking around I was getting reamed by command, and I don't like getting reamed. We're out of here, immediate exfiltration. You two don't get back within the hour, you'll have to make your own way out, plus the court-martial for you, Kitty, the way these people are talking."

Keeler said, "You didn't hear what I said, Calcutti. There's a missing operative up at Canada. We're not leaving one of our people behind."

He visualized Calcutti's face contorting into an angry rictus. "A, there wasn't supposed to be anyone to leave behind, B, it's not our operation, whatever they were doing there. Get your ass back here, Kitty, that's an order."

Keeler broke the connection and looked Karim in the eye. "Meet you back at Brooklyn. No need for overwatch. Capisce?"

The guy looking at him, intelligent eyes searching. Keeler dead-eyed him and hoped it worked. Karim finally broke the contact and looked away.

"My uncle's a truck driver here in Turkey. He goes cross-country all the time, and it's a big country. Those drivers like to talk. You know what, they still use CB radio to speak."

"Is that right, with the old-school handsets and everything?"

Karim looked at him. "These days they use apps on phones." He held up an iPhone. "You download it onto one of these and boom, you're suddenly talking to truckers."

Karim rose and tapped him on the shoulder. "You won't see me up in Çankaya, but I'll be in the truck, brother." He stood there for a moment. "I'll be Spiderman and you'll be the Flash. We'll use channel nineteen. Capisce?"

Keeler nodded. "Capisce." He hadn't wanted to ask Karim to come up with him again. For one thing, it was against orders. Another reason was that Karim was not an American, he was a foreign contractor with the company. But the man had understood the warrior's imperative.

Nobody on the team gets left on the battlefield. Period.

He watched Karim blend into the night, thinking about how quickly he'd set up a clandestine communications scheme using something as mundane as a CB radio, blending in with truckers. As if he'd done it before. Which, come to think of it, was pretty likely given Karim's age. He'd probably been a decent criminal before signing on with the United States Clandestine Services.

Keeler had a little laugh to himself. Criminal experience would be useful in this line of work.

Calcutti and the other guys working for JSOC came from a variety of teams: Delta, Seals, the Intelligence Support Agency. Serious teams with tough mottos, mostly about how resilient their operatives were. Keeler didn't know the other mottos, but he was a pararescue operator, and the PJ motto is *These Things We Do, That Others May Live.*

FOUR

Keeler took a taxi back to Çankaya.

In the back of the cab he found a CB radio app and downloaded it. As the nocturnal scenery went by, Keeler thought about what had just happened. A quick series of surprise events. Surprise number one, the clear evidence that there had been an operation running out of Canada. Surprise number two, three dead bodies. Surprise number three, what Calcutti had said about being ordered to withdraw from the safe house.

A weird exfiltration, as far as Keeler was concerned.

Clearly, someone, somewhere was doing some tricky shit. Dollars to donuts it would be an office-based type of person, comfortable with the commuter lifestyle, wearing clean shirts and sitting around conference tables in a Virginia suburb. Keeler had the earbuds in, listening to whatever was coming from the Turkish trucker band on channel nineteen. None of which he could understand. Mostly crackling and a voice here and there speaking in their language.

He tested it. "This is Flash for Spiderman. Out."

Karim's voice came through in a field of hiss and crackle, intermittently present as remote syllables and vowel fragments, essentially unintelligible. Keeler figured they were out of range. He made the driver drop him off five blocks from Canada. The night had brought a chill to quiet streets.

He thought, *Assume four operatives had been working out of the safe house.* Three were now dead and the fourth could have escaped or been taken captive. Another possibility, the fourth guy was out of the apartment when the attack occurred. Keeler remembered the empty takeout boxes, so someone was fetching dinner most nights. Which made sense. You don't order delivery to a clandestine safe house.

He came down the hill from a parallel street to the front entrance, where the taxi had been earlier. He cut through a gap between residential buildings, hopping the fence dividing the rear gardens. The ground-floor apartment was lit. Through the rear windows he could see a family of five eating dinner, the mother spooning rice from a large pot to three kids as dad waited hungrily.

He found a vantage point close to the street where he could see the building's entrance and crouched in a shadowed section of brush. Keeler pushed the volume up on the CB radio app. Still crackles and hissing. He spoke quietly into the microphone built into his earbuds.

"Flash for Spiderman, over."

Karim's voice came through. "This is Spiderman. I have oversight at the rear. Blue skies. Over."

The rear was good. Keeler was looking at the front, which was the image of calm. He said, "Flash for Spiderman. You stay on the rear and let me know if you see anything spicy, otherwise radio silence. There's too much noise on this thing. Over."

"Spiderman for Flash. Roger that. Out."

The CB radio was fine as a backup, but he wasn't about to keep that hiss and crackle in his ears while operating. Keeler got himself in the mission mindset, calm and collected. A minute later he was feeling good, letting the adrenaline settle. He let five minutes pass, watching and listening. If there was surveillance, he wasn't seeing it.

Keeler went up the staircase two at a time. The Yavuz 9mm encased in his large right hand.

This time, the apartment was dark, moonlight coming through the windows and casting the scene in a cold glow. He made his way past the corpse in the entrance. It was eerie seeing how the dead had remained perfectly still, like furniture.

Keeler canvassed the apartment again, looking for possible hidden panels but not finding any. The toilet's ventilation window was open. You could see right through to the building next door, maybe three or four yards away. He stepped up onto the seat and hoisted himself so that his head poked out through the small opening. It wasn't comfortable, but if push came to shove he'd be able to force his shoulders through. Head out the window, Keeler was facing directly down, four floors to a dark and tight alleyway below.

He twisted his body to the right. A fat drainage pipe ran vertically up the wall, definitely within reach of the window. To grab hold of it and climb would be an acrobatic act, for sure. Possible to perform, but not easy. The question was, if a fourth person in the apartment had come out this way, had they gone up or down?

Keeler pulled himself inside and sat on the closed toilet seat.

Down would be the obvious direction of escape for a nonprofessional, extremely risky because a competent attacker would cover exit routes. Up would also be risky because you'd be essentially trapped. He remembered the fifth floor, a construction site. Up would be better. Get to the fifth floor and into the best concealment available. Maybe even a hiding place prepared in advance.

Keeler took the stairs to the unfinished apartment on the

fifth floor. There were no lights up there, just the shape of construction materials and moonlight playing over the hard contours. Wind gusted through the window openings, whipping at plastic sheeting that covered a huge cement mixer and raising fine dust from the floor. On the far side Keeler could see a pigeon walking through a moonlit puddle. He kept moving.

Large plastic buckets were lined up by the window. Ropes hung from the pulleys he'd seen upstairs. They were making the cement down here on the fifth floor and sending it through the window up to sixth to pour the roof. Keeler had worked as a roofer in New Hampshire one summer. He'd carried stacks of roof tiles up a ladder ten hours a day for about eight weeks. At least these people used a rope and pulley system.

He raised the volume on the CB app, listening for Karim's voice, but hearing only static and the intermittent laughter and conversation of Turkish truckers. Keeler looked out the unfinished window, down into the darkness. He saw only trees and brush and built structures. Nothing moving and nothing human.

He thought, *No news is good news.*

From behind him, a sound, something alive, like pigeons. He turned and moved past a load-bearing pillar, stepping to the left and keeping it at his back. Keeler gazed into the darkness, letting his pupils fully dilate. The sound came again from the dark. He felt a chill creep up from his chest to the top of his head.

FIVE

HE WAITED to hear that sound again. A shuffle, or maybe some kind of vocalization. It came again as a kind of moan from over by the cement mixer. Keeler moved forward, the Yavuz 9mm up and tracking in sync with his eyes. The tarp covering the cement mixer was weird, not covering it, more like stuffed into it. He grasped the sheeting and tugged it out.

First he saw a pair of boots, or more specifically, the soles of boots. The legs were clad in black denim and pressed together, knee to knee. He could tell immediately that it was a woman, the position and small size of the boots.

Keeler said. "I'm here to help you. I'm American."

A shallow moan came from the dark cavity.

He pulled the woman out of the big cement mixer, like pulling something out of a huge sticky trap. She was alive, muttering something that he couldn't hear, maybe five feet tall with small bones and light to carry. Keeler was able to hold her in his arms and lay her down on the bare concrete floor. Her face and body were covered in dried and crusted cement.

It was dark and he couldn't see her properly, so he moved the woman to an area slashed with moonlight. She had dyed black hair and a lined face, maybe sixty years old. She was breathing softly and trying to say something. Keeler leaned in to hear, but couldn't make it out. He realized she wasn't speaking English.

He leaned over her. "I'm an American." He looked for a sign of recognition. Not finding any and figuring she was wounded, he said, "Show me where you're hurt."

The woman was pushing at Keeler's hip. He looked down, something was being pressed at him, a camera with a large lens. The tripod mount was attached. Keeler took the camera. He found the memory card and ejected it from the device. He slid it into the coin pocket of his jeans.

"Let's get you out of here." Keeler figured she'd been wounded in the belly or groin but he couldn't see.

He put the camera on the floor next to him and reached down to feel around the woman's lower torso. His hand came back sticky with blood. Either shot or stabbed, which begged the question of how she'd gotten out of there unseen. Climbing up the drainage pipe with a bullet in the belly was some feat, but then people are capable of all kinds of things in the panicked moments after being wounded, before the shock sets in.

There was a sound from outside as something passed from one side of the apartment to the other very fast, the sound louder when it crossed the windows. He felt the woman's body stiffen against him, she recognized the sound, as did Keeler—a micro reconnaissance drone. He glanced down at the woman and caught the glossy shine of an eye looking up in fear at the ceiling.

Keeler ran in a crouch to the closest window. He stood to the side, in the shadow. Looked down at the garden five floors below. Nobody in sight, nothing moving. A residential neighborhood at dinner time. He thought about Karim. No warning, either the overwatch was still unaware, or he'd been compromised.

He turned up the volume on the CB radio feed, crackle and hiss and foreign voices. No Karim. Keeler turned off the useless thing.

The drone was quiet. He kept very still and saw it moving in through one of the window cavities about fifteen feet away, long as the width of his hand, maybe five inches, whirring with a stealthy insectile sound. If this hadn't been an empty construction site at night, he probably wouldn't have been able to hear it. The drone flew slowly, scanning the darkness through an infrared sensor. Hover time maybe twenty minutes, range maybe a mile, maximum.

The operator would be closer than that.

But would he be friendly? Keeler moderated his breathing, slowing down his heartbeat and reducing adrenaline flow. He calculated the odds. Eighty percent chance this was an unfriendly force, twenty percent he was facing a team sent by the embassy after Calcutti had called in.

The drone found the woman curled up on the floor and visibly shivering with fear. The machine hovered, tough to see in the dark, sucking up her enhanced image and sending it down the line to the operator and whoever might be looking over his shoulder. A glowing red dot appeared through the front entrance, playing over walls, a laser sight. Someone was coming up the stairs. The dot was joined by a second, jerking crazily, dilating as the operators approached.

Keeler backed up, keeping the load-bearing pillar between himself and the drone. He arrived at the open window and zipped the pistol into his jacket pocket. No way of signaling to the people coming in, and no way of engaging, since he didn't know who they were. He grabbed hold of one of the ropes coming in the window and swung out easily, almost lazy in the movement. Letting his boot take the weight, he braced himself against the exterior wall for a moment, getting his balance. Keeler went up the rope, hand over hand, fast and silent. Each grab accompanied by a silent boot against the wall, grab, boot, grab, boot, getting a rhythm going until he reached the lip of the sixth floor, settling just below it.

He twisted the rope once around his right arm, feeling the steel muscle operating smoothly. He got his feet maneuvered around the line, gripping with the thighs first and then the feet, locking on and distributing body weight. A second micro reconnaissance drone whirred from above, checking out the sixth.

It was pretty nice up there, hung alongside the building, breathing easily. He scanned below him, six stories and maybe a forty foot drop.

Karim. What was going on with the guy?

Nothing was happening down below, it was like a very calm evening in a classy neighborhood, people finishing up dinner and maybe reading a book on the sofa, maybe watching a TV show or a movie. Civilians, people who believed what they saw on the news, unaware of these stealthy operators, which was at least some indication that they probably weren't Turkish.

Because if they were, they wouldn't need to be quiet about it.

SIX

From the fifth floor apartment below came muffled sounds and a weak voice that he thought was the woman. Above on the sixth Keeler heard the scraping of boots. Whoever was up there got close to the edge. Keeler could hear the rustle of clothing as the operator cleared the area.

Mixed into that audioscape were the whispering drones, probing and scouting. One thing Keeler knew: if the drone found him, he'd definitely have issues.

The current estimate was four to five operators moving above and below. The audio signature from below had changed. Shifting and scraping and shuffling sounds and a moan. They were taking the woman out and there wasn't a damn thing he could do about it.

The drones went quiet. He waited.

Four minutes later there were no more sounds from either above or below. He eased himself up the rope to the edge of the sixth floor and peered over the low wall. Nobody there, nothing moving. It was now just himself and the lifeless construction equipment and materials.

Fact: he was responsible for the woman, a wounded comrade on the battlefield.

Keeler turned up the CB radio app and got the usual crackle and hiss.

He came down the stairs quiet and fast, feet fluttering over the steps. Out of the building, he took a right through the alley he'd seen from the toilet window. Over on the other side of the property he hopped a chain-link fence and crept up to the street through the neighboring yard, careful that the dry leaves didn't crunch loudly.

Keeler stayed behind a low stone wall separating the garden from the street. To the left were figures in front of the building. He watched through the skeletal branches of a leafless bush, two men dressed in black with baseball hats and close-cropped beards, both of them out in the road. One of them spoke into a handheld device, the other paced back and forth. They were expecting something.

He waited. A car came from the other direction and both men turned. Keeler took the opportunity to roll over the wall and come up in a stroll like a regular guy out for an evening walk. If these people were American, he needed to make contact. If they weren't, his mission was to stop them from taking the woman.

The men spotted him quickly and adjusted configuration. One moved in toward the building, the other stayed out in the street, making a funnel for Keeler to walk through at a tactical disadvantage. When he was about twenty feet away, he saw two other men, deeper into the shadowed path leading to the building. One of them blocked a full view of the woman Keeler had found curled into the cement mixer. She was barely visible, a slouched figure propped up by the second guy.

Keeler passed between the outer-facing operators. He gave them an open and appraising look and they looked back, males of military age, with focused expressions and the calm demeanor of seasoned combatants.

None of them recognized him, which meant that he wasn't known to these people. No good way of engaging them without putting the woman into unacceptable risk.

A couple of steps past them, Keeler saw what they'd been waiting for, a van coming up the street from the main road, headlights on high beam. He could feel eyeballs on his back and imagined worse, laser sights between the shoulder blades. The image was so vivid, that he actually felt the itch. He stepped between parked cars into the street in front of the van, making the driver brake for him. He crossed to the other side.

The vehicle was a well-used white Renault van, maybe ten years old. One driver, no passenger. Driver wearing a black baseball cap with the close-trimmed chin beard a lot of young Middle Eastern guys sport.

On the opposite sidewalk, Keeler turned and looked at the van. No windows in the back, a good number of dents. He jogged back, pacing the vehicle and keeping in the driver's blind spot. The 9mm Yavuz was now in his hand, feeling solid and good. He was coming at the driver's side of the van, keeping away from the side mirror, but close enough that the van hid his presence from the operators on the other side.

The driver's window was half open, the man's face at a three-quarter rear angle, focused on the mission. A chiseled jaw covered in fuzz, thin mustache. He stopped the van ten yards from the front entrance. Keeler came up on him and reached in through the window, jamming the pistol under his chin hard.

He spoke in a whisper. "Authenticate." The driver moved his head slightly in Keeler's direction. The eyes were remarkable, grey green, the pupils tiny, given the low light. It was weird. It gave the driver a hard predatory look, somewhere between a fox and a wolf. Keeler pushed the weapon deep into the soft place under the man's jaw. "Authenticate. Two seconds."

If the driver was part of an American team, he'd understand. He'd say something, like a brevity code, or some other means of authenticating himself to a friendly combatant. Keeler was aware of his situation, the weakness of his position. He was a second away from blowing the head off a friendly combatant in a hostile battlefield. That was a possibility, as was its opposite, a hostile team capturing an American asset in the field.

He thought, *Either way you lose, but it's not about you.*

Two things happened simultaneously, broken down into multiple sub-actions, all of which precipitated a major third event.

The driver kept his head very still, but Keeler caught the movement of his left eyeball in its socket, to the right. He followed the look and made eye contact with an operator on the other side, looking directly at him. The driver hit the accelerator pedal and the van leapt forward. The window frame knocked Keeler's arm back and he almost lost his grip on the weapon.

When the driver had stamped on the pedal, two operators surged up from the driveway with the woman between them, gripped by the arms. Her face appeared momentarily in the van's headlights, pale, drawn and lined and unhappy, but alive, with open eyes darting frantically. Then she was in motion, propelled by the men into the path of the oncoming vehicle.

Keeler saw the impact as a sequence of very fast strobe images. A shock of dyed hair fanning up as the front of the van slammed flush into the woman's face. The hit made a solid sound, like a dull thud meets a bone-breaking smack. The body momentarily rose and disappeared beneath the vehicle. The van continued over her before stopping. The whole thing blandly simple and quick.

The van's door slid open on the other side. Keeler sprinted

up at the driver, watching the window lifting shut as he came, handgun up. The driver moved his head a little to look back at him. Those eyes again, grey-green and seemingly translucent. Not a wolf's eyes—more watchful and careful like a jackal's.

Keeler braced and squeezed three 9mm rounds into the glass, aiming for the driver's face and going for the same spot on the window. The glass spidered and fogged but the bullets didn't penetrate. The driver looked at him calmly for a moment before hitting the gas pedal and speeding away. The rear tire bumped over the body and Keeler was alone with the woman in the middle of a quiet residential street.

SEVEN

SHE LAY CRUMPLED, the road dark beneath her pale skin. The woman coughed once and her eyes opened to slits. He leaned down and heard her say three words "With the girl."

Like it was the end of a sentence.

He leaned forward farther, feeling her breath on his ear. "What girl?"

"You help the girl." The Middle Eastern accent was apparent now. The woman coughed again and rolled slightly, her eyes suddenly meeting his, hard and wounded. "You pledge." Keeler pulled back. A thin and hard hand whipped out to clutch his jacket. The eyes, not so much pleading as accusing. Her entire body seemed to strain from the effort of speaking, neck veins popping. "You make a pledge to help her."

Keeler wasn't sentimental about death. Any other person in that woman's condition, he'd walk away. But this was a fellow combatant, in her death throes on the battlefield. She was likely a team member, and you don't walk away from someone on your team. He had no idea what she'd been talking about.

Her fingers pulled in, clutching, eyes imploring. Keeler

gently put his hand over hers and she released her grip. He looked into her eyes. "Sure, ma'am, I'll help the girl if I can."

Not that he knew who the girl was.

The woman's eyes didn't change so much as turn dead. He'd seen it enough times, the eyes lose the shine of life and become simple reflective objects, like glass marbles. In this case, the glint of a streetlight became obvious in the convex bulge between eyelids like worn paper.

Keeler had noticed something else. The woman's blouse was unbuttoned, as were her jeans. They'd searched her body unceremoniously, without regard for her, fast and rough and efficient, presumably looking for the memory card from the camera. Keeler pressed his thumb against the change pocket of his jeans, felt the rigid rectangular outline through the denim.

They wouldn't be getting that card, that was for damned sure.

He remembered Karim, and the CB radio thing, which hadn't worked out at all. Keeler raised the volume on his device and heard static crackle and hiss, not even a trucker's voice.

"Flash for Spiderman. Over."

Nothing, just the noise of some kind of vast expanse, radio waves pushing through the air, going through foliage and thin walls, blocked by other walls, absorbed by bodies. The crackle and hiss of nothingness.

Already, neighbors were at windows. No doubt the police had been notified. No doubt, people were filming him on phones. He wasn't worried about the shaky blurred images they'd capture of him distant on the street. But it was time to get the hell out of there. Karim would have to make it back by himself, which is one of the things he'd been trained to do.

Keeler stood and looked once more at the woman's body, destroyed and disfigured. Getting angry was a rare event for him, but his head felt hot, and he got the buzz of rage.

He let the protocol take over. That amount of contact required an SDR route out of there. He broke up the pistol and the phone into their pieces and tossed them into street gutters and garbage cans. The iPhone and earbuds were simply liabilities at that point. The only objects he retained were the money belt strapped on the inside of his waistband and the memory card wedged into the little pocket of his jeans.

He needed to figure out what to do with that.

Keeler moved through the city, creating a surveillance detection route on the fly. He was barely conscious of a final destination, requiring only distance from the mess. By midnight he found himself once more in the northeast section of Ankara, not really knowing why he felt drawn to it.

He saw the same market where he and Karim had eaten—maybe that was it.

The neighborhood around the market was public housing, Turkish style. High-rise buildings for people nobody gave a shit about: immigrants, asylum seekers, refugees from the currently homicidal chaos of clan-based Middle East and Central Eurasian societies.

He had ditched the device he could have used to contact Calcutti. In any case, Calcutti was gone with the others. Withdrawn to the embassy is what he'd said, which meant Keeler had to use the clandestine service emergency contact. He picked up a burner phone and a SIM card from an all-night kiosk.

The market was closing for the night, but he found a shisha café doing brisk business in amber glasses of hot tea with paper-wrapped sugar cubes and baklava. He took a seat outside under a heat lamp and ordered when the guy came. He looked around, people sitting out there in the chilly weather. The place was crowded, but not a woman in sight, only men talking loudly, gesticulating and waving lit cigarettes in the air like breathing had gone out of style.

Now, sitting in the café, he removed the battery from the burner phone, slid in the SIM and activated the device.

It didn't take long to power up. Keeler thumbed in a text message to a memorized number with a local toll-free prefix: *Need to change my reservation.*

A few seconds later an automated response beeped in. *Please enter your booking reference.*

Back only a couple of years, the service had featured human operators, now it was algorithms. Keeler entered a ten digit number. The automated response came a couple of seconds later. *Thank you.*

Now it was time to wait.

He broke the situation down into sequential parts, paying attention to the known and unknown events. While Calcutti's JSOC team had been running training exercises in Ankara, someone had been using the safe house at Canada for a live operation. They'd literally received free protection, which meant there had been no budgetary paperwork, no admin, no data to trace—perfect for keeping it hidden from their own side.

Not that the free protection had worked out so well.

What Keeler wanted to know was who they were and what they had been doing. The memory card might provide clues.

The other set of questions related to the enemy. Who they were and why they'd gone so far as to not only kill, but cut the throats of an entire operational team. The throat-cutting part was symbolic, since it wasn't required. The symbolic action seemed intended to be received as a message for someone who would understand it. It was the kind of thing he'd seen in places like Syria, Iraq, and Afghanistan, clans and sects raising the stakes without hesitation, escalation and vendetta like a weird form of communication.

After Keeler's second tea, the phone made a chirping sound like a small bird. The reply to his text read: *We are pleased to confirm your reservation at the Holiday Inn Kavaklıdere, room 405. Gardens.* He paid the bill and got rid of the phone, ditching the various pieces into garbage cans and storm drains on his way out of the neighborhood.

EIGHT

The Holiday Inn was downtown.

A weird spot sunken into a hill, with a highway running alongside the building. A little past two in the morning and cars were still spinning around the curve, out of one tunnel, hurtling down the steep hill past the hotel before disappearing with a metallic echo into another. Keeler observed the backside of the building, a couple of delivery entrances, all shut, all covered by multiple cameras.

What Keeler was expecting: a welcome committee for initial debrief, not JSOC people, more like a team of clandestine services field agents from the embassy. The other thing he wanted but knew better than to expect was an operational backing and a plan for dealing with the bad shit up in Çankaya. Given that they'd pulled the JSOC team back to the embassy, Keeler wasn't so hopeful.

He turned and walked up the hill, away from the hotel. Narrow urban streets peppered with hostels, all-night kebab stalls, and all-night phone stores. The claustrophobic alleys opened up to a huge mosque, the building and grounds taking up maybe ten city blocks, minarets lit up by floodlights. All of it looking clean and well maintained—or maybe *pure* was a better word.

It took a while for Keeler to find a phone store that had what he needed. The operational funds he carried covered a used laptop, a set of jeweler's tools for computer technicians, and a USB memory card reader.

He was going to take a look at that memory card from the woman's camera before he handed it over to anyone.

Keeler approached the hotel from across the street, studying the main entrance. A revolving door with a doorman and security guard standing near a metal detector. Behind that was a baggage scanner with a second guard sitting at the console looking at his phone. Keeler crossed the street and the doorman got aroused, moving to the door and taking a step out. The text message had included the word *gardens*.

The doorman moved toward him and Keeler smiled broadly. "The botanical gardens closed late."

The doorman nodded, but the smile disappeared. "Yes, sir."

The lobby was large with heavily polished marble floor and a reception desk fifteen yards away, the female receptionist behind it in a neat Holiday Inn uniform and Islamic head covering. She was leaning back looking at her phone.

At Keeler's approach, she activated. "Good evening, sir."

Keeler said, "I'm in room 405. I left my key card on the way out." He gave her no name, wanting to see how it worked.

"Just one moment, sir."

The receptionist got busy with her keyboard, engaged with the computer. Keeler looked around, saw the lounge and the bar. Quarter to three in the morning, two bulky guys in suits at the bar talking and drinking with their backs turned to the entrance. A bartender was focused on cleaning a glass.

The receptionist reached into a drawer and produced a small envelope. "Excuse me, sir, this is for you."

Keeler took the envelope, the receptionist watching him, waiting for him to open it. He put it in his pocket and she averted her eyes to the computer. A few keyboard clicks later, her long fingers removed a blank key card from a stack. She swiped it twice through a scanner and slid it across the counter.

"Thank you, sir."

"Thanks." He took the card.

The elevator had mirrored walls on three sides. Keeler looked at himself, feeling the cubicle rising on steel cables, almost soundless. He was carrying a plastic bag heavy with the laptop he'd bought and the various devices.

On the fourth floor, wall sconces cast an amber light on plush beige carpeting. The elevator waiting area had a couple of leather benches. Signage indicated the direction to go for rooms, simple choices, left or right.

Room 405 was a right turn. Sometimes the last place you want to go is the one place you're supposed to be. Keeler took a seat on a bench by the elevator.

The fourth floor felt deeply quiet, like a funeral for an unpopular person. An exit sign pointed left, opposite direction from the room. One thing Keeler wasn't going to do was go into room 405. He'd pictured it on his way to the hotel. The silent corridors and muffled footsteps, the door snicking shut behind him. Once that hotel room door shut on him, he'd be a potential prisoner.

He was already pretty un-excited about being at the Holiday Inn. The place felt bizarre. It manufactured a sense of quiet and safety that he didn't trust. So what if one or some of the eighteen or twenty odd US intelligence agencies had operational control of the Holiday Inn, using it as an asset. The hotel wasn't ever going to be what Keeler thought of as safe.

The envelope he'd been given at reception was stiff in his pocket. He took it out and turned it around, looking at it. Inside was a breakfast buffet voucher card. The other side of the card was blank, no note or anything. The buffet opened at 6 a.m. Keeler enjoyed an internal chuckle. He'd expected something direct and operational. Maybe a team of hard-faced agents in a safe house somewhere, ready to debrief him and get nasty if necessary.

What he was getting was the full corporate experience, including a breakfast buffet. It felt suspicious, like they were setting him up for something. Or the answer could be more mundane even. Since the initial message to the clandestine service emergency contact, he'd been getting the normal automated response, no evidence that a human being was aware of his situation.

Figures. He was being managed by a computer, like a member of the laptop class.

Keeler sat by the elevator for seven minutes. He pocketed the envelope and got up. Walked in the opposite direction from the room, following the exit sign, and descended the stairwell.

The staircase was functional, ending in a rectangular concrete vestibule with a door to the lobby and another area with another door to something, maybe a kitchen or a parking garage. The door to the lobby had an octagonal window, giving a view of the bar and lounge. A leather armchair was positioned against the far wall with a power socket above the baseboard and a coffee table at knee height. Nobody was looking at him. The few people still in the lobby were at least discreet. The two guys at the bar were gone. The bartender sat on a stool at the counter, looking at a phone.

Perfect.

Keeler entered the lobby and took the armchair. He set the plastic bag with his purchases on the coffee table. The bartender came over, young with a gold tooth and thick black hair brushed hard into a side part.

"May I help you, sir?"

"Orange soda, please."

"Fanta?"

"Right."

The bartender walked away to fetch the drink, leather shoes sinking with a whisper into the lounge carpet. Keeler plugged in the laptop and powered it on. The laptop would most likely have malware installed, given where he'd bought it.

It took the better part of an hour to download and install the software necessary to begin using the computer. Applications to detect malware mostly, but also applications for encrypting messages and files correctly. By that time he'd drank half of the Fanta through a straw. He liked Fanta in Asia and the Middle East. Back home he'd drink Coke. Once the software was installed, Keeler turned the laptop over and unscrewed the back.

The Wi-Fi card wasn't soldered to the motherboard. He was able to use the jeweler's screwdriver and gently pull the clips away. The little card multitasked for both Wi-Fi and Bluetooth. Now, even if there was malware remaining on the computer, there wasn't any easy way to bridge the air gap between this machine and a network.

Keeler was all set to plug in the memory card reader and finally look at what that camera had captured. He had the thing in his hand and was pushing it into the USB interface, when the revolving door at the entrance activated. Two people came in from the cold. Keeler observed them, noticing first of all that they hadn't noticed him.

The first guy in was a well-built man in his forties. He had his hair in a crew cut and wore a beige overcoat. Keeler wrote the bio in his head. Guy was a linebacker in college. Got a degree in the problems of life, then got a job at a multinational corporation counting boxes on spreadsheets, or he worked for the CIA.

A couple of seconds later a much younger woman came through the revolving door.

The two were together, and the gap between arrivals made it seem to Keeler like they'd had an argument. He pictured them out front of the hotel, fighting about something, maybe inside of a big black SUV. He saw the guy get impatient and storm out to the hotel entrance, then the woman compose herself and go after him.

The two of them couldn't have looked more American. It was in the haircuts and the clothes, but most of all in their bearing and mannerisms, like they were entitled to an answer.

She was slim with Asian features, at least a decade younger than the big man, who was already up at the reception desk gesticulating like an asshole. Keeler watched them make it to the elevator. The guy got a phone out and started doing things to it. The woman was still, her eyes scanning the polished bronze elevator door's reflection, being a spook.

It made Keeler smile. One of the things you learn by experience, acting like a spy makes you suspicious to other people who might be watching. The woman wasn't exactly a noob, but she wasn't a veteran yet either.

The elevator came and the man entered and started punching buttons. The woman moved in and leaned back against the rail. She was smooth. Her eyes drifted up and met Keeler's a second before the doors closed. The display above the elevator mounted. It went fast, one and then two, and stopped at the fourth floor in half a minute.

NINE

TINA CHOI WAS quiet in the elevator. Not because she had nothing to say, but because she didn't want to say anything. The guy from the CIA was making enough noise for the two of them, doing things with his phone and forgetting about controlling his breathing. Consequently he was mouth breathing loudly.

Choi had long ago managed to control her general disgust and channel it into thinking.

Thinking about the guy in the lounge who'd made eye contact when the elevator doors had closed. One thing she liked to do was invent stories for people she saw. This guy, with unkempt hair and a week of stubble on his face. What was he doing in Ankara? Turkish people came to their capital to brown nose the government. Business to business was done in Istanbul, business to government in Ankara.

But the guy hadn't been Turkish.

Which meant he could fall into the second category, selling security or defense to the Turkish military. But he didn't look like a salesman. Not in any way. Curious. Also curious, she got an earworm. A tune popped into her head and looped over and over. She figured out what it was just before the elevator got up to four.

Tom Waits. Shoot, Choi laughed gently to herself when she realized which song exactly, the one about a guy and a girl in a bar and the guy's hoping he doesn't fall in love with her. It also occurred to her that the guy in the lobby could be the JSOC operator they were supposed to be debriefing up in room 405.

Since she was simply along for the ride, Choi decided to sit back and let it all happen. Anderson from the CIA could handle it.

The elevator stopped smoothly, the number four appearing on the screen. The door opened and CIA guy leered down at her. "You done laughing?"

Choi ignored him, followed him out the door and down the corridor. Room 405 was bang in the middle of the building. The guy stopped suddenly and turned to her. She anticipated the movement because she was agile and lithe and worked out every single day. She stopped moving before he turned, avoiding the hot stench of his four-in-the-morning mouth.

He bent down at her and whispered intensely. "What I said outside applies the same. I do the talking. You don't jump in until I give you a nod. You got that?"

She said nothing, looking into his florid face and holding her breath, which she was capable of doing for four minutes with the proper preparation, two minutes without.

The guy's eyes were popping out of his head. Anderson was his embassy cover name, but she'd done her research and knew about him. He turned and stalked off, pausing just before he arrived at room 405. She walked slowly after him, watching him remove the key card from the pocket of his overcoat. She examined him closely. The overcoat was camel hair, which was weirdly expensive for a government employee to wear.

Which most likely meant that he was a well-paid corporate contractor.

He knocked on the door and waited. Knocked again and waited more. Nothing happened and Anderson tapped the key card to the lock. The mechanism clicked and whirred and he pushed the door in. Choi waited a little just to see if he'd get shot or something, then followed Anderson into the room and closed the door.

The room was empty. There was no indication that anyone had been in there since it had been cleaned. Which was weird because they had expected the JSOC man to be nervously waiting for them, ready for his debrief and exfiltration.

That was the CIA fantasy. But Choi wasn't CIA, she was Defense Intelligence Agency, and the DIA did things differently. At least that's what Choi had heard from her colleagues back at Anacostia–Bolling in Washington.

The guy downstairs in the lobby. She figured that was him, a special tactics soldier traveling on an Australian passport in the name of Dixon. He'd been watching and waiting for them. Choi wondered what he was playing at and then immediately rejected that thought, self-correcting. The JSOC guy wasn't playing, he was an experienced operator being prudent. She saw the eyes again, watching her as the elevator door closed. He was still the *agent in the field*, which meant the call was his to make, not hers and not Anderson's.

Anderson was agitated, stalking around the room, pulling curtains and opening the sliding door to the balcony. Nothing out there but a folding metal table and two chairs, nothing inside. The room was fancy, like a junior suite. A bedroom with a good-sized seating area with a couch, an armchair and a coffee table. A minimal viable work desk built in to the wall with a power socket area including USB plugs.

She sat on the minimal viable desk chair and watched Anderson give off anxious vibes.

He turned to her, face incredulous. "What is this?"

She didn't even shrug, just gave him lazy ice from her eyes. She wanted to see the guy melt down.

The animosity between them began with the power play he'd made outside and before.

* * *

At two in the morning she'd been in bed when the iPad made its special sound, like a bamboo chime on a Tibetan mountain. She'd woken with a clear head, like crystal, awake and alert and well rested. In a couple of seconds she'd entered the necessaries and the device went into clandestine service mode, no longer an iPad.

First up was an urgent live call request from the Ambassador, currently on some kind of Mediterranean boondoggle down in Bodrum with the Turkish and Bulgarian NATO Intelligence liaison officers. The conversation had been brief, shit has hit the fan, Choi, get yourself up to date on the wire feeds and make sure DIA leans in to the mix.

She had *yes sir*'d him and checked the encrypted feeds on the tricked-out iPad.

The new rules, post 9/11, stated the Ambassador is coordinator for all clandestine activity under his remit, a measure brought in to avoid in-fighting among agencies. It was a little hard to untangle exactly what shit had hit what fan, but Choi was studious and had memorized all the acronyms and pseudonyms of the clandestine bureaucracy.

What she knew: the chief of a Joint Special Operations Command support unit downtown had called in, reporting they'd found a CIA Special Operations Group safe house with three dead operatives. Choi had stopped reading for a moment there because she hadn't been aware of any ongoing CIA operations.

The Ambassador had ordered the JSOC team back to the embassy for immediate exfiltration. This was going to be pure damage control.

She let her mind play over the complicated acronyms, recalling the distinctions. Joint Special Operations Command and Special Operations Group were not the same thing, although they often collaborated. The difference was the chain of command, but confusingly, that didn't matter in the field when the embassy was involved because the Ambassador was in charge.

She refocused on the information coming in.

The JSOC unit commander was now saying that a fourth operative up at the wiped-out safe house was presumed missing. Plus, a member of the JSOC team was still loose in the city and had activated the clandestine service emergency contact system that DIA had recently set up.

Total FUBAR situation.

Choi had lain back in bed, letting her mind wander over the complicated alphabet soup of joint operations. The mixture of agencies in the clandestine service created a situation of intense territorial conflict. It wasn't easy to keep track of who had what.

She got out of bed and dressed, got herself to the office, ready to represent at the debriefing session. The next thing she knew, Anderson was jumping all over her at the motor pool. He claimed the op was exclusively Langley's territory. But Choi had her own orders.

In the end they'd called the Ambassador in Bodrum and gotten him out of bed again. He hadn't been happy. He said, "Call me back in ten." Choi and Anderson circled each other in the underground garage, waiting for the bosses to talk. Five minutes later the Ambassador called back. He'd sounded tired and pissed off.

They got the phone on speaker in the underground garage. He'd spoken in a soft voice, Choi and Anderson leaning in to hear him.

"This is delicate. I've been transferred to Kabul as of last night. In fact I'm here already, not in Bodrum. That was a story we put out for the press." He coughed, cleared his throat. "I called Washington, trying to extend, but that's not happening. Since Election Day, everyone in DC's got their panties in a twist. Haven't seen anything like it since Giancana helped Kennedy rob Nixon in Illinois." He paused for a couple of seconds, as if to let it sink in.

Choi and Anderson looked at each other, silent and blank faced. Neither of them particularly cared one way or another who the POTUS was, or what team of political opportunists he'd brought to the White House with him. The Ambassador continued. "Anyhoo, Jim Miller is going to move up to Chief of Mission duties for the interim, until the incoming team decides on an appointee. You both know him. Miller's on the line with us. Jim, handing over to you right now, buddy."

James Miller, Deputy Chief of Mission, second in command to the Ambassador. Choi and Anderson looked at each other. One thing they could agree on: Miller was a big step down in quality from the Ambassador.

Miller came on the line. Choi imagined him in the situation room at the embassy up in Çankaya. Miller was an asshole. He gave a short pep talk that both Choi and Anderson eye rolled. Choi had to restate the jurisdictional question, insist on DIA participation. Miller had referred to the Ambassador, still on the line, but unwilling to influence the decision.

"Jim the ball's in your court now."

It took Miller a moment, but he'd managed to express an opinion in the end.

Deputy Chief of Mission Miller had said to Anderson, "CIA priority, interagency responsibility. You're in charge."

He'd said to Choi, "Take a ride with Anderson, represent your people and report back to headquarters. Tell them you've received cooperation at the embassy and agency level."

* * *

Now, they were in the empty hotel room at the Holiday Inn. Anderson was saying something with a question on it, like asking Choi her opinion on what to do.

Choi said, "Well Anderson, I'd guess that our man is in the building. Maybe he's waiting for the free breakfast buffet in,"— she checked her watch—"less than two hours."

Anderson was going to say something, but there was a knock on the door. Three knocks to be precise. Knock, knock, knock. He leapt at the sound, lumbering to the door and giving off relief vibes. Reminded her of a guy grateful that his date hadn't stood him up.

What Choi was wondering at the same time Anderson opened the door: They'd been alerted that the JSOC guy had received his key card from reception, so, why would someone knock if they had the key card?

Choi opened her mouth to say something, but the door was already swinging in.

She looked at Anderson's broad back, the room's entrance area narrow for the large man's frame. He opened the door, giving her a glimpse of someone on the other side of it. Choi heard a loud pop and Anderson's posture changed. Another pop and the back of his head exploded. She caught a flurry of skull fragments to her face in a hot, wet stinging slap.

TEN

CONTROVERSIAL OPINION: there's only one truly essential element to special tactics training—eliminate the instinct to flee and develop a counter-intuitive instinct to move to the source of danger. Everything else is like an à la carte menu. A little parachuting, maybe some mountaineering. Throw in underwater demolitions and maritime navigation. Maybe some weapons training would be nice.

Choi had been a good student, eager and ready for anything. She'd developed highly aggressive instincts in training, none of which had yet been put to use, since this was her first field posting.

When Anderson's brain pan received the bullet, she didn't move back from the violence; she moved toward it. The big man's body was falling and there was only one play, one important thing in the world at that very moment: seal the room. The open door was a breach, and she was in imminent danger of being killed. Choi tackled Anderson from behind and used the coiled strength in her legs to shove him into the shooter.

The CIA man was already a corpse on legs. His body tottered at the guy in the corridor. She kicked the door shut and didn't get to see the heavy dead man collapse into his killer. By the time the door slammed, Choi was in motion, counting the seconds in her head, knowing that she had one minute or less to get out.

There weren't two ways out; there was only the balcony.

Fourth floor. The wind whipped at her face, fresh and lively. The sound of traffic from below was like a cold shriek. Choi looked up and down and to the left and the right, four quick swivels of the head. The easiest and fastest option was a neighboring balcony. She got up on the railing, holding the separation wall with one hand while the other extended for balance.

There was a brief tricky moment where she had to use blind trust, swinging out across the divide and finding her footing on the other side. She didn't look down. A second later she was on the other balcony, probably room 406. The curtains were drawn. Choi made the call and did the lateral move again. Up on the next balcony railing, swinging out. She heard the sound of a sliding door from room 405. She didn't look to her right, but assumed that the killer had seen her.

The curtains were also shut on the next room over. Choi had a vision of a middle-aged couple sleeping on the other side of the sliding door. She peered over the balcony to the right. No sign of the shooter, or anyone else for that matter. What she visualized: a team of assassins mobilizing, communicating and triangulating on her position. She switched balconies once more, which brought her to the corner of the building.

Last stop, nowhere else to go.

She had to assume that the enemy was closing in on her from above. Two choices, climb to the fifth floor, or drop to the third. Dropping was going to be easier.

She rolled over the balcony and did a controlled upside-down slide down the vertical steel bars until her hands touched concrete. It left her in a very awkward position, her feet up in the air, balanced lightly, hands gripping hard steel and rubbing against the concrete.

Choi pushed through the pain and let herself swing gently out, controlling the movement. She built up momentum, four swings and then the big one, swinging out to the limit and coming back to release. Her body coordinating like a single well-formed muscle, agile in midair, making it past the third-floor railing. What she hadn't anticipated: colliding with a folding metal table.

She hadn't been able to see it from where she'd hung. The junior suites had the table and chairs and the regular rooms just got the plain balcony. Her foot hit first, sliding along the metal surface of the table, followed very quickly by the rest of her. She slid across it, collapsing the table and landing in a heap on the third-floor balcony.

Nothing broken, but she'd banged and scraped her elbow and knee.

The fall had been noisy, but the hotel was sound insulated. Given the traffic noise below, nobody was going to hear it. She looked at the sliding French door. The curtains were not closed. Choi put her face to the glass and blocked out the exterior light with a hand. The bed inside was neatly made and undisturbed.

She tried the sliding door, but it was locked.

No way around it. Choi picked up the folding table and swung it by the legs into the glass door, putting as much force into the impact as possible. The edge made contact with the glass and the window imploded. She stood back from the carnage, letting the shards fall.

Choi stepped over the threshold to the bed. She sat down and picked up the phone to call reception and then put it down. If she called them, they'd see what room she was in. She used her own phone to find the number and call the hotel reception desk.

A woman answered.

Choi said, "There's a man sitting in the lounge. Do you see him?"

The receptionist paused for a second. "Excuse me?"

"A man in the lounge sitting in an armchair with a laptop. Do you see him?"

"Yes."

"I need to speak to him now. It's very important."

A half minute later the guy's voice came on. "Yeah."

Choi said, "I'm the one you saw get on the elevator. The guy I was with is dead."

"Where are you?"

"Third floor. South side of the hotel on the corner. Must be the last room from the elevator if you take a right."

"Outstanding."

He ended the connection. Choi sat there getting her breathing under control. *Outstanding?* She wondered what had happened upstairs with the shooter and if there had been an accomplice. A couple of minutes later, there was the knock on the door.

Choi looked through the peephole at the guy standing there. It was a reassuring sight. She opened the door and made eye contact. He looked past her to the shattered glass. Back at her with a curious raised eyebrow, like he was interested. She looked down at herself. The guy's chin pointed at her elbow. The jacket she wore was torn there, but otherwise it was all right.

He said, "You ready to go?"

ELEVEN

Shortly before, down in the lobby, after he had seen the two Americans take the elevator to the fourth floor, Keeler had been about to pop the memory card into the computer. He figured the spooks would eventually find him. By the time that happened he wanted to know what was on the memory card. But that didn't happen.

Two black muscle cars pulled to a tactical stop outside, high-end Mercedes models, unmarked cars with blue flashers on the dashboard giving off serious no-joke vibes. A total of seven men emerged from the vehicles. Three of them came through the front door, each in plain clothes with balaclava hoods masking their facial features. Each wore a red Polis armband around his left bicep.

Turkish security services, maybe internal counter intelligence, is what Keeler was thinking.

He watched them deal with the doorman and the two running the security hardware. Two of the cops approached the counter and shouted harsh Turkish at the receptionist. She nodded and went to the back, maybe to wake up the duty manager.

Keeler ran a finger under the seat of his chair. Finding the seam, he pulled at it, using a fingernail to claw a rip into it. He pushed the memory card into the hole he'd made. Just in time because two of the hooded security men were up in his face, scanning him carefully. Evidently, they didn't have his face in mind.

He said, "Hello."

Which they ignored.

The men moved back to the elevator bank, one of them stabbing at the button while the others checked their six. No weapons out in the open, no more words shouted. Everything relatively quiet and fast.

Out front, four guys in the same outfits had taken up positions covering the exterior. They reminded Keeler of the men he'd seen outside Canada just before they'd thrown the woman in front of the van and killed her. They had the same disposition. He was getting a tingling sensation at the back of his neck, thinking that these were the same people.

If so, they were inside the US clandestine services communications. They didn't have Keeler's description, so what was it?

The woman at the counter looked shaken. If the leak had been human they'd have known Keeler was the guy who'd showed up. The emergency contact system was now automated, no human in the chain. He'd called in and did the thing with the codes, gotten the room number. Presumably everything set up by some computer with fancy algorithms or whatever.

One thing the computer didn't have was his name, his face, his identity.

A couple of minutes later, the phone rang at the reception desk. Then he was called over. The conversation had been brief. He went back to get his stuff and then made for the stairs.

Now he was standing in the hallway with the room door open, appraising the woman he'd seen down by the elevator, who'd made the eye contact and behaved like a spook right out of spook school. Up close she looked pretty fierce. Small in size and young, but focused and concentrated and hungry. The other thing was that she looked like shit had just happened to her, like she'd been in a wrestling match with a polar bear.

He turned his back on her and moved out, keeping a normal pace down the empty hotel corridor. He heard the door close and glanced behind him. She was following and caught up with him halfway to the elevator bank. "Where are you going?"

Keeler said, "What do I call you?"

"Tina Choi."

"I'm Keeler."

Keeler had come up the stairs from the lobby. He figured hotel guests don't normally use stairs. His plan wasn't complicated. Get out of there, most likely out the back. He figured there would be a kitchen down at the ground level and where there's a kitchen you can usually find an exterior door. He glanced at Choi. "Are you armed?"

"No."

They were at the end of the corridor.

Keeler turned and examined her. "You did just fine staying alive. That must have been a hectic situation. How'd you come down to the third floor?"

"I was good at high school gymnastics."

Two elevators, each of them currently serving a different floor, according to the indicator above. The elevator on the left showed the fourth floor, the one on the right showed the lobby. Keeler led them to the stairwell access door.

"We have to consider any person we encounter an enemy combatant. Do you understand what that means?"

She blinked once, processing the implications of his statement. "Yes, of course."

"All right. Survival isn't always pretty."

The heavy fire door opened inwards. The stairwell was brightly lit glossy grey concrete with thick white lines painted on the steps. Keeler stood inside, listening and watching. He thought he'd heard something from above and held up a hand to Choi signaling for her to wait. He went to the stair shaft and looked up. Nothing to see. He waited three beats, patient and making no noise.

They needed to keep moving.

Choi was good at moving quietly. They reached the ground floor without incident.

He wasn't sure that he hadn't actually heard something above them. At the bottom of the staircase was the door to the lobby. Keeler explored the vestibule on the right, finding another door with a P sign for parking, an underground garage.

No kitchen.

He hadn't thought of the parking garage before, but now it seemed like an okay way out. Not just yet though, if there had been a guy up in the stairwell, he wanted to know, being the kind of operator who loves contact.

Keeler opened the garage door and let Choi move through. He followed her and closed the door loudly, like a performance. Choi was watching him. He held up a hand for her to wait before reopening the door as quietly as he could, keeping it open a quarter inch shy of the jamb.

He crouched, ear glued to the crack in the door.

She whispered. "What are you doing?"

He looked at her. "I want to know who these people are."

She had been on the verge of saying something. Keeler held out the bag with his laptop and other items. Choi closed her mouth and took it. The memory card was back in the coin pocket of his jeans, nice and close. He figured that was what all of this was about in the end. Whatever that woman up at Canada had photographed, someone thought it was pretty important.

A minute later, he heard movement coming down the stairs. The footsteps were quiet, it was only really the shift of clothing that gave the man away, an approaching rustle that became progressively louder. Choi's eyes had gone wide, alert, sensing something in Keeler, maybe a restlessness, the barely contained violent tendencies. Keeler nodded to her, noticing that his jaw was clenched. He relaxed it, preparing himself for rapid deployment.

Anybody using the stairs was going to be fair game according to the rules he'd set out already. Choi seemed to have concerns, but kept them buttoned in.

He opened the door and moved through smoothly. A man was coming off the last step, therefore slightly unbalanced. His hands were empty and he wore a shiny black jacket. Keeler came at the man smiling, goofy like a half-drunk hotel guest who was just going to walk up the stairs past him.

He noticed white earbuds. The man's eyes scanned him, top to bottom and fast. His mouth opening to say something.

Keeler didn't want to give the guy any time to converse with colleagues. He timed his movement, letting the man's right foot land on the solid ground floor. As it did so, Keeler stepped in and stomped on the guy's knee with a heavy boot. The stomp landed obliquely, glancing off and saving the guy cartilage, ligament, and bone. The target lost his balance and fell back against the wall, using both hands to keep himself upright.

Keeler saw the eyes darting around in a desperate bulge. The man's brain was in a state of perfect chaos. Code black, too panicked even to speak.

Not that Keeler was prepared to let him.

He jabbed the stiffened fingers of his left hand into the soft part of an exposed throat. The man fell back against the wall, gagging. Keeler pushed a hard hand against his chest, pinning the man in place. He frisked him, finding the phone, ripping out earbuds, car keys, and a wallet and dumping it all on the floor.

No weapon.

Keeler opened the wallet and found an ID. The target's face with a Turkish name. Halid Semiye Gökalp. One heck of a name. He handed the wallet back to Choi. "Is this the guy you saw?"

She examined the ID. "I didn't get a good look at the shooter." Choi stepped forward to examine the man, currently trying to catch his breath and clearly terrified. "I don't think so. This guy's bigger and fatter." She approached the guy and spoke in Turkish. He shook his head, negative.

Keeler couldn't understand the language, but he got the vibe, some kind of plausible denial.

Choi picked up the man's earbuds and phone. She held the device for him to unlock with a thumb print. Keeler watched her hunting around in there.

She deadpanned him. "This guy's a civilian. He was going down to the garage because he couldn't sleep and figured he'd wait at the bakery for the first batch of fresh pastries his wife likes. Some famous Turkish bakery. They're on vacation, came down yesterday to Ankara from some town by the Black Sea."

Keeler had the guy's car keys in his hand. A BMW fob. He held it out to Choi. "Tell him we're going to borrow his car. Tell him to go back upstairs to his room and shut the door."

She said something to the man, who scowled. He took another glance at Keeler and leaned back against the railing, dropping his head in submission.

Keeler made a gesture. "Go upstairs."

The man hurried up the steps. He'd be in his room within two minutes. Choi had blood splatter on her face. Keeler hadn't even noticed before.

"Stay still."

She allowed Keeler to wipe it off with a thumb.

TWELVE

Keeler roamed the garage. Flat concrete covered in a layer of dust. The wind whipped in from the exit ramp up ahead. Nothing was moving, nobody in sight. He peered into vehicles, cabs empty. Cold cars and fluorescent light, paint and Tina Choi, left back by the entrance, looking for the BMW to which the keys belonged, while Keeler scouted ahead.

The exit ramp sloped steep, twenty degrees. At the top was a rectangular opening to the street. Butting up to it on the right was the simple form of a guard booth. Mirrored glass tinted blue, something you saw all over Ankara.

Keeler went back for Choi and didn't have to go far. The headlights of a glossy black BMW sedan flicked on. There she was behind the wheel. The car looked powerful, even wicked. Keeler climbed in. The bag with his stuff was in the foot well. He kicked it aside and the engine growled.

Keeler pointed toward the exit. "Guard booth up there. Go easy until you hit the ramp, then gun it." He looked at her, saw the determined face and had to smile to himself. Looked to him like Choi had enjoyed her training. "I don't want them coming out of the guard booth, you go too slow and they'll come out."

Her eyes moved in his direction with a kind of distasteful expression. "Roger that." Choi got the BMW moving.

She kept the lights off until the base of the ramp. The mirrored exterior of the guard booth was unreadable. Keeler refrained from commenting. Choi hit the gas, smoothly flying up and cresting the rise. Nothing happened with the booth and a second later, they were out.

The hotel entrance was directly to the left. There had been four men and two vehicles, now Keeler saw two men and a single vehicle. Balaclava hoods and Polis armbands. The men outside already turning to look at them.

Choi said, "They've seen us."

Keeler didn't respond. One of the men started to move in their direction. The other grabbed his jacket and stopped him. Mouth moving, speaking into a communications device.

Choi made the right off the ramp, away from the Holiday Inn. His eyes searching and seeking, Keeler thought about the second vehicle, missing now. Totally possible that a second team had been called somewhere else. The street resembled some kind of urban canyon, large buildings on either side, hemming them in. Keeler felt a strong desire to break out of there.

Choi let up on the accelerator and allowed the car to coast. Up on the right was an alleyway, Keeler's side of the car. Same thing on the left side. On the other side of the left alleyway was a big building with a series of loading docks for trucks. Each loading dock possessing its own sloped driveway that the trucks would back into.

A movement caught his eye. His head whipped to the right, eyes sharp and focusing in on the next alleyway. Choi hit the accelerator hard, sensing something. Keeler saw a shadow flitting over the wall on the far side of the alley, something moving in there.

Choi said, "Oh boy."

Keeler didn't comment. They came abreast of the alley's entrance and it was too late. The second Mercedes had been waiting, maybe on other side of the alley. They'd been summoned and were now moving at high speed, raising dust and just about erupting from the narrow entrance. Keeler, anticipating the coming impact, sensed words moving from his brain to his mouth but materializing as weird sounds between a groan and a growl.

Choi spun the wheel to the left, attempting to get out of reach and mitigate the impact. Keeler was looking through the passenger side window at the guy behind the wheel. The driver wore a balaclava hood like the others. That didn't stop Keeler from recognizing his weird clear jackal eyes. The same eyes he'd seen on the driver from the night before, the guy who'd run his van into the injured woman and killed her.

That was why they hadn't noticed him in the lobby: the guy with the jackal eyes had been outside.

The Mercedes closed fast. Choi's defensive maneuver avoided a direct impact but there was no avoiding the collision. The two vehicles crunched together. Choi hit the gas and spun the wheel hard right, trying to get distance, but the bumpers had caught together like mechanical Velcro.

Centrifugal force spun the Mercedes into the side of the BMW. The vehicles got parallel, and Keeler looked to his right through the window, directly at the driver.

Who didn't notice, focusing hard on the physics and mechanics of a double-vehicle disaster ballet. Eyes straight ahead, trying to influence the trajectory. Keeler pushed the window button. The glass came down and he prepared to seek contact with the enemy.

"Stop the car."

Easier said than done: the two big German cars were careering down the urban canyon, locked together with metal tearing and sparking. Choi screamed with the effort and got the wheel turned hard to the left, pulling the fused vehicles straight toward the first loading dock. She got them half on the sidewalk and half off, the vehicles grating against the curb. The dip in the loading dock came fast and they dropped with a vertiginous lurch and a hard bang and a jolt. Keeler's face bounced off the dashboard. His mouth flooded with the mineral taste of hot blood.

Choi was okay, protected by the steering wheel, now struggling with her seat belt. Keeler turned his head to the enemy. The window open, the driver of the Mercedes right there, eyes darting around. No possibility of opening his door because the two cars were crushed together.

A long braided lanyard with hand-embroidered edges was looped from the rearview mirror in front of him, the photograph of a young girl dangling from it. The girl was maybe eight or ten years old. Keeler un-looped the lanyard from the mirror and got it in his fist as a potential weapon, fleetingly aware that this was a gift to the civilian he'd assaulted back at the hotel, probably from his daughter, something she'd made in school maybe.

The world was full of curious and beautiful forms, many of them available for multiple purposes.

THIRTEEN

KEELER CAME out of the car, vaulting through the window, using the sill as a foot hold. He got up on the roof of the Mercedes, wondering if the enemy had noticed, given the confusion and chaos of the car crash. Below him, the rear passenger door flew open, kicked by a booted foot. A man pulled himself out.

Keeler was looking at the top of his hooded head and the pistol held in his hand. The guy's head was swiveling, left and right and then back to the BMW. Keeler knew what he was seeing with his predatory eyes. The body language adjusted, like a question mark morphing into an exclamation mark. He'd seen Choi. Maybe she was still working on getting loose from the seat belt.

The man's gun arm came up and it was time to engage him.

Keeler dropped off the car and landed behind him. The braided lanyard came around the man's throat, secured to Keeler's wrist with a quick loop. The man was taller than expected, which made the angle uncomfortable. It didn't help that the neck was heavily muscled, the balaclava riding up with the struggle, revealing a neck tattoo, some kind of tribal design.

Keeler tightened his grip on the lanyard and used his free hand to grope for purchase on the man's weapon. The huge back and shoulders pushed against Keeler's chest. Keeler tucked his chin into the hollow between the man's shoulder blades and pulled him away from the open car door, not wanting to be an easy target for his colleague.

The man's throat quickly became hot against Keeler's fist, then bunched and hard as he continually ratcheted the grip on the braided garrote. He was losing time; the guy's neck was too strong for a quick strangle. Time for plan B. Keeler swept the man's feet out from under him and flipped him onto his back.

The pistol clattered onto cement. The man drove huge hands for Keeler's throat.

Which wasn't a good thing. Keeler pulled back from the hands, sinking his left thumb through the hole in the balaclava, into the man's right eye. He got his whole hand in there, groping fingers went to the man's ear, looking for a good hold. The man grunted, which Keeler took as a good sign. He let his muscular digit move freely in the eye socket, mashing the soft inner parts, making pain and involuntary fear fire off in the brain. A choked sound came from him and his hands flew up, incapable of doing anything except defend, a purely instinctual drive to alleviate the danger to his eye.

Keeler snuck his other hand under the balaclava, stretching the fabric as he grasped hold of the man's other ear. He raised the big head up and smacked it into the ground twice in rapid succession, looking for something to break. Nothing doing, the guy was still fighting. He'd given up on the eye and was getting the hands back on the offensive, pounding Keeler in the kidney.

The guy wouldn't quit. Keeler grabbed the pistol and pushed it into the meat of the man's thigh, pulling once and receiving the jolt and bang of discharge. The man's hands quit finally, possibly tricked by the brain into pure submission.

Keeler took a look at the weapon, a very new Heckler & Koch VP9.

In the edge of his peripheral vision, he was aware of a second man coming out of the Mercedes on the other side. Keeler scooted around the back of the car in a crouch and rose to meet him. The other man, moving fast and furious, was not expecting to find a big American coming up on him around the back of the car. Keeler pushed the H&K point-blank into the man's chest and pulled, his left hand pushing the enemy's weapon away.

The 9mm round ripped through muscle and bone and organs. Keeler took control of the man's weapon, aware of Choi, yelling something incomprehensible. He saw a blur of move-ment and knew immediately that the driver was coming out, weapon up. He made himself as small as possible, pulling the man he'd just shot close and tight. Two bangs echoed off the close walls of the loading dock. He felt two distinct thuds as the driver's bullets hit the man in the back.

Keeler pushed the body away and got his weapon up and ready. The driver had vaulted onto the loading dock and was pulling open a door. Keeler squeezed the trigger and watched over the sights as the first round took out part of the brickwork by the door frame. A second round passed between the door frame and the driver's neck, raising a pink mist as the bullet grazed through skin and flesh. The driver disappeared into the building.

Keeler flipped the man he'd shot onto his back. The guy's eyes were open, looking at him vacantly. He looted the man's clip-on holster. Choi was there, hand out for the man's weapon. Keeler put the VP9 in her hand and saw her push off, looking like she wanted to chase the driver.

He snatched a grip on her jacket and pulled her back. "No." Choi was breathing hard, scowling at him. He could see in her eyes, adrenaline flooding through her system. Keeler said, "Not now."

She stared at him, eyes shining, overcome with excitement. "Did you hear them talking?"

"No."

Choi pointed where the driver had gone. "That guy yelled to his buddy, while you were dealing with the first one."

Which reminded Keeler that he'd shot the other guy in the leg. He went around the back of the BMW, looking at the man, unconscious now, or faking it. The leg wound was serious, blood pooling underneath the man.

Choi had followed him. She pointed back at the guy. "Listen to me. That guy called back to his buddy who just ran into that building." Jerking her finger at the spot the driver had disappeared into the building. "They weren't speaking Turkish."

Keeler wasn't completely understanding Choi's point. "What were they speaking?"

"I think they spoke Uzbek or Tajik." She was looking at him in *that way* now, impatient.

He got it though, the meaning of what Choi was saying. Turkish security services would not be Tajik or Uzbek. This was a hit team disguised as Turkish security, a bold and dangerous thing to do given where they were doing it.

He said, "So, they've got *cojones*."

Choi was nodding. "Yes." She was crouched down now, checking out the man with the leg wound. Saying something about getting information out of the guy, patting his pockets. Keeler heard sirens. It was definitely time to go.

He grabbed her shoulder, but Choi pushed his hand off angrily. "Don't grab me like that."

"We have to go."

She stood up. "The guy's clean. Carrying nothing, not even pocket litter."

Keeler nodded calmly. "Fine. Let's go."

He watched her, looking back at him, her face full of fear and doubt and disgust. Horror mounting in her eyes, she said, "We've got to report this." Insistent and confused.

Keeler said, "We will. But not to the Turkish spooks in some dungeon." The sirens were getting louder. He twirled a finger in the air. "It won't be a very good look at the embassy if they have to try to get us out of a Turkish prison. You ever see the movie *Midnight Express?*"

"What?" Choi said, maddened and confused.

Keeler started moving. A minute later he looked behind him, just to verify that she had followed. There she was, keeping pace. Moving fast but not running, head down. He let her catch up with him and then moderated the pace. Time to get distance between themselves and the howl of incoming sirens.

FOURTEEN

The Acting Chief of Mission, James Miller was looking at a live video feed from Incirlik Air Base. He watched as the JSOC team boarded a C-37 Gulfstream brought in for their extraction. Three American operators were walking up the stairs from the tarmac. Miller said the names to himself, as if ticking off a list: Bratton, Calcutti, and Cheevers.

Calcutti was the unit commander of the team, the usual voodoo mix of dangerous killers whom the embassy had to infrequently deal with. These people were simply bad news, running amok with the gleeful approval of the shamans at Fort Bragg and Langley. There wasn't anything that the foreign service could do about them, since they had privileges going up through the State Department all the way to the Executive.

What Miller did understand, Calcutti's team was involved in something called an Intelligence Support Activity, whatever that meant. The command chain went from Calcutti, straight into some kind of atmospheric zone, where the CIA's Special Activities Center and the Pentagon intersected.

Strangely, Calcutti seemed to have a scary degree of autonomous command.

He hadn't been easy to brush off, but Miller managed to bullshit him with a couple of half-truths and one outright lie. He'd lied and said Keeler was safe at the embassy and would be extracted via a land route within twenty-four hours. A Regional Security Officer was taking care of the exfil.

Part of which was sort of half true.

Then there was the question of the foreign national, a private contractor by the name of Karim Hassan Ahmadi. Apparently Ahmadi had been attached to Calcutti's unit in some capacity. Ahmadi was still unaccounted for, but Miller was willing to bet he'd show up demanding his paycheck.

Anyway, Ahmadi was not an American, so he didn't count.

Miller was in the situation room at the Ankara embassy, at the head of the table where the Ambo used to sit. Normally it would be just him and the Ambassador with the CIA and DIA liaisons, unless there was other shit to deal with, in which case there could be a full house.

Now it was just him, which felt good. Whoops, he'd almost forgotten the guy at the other side of the table, Dinglewort, or Dinkleworth, or something like that. Anderson's lackey in the embassy's CIA office. The guy was young, early thirties, poking around on a laptop and looking useless.

Miller leaned back in the Ambassador's leather chair, loafers up on the desk. He watched as Calcutti passed into the Gulfstream, the last of them. What a dick. Miller couldn't stand military nut cases like Calcutti.

Up on screen number two was Kathy Jensen, Counselor for Agricultural Affairs. Since Miller had been jumped up to Chief of Mission, Kathy Jensen had been jumped up to Deputy Chief of Mission. Which Miller figured was too high of a jump for that particular farmer, currently calling in from Malatya where she'd been getting a tour of an apricot-packing plant.

Miller watched her for a second. Jensen was distracted,

sitting in a hotel room with a cup of coffee and looking like she'd been unhappily woken up. He had an unkind thought and enjoyed it. At sixty-three years old, Kathy Jensen needed her rest more than he did. Miller figured she was holding out for a couple more years, angling for a legacy retirement package.

"You get that, Kathy? They're on the plane now."

Jensen shifted her eyes slowly to the camera. "Oh, okay. Gotcha, Jim. Is that going to be all?"

"No."

Miller shifted his weight forward with an outstretched hand. On the desk was a cardboard box packed with pistachio-stuffed baklava from Faruk's. The designer office chair smoothly catapulted Miller's body to the desk, allowing his thumb and forefinger to close around a tightly bound filo package, heavy with honey and rose water. He let himself fall back in the chair and brought the pastry to his mouth in the same fluid gesture. One bite and a half second later the sugar surged into his bloodstream.

Damn that was good. He allowed the chair to spring forward again and this time secured the coffee cup beside the baklava box. Miller allowed the movement to translate into his rising from the chair, feeling graceful. A sip of hot black coffee knocked back the sweet baklava, and he felt awesome.

He looked at the CIA man across the table. "Want one of these?"

The guy looked up from his laptop and made a declining gesture. Like he was on a diet, or he was trying to cut out sugar, or some other disapproving thing.

Miller called out to his new assistant in the other room. "Patch the Undersecretary in on screen three." He fixed a look at Kathy Jensen. "We have to notify the Undersecretary, Kathy. Probably won't take more than a minute. She's a busy lady."

"You betcha."

The assistant called from the other room. "Undersecretary Neuman's only doing voice, sir."

"Fine."

The call came through just as the Gulfstream lifted off the tarmac. Done.

Vicky Neuman didn't mess around. Her voice was a low growl. "I've got three minutes, Miller."

Miller said, "Thank you Madam Undersecretary." He glanced briefly at Anderson's man, thought about mentioning his presence and decided that non-playing characters don't count. "I'm here with the Counselor for Agricultural Affairs, ma'am. She's Acting Deputy Chief of Mission at the moment."

"Who's that now?"

"Her name is Kathy Jensen." Miller looked up at Jensen, smiling on screen two. Why was she smiling?

"Kathy Jensen from Kansas?"

"Yes, ma'am."

Neuman's voice became uncharacteristically friendly. "Hey, Kath. Long time no see."

Miller felt a bolt of fear run up his spine. Not only had he never heard the Undersecretary of State for Politics sounding friendly, but this seemed to be a genuine and involuntary event

Up on screen two Jensen looked happy. "Good morning, Madame Undersecretary. How are you?"

Miller couldn't stand the fact that these two seemed to know each other. He cut in. "We've just watched a live feed of the JSOC men leaving the country. We're clean, Madam Undersecretary. Everything is backed off like you said."

Miller strategically left out the part about the remaining guy, Keeler, still in country. He'd be out soon.

"The CIA thing got cleaned up?"

Miller looked at the CIA man, gazing back at him through black-framed glasses. He moved a stray piece of baklava from a molar with his tongue. "American involvement was confined to the hotel thing, which is a DIA setup. CIA tells me that there are no American nationals involved in the other thing. A hundred percent deniability. We haven't gone near it, just going to let the locals find it and deal with it."

The CIA man nodded and went back to his laptop.

Neuman said, "So there's been nothing from the locals. No Turkish grief?"

"None at all."

"Good." Neuman paused, like she was having some last doubts before allowing herself to relax. "So, there's no reason to involve Political Section."

He said, "No, Madame Undersecretary, I think we're clear on that."

Neuman said, "What about you, Kathy? Do you have any thoughts?"

Jensen said, "To be honest, I've been working my way around the apricot-growing regions of Turkey." She laughed. "Quite its own world. I'll be back in Ankara in a couple of hours. Planning to get up to speed on the flight if Jim can send me the relevant files."

Miller almost choked. Yeah right.

"You do that, Kathy." Neuman sighed, one long breath out. "Shit, it's total chaos in DC." She did something between a laugh and a cough. "To say the least. You'll probably be talking to someone else in a week, I'll be sent back to the think tank for the next four to eight years."

Miller already knew that, which was why he didn't give a shit one way or another what Vicky Neuman thought. There would be a new Undersecretary of State for Politics soon, and Miller wasn't even going to try to guess who that might be and what the new guy or gal might think about the world.

Undersecretary Neuman ended the call. Miller turned to

see his new assistant with the red hair, a glimpse through the open door to the waiting room. She was new to him, not to the embassy. The incoming administration wouldn't make him Ambassador but at least he could enjoy the perks for a while.

Kathy Jensen wasn't gone yet. She was looking at the camera, coffee cup up in front of her face.

"Anything else, Kathy?"

The coffee cup came down. Jensen's lips were tight. She said, "You really have no idea who might have been responsible for what happened?"

"Uh, no, Kathy, I don't. I'm pretty certain that we won't find out either, since we've just been told to back the hell off."

The CIA man had perked up, flicking his gaze between Miller and the woman on the screen. Jensen nodded and for a moment, in her blue eyes, Miller glimpsed anger. It was like a sudden glimmer that shot out and scared him for a second.

She said, "Mmmm hmmm. Well, whoever it was chose a good time for it."

FIFTEEN

UNDERSECRETARY OF STATE for Politics Vicky Neuman was in bed, fully clothed, looking at her phone. It was 11:00 p.m. in Washington, DC. Her husband, Bob, farted loudly from the bathroom.

Neuman shook her head in wonder. "Jesus Christ."

Bob's deeply resonant voice came through the door. "Thanks for the appreciation, babe."

"You remember Kathy Jensen?"

Bob didn't respond. Neuman figured he didn't remember that Jensen had been her roommate at Brown for three very fun, desperate, and naughty years.

Bob liked to sit on the toilet, read through stuff on his phone. He said he got most of his intellectual work done that way, ensconced on the throne, so to speak. Bob was a big-time political philosopher, currently a member of the Republican party, but quickly rethinking his membership in light of the election results. Neuman was a Democrat, in the sense of aligning with the political party. The political concept itself was more negotiable.

Bob came through the door and stood over her in his bathrobe. "So what's the deal?"

Neuman looked up at him through heavily lidded eyes. "Miller says it didn't happen, fully deniable." She was nodding to herself. "Last thing I want is to get involved in anything right now." Bob was looking at her intensely, as if he'd had a thought. She said, "What?"

"Some of our people got killed. That's what happened, right?"

"One. The others weren't Americans, apparently."

"But they were working for us."

"Deniable."

He insisted. "They were working for us, Vicky."

She didn't avoid his gaze. "No, Bob, they were not working for us. They were working for themselves. One was a local contractor and the others were on their own team. Some kind of CIA witchcraft. The agency gave them some support, but nothing is official, and we're out of the game, bubbie."

Bob sat down on the edge of the bed. "Except someone came after your people, took them out, and you don't know who it is."

Neuman looked at him, eyes hard. "Now, now, Bob. We don't know *precisely* who it is, but what are you going to do? It's an unknown unknown type of situation. We're going to take the hit and not engage, because we can, Bob. We're the United States of America and they're probably not even a nation state, probably some bunch of foreign deplorables. What do you people call them? *A shit-hole country.*" She shrugged.

Bob indicated the bathroom. "I got a text, while I was on the throne. My guy in Jerusalem. Says the Israelis have been in touch with State about this, demanding things as usual."

Neuman shrugged. "Yeah, so what? It's like you always say,

Bobby, give those people an inch and they'll take a mile. We always push them off at first, you know that."

Bob said, "In this case, maybe they know something you don't."

"Right, like always." She scratched her ear. "Look, these people, whoever they are, managed to take out a CIA man, which makes it a CIA problem, and by the way, CIA is very capable of speaking with Jerusalem if they so wish. All of this has the added benefit of not being my problem. I hear CIA never closes the book, so justice will be done, eventually. Just not with me involved."

Neuman lifted her left foot and removed a high-heeled shoe. "The world is full of problems, Bobby." The shoe went flying across the room and the other shoe was removed. "The problems are endless, and they just keep coming. Problem after problem after problem." Her denuded foot now moved to part Bob's robe, seeking the inner folds below his waist. Neuman played it surprised. "Oh my, what kind of problem do we have here?"

She was genuinely surprised at the hot flush coming up through her middle. Blood and guts used to get her going back in the day, five or ten years ago. Maybe she was having a second youth. Bob put a meaty hand on her leg. Moving it up from the knee to the thigh. Neuman smiled, knowing that her husband was going to say something funny.

"What you've discovered there is a very hard problem, honey," he said. "Hard problems often demand soft and delicate solutions."

She lifted her eyebrows, letting herself slide into a deeper recline. "Oh, Bob, you've got such a way with hard-to-grasp concepts. I always wonder about those post-grad students of yours, how you can fend them off so diligently."

Bob laughed and gripped her harder around the thigh,

squeezing and sliding his hand farther up, letting the finger tips tease the regions above. "It's one thing being Professor Bob with a PhD, and quite another getting laid with it."

"Yeah, right."

Neuman reached her left hand out to the night-light, finding the dangling chord, and in a click, the room was in a perfect half-darkness.

SIXTEEN

Tina Choi was a silhouette at the batik-covered window, moving this way and that. Kind of swaying in fact, her phone held up to her ear, in conversation with someone at the embassy, pacing like some kind of restless animal. Keeler was full stretch on the sofa. Half listening to Choi's conversation, the few times she got a word in.

Keeler was a little tired, but he liked what he was looking at. Watching her made him feel good.

She was saying things like, "Yes, okay. Yes, yes. No." Mostly yes.

They were back at Brooklyn. Keeler had figured since the safe house was abandoned, it would be overlooked. The key was hidden at the back of an unused garbage chute, still there when Keeler reached for it. He couldn't think of a better place to hole up, since he'd made the executive decision that hotels, hostels, and guesthouses were off-limits.

Turkey, the kind of country where the military's main job is to occupy and suppress their own people. Pretty much every other person you saw was a police informer. That would be true for eighty percent of hotel staff.

Keeler was enjoying a highly meditative mental state, letting the interesting recent events come in and out of his mind, filtered through the vision of Choi at the window, fine boned and very beautiful. She had straight black hair which she kept having to push back behind her ear.

Slim in the right places and strong in the right places. Like an acrobat or a dancer.

Keeler wasn't any kind of jewelry expert, but the ring on Choi's left hand looked significant, in the sense that it might signify that a wedding had taken place, or was scheduled to take place at some point in the future. She wore a silver crucifix on a silver chain. Choi had it out from under the sweater and was fooling with the charm while listening to someone talking down the line.

An hour before, things had been different. They'd been running and ducking and diving through the narrow streets of downtown Ankara. There had been a moment when Keeler, realizing that Choi hadn't kept up, had gone back and found her bent over, puking her guts out. Keeler had pulled her hair out of the way, and she'd looked up at him, face full of tears, eyes red.

What she'd said exactly: "It's my first day."

Somehow, Keeler had understood what she meant by that. She'd never seen killing before. He'd seen a lot of it, it wasn't his first day. He'd used his sleeve to wipe away the vomit on her chin.

He'd said, "Everybody gets a first day."

Choi had glared at him and turned back to the wall. She'd opened her mouth and screamed and howled, putting everything she had into it. When she was done, Keeler had taken her shoulders in his hands and looked at her straight. She'd looked back, defiant and vulnerable all at once.

He'd said, "Good?"

Choi had nodded. "Good."

In the back of a taxi, they'd been silent, each looking out the window and seeing something else. Once they'd entered the safe house, Keeler had taken her into the kitchen, sat her down, and tried to make coffee, but there hadn't been any coffee, only tea. Which worked for Choi, which is what mattered.

Choi cradled a mug in two hands, listening to Keeler telling her everything that had happened up to that point, giving her a full debrief. Which he figured was the least he could do, since she was now deeply implicated. He told her about the scene he'd come across at Canada, the woman in the cement mixer. He'd left out the memory card and the camera, wanting to hold it back until she'd spoken to her people, interested to see what questions they would ask him.

Because Keeler didn't trust the bureaucrats. He wanted to know what they knew, what they would say.

Choi told him about the escape at the Holiday Inn, what had happened after that CIA guy Anderson had been shot. She'd been angry, to the point of panic, worried about how the enemy had gotten into their communications cycle, if there was a mole.

Keeler had told her about the lobby, how the perpetrators had passed over him, not recognizing his face. Choi's eyes flicked up in alarm.

She said, "So you're saying they're in the system."

"Yes. I think they must have hacked your system. You need to shut it down."

Choi looked away, face flushed.

Once they'd finished the tea, Choi called in on her secure device, a professional after all.

* * *

SHE FINISHED her phone conversation and turned to Keeler. He swung his legs off the sofa to give her space and she took a seat, her face coming into the lamplight. Keeler could see that she was beat to hell with fatigue.

He said, "So?"

She glanced at him briefly and leaned back, staring up at the ceiling. "DIA will send a team in to audit the system. As of now it's dead. But, you're not going to be happy. First of all, nobody is coming for us and they've already exfiltrated your team to Amman."

"Why did they do that?"

Choi didn't know. "Well, it means they're backing off, right?"

"Who else is involved?"

"What do you mean, at the embassy?"

"Yes."

She said, "Depends on who needs to be involved. There's a CIA guy who was working with Anderson, and there's me on the clandestine service side. The Acting Chief of Mission and the Deputy Chief. Miller's acting Chief and I don't know who they brought up to replace him as deputy. He could bring in the Counselor for Political Affairs, if the locals get a whiff. I guess a lot depends upon what the CIA wants, at this point." She shrugged. "Anderson was theirs. It's possible they'll want to play it their own way."

Keeler said, "*Acting* Chief of Mission. What happened to the Ambassador?"

"They moved him to Kabul, apparently. I only heard about it when they woke me up." Choi gestured around. "For this."

Keeler said nothing, waiting for the real information.

Choi said, "And that's it. Bottom line is they're going to get back to me about exfiltration. I think they just want you out of the country, period."

"Get back to you, huh?"

"Yeah, he said four hours max."

Unsatisfying. "And Canada, what happened up there, what are they planning to do about that?"

Choi was tired. "Your role in this is over, Keeler. I know how you guys normally like to cowboy, but you're working for the State Department here, which means the Chief of Mission ultimately calls the shots. Our job is to advise and propose. He gets to decide."

A thin smile crawled up Keeler's face. "There's a zero percent chance of me exfiltrating. I'm not going anywhere. I require information relating to what happened last night. Call your guy again and let me speak to him. I don't give a shit who he thinks he is. We're not in Maryland."

Choi looked at him weird, like there was something she wasn't saying.

"Spit it out, Choi."

She looked away, rolled her eyes. "Miller just told me your unit commander didn't want to leave the battlefield, like that's some kind of taboo for you people. Miller warned me about you. Are you going to make this complicated, Keeler?"

"It's already complicated." Keeler was smiling—not because it was complicated, but because he was thinking about Calcutti acting the hard case. He looked at Choi and made his face hard and serious. "Yeah, so I'm not leaving, Choi. Tell your chief actor, or whatever that pencil neck is called, to wake up. You didn't say anything about the other guy, Karim Ahmadi. Has he checked in yet? Because if he hasn't, I'd take that very seriously."

Keeler half expected Choi to react in a negative way to his blunt manner, but she didn't. Quite the opposite, Choi looked at him for a second and then her face opened up like she actually believed him.

Choi said, "Roger that. I get you." She paused, thinking. "But let me ask you something, there's something else, isn't there? Something makes this special, or different for you. No?"

Keeler didn't hesitate. "Affirmative. That woman I told you about, the one I pulled out of a cement mixer and then watched die in front of me, we had some words—not exactly a conversation, but there were words exchanged. She made me promise her something. Actually, she used the word *pledge*."

Choi looked at him funny. "Pledge. That's cute. What did you pledge?"

Keeler was aware how old-fashioned the phrase sounded, but was unashamed of it, owned it. He said, "I don't exactly know, but it's something about *the girl*. What she'd said up there, dying on the street and looking up at me. She said, *Help the girl*."

"Who is the girl?"

Keeler shrugged. "I really don't know. But we're going to have to find out."

He felt content in the knowledge that it made no difference that he had no idea who the girl was. He was neither happy nor unhappy about the pledge, something he'd promised impulsively. A pledge like that was a deed already done, not a negotiable variable in any kind of complicated equation.

Choi turned her head, looking at the batik-covered window. "I don't know how to feel about your *pledge*. It's not very professional."

"Remember that it's your first day, Choi. This is my four thousandth day, or something. I haven't counted. Right now, I could use your help. I figure you've got at least two college degrees." He came upright. "And we've got four hours to kill, right?"

She didn't shrink away, but turned toward him. Curious to know what he was talking about. That was really the moment he felt something for her, understanding that Choi wasn't simply another suit from the embassy. He'd already seen it in her behavior back at the Holiday Inn. He saw it again in the way she attended to what he was trying to do, the combination of curiosity and professionalism, so rare.

Keeler swung the bag up from the floor and let it drop perfectly to the coffee table.

"Am I right?"

"About what?"

"The college degrees."

"Almost, I mean, yes, I have two or three degrees, depending how you want to count. I did a double masters in chemistry and international relations at Johns Hopkins." She shrugged. "Plus, you know."

The laptop came sliding out of the bag. Keeler removed the memory card from the change pocket of his jeans and inserted it into a slot in the machine.

"I want you to look at something with me."

He felt her physical presence as she slid closer, warmth and the smell of dried sweat.

Choi said, "What is it?"

The screen came to life and Keeler did the necessary password input. The memory card was filled with image files. He used his thick forefinger on a trackpad to select the files and open them. He sat back as the screen began to fill with boxes animating and opening, loading and rendering.

SEVENTEEN

Choi was leaning toward the laptop screen, examining a photograph of a guy smoking a cigarette. This was the last of six hundred and eighty-two image files.

She turned to examine Keeler, something dispassionate in her eyes, like he was being evaluated. "Why didn't you say anything earlier about this?"

He had anticipated the question. "I assumed you were going to ask me about it, but you didn't."

She didn't get it, busy now copying the contents of the memory card to the laptop's hard drive. "What made you assume that I'd ask? It was a CIA operation, apparently."

"There I was, thinking you were the CIA."

Choi scowled. "I work for the DIA."

Defense Intelligence Agency. He said, "Oh."

She looked back at him. "I've got a double posting to Ankara. MASINT plus DIA rep at the embassy. We coordinate nonproliferation work, plus DIA runs the technical networks, like the one that got you into the Holiday Inn."

MASINT made sense, he thought, looking at Choi. Measurement and Signature Intelligence, the agency that does things like dropping sensors into various advantageous positions in places all over the world. Getting readings on chemical and nuclear substances, stuff transiting in and out of ports, trafficking of various flavors.

He said, "Are you declared?"

"Yes."

Keeler nodded. *Declared* meant registered with the Turkish authorities as a US intelligence official working out of the embassy. It could be advantageous, at least in the sense that it gave her diplomatic cover. Further questions could wait, for the time being.

Choi turned back to the computer and started again from the beginning. Clicking slowly through the images. The photos were of three locations, each of them captured through a high-power telephoto lens from that living room up in Çankaya. All three of the photographed locations were from the same building, sharing the same glossy white exterior cladding, giving off high-tech vibes.

Keeler remembered the tripod, set high in the middle of the room. Judging by the sequence of shots and repeated locations, the team at Çankaya had been operating for more than a week.

CIA operation, indeed.

Recalling the bodies and the dental work, and the fact that nobody seemed to know who they were, Keeler couldn't help but see the comedic aspect, the basic truth. Eighteen intelligence agencies and ten times as many corporates were all feeding off the federal tit, creating a shit storm so intense that nobody knew what they were doing, let alone what anyone else was up to.

First up was a photo of a courtyard shot from a very steep angle. It was the smoking area out back of a building, a patio with slate flagstones, plant beds, and a standing ashtray. There were quite a few people moving in and out of the pictures, flicking ash, drinking coffee, stubbing butts, looking at phones, and jawing at each other. Many of them wore medical outfits. The outfits were color coordinated, pink for the female nurses and dark blue for the male surgeons.

So, some kind of medical facility. Maybe a private clinic.

Looking at the nurses, Keeler imagined how it would be, lying back on the operating table as the opioids enter your bloodstream, pink-clad women hustling around, sticking things into your arm. It made him laugh.

About half of the shots from the outdoor location featured a bearded guy wearing a leather jacket. Not only a heavy smoker, but a classic military-aged male, with a full head of hair and a full black beard. Keeler had leaned in and taken a good look at that guy. Never smiling, watchful eyes, athletic build. A guy who looked like he'd taken scalps. Keeler figured he was the main focus of the surveillance on that location. The other half of the images from the smoking spot looked to be pure data collection, getting workable face shots of people associated with the place, just in case.

Another location was a room, photographed through a window maybe thirty degrees down from the camera's position. It looked like a fancy waiting room or a lobby. The images showed half of a cream leather armchair, a leather sofa, and a coffee table. The foreground had floor space. Above the coffee table was a framed illustration of a pink landscape.

The bearded man featured in many of those shots, mostly sitting back in the leather armchair looking alert, but sometimes standing by the window and looking out, like he was already jonesing for a smoke. There were other people in the shots, besides the beard, two of them repeatedly photographed: a young woman in her late teens or early twenties and an older man hovering around sixty. The older guy was tall and skinny and liked to keep his face cleanly shaved.

Sometimes he wore a suit and tie and sometimes a navy-blue surgical outfit.

The young woman had a large hooked nose.

The third location was out front of the same building. A big lit-up sign read *Zaros Aesthetica*, evidently the name of the clinic. The logo was in light blue, giving off soothing medical vibes. The shots were taken through the windshield and side window of a vehicle. They showed the clinic as well as part of an adjoining building.

These shots were classic stakeout material. Keeler was wondering about the vehicles. What would fit in and not draw attention? Taxi cab, or maybe they'd rotated rental cars parked out front, switching it up enough so it didn't make a pattern on the CCTV feeds.

The first angle was from directly in front of the clinic. Subjects came in and out of the front door. Mostly the surgeon from the waiting room, wearing his sharp suit and carrying a slim briefcase. The well-dressed surgeon had a clear pattern of life, emerging in the morning light from a late-model Land Rover, handing off keys to a valet. Later on, he'd be coming out of the building and getting back into his car, usually after dark.

Keeler said, "Hard worker and maybe a family man. Leaves work, goes home expecting dinner. Comes back to work the next day."

Choi clicked in to a close-up shot of his license plate. "You think he got a visit already, from our dead friends?"

Keeler raised his eyebrows, easily picturing a home invasion in a fancy suburb of Ankara, probably a gated community. He said, "I have no idea."

The second angle of the clinic included an adjoining building and a passage between the two structures. The passage was covered, and it was clear that the two buildings were related. The shots were all of the young girl from before, exiting the adjoining building and entering the clinic by a side door. The bearded man was omnipresent.

In the final images, the woman had a bandage covering her nose.

Keeler and Choi had said it in unison the first time they'd seen the photo: "Nose job."

Choi giggled. "What about the adjacent building?"

Keeler called it. "Accommodation. Patients stay there while they're doing the procedure and for the recovery."

"Right."

Keeler was looking hard at the bearded guy who constantly accompanied her. Watchful and alert, opening doors and letting her through. Following right behind her and checking his six. Keeler put a finger on the guy's image. "Bodyguard or captor?"

Choi said, "Why captor?"

He'd shrugged, didn't know why. It was just a thought that came to mind. Maybe it was how the man was alert and predatory. He revised that thought. The vibes coming off the young woman were more significant, even in still images. It was her posture, the way her body oriented to the guy, like she was afraid of him. Choi yawned deeply, leaned back against the sofa cushions and closed her eyes.

Keeler took her place at the computer, zooming in on an image showing the young woman's face, before the surgery. He got it nice and big on the screen.

The woman dying up in Canada. *Help the girl.*

This was the girl.

Choi had turned over on her side and was leaning against the sofa's armrest. She mumbled sleepily. "Jeez. I wonder if the CIA even knows about these photos."

Which was a damned good question.

Keeler was still looking at the girl's face, letting it burn into his memory. Thinking that he might have to recognize her with surgically altered features. Maybe the surgery wasn't voluntary. Choi yawned.

Keeler said, "Go into the bedroom and get some sleep."

She stood up stiffly. "Okay. Wake me up in an hour?"

Keeler made a mumbled sound, which was meant to be interpreted as either something or nothing, not wanting to make any more promises or pledges.

* * *

WHEN CHOI WAS GONE, he flipped the laptop over to access the back and used the jeweler's tools to get into the guts of the machine and reconnect the Wi-Fi card to the motherboard. It took a minute for the laptop to reboot. Cheevers had hacked the neighbor's Wi-Fi password. Keeler connected to it and looked up the clinic.

Zaros Aesthetica had a website with an English language option. Keeler read the menu of what the clinic offered. Hair transplantation and dental surgery seemed clear. Breast augmentation made sense, like Botox, face-lifts, and liposuction. But things like blepharoplasty, brachioplasty, and vaginal reju-venation remained mysterious.

He found what he was looking for in the *about* section of the site. A list of their top surgeons with short biographical data and a head shot. Doctor Fatih Erkin was the guy in the photographs they'd seen. He was fifty-eight years old and a co-founder of the clinic. Keeler memorized Erkin's face and then wiped the historical search data off the computer. He removed the memory card from the computer and put it back in his jeans.

Choi was fast asleep in the back room, purring like a cat. The Heckler & Koch VP9 was on the night table next to her phone.

Keeler left the apartment quietly and descended to the

street. The city was in full flow and he felt liberated to be out there, operating among the civilian population. Better still, he felt like a hunter.

He bought a new burner phone and SIM card from the store on the corner. Powered it up and got it working, just in case.

Keeler was about to move out, but something held him back. Thinking about Choi, sleeping there all cute with her wedding ring, or engagement ring or whatever. He went up to the apartment and entered, quiet as possible. The SIM he'd just bought came in a punch-out card. The phone number was on the back of it.

Keeler left the card on the table, just in case Choi needed to get in touch.

EIGHTEEN

Tina Choi was in church, weird. No, not church, a blessing ceremony with around five thousand other people. Everybody was chanting the same words, but for some reason, Choi couldn't remember what to say.

Our family pledges to build the universal family encompassing Heaven and Earth, which is God's ideal of creation, and to perfect the world of freedom, unity, and happiness, by centering on true love.

Words that were supposed to be joyful, but to Choi, unaware she was dreaming, they sounded menacing and foreign.

She snapped awake, rudely broken out of the dream, disoriented. Her phone was ringing silently, vibrating against the night table with a soft buzz. Next to it lay the 9mm pistol Keeler had taken from the dead man and handed to her.

Acting Chief of Mission Miller was on the line. "We sent a car to get you. Be downstairs in five."

For some reason it caught her by surprise, even though it should not have. She said, "Where to?"

"Back to the embassy. We can figure out logistics from here. Five minutes."

She rolled off the bed, a little groggy. Maybe the call had interrupted one of those ninety minute sleep cycles she'd heard about. Or maybe that was all bullshit and she was just tired. She looked at the time: ten. She'd been asleep for an hour and a half.

Choi went out to find Keeler and tell him to get ready.

The laptop was on the coffee table, and a new SIM card next to it. No, not the SIM, just the card, with a phone number on it. Keeler wasn't in the safe house, which meant he'd gone out on his own. Choi wasn't surprised, which was interesting. She pocketed the phone card and wondered what to do with the pistol in the bedroom. She wasn't going to bring it with her, so she just left it on the coffee table for Keeler.

Several minutes later she was climbing into the back of an SUV with blackened windows. The two guys up front were marines in plain clothes, wearing earpieces with coiled cords running into the collar. Their identical bull necks reminded her of elephant legs she'd seen on a family trip to the zoo once.

She'd slid into the back seat, the passenger looking back at her. He had hard eyes.

"Ma'am, Staff Sergeant Leonard, I'm the Marine Detachment Commander here in Ankara. We were expecting two of you."

"The other guy's not here." The man looked at her, expecting more. She said, "Isn't Staff Sergeant a little light to be Detachment Commander here?"

Leonard gave a slight dip of his chin. "Yes, ma'am."

But he didn't explain more. Just kept on looking at her. The driver didn't look back, his head swiveling between mirrors and the windows.

She said, "I don't know where he is."

Leonard said, "Unofficially, ma'am, is it true that he's a PJ, Captain, name of Keeler? It's what we heard from the team that just exfiltrated."

"You know him?"

"Haven't met him personally, ma'am." He corrected himself. "I mean, not shook his hand or anything."

"Well, he's not coming, so let's go."

Leonard used a mobile phone to call it in, said a couple of words in a monotone and handed a phone to her.

Miller was pissed off. "How did you let him leave the safe house?"

She had no excuse, so didn't try to give one. Fact was, with Anderson a corpse, Choi was now the senior intelligence officer in Ankara. The Chief of Mission always called the shots, but neither Miller nor the Ambassador were from the clandestine service.

The driver was looking at her in the rearview, impossible to read behind the sunglasses. She hung up when Miller was mid-sentence because she didn't like the way he was speaking to her. She handed the phone over to the front. Choi said, "Okay, let's go."

The marines were happy to receive a command. They rolled up their windows and got the vehicle moving through the tight Ankara streets. Out through downtown and up the hill to the diplomatic district in Çankaya.

Choi took out her phone and the SIM card thing Keeler had left on the coffee table. She dialed the number.

Keeler picked up on a single ring. "Yeah."

"I'm in a car going up to the embassy. Why did you leave the apartment?"

"Wanted to check out the clinic."

"And?"

"I'm getting there. I thought they said four hours?"

"Well, they sent a car now. It is what it is."

Keeler said nothing, which Choi found infuriating. She said, "I need the password for the laptop. I'll have to show the photographs to people at the embassy, try to get things moving."

He gave her the password and hung up, abruptly ending the conversation. She called him again and he didn't answer. An SMS message came a minute later. "Do your thing at the embassy. I need my team back in Ankara. Tell them that."

Choi let out a breath. Here was one guy who didn't understand how things actually worked. Living in his own bubble world of special operations. DIA was military, although not strictly speaking in the chain of command. Still, she had enough association with military types to know what she was dealing with.

An American embassy abroad is designed to project real power in the world. The embassy in Ankara was no exception. Coming there to work every day, Choi was always impressed by the building, a squat and sprawling two-story fortress behind iron gates and concrete bomber-prevention blocks. That stuff wasn't academic either, a couple of years back a guy with a suicide vest had killed himself and two Turkish guards just outside the embassy, blowing a hole in the wall.

Things had been adjusted after that.

They came in through the rear entrance, a set of iron gates backed up by a truck bomb-stopping thing that looked like the inside of an alligator's mouth. Two Turkish guards with assault rifles and body armor were posted out front. They'd be the ones who'd get blown to pieces if another bomber showed up. Four marines were deployed inside the gates: two up front and another two stepped back twenty yards.

The SUV came through, and the marine in the passenger seat spoke to the air. "We're inside."

They crested a hill, and the parking garage opened like a dark mouth, devoured the SUV and closed behind them.

The marine up front turned his head ten degrees. "They're waiting for you up in the situation room, ma'am."

NINETEEN

THE SITUATION ROOM was a weird combination of busy and calm. Busy, because the screens were filled with concerned faces. Calm because, besides the three people beaming in remotely, there was only the Acting Chief of Mission and Anderson's CIA sidekick, whose name escaped Choi, Dinkle-bat, or Dilbert or something of that nature.

Choi stood in the doorway for a second before anyone acknowledged her presence. She wasn't a complete noob, but she was young. Six months so far in Ankara and still getting used to how things operated. Most of the six months had been spent either getting up to speed on existing MASINT opera-tions, or researching future potential projects, none of which had yet moved beyond the planning stage.

Her mentor had always told her to read the room.

Five people, if you included the remote presence populating screens one, two, and three. Miller, the other guy, and the three remote participants were concerned with devices in their hands, staring into the small screens and accessing virtual worlds, both highly public and specifically private, in complicated ways.

She counted the men in the room and the women, herself included. Four to two.

Another two screens were devoted to data display. Currently showing a real-time heat map of the planet, *World Freedom Index* in large white text up top. Parts of the world were more blue than others, parts were red. Russia and China were red. Turkey was orange. The United States and Canada were deep blue, along with some of Europe and Australia.

Reading the room, Choi noticed there was no representative from the Political Section, no Regional Security type, which indicated a lack of concern for security, and the feeling that this issue was contained.

The other thing her mentor had said was if you walk into a room full of people waiting for you, they've got the power. You need to mess something up.

The situation room was secured against electronic surveillance. A SCIF room, for Sensitive Compartmented Information Facility. Choi pushed the heavy door, and it closed with a sucking sound. The air pressure adjusted, as if a new altitude had been reached.

Faces turned to her. She locked eyes with Miller and stalked to the conference table, the most underrated of foreign service hunting grounds.

"I'm ready to debrief. I don't see the Deputy Chief of Mission here." She made eye contact with the remote faces. Looked back at Miller. "I don't want to have to do this twice, fellas, can we get going?" She snapped her fingers twice.

Miller shook himself awake. "Uh, if you're asking about the new *Acting* Deputy Chief of Mission, it's Kathy Jensen, our Counselor for Agricultural Affairs." He indicated the screens, two middle-aged men and a younger woman, none of whom Choi had met. "We're thinking it'd be good to keep this small, kind of a need-to-know basis." He managed a cough that might have been intended as a laugh. "Last I heard Kathy Jensen was out there inspecting hazelnut trees, or getting taste tests from the apricot harvest." He looked up, hoping that Choi would be satisfied.

She said, "No," then watched Miller's face turn red, knowing her mentor would be pleased by that.

Choi wasn't being frivolous either, she was just working it like a professional. It was precisely at moments like this that protocol was important. It was designed for panicked idiots like Miller. She moved to the teleconference console at the center of the table, punched the button for the assistant to the Chief of Mission.

Choi said, "Can you get the Counselor for Agricultural Affairs up here, please? Kathy Jensen."

A female voice made positive sounds from the other side of the electronics.

Choi glanced at Miller, who looked like death. Droplets of sweat on his forehead, face the color of chalk. "What happened to you? You look terrible."

Miller blinked. "Must have been something I ate."

The assistant's voice hissed and crackled. "Mrs. Jensen is coming up from her office now."

The man on screen two coughed and spoke. "Miller, you want to get this started?"

Miller pointed at the faces on screens and made introductions. Screens one and three were CIA. One, an executive type from a corporate contractor firm and three, a legal advisor from Langley. On the screen in the middle was a man from the State Department, who said he was just sitting in as an observer, not a participant.

Choi said, "While we're waiting for Jensen, I was

wondering if we had the file on Keeler." She could see that the name was drawing a blank for Miller. "That's the JSOC operative Anderson was supposed to debrief at the Holiday Inn. Guy I was with earlier."

Miller looked at the CIA man in the room, who shrugged and looked at Choi.

Miller said, "Uh, that's out of Fort Bragg, Choi. We'll have to go to Defense if we want the file on this guy. Why don't you debrief us on what happened, and we'll address that offline."

The observer from the State Department leaned forward and activated a microphone. He said, "I don't see why that's necessary, Miller. Caution is the byword here, minimizing blowback, which includes putting a ring fence around the amount of paperwork that gets generated."

Miller was nodding vigorously. "Choi, you have any idea what's going on in Washington? It's total chaos."

Choi wasn't completely understanding what the heck these people were talking about.

She tried being polite. "I'm sorry about the difficulties in DC. Here in Ankara we've got Americans being killed. I was lucky to get away from the hotel. After which, I was attacked once again. If that JSOC operator hadn't been around, I'd be a corpse too."

Miller was holding up his hand, like it would protect him. "Look, we've got instructions, directly from the Undersecretary of State for Politics. We're to stand down. Neuman wants us to back off completely."

Choi was having some kind of flashback to what had happened just a few hours earlier. The sheer physical reality of the thing. She could feel her fury rising.

"What do you mean by stand down, exactly?"

Miller swallowed. Choi watched as he looked up at the screens, appeared to be trying reasonableness as a rhetorical tactic. "Let's slow down. It's turmoil over there in DC. Incoming administration's already got the transition teams in place, and they're moving aggressively. The feeling coming out of Washington is that this isn't the time for anything, uh, significant to actually happen."

As if significance waits for the prepared.

Choi said, "Which means what to me, exactly?"

The door sucked open and the atmosphere adjusted. An older lady in a red business suit was in the doorway, white hair in a coif. "Sorry, am I interrupting?"

This time when the door sucked closed, Anderson's assistant put his fingers in his ears. He mumbled. "I hate that feeling."

Miller waved his hand. "Come on in, Kathy. Maybe you can enlighten Ms. Choi as to the strange doings of our political masters in Washington."

Jensen came over to the table. "I don't think I know what you mean, Jim." She looked at Choi. "Hi, we haven't met. I'm Kathy Jensen. Counselor for Agricultural Affairs." She moved a hand around the table and gave a tight smile. "And um, Deputy Chief of Mission as of right about now."

Jensen held out her hand politely, making eye contact. The hand was cold and soft. The eyes were more promising, containing residual ambition.

"Tina Choi. Defense Intelligence Agency liaison."

"I've never met you, are you new?"

"Six months, so yeah, I guess I'm new." Jensen was still looking at her, like she expected more information. Choi said, "I'm a MASINT specialist."

The woman nodded with eyes that sparked with intelligence. "Ah, you're a scientist, someone who actually knows something about something. I'm in agriculture, we have to deal with the real world too." A flashing smile. "Like soil and rain and fertilizer and droughts and stuff. When the crops don't grow, it's a real problem, not a theoretical problem."

Choi noticed Miller staring at Jensen with malice, as if he had a problem with her, which was ridiculous since Choi had quickly found a lot to like.

TWENTY

KATHY JENSEN TOOK A SEAT. She looked at Miller. "Are you okay, Jim? You look sick."

Miller got red in the face. "If another person tells me that, I just might pop a gasket. I'm all right, thank you. Something I ate didn't agree with me." He looked at Choi directly. "You've got Kathy up here now, so without wasting any more time, can you tell us exactly what happened?"

Choi had the bag containing the laptop with the images that Keeler had retrieved from the dead woman at Çankaya. Would any of them ask about the files? She laid the bag on the table and told them what had happened, from beginning to end, leaving out the part with the laptop and images.

When she'd finished, Choi put both of her hands flat on the table and looked up, ready to observe reactions.

Miller was looking at the screens, clearly deferring to someone up there. The two CIA people were nodding. The State Department man had his chin in hand and was scratching at an ear with his other.

Miller seemed to realize that everyone was waiting for him to speak. "Okay, wow, thank you, Tina." Like this was an Alcoholics Anonymous meeting. Choi half expected a round of applause.

If she was expecting more from Miller, she didn't get it. The State Department observer filled the silence. "Can we get an update on the KIA, guy name of Anderson?"

The CIA man on screen one was looking at something off camera. He drew out the first word, "Yes." Looked up through rectangular glasses. "Anderson was with Booz Allen, not a direct employee. So, the blowback on that is to be absorbed by his legal employers and not something we need to worry about. Booz Allen always has a generous package in place for next of kin." He looked up. "Simon?"

Anderson's assistant now had a first name. He said, "Corporate is maintaining a holding pattern off-site, monitoring the situation and preparing to deal with the local authorities as and when necessary. Local law enforcement is going through the motions. And, uh, once that's complete, the body will be repatriated."

"Okay, so that's all corporate, not our problem," Miller said, waving a hand around like it was a lasso designed to capture only foreign service personnel.

"Correct."

The man from the State Department seemed happy. "Great."

Kathy Jensen spoke. "Ms. Choi, that must have been a hell of an experience, I'm glad you got through it. I have a few questions." She looked at Miller.

"Uh, shoot, Kathy."

Jensen said, "I was a little surprised, getting up to speed earlier on the plane." She counted on her fingers. "An American killed at the Holiday Inn, plus, an operational team a hundred percent wiped out? I mean Jeez, Louise!" She looked around the room at the faces, clearly dissatisfied. "Is there going to be a response to this? You say that you're planning to back off it. What was the operation? The entire team was executed. I'm the first to acknowledge my lack of expertise, but there must be a reason why somebody thought that was necessary." She was searching for words. "I mean, what *normally* happens in this kind of situation?"

Miller waved his hands in the air for the remote faces. "I can probably take this one." He made another reasonable face and spoke deliberately, as if to a child. "Kathy, all good questions. When it comes to the clandestine operations in an area under the control of an embassy, there are no normal situations. The purpose of this meeting was for our DIA liaison, Miss Choi, to brief us on what has just happened out there. After which, our task is to arrive at a sober assessment of the political, diplomatic, and security ramifications for the United States Mission in Turkey. That is our primary role." He nodded to the man from the State Department.

The observer from the State Department realized that he was being addressed. "Yes. From where I'm sitting this unfortunate chain of events can be wrapped up. You'll have to exfiltrate the remaining JSOC asset, Jim. Do you have an ETA on that?"

Miller said, "He's safe, on ice at the moment." He glanced at Choi. "Plan is for him to slip out in a day or two. I think it's prudent to let the events settle."

The State Department guy was staring into the camera. "Do you require additional resources?"

"No, sir, that's why I think it's best we let him cool down."

Choi had a cold feeling come down from the top of her head to her toes. This guy Miller was a coward, simply telling them what he thought they wanted to hear.

The State Department man nodded once, curtly. "Well great. Once that's accomplished, I think we all want to step back and clear the slate over there. Sometimes that's best. We can start over when the new administration's ready to get their feet wet." He laughed hoarsely.

Choi slid the laptop out of the bag. "I've got images here, retrieved by the JSOC asset from the operational team up at Çankaya. They were engaged in static surveillance of a target, which is, I assume why they were in the safe house to begin with."

She made eye contact with Jensen. "Who do I give this to?"

Miller looked surprised, but he had an answer. Pointed to Anderson's man from Booz Allen, yet another CIA contractor. "Uh, I guess that should go to you, yes?"

The man nodded. "I'll take that, thanks."

Choi watched as he got his hands on the laptop and pulled it toward him, then lifted it carefully from the table and inserted it into a large briefcase. Would they look at the photos? This was an educational experience for her, an eye-opener. She looked at Jensen, who had been watching the same thing. The older woman looked pissed off.

Jensen actually raised her hand, like she needed permission to speak. She said, "Just so I'm clear on this." She indicated Anderson's CIA assistant. "There isn't any actual agency presence here; you're a contractor. Correct?"

"Yes, ma'am."

"Okay, gotcha." She pointed up at the screen. "And you up there. Screen one. Are you in Langley, or are you also corporate?"

The CIA man smiled broadly. "My office is in Fairfax, but they know me very well over at Langley."

The woman on screen three chirped up. "I'm at Langley, ma'am. We work with a lot of people, including many in the private sector. If you have any questions we can talk offline." It was the first time the woman had spoken, and now she smiled with very bright white teeth. "Guys, I've gotta jet. Far as legal is concerned you're all good."

Choi watched Kathy Jensen keeping a lid on it. She could see that the older lady was frustrated and felt it herself upon seeing the alarming rate that things were being swept under the rug. These people thought that was okay, even business as usual.

Jensen simply nodded and smiled. "Thank you."

Choi stayed in her seat once the meeting ended, looking at the screens blink off as people ended the online session. Anderson's assistant packed up his briefcase and got out of there. He'd be going down to the clandestine service's offices. Miller had rushed away as soon as he could, looking like he badly needed a bathroom.

The phone in her hands vibrated as soon as she walked out of the SCIF. A message from Keeler's burner. Choi tapped the icon to open it. The text message was like a military command. "I need you up at the clinic. Get here."

Choi stared at the message, thinking about Keeler, The hotshot from JSOC who'd saved her life. She hadn't met many of those special tactics types, and he was certainly special. Still, there was no reason to let him control the situation. That was their default mode, people like him: control the situation.

She tapped a message back, "Negative."

TWENTY-ONE

KEELER WAS CHEWING on a toothpick he'd gotten at a kebab stall, sitting at a bus stop, obliquely angled to the front entrance of the clinic. Zaros Aesthetica was a busy place, people coming and going. Much of it looking like client traffic, shiny black luxury vehicles disgorging and receiving patients.

The phone bleeped and he read the message from Choi. "Negative."

Figures, she was an actual person, unlike most. The tooth-pick was shredded already. Keeler gave it a death grind and spat the shards out onto the sidewalk.

He'd been thinking about offering Choi up for a breast implant, using her as a decoy to get in there and poke around. That was plan A. Now it was time for plan B, use himself. Biggest issue was his full head of hair, but since he wasn't a conventionally handsome guy there wasn't going to be any trouble finding an appropriate cosmetic modification.

Keeler went straight into the clinic through the front door. Smiled amiably at the security guy and made it to the shiny front desk, literally glowing with health from some internal light source. Two young women in pink scrubs were looking at him with fresh faces; behind them an office door yawned open.

He smiled broadly. "I've got an appointment, Martin Van Buren."

The name had come directly from the back of his mind to the tip of his tongue, leaping off before he gave it a thought. It took a second for Keeler to recall who that was. Van Buren, eighth president of the United States of America, little Dutch guy from New York, stood five foot six and was unlucky enough to have taken office just before the country sank into an economic depression three months after his inauguration. The shit wasn't his, but he'd eaten it anyway and come out smiling.

Which made Van Buren a role model.

One of the women in pink approached. "Please, your name again?"

He spelled it out and she made a show of looking on the computer. Keeler moved to the right and saw into the office. The edge of a desk and two fingers with dark nail polish, nothing more.

She said, "Who was the appointment with please?"

"Dr. Erkin." He touched his nose. "It's for my nose."

She gazed into the screen. "You have appointment confirmation?"

He held up the burner phone. "Battery is dead, or I'd be able to show you the email."

She was looking at him. "Please wait." She nodded at her colleague and said something in Turkish. The colleague said something back to her and she addressed Keeler once more. "Rhinoplasty." Looked at Keeler, clearly expecting him to know this word. "For the nose?"

"The nose, yup."

She indicated a waiting area, visible through a glass partition. "Please."

Two teal green couches were arranged in L formation around a coffee table laden with flowers, brochures, and a bowl of candy in plastic-wrapped twists. A large TV on mute showed a loop of before and after videos. Keeler sat on the couch. The clips were strangely interesting. Women with bent noses made straight, aligning to some kind of standardized ideal. Bald men suddenly appeared with thick hair, and the camera panned to their confident eyes. Combs caressed through heavy locks, proving each graft true. Women stretched their arms upward in skintight tank tops and bikinis, breast augmentation and liposuction fantasies. Natural smiles and glistening white teeth gnashing. The whole thing looked incredible, as if anyone who walked in there would come out a winner.

A little red-faced dandy dressed in tweed, with a goatee and a hat appeared.

"Mr. Van Buren?" He spoke in a British accent.

Keeler nodded. "Yes."

A hand the color of a blended radish was extended, and the guy introduced himself. He was a *patient coordinator*, with a name that Keeler couldn't understand. Presumably, it was easily comprehensible in the local language. Keeler simply nodded and the man sat down, maintaining intense eye contact. "Apparently you have an appointment?"

Keeler tugged on his nose. "Tired of this damn thing looking at me sideways every morning. I'm supposed to be getting a tour of the clinic and meeting the specialist." He indicated the reception desk. "Why didn't they have it on the schedule? I got an email confirmation two weeks ago."

The man waved it away. "That doesn't matter. Here's what I propose: I'll give you the tour myself right now, answer any questions you've got. After that, you can have lunch in the cafeteria, on us with coffee and dessert, of course. In the afternoon you will have a private consultation with our chief rhinoplasty specialist, okay? We'll discuss options once you've met him. Does that sound good?"

"Outstanding. Is that uh, Dr. Erkin?"

"Yes, that's right."

"Excellent." Keeler felt lucky but knew that he wasn't. Hard work and opportunity collide and make results.

The little guy showed the way: up the elevator to the third floor, to another waiting room that led to rooms where hyper-sharp steel blades and tools met flesh and bone in an unequal collision.

The guy said, "This is where we perform the skin procedures. Fourth floor is for hair transplantation."

Color-coded teams of nurses and surgeons moved around, busy with the day's schedule. Women sat on chairs leafing through magazines and watching before and after videos.

They went up to the fifth floor, another lounge. "We do some of the more complicated procedures here. Basically the same as downstairs, with a few extra facilities."

Keeler thought about silicone implants littering stainless-steel surgical surfaces. Thought about the surgeon, Doctor Fatih Erkin. He was looking forward to a one-on-one. They went down to the lobby again, and the man took him through a side entrance, which he'd seen in the pictures, the covered space between the main building and the neighboring structure.

The residential building had hotel suites and single rooms on the third floor and a cafeteria on the fourth, used by patients and staff, with segregated seating areas for each. The second floor had a cosmetic dental section and the top floor was an events space. The guy was talking up the clinic, saying how Zaros Aesthetica was an industry leader in research as well as practice, how they hosted conferences and other industry events.

They entered the cafeteria, all gleaming white Formica and

spotless marble. Floor-to-ceiling windows looked out on the city. The little guy wanted to leave him there.

"I hope it's not too early for lunch?"

Four men were gathered around a table shoveling cafeteria food into their mouths, each of them with a fully bandaged head. "What did those guys get?"

"Hair transplants, it's approximately half of our business."

"What's the second half?"

He pointed to Keeler's nose. "Rhinoplasty is a specialty. Although, it's not so common for men." His fleshy lipped mouth smiled. "You might find yourself surrounded by women, Mr. Van Buren."

A woman sat alone in the corner, looking out the window and nursing a cup of coffee; nothing was visibly damaged.

"What about her?"

"I'm not sure." He was watching Keeler with a little smile. "Are you hungry?"

"Always hungry."

The guy actually nodded. "You look it."

The funny man left him there, in the hands of an older woman who hustled back and forth from Keeler's table to the kitchen, bringing him a bowl of soup with Turkish bread and a plate of meatballs on rice. Keeler took it slow, eating methodically and ordering coffee once the plate was clean.

Free lunch.

Zaros Aesthetica had the healthy ambience of a busy and professional private clinic. People came and went. He didn't see anybody resembling the characters in the surveillance photographs. There had been several women with nose bandages, but not the woman he was looking for.

Something caught his attention in the periphery, and Keeler turned his head.

A man with a head bandage sat at a nearby table, a lunch

tray in front of him. The man was looking elsewhere, but held a phone in his hand, the position of it casual but too perfectly angled in Keeler's direction. Keeler looked at the man and at the phone, thinking the guy had just taken his picture. The man hadn't made eye contact and the phone hadn't made the camera sound.

Interesting.

He watched the man put the phone on the table and pick up his fork, stab at a cucumber. Keeler couldn't be sure that the guy had taken his picture, but he'd learned to trust his instincts. Two possible paths: let it go, or don't let it go.

No contest.

Keeler rose from the table. Took two steps toward the man, who still hadn't looked at Keeler directly but clearly sensed his presence and was now focused on his phone, thumbs and fingers flying. Keeler smiled. What he now knew, the guy was sending the picture and deleting it. A couple of steps closer, Keeler checked angles and objects, his eyes honing in on a shiny hotel suite key card on the white Formica table by the tray. A cup of weak coffee, a bottle of mineral water, the leftovers of rice and meatballs and salad.

The man looked up and Keeler smiled.

What he would have liked to do was lash out with a quick hand and trap the guy's phone. Pull the man's body over the table while simultaneously shoving the food tray and drinks into his lap. Keeler would watch the man's reaction, judging whether to keep going: push the chair over, get him on the floor, give him a quick double-knuckle punch to the throat.

He'd stand up and pretend to be sorry. It was an accident, I tripped. Patients and staff wouldn't know shit, and if the guy had taken Keeler's photo he'd keep his mouth shut. Checkmate.

But that's not what happened.

What happened was Keeler smiled and said, "Hey, Bud."

The guy looked up, like he'd been distracted by his phone. Keeler put a hand on the white Formica table, trapping the key card. He leaned over and pointed a thick finger at the guy's head, almost touching it.

"Did it hurt?"

The man drew his head back defensively. "What?"

"The surgery. Did it hurt, or do they put you under or what?"

The man spoke English with an accent, not easy to place. American mixed with something else, maybe Turkish. "They only use local anesthetic. That hurts, not the procedure." He looked critically at Keeler's head. "You must have already had work done."

Keeler stood up. The key card palmed. "Yeah, but it was in the USA and they didn't finish the job, so I was wondering how they do it here. I guess it's cheaper."

The man nodded. "Much."

"Nice, so only the needles hurt, otherwise all good."

The man had a pleasant tanned face. He smiled at Keeler, picked up an olive and popped it into his mouth and spoke around it, tension visible in his eyes. "Indeed."

Keeler held the eye contact and grinned. "Incredible." He indicated the tray. "Going back into it after lunch?"

The man passed the olive stone from his mouth into his hand and set it on the tray. "One last round before I'm done, yes."

"Good luck with it."

The man smiled stiffly, guilty, Keeler thought.

Back at his table, there was time for a milky Turkish dessert and another cup of coffee before the patient coordinator came to bring him over to the main building again.

TWENTY-TWO

FATIH ERKIN WAS A DAMNED good-looking guy.

It was the first thing Keeler thought as he took the outstretched hand, feeling it strong and dry and experienced. The skin soft and fingers fine boned, but laced with muscle. The man's eyes were blue, pale, and intelligent, set below a noble brow and a head of salt-and-pepper hair that looked tough to tangle.

Keeler's take: a guy with great genes selling products to the genetically challenged.

Erkin said, "Mr. Van Buren."

He walked back behind an oak slab, the kind of classy doctor's desk upon which you'd never in a million years find a computer. Keeler almost chuckled. The desk was polished dark wood with a leather writing pad and a lined yellow notebook. The pen was pure class, a black Bic, finely pointed.

Erkin stretched out a hand, pointed at a chair. "Sit in that. You'll be more comfortable."

Keeler sat.

Erkin folded himself into his chair, put up his feet, and breathed deeply.

"Tough day?" Keeler said.

"You could say that. I started at six a.m. with my daughter in tears, pure despair." He leaned forward. "You see, it was her first attempt at making American pancakes and she completely failed." Erkin smiled and leaned back on the chair, feet wiggling. "Forgot the eggs. Just milk and flour, which made the pancakes borderline inedible."

"You didn't eat them?"

"Of course I ate them. Luckily, I am Turkish and we are in Turkey. Here, we are the world's leader in two things, besides cosmetic surgery, apricots and hazelnuts. The summers, I go out to my family's farm and help the pickers in the orchards. I make a jam from the ripest fruit of the harvest." He stared at Keeler, serious. "That jam, spread and sprinkled with roasted hazelnuts, simply elevates anything it touches. You want to take it to the next level, you drizzle it with olive oil and add a sprinkle of sea salt flakes."

Keeler was almost salivating. "Damn, doctor, that does sound tasty."

"It is." The surgeon chuckled, pulled at the sleeve of his navy-blue uniform. "So, what were you thinking about doing?"

"The nose job?"

"We call it rhinoplasty." Erkin came out of his chair, around to the other side of the desk, and took a seat. "Lean forward, so I can introduce myself to your face."

Keeler leaned forward. Gave his face up for an examination. Erkin's fingers traced both cheekbones. Made their way in to the outside of his nostrils. Keeler was looking at Erkin's eyes, which were closed, as if the visual sense was getting in the way of something more pure. The fingers came over and met at the bridge of the nose, traced down and over the bump and then started feeling around and squeezing.

"Very good cartilage, with a significant buildup of scar tissue in a few areas. Your nose has been broken several times. You're a fighter?"

"I'm just clumsy is what I am."

"Mmmm hmmm." Erkin danced back, sliding off the desk and swiveling himself to the chair. "So you had something in mind, a nose that you'd rather have on your face?"

"I was thinking of Brad Pitt's nose."

Erkin picked up his pen and twirled it. "Uh-huh. How would you describe Brad Pitt's nose?

Keeler had no idea. He assumed it looked pretty. "Good-looking nose, everything's straight on it."

"Yes, Brad Pitt's nose is a very regular nose, it's also a medium size for his head, which is actually quite small, given his shoulders. The nose sits nicely between the relatively intense brow and the full lips below. As you said, it's a very good nose." The doctor nodded and pointed. "You tell me you want Brad Pitt's nose, I'll give you Brad Pitt's nose."

Keeler leaned back in his own chair and cracked a smile.

"Well, that would be a good nose to have doctor, but unfortunately it isn't my own nose I've come to discuss with you."

"Oh?" he said, eyebrows raised.

"Yeah, I was messing with you about that. I represent a third party. My client has heard of your work and would maybe like to have a little more than just a better nose, he's quite concerned about his privacy."

"More than a nose." Erkin's face had darkened. He said, "I don't know exactly what you mean, Mr. Van Buren. You're being purposefully obscure, which is all right. In my business there isn't much room for ambiguity, strangely enough." He tapped the oak desk. "The buck stops here, as they say in your country, so I'll be direct. There are two kinds of procedures that we do here. The first kind doesn't guarantee a change to your facial recognition profile, the other kind does. The Russians have invented a device that can map your skull in three dimensions using simple digital images and artificial intelligence. No amount of skin work can protect you from that, if the machine just sees right into your skeleton. For that we need to change the bone structure. Recovery time needs to be factored in, of course."

"And you'd perform that here?"

"We have a total solution. Private suites next door and a private surgical chamber here in the clinic."

"What about staff?"

"For the special projects I have my own team. Handpicked people, the best in Turkey. They're paid executive wages. We have full dossiers on all staff going back seven years, if your principal requires verification."

"Ballpark cost for the procedure?"

Erkin laughed. "I can't know that. I will need to thoroughly examine the patient, and see what their expectations are."

"Price of a house or something, right?"

The doctor just smiled.

Keeler had a hard grin set on his face. "Right, Doctor, like a house?"

The doctor's smile remained, eyes hesitant. "If you say so."

Keeler came to the edge of his chair. "I do say so. What my client said was find out what kind of house the guy lives in."

Erkin's smile wiped. "Excuse me?"

"Your house, Doctor. My boss asked me to find him a surgeon who lives in the kind of house it costs to get the job done. Said he wouldn't trust a doctor who goes either too high, or too low. In the man's words, I want to get cut by a guy who lives in a house that costs as much as a good face."

Erkin was amused. "Your boss sounds like a man with a sense of humor."

"Oh, I wouldn't put it that way, Doctor. I'd say the boss is eccentric. Because, sometimes what you think might be funny, the boss doesn't find humorous, and then, when you think something's deadly serious, the boss might suddenly crack up."

"Which makes him sound insane actually." The doctor examined Keeler for a moment, like he was thinking deep on an evaluation. He looked at his watch. "I have to get back. This is a strange profession, Mr. Van Buren. The kind of job that requires dedication. You've just elaborately invited yourself over to my house, so why don't we make it dinner?"

"That works."

The doctor wrote his address on the back of a business card. Slid it over the desk. "Come at seven. You're not planning on taking photographs are you?"

Keeler tapped his head. "Got a killer memory for visuals, Dr. Erkin."

Erkin rose and chaperoned Keeler to the elevator. The doctor leaned in and pressed the button for the lobby. After the door closed, Keeler hit the button for four, where the hair transplants were done. He got off the elevator into another waiting room. Two men looked up at him from the sofa, absorbed in magazines, heads bandaged. Neither of them the guys from the cafeteria.

He went back into the surgical area, poked his head around the door. There were four rooms back there, each with a large glass door. The place was well lit and ventilated. Each room had a surgical bed. On each of the beds was a man draped in surgical sheeting, shaven head offered up to the surgeon who sat behind him, poking at it with something sharp. The patients looked equally vulnerable, but the heads had to be different.

Keeler's goal was to identify the man from the cafeteria, verify that he was out of the way, and then use the key card he'd palmed to go into the guy's room and search it. Problem was, the patients all had shaved heads. Out of the four, one had a beard and one had very pale skin, which left two possible candidates. Keeler stood for a while, staring at a man's head through the glass. Looking at him lying back on the surgical bed having his skull poked with some kind of implement by a blue-clad surgeon wearing a binocular loupe headset.

Bottom line, it was too hard to tell. But, whatever, what was the worst that could happen?

TWENTY-THREE

KEELER WENT BACK DOWN to the clinic's lobby and out the side entrance to the neighboring building. None of the pink ladies looked at him twice, having seen him already. Crossing between the buildings, the air had a cold nip. People were hanging around over by the smoking area to his right, the place that had been featured in many of the surveillance images he and Choi had seen.

There were two bearded men in monochrome outfits, one in pink, the other in blue, puffing and chugging on tobacco and coffee. One hand up at the mouth, the other holding a small cup.

Keeler entered the second building. The older lady who'd served lunch passed him on the stairs going up, smiled, and said something in Turkish. He mumbled in return. The hotel area had a receptionist's desk and an office behind it. A woman sat at the office desk, eating with chopsticks and watching something on her phone, which she'd propped up against the base of a lamp.

She glanced at him and he mumbled a greeting and moved

on, hearing her response a second later. The white key card was in his hand, ready to meet a matching electronic lock.

He made his way along the corridor, reaching out with the key card to each lock as he passed. Keeler only tried rooms on the right side, aware of the ceiling mounted cameras at each end of the corridor. He'd appear on the surveillance footage, a figure moving down the hallway. Only a close look would reveal his arm, extended at each door.

What Keeler saw was a whole lot of carpet and identical electronic locks blinking red at him as he walked by. He came back for the second pass, trying the other side of the corridor. Same thing, red winks and no whirring snick of a lock bolt releasing.

The woman he'd seen eating sushi in the back office was now out front at the reception desk, perpendicular to the corridor, which meant that she wasn't looking in his direction, but focused on something in front of her. One more room on the right, before the corridor branched off to the stairs and an elevator vestibule.

Keeler extended the key card and the light blinked green. The lock whirred and clicked as the bolt drew back. He didn't wait to see if the woman noticed, just pressed the lever and pushed the door open and stepped through, letting it close behind him.

* * *

WHEN KEELER STEPPED into the room, an older guy was sitting on the bed. the man's eyes immediately latched onto him and flicked to the bathroom and back. He had steel-gray hair and wire-framed glasses. The eyes were the same color as his casual suit, pale blue.

The man was very calm. "Can I help you?"

"I don't know."

Keeler scanned the room, taking in objects scattered around it. There weren't many of them, besides the equipment that came with the hotel. A brown leather duffel bag sat on the bed, unzipped and packed with clothes.

The man smiled. "Well, you just let me know when you've decided." He held a phone in his hand. "They must have given you the wrong room."

Keeler took a single step in and pointed to the duffel. "You're leaving?"

"No, I've just arrived."

Which made more sense. The man didn't look damaged in any way, no post-surgery bruising or bandages. The silver hair wasn't exactly thick, but it wasn't anything you could shine with a rag either. The man stood up and yawned.

"I've called reception. Maybe they can help you." He held out the phone to show Keeler the number. "Excellent service here, by the way. Congratulations on the choice. I think we're in good hands." Another disarming smile. "I mean, I guess you've also just arrived, yes?"

A knock at the door.

"That's probably her." The man was capable of an honest expression of sympathy. Held up a perfectly white key card. "These things all look the same, it's easy to confuse the rooms."

Keeler took a step farther in, coming alongside the man with the silver hair. He looked past him, into the bathroom. The door was mostly closed; a small gap revealed a tiled shower stall and little else.

The man wasn't freaked out enough. A stranger walks into your hotel room and doesn't leave, and what, you're cool, calm, and collected?

The guy glanced at Keeler and walked past him to the door, opening it. He said something in Turkish. The receptionist stood in the doorway, concern written on her face. She spoke back to the man and both of them turned to look at Keeler. The man had that same smile on his face.

Keeler showed the key card. "Found this on my table at lunch."

She took the card from him and studied it, as if she could see anything in the blank white plastic. Her concern seemed about to turn into questions. Time to go.

He nodded at the man with the silver hair. "Take it easy, buddy."

The man grinned and faked an American accent. "I'll take it any way I can get it."

Keeler smiled in return. "You're pretty good."

"You're okay. I'd give you a C."

The receptionist was still standing in the doorway.

Keeler said, "C's what, satisfactory?"

"It's a passing grade, which is better than a failing grade."

The configuration was amusing, like two predatory animals making conversation around a clueless Bambi. The receptionist still had no idea what was going on.

Keeler wasn't completely finished. "What's he in here for?" he asked, pointing at the guy.

The woman dragged out a phone and got up a translation app. "Please say here. I don't understand."

The man was shaking his head like he was disappointed. He said something to the receptionist in Turkish. She laughed and put her phone down. The man's eyes turned to Keeler, bright with humor.

"Nice try, my friend. Unfortunately it's been a long day, and I need to take a shower. I'm so sorry." He said something else to the woman in Turkish, a lashing of vowels and consonants and some guttural sounds sitting somewhere between the two.

The woman jumped back, instantly apologetic. Said something back to him and literally tugged Keeler away. The door closed and they were standing in the corridor. The receptionist was tapping at her phone and shaking her head. She looked up at Keeler and spoke into the device. Someone said something back to her and she nodded, passing the phone to Keeler.

She said an unpronounceable word in Turkish.

He took the phone. It was the dandy with the British accent, the patient coordinator. The voice was cheerful as ever. "We seem to have lost track of you, Mr. Van Buren. If you come downstairs, I'll be there, and we can discuss options over coffee."

Keeler handed the phone back to the receptionist, who took it gratefully. He went downstairs, thinking about the guy up there in that room. It wasn't completely clear what had just taken place. Only that he had the strong intuition he'd met a smooth operator, an espionage professional.

Downstairs, he called Choi as the patient coordinator was coming out of the clinic, a salesman's smile on his little face. Keeler ignored him and turned away when Choi picked up.

He said, "Choi, we're invited to dinner tonight."

"Oh." Followed by a longish pause. Her voice was hushed, as if someone else was in the room and she couldn't speak freely. "I need to call you back. Fifteen minutes, okay?"

"Sure." Keeler grinned. He liked the fact that he'd thrown Choi off.

The patient coordinator came up smiling, obviously thinking that the grin was for him, but he was wrong.

TWENTY-FOUR

Tɪɴᴀ Cʜᴏɪ ʟᴏᴡᴇʀᴇᴅ the phone from her ear.

We're invited to dinner tonight.

What was that supposed to mean, was this guy asking her out?

She was in Kathy Jensen's office down in the Commerce and Agriculture section, and Jensen was looking at her kind of funny. Choi smiled and breathed, hoping it was a reassuring kind of smile that didn't reveal the tension inside.

Earlier, after the meeting, Jensen had approached her in the cafeteria.

She'd set a tray down and said, "I think we should talk."

Choi had said, "Sure."

"Let's eat lunch and then go down to my office."

Turned out that neither of them were too comfortable with how the meeting had gone. Choi didn't have much leverage. Her involvement had initially been confined to DIA rep along for the ride with Anderson on a CIA/JSOC gig. It had been a matter of interagency cooperation at the time. Jensen also lacked leverage. She was the Counselor for Agricultural Affairs and Acting Deputy

Chief of Mission only by some kind of weird bureaucratic fluke.

"It's because I'm old, Choi," she said. "It's the foreign service hierarchy."

Choi said, "What depresses me here is the ass covering, even with all that's going on, you know?"

Jensen had agreed, without even the trace of a smile. "It's ugly. They're running for cover like a bunch of rabbits." She looked up, grim line of a mouth. " So, what do you think, Choi, what would you suggest, if anyone gave a shit?"

Choi said, "Let's set up the problem. The relevant operations are CIA responsibility. They're getting off the hook because the casualties are either contractor or foreign. We have to admit that it works technically, which is why they're doing it, backing off like that."

Jensen said, "Ass covering is built into the system Choi, fact of life."

"Yeah, I'm learning that. It's what allows them to carry on with their careers, not get attached to trouble." She looked up to see Jensen nodding at her, following the train of thought. "It's a profession, right?"

Jensen said, "That's right, Choi. But?"

"But sometimes it shouldn't matter."

"I agree."

"There are greater things, higher things than career." Choi realized how she sounded, an idealist speaking with passion. She didn't care anymore.

Jensen smiled and shook her head in amazement, raising her eyebrows. "Go on."

"I see two issues. One is the operational standing of the United States. Someone just went to the bathroom and wiped himself on our flag. Excuse my French, but that shouldn't get a pass. The second thing is we need to hold ourselves responsible for the people we go to bed with, period. You get a foreign national involved, like that guy Karim Ahmadi, then you have to demonstrate that you care. You don't just throw him to the first wolf who comes to blow the house down."

Jensen looked like she couldn't agree more. "All right, so what do you suggest?"

"I want a follow up on the surveillance material Keeler took from the operatives up at Canada. Even if it's only to understand what the hell was going on up there. I've seen the pictures but I don't have context. We need to have a grip on the operational outlines of work that the United States Clandestine Services has been supporting." She felt herself getting hot behind the ears. "Did you see how that weird CIA contractor guy just took the laptop and put it in his briefcase? Will that thing ever be examined, or will they just delete all evidence of association?"

Jensen stood up from her desk. "Let's go upstairs and give Miller some hell." She pointed at Choi. "I'm a nobody, but you're the ranking clandestine services officer at the embassy now that Anderson's dead. Your recommendation needs to be heard."

* * *

UPSTAIRS, Miller's assistant looked up at them weakly. "He's been in the bathroom for a half hour. Must have eaten something that didn't agree with him." She put her head in her hands. "I'm not feeling so great either."

A half eaten baklava pastry was perched on its paper doily, the assistant's teeth marks visible in the congealed butter, shredded wheat and honey wedge. A sound between a belch and something worse emanated from the bathroom at the back of the office

Jensen looked at Choi, raised her eyebrows, and got red in the face. She strode across the office and pounded the bathroom door twice. "Jim. It's Kathy Jensen. I need a word."

From inside, a muffled grunt and a moan. Some other kind of noise and the water was running furiously. A minute later, Miller emerged with a wet scrubbed face and hair that had just been slicked and combed. He looked at Jensen and Choi with red eyes.

"What is it?"

He was actually pretending to be operational. Miller eased himself into the leather chair behind his desk without offering a chair to his standing visitors. He was barely able to make eye contact. Miller looked worse than bad, absolutely awful.

Choi stepped forward and made the case. She laid it all out there in a logical progression of reasons and facts. The narrative was structured on the fly, a gradient moving from the coldly logical to the warmly moral. She ended her presentation with an ethical evaluation of the situation, filtered through the lens of American values and what they were in Ankara to promote: *Jim.*

At first Miller had been looking at her, watching her, Choi felt, like he hadn't actually expected her to speak. After half a minute, his head had fallen onto his chest, and he kind of nodded there. Occasionally he'd glance up and then put his head down again in a more energy-efficient position. When Choi finished speaking, Miller leaned back in the chair and found a modicum of comfort.

It looked like he'd have a hard time moving out of there.

Miller said, "So you think I should get the surveillance stuff back from Anderson's guy, whatever his name is." He glanced at Choi. "What's his name, again?"

"Dingleworth, I believe."

"No, it's something else. Anyway, okay, imagine we get the laptop from him. What then?"

Jensen stepped up. "As Acting Chief of Mission, you can request that Langley briefs you fully on the material. They need to explain what they were doing in your territory, Miller. You can't just give them a pass." She feigned shock. "I mean, Jim, that's my opinion. I'm just the lady from Kansas who doesn't know shit about clandestine operations."

Miller was nodding his head, like he agreed about Jensen's ignorance and limitations, which made Choi dislike him even more. When he looked up, his eyes were bloodshot, pupils reduced to pinpoints.

"Not going to happen. I think they've already destroyed the computer with that machine they have. It's all about deniability at this point." He shuddered. "Anyway, you heard the guy from State. This episode gets shelved. When someone from the State Department says it like that, it's going to happen."

Miller cursed and staggered up, supporting himself on the desk. "Sorry." He lurched against the wall and made it to the bathroom door.

Jensen looked at Choi. "What machine is he talking about?"

"After Tehran in '79. The Iranians broke into the embassy and found shredded CIA documents. They spent like a million man hours putting them together again, like some kind of a jigsaw puzzle. So, we've got better shredders now. Nobody's going to be putting anything back together again. Now it's not just paper—they can shred hardware as well."

"Gotcha. So, they shredded the laptop." Jensen's face had gone slightly flaccid.

Choi said, "Miller's not cooperating. He's obviously not well and he's panicked by that bully from State."

Jensen said, "And whatever other phone calls he's been getting from DC."

"Right. We could put something into writing."

"Not a good idea." Jensen gnawed at a thumbnail. "I could make a phone call, but my fear is that I don't have any leverage right now." She looked up at Choi. "I've been around long enough to have a few friends, but you need to give me something, anything."

"Like what, exactly?"

Jensen bunched her fist up and twisted, as if she holding a rope. "Something that I can use, some piece of information that would make someone scared."

Choi wasn't understanding. "Scared how?"

"You know the one about scaring whores?"

"Uh, uh."

Kathy Jensen's eyes went clear and hard. "You can't scare a whore with a cock, Choi."

The vulgarity momentarily distracted her. It took Choi a second to understand that it wasn't a joke, it was a proverb or something. Jensen looked at her with a softened expression.

"What can you scare a whore with?" Choi asked.

"Probably a lot of things, just not a penis. You married?" She pointed at the ring. "I noticed the diamond."

"Engaged."

"How nice."

Choi twisted the ring on her finger and nodded because that's what you usually did. She was thinking about Keeler and how one might put the scare on a whore.

TWENTY-FIVE

KEELER GOT RID of the patient coordinator and walked away from the clinic, down the hill toward Kuğulu Park, and then back up again through the narrower streets around the Sheraton Hotel. He picked up a fake Gucci baseball hat and a pair of sunglasses at a kiosk, trying to adjust the look. As someone once said in training, a little bit can go a long way. A half hour later he was across the street from the clinic again, eating yet another sugar-soaked baklava with another black coffee.

The guy in that hotel room with the silver hair, there was something about him that Keeler both liked and was wary of, like the man was playing at half speed, as if he was someone who could go up a couple of gears on you with a finger snap. He somehow reminded Keeler of a middle linebacker he'd played with, way back in high school when his family had spent a year and a half in Oklahoma. Keeler was the new guy, playing running back, practicing with the team. This linebacker was languid and relaxed, but when you least expected it, there he'd be, hot on your tail, bringing you down.

The burner buzzed, Choi on the line, stressed out and

unhappy, speaking louder than he imagined she could, maybe taking her frustrations out on him. "A, I'm not going to dinner with you. B, I need sleep. C, You need to get back to the embassy."

Keeler had to hold the phone away from his ear until she was done.

"Choi, the dinner isn't personal. I got us in with the guy in the pictures, the surgeon. We're invited, but I'm not even sure we'll eat, so maybe you should get some sleep, have a good snack, meet me up at the safe house around six thirty."

There was a significant pause, and he thought about Choi on the other end of the line contemplating new information.

"I don't understand," she said. "How did you get us invited to the surgeon's house?"

"I used my charm."

"And why won't we be eating?"

"Because we might have to extract information from the surgeon, maybe he's got some tools up there we can use, like in that old movie with Dustin Hoffman about the Nazi dentist."

"This isn't funny Keeler."

"No."

She wanted more information, but he didn't give it. Better to have her up there with an open mind. He ended the call.

He kept one eye on the clinic entrance. A couple of glossy black SUVs came and went, the city operating at a slow pace until an hour later, when the guy with silver hair walked out of the residential building carrying the same brown leather duffel bag Keeler had seen on the bed in the room.

The first thing Keeler felt was a kind of victory. He'd been right: there was definitely something off about the guy. Then he stifled that feeling and got to thinking about who the man could be working for, what role he was playing in the game. The guy walked out of there like he had no concerns, as if it was a regular hotel and not a high-end plastic surgery clinic specializing in custom knife jobs for whoever had a suitcase full of cash.

Plus, the silver-haired man hadn't been cut, there were no bandages or any visual evidence of work performed, so what was he doing there? Instead of getting picked up by a private car, which Keeler had anticipated, the man came out front and started walking west on a narrow sidewalk alongside the busy road.

Walking on sidewalks didn't seem to be a popular activity up there in Çankaya. It was more the kind of place people tended to drive, maybe due to the steep hills. Keeler gave the man a good lead before moving out in pursuit. The guy led him around the neighborhood for a half hour before disappearing into an underground parking garage at the base of the Atakule shopping mall, where Keeler had been the day before on the last SDR with Karim.

Pro move.

The garage had six levels and multiple entries and exits. Thresholds to the outside and the mall interior, plus the park, by foot and by car, by elevator, stair, or vehicular ramp. A nightmare scenario for surveillance. The guy might have a car parked, or not. Even if he did, there could be an accomplice meeting him, hiding the silver-haired man in the back. This was the kind of place that demanded a large team of street artists.

A team of trained local operatives like Karim Ahmadi, exactly who Keeler didn't have at the moment.

Which meant no dice.

Keeler sat on a bench looking out over the park, not exactly feeling lonely, but feeling a little empty, like he was playing the game without a full hand. The autumn leaves golden and the air light and beautiful. What he suspected: the silver-haired man had entered the residential part of Zaros Aesthetica to pick up the belongings of his colleague, the man with the head bandage Keeler had encountered in the cafeteria. Which meant two things, that these people were professional enough to evacuate in an orderly fashion, and that the bandaged man was out there somewhere, possibly carrying an unfinished hair transplant, which would make him one very unhappy operative.

He gazed around, knowing that if an experienced operator was watching him, he wouldn't notice, which meant yet another long SDR route.

* * *

BACK AT THE SAFE HOUSE, Keeler stretched out on the sofa and looked at the ceiling. He let himself doze off, thinking about stuff, trying to get some perspective. He'd been up in Ankara with Calcutti's JSOC team for about a week, six days to be exact. Running this guy Karim into the ground and building him back up.

Keeler had a reputation as someone who was good at breaking in new guys. Guys who might have come up out of BUDS, but who still needed to get dirty with operational stuff, like walking backward and looking through your gunsights at the same time, tricky shit that they didn't teach at Coronado or Warner Springs.

He'd worked with Calcutti before, liked him enough, mostly because he was a tough operator and a decent commander, but not someone he'd go on vacation with.

A week earlier, he'd been working with another JSOC team outside of Al-Khafsah, Syria, not far from Aleppo.

What Keeler saw on the ceiling, allowing sleep to come over him, spreading by diffusion across the brain, were images from his last night down there in that weird Syrian death zone.

About one in the morning, climbing out of the valley with

his crew of the last three months or so. Their mission had been simple enough, a mobile kill squad. Live off the land, find weak links and exploit them. Harass the enemy and take scalps for Uncle Sam. Make it hurt and make it bloody. Make it so they're afraid of the dark. Own the night.

And ten points if you take a Wagner scalp.

That particular operation had been down by the river. An ISIS crew they'd ID'd after tracking them for a couple of weeks with a recon drone. They had full facial recognition, a dozen assholes with a juicy pattern of life. These guys were foreign fighters from France and the UK. They liked to take girls down to the water and party, far enough away from town and the more sincere members of the Caliphate.

That particular raid, Keeler was breaking in a greenhorn SEAL. Their unit was a mix of special tactics operators brought together like a killer salad, or like one of those superhero movies where each one has a special power. This guy had come through the gauntlet at Niland without having attained several very important but highly specialized skills.

So Keeler had taught him and the kid had done all right. Taken three scalps as well as a bullet fragment to the leg. Keeler had pulled that out of the kid, under fire, with his Leatherman and a mini-Maglite.

Five hours later they'd crossed to the eastern side of the Euphrates and were back at their base, a requisitioned super-market outside of a town called Hulayhilah, which they pronounced *helluva-hill-ya*. The supermarket had a crazy name, Sniper Super. You couldn't make it up. Syria was a hundred percent out of control.

The message had come through for Keeler. *You're outta here.* Twelve hours later, he'd landed on a dusty square of concrete near Amman, Jordan. They'd handed him a shaving kit, the money belt, and a set of civilian clothes. Told him he was going to Ankara to join the team at Brooklyn. And now this shit had happened.

TWENTY-SIX

CHOI WOKE HIM, calling from downstairs. He buzzed her up and yawned. Sleep had been excellent and he felt like a million bucks, maybe more. A million bucks wasn't what it used to be, apparently, according to a guy he knew who owned property in a fancy part of North Carolina.

Waiting for her to come up, he lifted one of the fancy H&K VP9s they'd liberated from the killers outside of the Holiday Inn, admiring the beefy grip and slick hammerless rear of a striker-fired pistol. Luxury assassin hardware. Keeler wondered what had happened to the driver with the weird eyes, the Jackal. He'd definitely been touched by a round, but maybe not enough to put him down.

Choi had changed clothes. She'd been back to her apartment and slept, showered, ate, and now here she was, looking as good as before and smelling like someone's fancy bathroom. Coming in the door she sniffed and looked at Keeler.

"Oh wow, you smell terrible." Which surprised him, since he'd never considered the subject to be of even the slightest importance.

He said, "So what?"

"So, you can't go to dinner smelling like that. Go shower." She made a shooing motion to the back.

Keeler stood his ground. "We're not actually going to eat dinner, Choi. You understand, the social call is just a way of getting in there. What we're looking for is information, and I'm not choosy how I get it."

"Meaning what exactly?" Confusion and concern were etched all over her face.

"Meaning whatever works. Tying him to a board and putting his head upside down with a wet rag and a pitcher of water would work very well." He thought for a second. "You know, depending upon what's available in the house." Keeler still had the pistol in his hand. Noticing her watching it, he said, "Shooting his wife in the head would probably be counterproductive, but amputating his kid's little finger could work."

"Seriously?"

"Hopefully not." Keeler shrugged. "We'll see. Think about those men this morning in their balaclava masks and fake police armbands. These are bad dudes. Think about the people they've already killed and the people they're going to kill next. It's a wicked world out there and sometimes you need to choose the least of all evils."

Choi was watching him, very serious and flushed. "You're right. I'm sorry. I didn't mean to judge."

Which he thought was an interesting thing to say.

Keeler didn't extend the conversation on ethics. He got to business, filling her in on the day's events. The clinic, Dr. Fatih Erkin, and the dinner invite. He left out the silver-haired guy, since that was a tangle he hadn't yet begun to unthread.

She said, "Pretty smart, how you got invited to dinner. I'm not sure I would have thought of that. What were you planning to do, if I had come up when you asked?"

"Check you in for a boob job."

"You think I need one?"

"Nobody needs one, Choi, but sometimes you gotta take a bullet for Uncle Sam."

She looked at him strangely. "You *are* kidding, right?"

Keeler deadpanned her. "About what, exactly?"

She was just too easy to provoke.

* * *

DR. ERKIN'S place was south of the city in a neighborhood called Gölbaşı. Keeler wouldn't risk a taxi driver, so they took the bus, which took an hour and eight minutes and made them late for dinner. He said it didn't matter because rich people always like to be fashionably late. Not that Choi understood the concept. She was always on time because that's how she was brought up.

The house wasn't much of a house, more of an estate surrounded by ten-foot walls, floodlights aimed at the barrier from a grassy verge, spaced out every twenty feet. The gate was steel topped with some kind of ornate bronze and no guard-house, just an anonymous intercom system with a large camera eye.

Choi watched Keeler as they walked up from the bus stop, confident and alert. She even saw him sniff at the air, like he had super-human animal powers. He observed the intercom system from a distance, finally turning to her.

"In for a dime, in for a dollar."

He pushed the button and waited. Nothing happened for a full minute. He pushed the button again and waited another two minutes.

A man's voice answered in Turkish.

Keeler said, "Van Buren, for dinner."

"Wait, please."

It took a while, like another minute and a half, which is long when you're standing at a gate. No voice came through, simply a clicking sound and the huge gate swung open exactly wide enough for them to walk through.

"Come on."

He stepped in and she followed. The gate hummed shut behind them, secured with another loud click. She looked back at it, wondering if there was a manual override down here, or if it was simply controlled from the house. The main building was enormous, a mess of ninety-degree angles shooting off in every direction and strategically illuminated by floodlights, making its angular contours even sharper and less friendly.

She whistled. "Nice house."

He shot a look at her. "Yeah, place probably costs less than a studio apartment in San Francisco. I wonder how much a nose job goes for."

There were gardens and what looked like an orchard, rolling grass hills and a swimming pool, all of it illuminated by strong halogens. Keeler slowed down, looking out to the pool.

She said, "What?"

"I don't know." He squinting at it and pointed his chin. "See that thing down there on the tiles?"

Choi saw something pink on the slate deck. "Looks like a pool float."

He nodded. "Oh yeah."

It was hard to tell where the front entrance was, but they didn't have to know. A door opened on their approach and a young man stepped through. He had gelled black hair in a side part and wore a servant's vest.

"Welcome."

The man showed them into the house, taking them through

a huge cathedral-ceilinged entrance with the largest chandelier she'd ever seen hanging like an obscene pendulum from the rafters. Keeler shot a look at her and she raised her eyebrows. The house was deathly silent, the ambient temperature on the chilly side. They were brought through a series of corridors to a lounge area with low couches, all of it slick and rectangular. No rounded shapes at all. Whoever had designed the place had been very conservative with the protractor.

The man swept his hand to the coffee table, laden with small bottles of spring water and bowls of nuts and dried fruit. "Please."

Keeler said, "Where's the doctor?"

The man smiled falsely. "Please. No English." He gave them a last look and walked out of the room, leaving them in the silence.

She said, "I guess the doctor's getting ready."

"Wonder where that guy went."

As if in response, music piped in from unseen sources, something jazzy with a beat.

He said, "Exactly what I expect they'd make you listen to in hell, tied to a dentist's chair."

"Shhh, maybe we're being recorded."

Keeler looked around. "Assume that we are." He took a seat on one of the couches and cracked open a bottle of water.

Choi didn't feel like sitting. She walked around the back of the couch, where a full-size grand piano took up real estate in front of a picture window looking out onto the pool deck. The thing that Keeler had seen was there, and it wasn't a pool float.

She said, "Keeler."

He was at her side in a second, alert to her tone. Not asking what she wanted, but looking through the window with her at the body of a child sprawled on the cold stone. A girl with long dark hair in a pink fleece onesie, maybe ten years old. Blood pooled beneath her head and ran in a thin rivulet to the infinity pool's catchment trough.

Keeler drew one of the pistols from his waistband and snicked back the slide. He glanced at her and she did the same with hers. A chill went up Choi's spine and it felt indecently good.

TWENTY-SEVEN

SHE LET Keeler hustle her over to the other side of the room. She was wondering why he was moving there, then realized it was because of the cover provided. At first she was thinking that a bullet could come from anywhere. She wondered where the servant had gone and if he was an enemy. Keeler put a large and comforting hand on her shoulder.

He pointed at the weapon she held. "You trained on that?"

Choi swallowed and breathed deeply. "I'm okay with it, yes."

"I'm beginning to feel like I'm always fifteen minutes too late for the bodies."

She didn't respond, too busy dealing with the fear. That initial spine chill had spread and now she felt a weird numbness.

Choi shook it off. She said, "What about that guy, the servant?"

"I don't know. We're going to clear the house, see what's going on here. I'll lead and you stay with me, non-shooting hand grabs the back of my waistband." He pulled at it. "Right here. You don't need to pull at me, just make sure we're in touch.

That way I can operate out front and know that you're with me without having to look for you. Got it?"

"Yeah."

"See if you can cover our six."

"Okay."

They moved quickly through the ground floor, moving from room to room, following Keeler's method. She held on to the waistband of his jeans, the back of her fingers and knuckles feeling the coiled muscles moving beneath his skin. It wasn't very easy to cover someone's rear like that, probably something that these guys trained at for months. She did her best, holding on and moving forward, while simultaneously turning to see behind her.

After a while she got used to the movement. She adjusted her footwork and they started moving faster.

There weren't many actual rooms. The house had a modern approach to open spaces, which meant areas with a lot of nooks and crannies and then a section with normal rooms off corridors. Keeler moved smoothly and quietly. She let herself get into his rhythm and strangely, the action felt good, like a choreographed routine starting to come together.

Nothing was happening on the ground floor. No sign of the servant. But they saw the front door was gaped open.

Keeler said, "The guy probably brought us in here and then left."

"Why?"

"I'm sure we'll find out."

A set of fancy floating stairs went from the huge ceilinged living room to a mezzanine above. The second body was on the landing, a teenage boy sprawled out on the gray wall-to-wall carpeting. He'd been shot in the back twice, one arm pinned under his torso and the right leg at an impossible angle.

She noticed that Keeler was observing her, seeing how she was handling the death scene.

Choi said, "Don't worry about it. This is my second day."

He grunted, apparently satisfied by this response.

They cleared a bathroom to the right, spacious, with its own sauna and a hot tub below a mirrored ceiling. No bio mass in the sauna and nothing floating dead in the hot tub. Keeler made eye contact and the stench hit her like a hammer, death and other things, acrid and wrong.

He didn't hesitate. He moved into the adjoining master bedroom, then pulled back, pushing her out of the doorway.

"You don't want to see this."

She blinked and stood her ground. "I need to see it."

* * *

DOCTOR FATIH ERKIN hung in the center of the room. Below the corpse, his blood had pooled and blackened, congealing from the outside in, an effect that she knew from the textbooks but had never seen herself.

A nautical rope had been looped around a rafter beam and bound to the surgeon's neck, wrists, and ankles. The procedure was sophisticated, the kind of arrangement of knots and loops where the guy chokes himself if he struggles. A man gets hung up like that and one of the torturers holds the other end of the line, letting the victim take the weight on his feet if he's being cooperative. If not, the weight can be quickly displaced to the vulnerable wrists and neck.

In addition to the strangulation, someone had gotten carried away with a knife.

The exact details were tough to see through all the blood. Keeler noticed it right away, but it took Choi longer. She recoiled with an involuntary gasp and turned away, staggering to the doorway to suck air.

It wasn't just simple knife work, the perpetrator had been a true artist with serious skills. He'd run the edge of a blade between Erkin's epidermal layers, flaying skin from the torso, working from the upper pectorals down so that translucent layers dangled over Erkin's genitals.

It looked like this scene had played out slowly.

The boy on the landing hadn't been shot so recently either, Keeler figured it had been maybe three hours. Which is a long time to be slowly strangled and flayed. Worse yet was the other thing, the inhuman corpse occupying Erkin's king-size bed. Choi's eyes were tearing up, red and swollen already. She was forcing herself to look at the terrible things these people had done to the doctor's wife, presumably while he was made to watch.

Her naked corpse had become rigid. The pale skin a mess of blood, blackening and clotting. The arms and legs splayed and tied off to the four corner posts. She no longer looked entirely human. Keeler forced himself to examine the corpse. The perpetrators had raped her so violently that her genitals were no longer recognizable, which suggested that they'd used tools.

A cold rage came over him. He saw that Choi was experiencing the same thing, shivering with anger. "We need to stop these people."

Keeler had seen worse, but not much worse. He also knew that this kind of thing was common in some places, in certain situations, a part of human behavior that was really just the other side of kindness. Like that god Janus, facing both directions.

First the team at Canada, a surveillance operation that uncovers images of the doctor and a young female patient. Now this. Keeler couldn't help suspecting that his own involvement had somehow condemned Erkin to this fate. The other question was why he and Choi had been invited into the house by that young guy in the first place.

Maybe their showing up had surprised the killers. In that scenario, Keeler and Choi had been brought into the house and in the meantime the killers had gone out. But it didn't matter now; they needed to leave.

He said, "Let's get out of here."

As they moved out, the music still played and the same chill hung in the air, but the house had become spooky. The stench of murder was beginning to thicken and spread, despite the spaciousness of the house. The thought occurred to him that this house would eventually be sold. People would live there again, ultimately going about their lives and pushing away the past.

They exited through the front door. Nothing was happening outside but a clear and chilly night in the suburbs of Ankara. Once he closed the front door, the music from inside was gone, replaced by the occasional owl hoot and dog bark. In the distance was the sound of traffic from an unseen highway, a never-ending rush of tires on asphalt.

The gate had a button on the right side stone pillar. Keeler pushed it and the barrier swung open.

Choi said, "Back to the bus?"

He shook his head. "No bus. We walk."

The road was asphalt with a gravel verge. Dogs barked from suburban houses set back behind walls and gardens. They were on a ridge, looking out across a plain. Below, new high-rises emerged in front of a liquid stream of headlights, cars eating asphalt, going places.

They heard a vehicle approaching from behind. Choi looking at him, concerned, face pale in the darkness as if her skin had an internal source of luminance. Keeler's fingers wrapped around the beefy grip of the VP9. He slipped it from his waistband, a round already in the chamber, and let his hand hang down, masked by the leg. He motioned for Choi to stay cool and keep walking, as he thought about the timing. When the moment would come to whip around and put rounds through the windshield.

The vehicle flashed lights and accelerated, pulling up to them. Keeler turned. It was a black model S Mercedes. The window hummed down and the silver-haired man from the clinic was in the front passenger seat, looking at him through the steel-framed aviator glasses.

"Get in," he said. "There isn't much time."

Before he had the last word out of his mouth, Keeler was putting the H&K's barrel into his forehead. "Talk."

The man kept eye contact, cool as a cucumber. "There are four corpses back there, two of which carry entry wounds made by an identical weapon to what you're currently holding. I have more to tell you, but we should leave this area as quickly as we can, and not just for your sake."

The second guy, who was driving, had a head bandage. He didn't look too happy.

Keeler was thinking about it, thinking that the man was right. Thinking also that if he was honest with himself, let his intuition speak, this guy wasn't an opponent. Not in the strict sense of enemy versus friend.

He glanced back at Choi, who looked like she had questions and concerns. She was doing great for her second day. He lowered the weapon and opened the rear door of the Mercedes for her.

She said, "What's going on?"

He said, "Just get in."

He watched the conflict playing over her face, not a submissive person by nature, and smart and competent, but confident enough to make tough decisions like when to trust. She gave a curt nod. They slid into the back seat and the guy with the bandaged head hit the gas, not even waiting for the door to be closed.

Choi elbowed him in the ribs, hard, hissing at him. "Who are they?"

He said, "Still an open question, but I'm guessing they know their way around Tel Aviv."

The silver-haired man turned and raised his eyebrows once, fast, like a signal of humor. As if, in spite of all this killing and death, the world had to continue.

He said, "I can neither confirm nor deny." He reached a hand back, addressing Choi. "I'm Joe."

She took it. "Hi, Joe."

Keeler opened the window to let the air rush in, chilly and clean out there in the hills. He had the pistol in his lap and un-chambered the round, put it back into the magazine, and tucked the cleared weapon on the seat under his thigh.

2

SPARROWHAWK

TWENTY-EIGHT

FIVE MINUTES' drive from Dr. Erkin's house they came down from the hills, descending on a switchback to find the glare and flicker of police lights reflected off the steep rock face.

Joe opened the glove compartment and pulled out a folded square of cream-colored cloth. He passed it back to Choi.

"Do you know how to do this?"

Keeler watched as she unfolded the hijab head covering and expertly manipulated the scarf so that it covered her hair and ears loosely. Joe nodded to himself and turned to the front. They came around a final turn, an intersection below them, thick with security vehicles and personnel.

Joe opened the compartment between himself and the bandage-headed driver. The cavity had a false bottom with a secondary hidden compartment below. Keeler got it and handed over the weapon. He gestured for Choi to do the same.

They joined a line of vehicles moving through the checkpoint. Joe lit a cigarette and rolled his window down. He put an elbow up on the sill and drew in, blowing out a strong plume of tobacco smoke. Keeler noticed that he was holding prayer beads, fingering the polished wooden globes like a local.

Joe said, "They'll be looking for two people, not four."

A uniformed policeman pointed at their vehicle and waved them to a stop. Three men converged on the Mercedes, examining it from different angles, gazing into the windows. The bandage-headed guy brought the car to a halt and his window hummed down. The policeman had an unslung MPT assault rifle, Turkish military NATO standard. He stepped aside and an older man in civilian clothes approached. The man wore a handgun on his hip and looked like the kind of person who could give orders.

He looked in through the open window and spoke to the driver in Turkish.

The driver leaned forward to release the trunk. Behind them, several uniformed men busied themselves with the contents. The driver brought out his identity papers and Joe rooted around in the glove compartment for the vehicle registration. The plainclothes man looked over the documents and handed them back.

Joe leaned across the driver's lap and spoke to the security man. He must have said something funny because the guy smiled. Joe offered a cigarette and was declined with a gesture. The trunk was closed and they were waved on.

The Mercedes moved forward. The driver's window hummed shut and neither bandage-headed guy nor Joe remarked on what had just occurred. When they got to the city, Joe passed two black hoods back to them.

"If you don't mind."

Choi handed the hijab back to him. "You serious?"

Keeler said, "Put it on." He knew it was standard operating procedure. Their new friends didn't want to disclose the location of a safe house.

Fifteen minutes later, the hoods came off and Joe handed the weapons back. By then the Mercedes had entered a walled compound somewhere in the city. The compound had several outhouses, but the main building was a red-tile-roofed villa. Joe led them inside, a slight limp in his walk. He hadn't walked like that earlier in the day, when Keeler had followed him from the clinic to the underground parking garage. He caught Keeler looking.

"Mortar shell fragment in the left calf. Still have a nice scar. Now you can identify my body if something goes wrong."

Joe opened the door and Keeler walked in after him. The entrance was large, but the first thing he noticed was the tall woman with auburn hair, midthirties, standing in the archway to an open-plan kitchen, dipping a tea bag into a large mug, a phone clamped between ear and shoulder as she made uh-huh noises in another language, maybe Turkish. She met Keeler's eyes, then looked away.

The eyes were green, set into a good tanned face.

Choi and Joe came in after him. The woman said something else into the phone, then let it fall from her shoulder into her right hand, left hand holding the mug. She walked across the room to a door and kicked at it twice. The door was opened by a large bearded man whom she ignored. The woman gave one last look at Keeler before disappearing into a corridor on the other side. The door shut.

Joe didn't say anything about her. He ushered Keeler and Choi into a dining room that had been converted into a mini operations center. A woman and a man, both in their twenties, sat side by side at a family sized table, looking into screens and tapping, swiping, and murmuring to each other.

Keeler cast his eye over the hardware. Laptops, large computer monitors, a bank of burner phones plugged in and charging, plus other objects cabled into the machines: boxes with CPU cooling fans that would contain circuit boards stuck with custom-made silicon, memory chips, and logic chips planted into fiberglass and copper and impossible to identify visually.

A thick power cable snaked across the floor and out a window, cracked open. A super-quiet generator hummed. These people were avoiding an excess energy signature at the property, a pro move, given the hardware.

The two working the keyboards looked up briefly when Joe led Keeler and Choi into the room, then went back to clicking and swiping. Joe put his hand on the young woman's shoulder and spoke to her in English. "Show them before."

She nodded, her hands making a furious chatter on the keyboard. Joe stepped back, allowing Keeler and Choi to crowd around the screen.

The display showed time-stamped CCTV footage from Doctor Fatih Erkin's house. Keeler and Choi walking around, following the servant who'd let them into the house. The woman let them watch themselves, until she received a nod from Joe. She pressed a key and they were looking at the bodies: the two kids and then the bedroom with Erkin and his wife. The time stamp remained the same, different cameras.

Joe said, "So, as you can see, you two are walking around in Erkin's house, by the murdered family. Yes? It's not very complicated."

Keeler said nothing. The CCTV footage clearly implicated him and Choi in the murders. Up on the screen, Keeler and Choi, now alerted to the first body out by the pool, were moving tactically through the house with weapons ready. From a naïve viewer's perspective they looked guilty as hell. Keeler was getting it, the setup.

"Show me before we showed up."

The woman turned to Keeler and arched an eyebrow. "They had the system deactivated before you showed up."

Joe said, "What it looks like, the opposition improvised when they recognized you at the gate."

Keeler said, "The intercom camera." He thought back to the pause, a minute or two long, before they were let in.

The young man keyed in a command. The screens showed an empty house, time-stamped a few minutes before the initial shots of Keeler and Choi walking around. The servant was in the shots, moving to the front door presumably.

Choi said, "And what, this guy gets sacrificed so that we're trapped?"

Joe shrugged. "Or, he's already out of the country so nobody will ever know him."

Keeler said, "Someone on the red team's a thinker."

Joe said, "Oh, yes. Don't underestimate the enemy, assume that at the upper level they're as intelligent as you are." He tapped the woman on the shoulder. "Okay."

She attacked the keyboard and flicked at something with a mouse.

The same scene, Keeler and Choi moving. At the click of a key they were no longer there, and the house was exactly as before, just empty.

Joe said, "And now you were never there."

The woman looked back at Keeler and smiled. "Magic."

She switched to the exterior scene, Keeler and Choi walking up the driveway. With the click of a key they were gone, the scene now bucolic and suburban, an empty driveway and gardens. The young man sitting next to her was paying attention to the show, obviously enjoying the work they'd done.

Choi said, "What, this is just a scene from before we arrived?"

Keeler pointed. "Look at the time stamp. Same as before."

The woman said, "Correct. Not exactly *just a scene*."

She flicked the keys back and forth, summoning the images

of Keeler and Choi and then disappearing them at will, the time stamp remaining the same.

Choi said, "Okay, but how are you doing that?"

The woman looked at Joe, who nodded. She said, "We're tapped into the network so we've got access to footage from earlier. I took a shot from last night same time, similar weather. Painted you guys out of the scene."

The man next to her said, "Just like in Hollywood."

What Keeler knew: the technology they used for erasing him and Choi from the scene wasn't the big deal; the access to communications networks was. He said, "You can make this stick, inside their servers?"

Joe said, "Show them the bus."

She stroked the keyboard and the CCTV camera from the bus came on screen. Keeler and Choi traveling from the city to the suburbs. Another flick of the keys and they were no longer present. Impressive. This team was deep inside the CCTV networks of the Turkish security state.

The woman chuckled. "You're very welcome."

Joe smiled. "Do you like Turkish coffee?"

TWENTY-NINE

Sitting around the coffee table, Joe insisting on some kind of Turkish coffee ceremony before getting down to business. A plate of baklava and a round tray with the thick dark local brew, poured out of a bronze pot into thumbnail-sized porcelain cups. Choi observed Keeler unselfconsciously wolfing down three baklava pastries in a row, maybe a two-second break between each. He was making small talk with Joe.

She watched them, waiting for this man who called himself Joe to get down to business. She was playing along and analyzing behind her inscrutable expression.

Take Keeler. This wasn't the usual guy she'd known from the special teams. Being DIA, she ran into military people all the time. What appeared usual for those JSOC types was the ability to operate with no bullshit. In the kinds of situations they got into, it was essential to trust the guy next to you. Nobody trusts bullshit, and when it comes down to the wire, trust is all-important.

Keeler fit the bill there. No bullshit, like a model example of that trait. But it wasn't only that, he had more dimension than most of those guys. Charisma and charm coming from some wider kind of intelligence. He had the practical skills and apti-tude—and something else.

Which brought up an old memory of grad school. She'd had to take a European philosophy class at Johns Hopkins, where she'd learned the French concept *je ne sais quoi*, which means literally *I don't know what*, but also refers to *that thing that you know is true but you can't quite put into words*. What is it about Keeler that she felt drawn to? It was more than physical attrac-tion, which she knew he felt as well. *Je ne sais quoi.*

She nibbled at her first pastry and sipped, liking the strong coffee. A nibble and a sip hit the spot after what they'd been through so far that night. Joe was telling them how crazy he was about Turkish coffee, that you had to boil it seven times. Bluffing and leading them on, waiting for them to get impatient, a sure sign that he was trying to bullshit them.

The tall woman who'd been on the phone earlier entered the room and handed Joe a tablet, leaning over and saying some-thing quietly into his ear. She gave Choi a half-curious lingering glance and then departed. Auburn hair, tall, tough looking and discreet with fierce light-green eyes. Choi figured that she might be Joe's superior. That would be good operating procedure, don't divulge the chain of command to rival operatives.

Finally, Joe was ready. He said, "Right." And ran his fingers over the tablet's surface, holding up a hand. He had a low growl of a voice, like he'd had his larynx shot out somewhere in prox-imity to the Sea of Galilee. "I'm going to share several items of significant intelligence value. However, there are things that I won't disclose, for example, the source of the intelligence." He shrugged. "You may not like that, and I'm sorry. You'll have to decide for yourselves what you wish to do with the information I am going to give you."

Choi chose a casual tone. "Go ahead, Joe. Let's see what you've got."

He nodded and set the tablet on the coffee table so that everyone could see. Choi shifted her chair, feeling Keeler's eyes on her and flashing him hers, before fixing on the show.

Joe got busy, flicked his fingers over the tablet's screen, pinching and spreading thumb and forefinger and then swiping left. He landed on an image that she recognized, the bearded man from the surveillance photographs at the clinic. The guy who had accompanied the young woman with the nose job, like Keeler had said, either bodyguard or captor.

Joe pointed to the photograph of the bearded man. "Meet Amal Nizar Ezzedin, born in the southern Lebanese village of Ain Qana, now a senior commander in the Hezbollah. He reports directly to Sayyid Hassan Nasrallah." He looked at Choi. "Secretary General of the Hezbollah, yes?"

A big name. Choi deadpanned. "Go on."

Joe licked his lips. "When Mughniyeh was killed in 2008, Ezzedin went up the ladder. Fun fact, he was the Lebanese Shooting Federation champ about ten years ago, apparently still likes his target practice. Now, he's busy taking care of special projects for Nasrallah." Joe looked at them, wanting to be sure they understood what this meant.

Choi knew her Middle East politics better than most. Hezbollah, the Party of Allah, a Lebanese Shia militant group and the major political player in Beirut. Not only a power at home in Lebanon, but also a major Iranian proxy, funded, supported, and at times commanded by the IRGC, Islamic Revolutionary Guard Corps.

Joe swiped the tablet's screen to a photograph of the young woman who had been the focus of activity at the clinic, the recipient of a rhinoplasty procedure.

He said, "According to Zaros Aesthetica's books, this is Fizza Hamieh, twenty-three years of age. We believe this to be an assumed name. Her real identity is unknown at this time."

He swiped back and forth between the two images. Ezzedin and Hamieh, the menacing guy with the beard and the young woman. "At the moment it's a mystery. On the one hand, we have Nasrallah's man in Ankara, on the other a young woman who is evidently of some importance. Is she important only to Ezzedin, or is he acting on behalf of his boss? Currently, we don't have answers."

Choi glanced at Keeler, keeping a poker face. She was guessing what he might be thinking. The woman who'd died up at Çankaya, she'd certainly felt that the girl was important, at least enough to get a pledge out of a hard guy like Keeler. From what he'd told her, the pledge had been personal, *Help the girl.*

Joe was filling in some gaps, but his team had limited information. Did he even know about the safe house in Çankaya? The other thing was the Hezbollah connection. This was clearly the bait Joe was dangling. Nasrallah, the leader of Hezbollah and maybe the most-wanted man on earth, presumed to be living underground, literally, since the 2006 Israel–Hezbollah War.

Joe was sitting back with a *there you go* expression on his face. He lit a cigarette, leaned in to take a sip of the thick and sweet Turkish coffee. Kathy Jensen's face swam into Choi's mind for a moment, and with it a question: *Would this information scare a DC whore?*

Probably not.

Choi said, "Semi interesting. What are you hoping for, Joe, that we'll go in there and connect the dots? You want to know about this girl, get inside the clinic and extract some DNA, run it against your database, send it to CIA. Maybe something will come up."

Keeler looked at Joe, exchanging a meaningful glance, which she didn't like.

She said, "What?"

Keeler said, "What I didn't tell you is I met Joe in the clinic." He turned to Joe. "She's right, why didn't you get a sample from the girl?"

Joe coughed and stubbed out the cigarette. "We tried, but it didn't work. Ezzedin and the girl were always together. He had men on overwatch and others preceding them, sweeping for surveillance. We judged it to be a delicate situation."

Choi said, "What about bio waste, couldn't you get to it?"

He waved a hand. "Not a chance. It's why they chose this clinic. Anything of a biological nature generated from the procedure: blood, fluids, cellular material, hair, whatever, everything is incinerated on the spot with a purpose-built machine, right in the surgical theater. They have personnel whose sole function is the elimination of DNA trace."

Keeler said, "You could have gone for something more aggressive."

Joe lit another cigarette, pretty much chain-smoking. He looked up at Keeler. "Look, we're not in that situation. People back home don't want me to continue this operation; they're telling me to pull back. This is a what-do-you-call-it, a speculation." He took a drag, shaking his head.

Choi sat back, thinking she now understood the game here, what Joe hoped for. He was betting on the girl's being significant, hoping that he could use her to put the squeeze on Nasrallah. Problem was, he didn't have the girl.

She said, "Okay, Joe, Hassan Nasrallah and this young lady, I get it. It's sort of hot, but also half-assed, if you don't mind my saying so." She screwed her face sour. "It's got sex appeal, no doubt. But it's more *Vogue* than *Hustler*. I'm asking myself, so what? Why should I care? Show me the centerfold, Joe."

She saw the glint in Keeler's eye, liking her question, looking at her and admiring her. It made her feel warm and fuzzy and good. She watched Keeler relaxing back into the sofa, enjoying himself. He put yet another baklava into his face.

Joe laughed and put down the cup. Tapping his cigarette into an ashtray.

"You sound like my boss, a tough cookie. I bring you a diamond and you tell me it's shit. Isn't this what you went up to the good Dr. Erkin's place to find out? Why else would you be up there?" He looked at Keeler. "You're also a believer. You know I was a soldier too once, same stuff. You've got your gut, right?" He pounded his belly. "Soldier's gut."

Keeler said, "Sure, but the problem is you've only got half the information. Like my friend just said, it's half-assed."

Joe said, "You want more?" Both Choi and Keeler stayed quiet. Joe smiled. "I've got more, don't worry, my friends. I didn't come to the party with half a case of beer."

His fingers played once more over the tablet screen. Joe turned the device around for them to see a full-screen photograph of a man chained by his ankles to a stake in the dirt. He was dirty, naked, bloody, and looked Middle Eastern.

"Do you recognize this man?"

Choi didn't, but Keeler shot forward. "Let me see that."

Joe handed over the tablet. Keeler pinched his fingers and spread them to enlarge the image. Moved the photo around carefully, examining something. He glared at Choi. "Abdominal bruising and the left leg looks broken."

She craned her neck and looked at the image, not understanding why Keeler was so hot and heavy all of a sudden. She saw the awkward angle of the leg and the discoloring to the skin.

Joe, nodding. "Blunt trauma to the torso. Our analysis, they hit him with a vehicle to put him down."

Choi said, "Who is it?"

Keeler glanced at Choi. "He's ours," He said, obviously not wanting to say more in front of Joe. She had to connect the dots.

It was Karim Ahmadi, the local guy contracted to CIA for their street teams, the guy who'd failed to check in.

Choi felt a burning sensation at the top of her head, an alert. What had that asshole Miller said? *He'll call in when he wants to get paid.* What a dick.

Keeler, looking coldly at Joe, said, "What's the provenance of this image?"

"We're up on some of the IRGC communications channels. This image was received as a signals intercept, among other data that I won't disclose." He drained the last of his coffee. "Thanks to your vigorous action outside of the Holiday Inn, we now know that their operational squad in Ankara are Tajiks. At least, the corpses retrieved by Turkish security services have been identified as such. We can assume that they are under the command of the IRGC, or the Hezbollah."

Keeler said to Joe, "We're interested." But Choi felt his eyes on her, boring in hard and hot. "Right?" He turned back to Joe. "Where are they holding that man?"

Choi understood the look and the heat, but she wasn't entirely sure that this information would be enough to kick the political players into action, given what she'd heard in the situation room back at the embassy. Those people would find any possible excuse to avoid risk.

Joe retrieved the tablet from Keeler. He pinched and fingered the screen until he had a map to show them, pointing to a spot near the Syrian border with Turkey. "As of now, we know that they've taken your man to this village. The operational assumption is that they will attempt to exfiltrate to Syria as soon as they can. From there, who knows."

Keeler said, "What's holding them up?"

Joe shrugged. "There are a few theories." He raised his thumb. "Hezbollah and the Syrian regime people are not very popular in the north, to put it mildly. Not so mildly, ISIS are liable to execute any regime-connected captives immediately. So, getting through the north will be tricky, but of course they have their ways." He raised his forefinger to join the thumb. "And then we have your wounded friend. They'd consider him valuable, and they wouldn't believe that he's not American, as you know." He shrugged. "It's possible that your friend is too injured to move at the moment, or at least tricky to deal with. We really don't know."

Choi said, "What do you want, Joe?"

He shrugged. "What do I want? I want you to go get your man, and while you're doing that, I'd like a DNA sample from the girl. We believe that she's with them."

"And then what?"

"And then we'll see. If we get a good result from the sample, sky's the limit."

Keeler was looking at her. She caught the glance and he tilted his head toward the outside. He wanted to talk to her in private.

THIRTY

THROUGH THE FRENCH DOORS, Keeler could see Joe sipping from a glass of cognac. The auburn-haired woman who'd handed him the tablet was speaking, Joe was listening. It had occurred to Keeler that she might be Joe's operational commander.

Keeler sipped at the two fingers of cognac Joe had poured for him, sweet and strong. He wasn't a big fan of the stuff, but his mom had been French, so whatever. He didn't know anything about perfume, but Choi had something about her that did pleasant things to his olfactory senses. Even without looking at her, he had a precise idea of her proximity.

He'd asked her what she thought and she hadn't answered the question yet. They were standing by the pool house, about a yard apart. The pool itself was covered with a thick tarp, waiting for spring. He couldn't help analyzing the logistics.

The villa would have been rented by a cutout, someone with zero connection to whatever intelligence service Joe and his team belonged to. How many villas like this were out there in Ankara, and in every major city around the world. Spooks, scheming and surveilling each other, jockeying for an advantage.

And in between them were people like the young girl, Fizza Hamieh. What was her story, what was she thinking?

Choi said, "I think it's obvious that we take this to the embassy. We need to disclose the contact with these..." She waved her hand at the villa. "Israelis or whoever they are. I don't know if Miller will bite. I can send it up the chain on my side, but DIA doesn't move fast." She indicated the villa again. "This is also seriously speculative. I'm not sure how far we'll get, but what's the worst that could happen?"

He looked at her, a wry expression asking her how naïve she could be. "Worst that can happen is we go back to the embassy and they confine me to quarters with a bunch of marine guards. No one does shit and Karim dies, or worse, spends the rest of his life in a dungeon. He's got a family here. Karim's kids grow up without a dad, possibly without knowing that their dad died a warrior. They grow up thinking that he just disappeared, maybe even left them. That's the worst that can happen." Choi smirked. He said, "You think that's funny?"

She said, "No, but I think we're getting somewhere. If that's the worst-case scenario, what's the best?"

No reflection was necessary, he'd already decided on the best course of action. "I put a call in to Calcutti and we get the team back together. We go do some gangster shit and get Karim and the girl out. Send the Iranians and their proxy team to heaven or purgatory or wherever they go after life. End of story."

She gave him a 'you know very well' look and added, "And that fantasy needs to be sanctioned by command."

He shrugged. "Technically true. I don't know how long you've been around, maybe long enough to know what's possible.

Anyway, you asked for the best-case scenario, not the most realistic one." He flashed a grin at her, surprised to see the way she was watching him, suddenly quiet, her body language introverted.

Choi leaned against the wall of the pool house. When her head came back against the stone, the light from an outdoor lamp caught her face, perfectly illuminating the high cheekbones and full mouth. The hair cut in a bob, eyes gleaming from the shadows.

They made eye contact and he could see that Choi was blushing. She said nothing for a moment until it was almost uncomfortable. Then she said, "What are you looking at?"

"Nothing."

She maintained eye contact until she turned her head away and pushed her hair back with a quick gesture. The light caught her ring finger and Keeler got distracted looking at it.

She was watching him again. "Okay."

Keeler said, "Okay, we go inside and tell them we want the documentation they've got. We'll bring it to the embassy and push it up the chain of command, see what happens. Right?"

Choi looked at him and he realized that wasn't what she'd meant by saying *okay*.

She said, "Sure."

He turned toward the villa. She grabbed at his jacket. "Wait."

"What?"

She pointed to the glass in his hand. "Give me a sip of that."

He handed her the glass and watched as she took it down at once. Clearly not a drinker. Choi gasped, her face flushing.

She approached him, put her hand up to his chest and pushed him hard against the wall of the pool house. She brought her mouth to his, searching. They met, warm and welcome, her lips delicate, tasting of cognac. He touched her hip, resting his fingers on her waistband. He slid his hand farther up, until he brushed against the initial rise of her breast. Both of her hands flat against his chest, the left snaking up, fingers at the nape of his neck. Her body pushed hard against his, almost reckless. Soft. The kiss became more insistent until she pulled her head back a half inch, fingers clutched tight to his shirt.

"I needed to do that." Her eyes glinted in the light. "You know, get it out of the system. So that's it, okay?"

He wasn't sure anything was out of the system yet, but said nothing.

She said, "I'm not married yet, in case you're wondering."

"I was."

"Well, I'm not, but I will be."

"Congratulations."

"And I've never done that before, kissing a random guy."

"You seemed to like it."

She shot him a look and pushed away. "Yes, it was good. Let's go."

THIRTY-ONE

SHE WALKED BACK to the villa, and Keeler watched, breathing easy and getting his heart rate under control. His brain chemistry was going haywire, and it took about ten seconds to flush it through his system. He laughed to himself, thinking about Tina Choi. Shit happens and you'll never know how or why.

Keeler estimated an eighty percent chance that Joe and his team had the pool area under surveillance. Listening, maybe watching him and Choi. Keeler didn't care about that, not even a little. What he cared about was getting Karim out of whatever hole they were holding him in.

Seeing the picture of Karim chained naked and injured to a stake in the dirt, he knew that the prospects weren't good for the guy. In his experience, only a handful of people get out of a situation like that. Mostly, they end up dead and sometimes headless.

He stared into the dark. The images came at him hard and fast, that situation outside of Al-Khafsah just a week or so earlier in Syria. The ISIS guys had been down by the river in a fisherman's shack. What Keeler remembered, the way it felt to push a knife into a man's throat.

Keeler had come out of the river, feeling like the Angel of Death. His skin and clothes, glistening from the glossy mud his team had applied to themselves before the attack. The ISIS guy from England had been bragging to his friends, speaking loudly in his London accent about what he was going to do to the girls they'd brought with them. Unlikely that the girls spoke English. The ISIS guy was vulgar, drunk, and dressed like some weird idea of an Islamic fundamentalist, essentially a loser from London, LARPing as a Jihadi.

Begging for the blade.

Keeler saw the girls in the shack. The ISIS men had set up a scene, inspired by the thousands of hours of internet porn those people watched on their phones. He listened to the other guys inside, laughing and talking loudly. They were from London or the Paris suburbs, Westerners, just like Keeler except different. They'd taken a lazy way out of life, coming here to destroy someone else's country, someone else's daughter's life. They didn't believe in anything except power, were basically nihilists.

The English guy stepped outside to take a piss. Keeler's knife went into his neck like a long needle moving through Jell-O. He pulled the man off the deck and into the mud. Put a knee on his face and confirmed the kill with a hand signal. The rest of the team came out of the river behind him, and the other ISIS men died and the girls were released.

That had been real and clear and had taken exactly fifty-two seconds by Keeler's watch.

And now this.

The entire situation had been FUBAR from the moment he'd entered the safe house in Çankaya.

Now it was worse.

It hadn't been Joe who had brought up the Çankaya safe house. Keeler had been waiting for that to drop into the explanation, but it hadn't. It had been the tall woman from earlier, with the auburn hair and the emerald-colored eyes. She'd come into the room and stood there for a moment, looking at them. Joe had been surprised when she intervened, giving away the fact that she'd been listening in on the conversation from another room.

She didn't introduce herself and looked at them and spoke like she was addressing students. "You don't know shit about the CIA safe house in Çankaya, right? You're not just hiding the information from us, you simply don't know. Am I right?"

Keeler and Choi remained silent. Joe looked down into the remains of a coffee cup he'd turned over on its little saucer, searching the grinds for patterns telling the future. It was almost embarrassing. The woman had rolled her eyes.

"Okay, so maybe you can't talk about it, or maybe you actually don't know." She said, "So, I'll say it. That apartment in Çankaya was a CIA safe house in which your colleagues were hosting an MEK team. Those people whose throats were cut were MEK. Do you know who that is?"

Keeler said, "No."

Choi said, "Mujahedin-e Khalq. Iranian opposition militant group. They're a kind of weird cult, were designated as terrorists by the CIA at one time, but now apparently they're kosher. The Israelis work with them inside of Iran and presumably we do too."

The woman's chin dropped, not exactly a nod, but a gesture resembling agreement. She watched Keeler. "The Tajiks had orders to cut their throats because, for the Iranians, MEK operatives are traitors and therefore deserve special treatment. Just so you know who we're dealing with. I wouldn't be at all surprised if the kill team included an IRGC operative whose sole purpose was to oversee the ritual slaughter."

Keeler was thinking about the woman up at Çankaya, looking up at him from her death throes on the road and clutching at his shirt. *Help the girl.* If she'd been an Iranian opposition fighter, why did she care so much about the girl?

The tall woman walked away, disappearing into the door on the other side of the living room.

Joe looked up and his fatigue had become very obvious. He said, "The enemy of your enemy is your friend."

Keeler didn't care about that. He was too busy being pissed off at his own people. The conversation with Joe and his commanding officer shouldn't have been necessary.

* * *

IT WASN'T Joe who took them back; it was his superior, the woman with auburn hair waiting for them in a dusty Russian Lada 4x4, its engine rumbling, the exhaust pipe blowing black and gray into the night. Keeler sat up front, Choi in back, thinking.

Mostly thinking about the kiss. Fifty percent strategic, fifty percent because she wanted to. Hard to decide, maybe a little more on the side of the wanting to, if she was honest with herself. The strategic part was the microdot tracker she'd firmly pressed into the tag at the collar of Keeler's shirt, while doing the other thing, the kiss.

She was attracted to bad boys, knew they needed to be kept under close surveillance. A little smile passed over her mouth, the memory of it coming back.

Choi had another microdot, which she now deployed under the driver's seat of the woman's Lada. Working DIA, Measurement and Signature Intelligence, those things were a dime a dozen back in the office. More specifically, a microdot particle sensor with GPS tracking capabilities, the things designed for nonproliferation surveillance. Six months into the job and this was the first time she had actually deployed one herself.

Hard to believe, but better late than never.

The woman dropped them off in downtown Ankara. Choi got out of the Lada first and saw the woman lay a hand on Keeler's arm, holding him there. She was giving him a business card. Choi saw it in the side mirror by Keeler's door, watched him examine the card.

She kept the rear door open a touch, listening to the conversation.

The woman said, "Call the number and ask for Ibrahim. We'll get back to you."

She watched the woman give a head jerk in her direction.

"Complicated work relationship?"

Choi felt the blush.

Keeler said, "No."

The woman said, "Call me Ruth."

"Okay."

Choi knew what was next and she had a moment of distaste for the future. Now, they were going to have to hustle back to the embassy after midnight and encounter layers of bullshit so thick they couldn't be cut with a Ka-Bar knife.

THIRTY-TWO

A THEORETICAL POINT made concrete by Acting Chief of Mission James Miller.

Miller was speaking to Choi, completely ignoring Keeler, which gave Keeler an opportunity to examine the man.

Miller was sweating all over himself, looking like he'd had a meeting with death and gotten a couple hours reprieve in exchange for what remained of his soul. Keeler had never met him before and had assumed he was only an asshole because of his position in the bureaucracy. What he was looking at was truly unbelievable, off the charts.

For one thing, he was obviously in bad health, like he'd been poisoned by something. The man's eyes were red, like all the blood vessels had burst. He seemed short of breath, clearly working hard to suck oxygen into his lungs. The sweat indicated a high heart rate, among other things.

It had taken Miller four hours to mobilize from his apartment to the embassy. During that time, Keeler and Choi had racked out in embassy hospitality rooms. With access to clean sheets and running water and soap, Keeler had stripped down and washed. Now he was feeling good, even with the same old clothes. Clean and ready for whatever came next.

It was six in the morning and Miller had been looking through a pile of documents on his desk for ten minutes without saying anything.

Joe had given them the dossier: real paper and cardboard and printing ink, or whatever those machines use these days. The dossier had dynamite information. One of the most senior members of Hezbollah was accompanying a young woman traveling under an assumed name to a cosmetic-surgery clinic in Ankara. The clinic had been the subject of a MEK surveillance team operating out of a CIA safe house. That team had been wiped out and ritually slaughtered.

Additional documentary evidence showed that their man, Karim Ahmadi was injured and being held captive in difficult conditions. You didn't need to be a genius to presume they'd be taking him over the border to Syria, where they could keep him hostage indefinitely.

The list was beyond convincing.

A CIA safe house liquidated, a member of the response team kidnapped, a CIA contractor shot dead at the Holiday Inn. Add to that what had almost occurred at Dr. Erkin's house and you had the headline events of a coordinated attack on United States' interests in the region.

The more he thought about it, the more Keeler was convinced of a setup. The recent US elections had produced a kind of political fog, which made it a perfect moment to strike at American interests and get away with it. To his mind, this was an unacceptable result.

These people needed a three-in-the-morning visitation by a team of hooligans. Calcutti's team would do just fine, as long as Keeler got to be the point man with a knife.

That's not what Miller had concluded. His first response

had been incomprehension. He'd completely ignored the information about Karim, as if that didn't matter. As for the Hezbollah guy and the girl, he simply didn't see the utility.

Miller waved a lazy hand at the uniformed marine guard, detailed to shadow Keeler around the embassy. "Can you wait outside, please?"

The young guard did an about-face and exited the room, closing the door after himself. Keeler and Choi turned to Miller.

He said, "So what?"

Choi had tried to explain it, not mentioning anything ethical, like protecting a young girl from barbarism. She went rational and realistic like a good spook. "It's about leverage. We're not gunning for the Hezbollah guy, a drone can do that. We're going for the girl. If she's important enough for Nasrallah to send Ezzedin, she's very likely to be important enough for us."

"Who said Nasrallah sent him with the girl?"

"We already know that Ezzedin takes orders from Hassan Nasrallah. He's not here on vacation, Miller. My assessment is that he was sent under orders. There's something substantial here that we need to get into."

"Uh-huh. To do what with? I mean, if somehow you manage to get this woman's identity?"

Keeler was half expecting Choi to just walk away. Clearly this guy wasn't going to be helpful. As she'd explained it, the Chief of Mission has the final say on clandestine activity. The idea behind that protocol had been to avoid agency infighting overseas, away from DC.

The solution arrived at had been to make the Ambassador the final arbitrator for operations in his area of operations, make him Chief of Mission. But Miller wasn't ambassadorial material, he was an ass kisser who'd accidentally found himself Acting Chief of Mission.

Choi persisted. She tried to smile. "Do you have kids, a family?"

Miller coughed, annoyed. "Yeah."

"Wouldn't you do anything for your kids, Miller, for your family? Do you see how this could play out? Could give us a hell of a lever, maybe use it to pry open someone high up in Hezbollah. Who knows what you could get him to do, or give you, or agree on. Imagine you get to this girl's mother, and she's the wife of some bigwig in Lebanon, or Iran. Shia women don't have public status, but that doesn't mean they have no status or no power. If you have a family, you know how that works."

Keeler looked at Choi's left hand, the engagement ring. She certainly had ideas about family.

Miller had finally found an acceptable seated position that was temporarily easing his discomfort: behind the desk in the ergonomic chair, leaned back slightly, trying to maintain appearances, suppressing a rising nausea. Keeler and Choi were standing on the rug in front of him

"You're not going to convince me on a purely intelligence basis. That's not my remit, it's yours. My obligation is to the mission, and we've been clearly told to keep things cool. You want to pursue this, go ahead. You need to go through channels. Send it up the pipe to DIA." He put a finger on the dossier. "Anderson's KIA and his guy was recalled last night. I'll send this up to Langley myself." He gave a skeletal grimace. "We'll see what they say."

Choi put a hand on her hip, it was obvious that she didn't like begging.

She said, "I'm sending it up my chain of command, but they take time to analyze, and then to decide. We won't have an answer for like, forty-eight hours." She stepped up to Miller's desk. Jammed a finger into the closed dossier. "This is actionable immediately. Ezzedin has the girl at this location, right now.

Plus our guy Karim Ahmadi, right now. He's looking to get them across into Syria. We need to get him out now. Not tomorrow, not the next day."

Miller said, "Not *exactly* our guy."

Keeler thought about ripping his head off, figured it would be excellent immediately, but counterproductive in the medium to long-term.

He spoke to Choi. "Let's go."

Choi glanced back at him, angry, face red and forehead shiny. She turned back to Miller.

"I'm calling an emergency meeting. I want Jensen there and I want the Regional Security Officer and the Counselor for Political Affairs."

Miller deadpanned as best he could. "Counselor for Political is in Istanbul. We can get him remotely, but he won't be able to securely access these documents until he's back in the embassy tomorrow. There's a reason we haven't brought the political officer in yet, at the request of the Undersecretary of State for Politics, we've fire-walled this kerfuffle. No counselor for Political, no Regional Security Officer." He opened his eyes wide, gave a kind of salesman-like spread of his hands. "I didn't make this up, Choi, okay? This is direct from DC. If you wish to pursue this, I'll set up a meeting for you with the Under-secretary."

"Okay, do that."

Miller smiled. "Fine. I'll see when she can be available."

If Choi was expecting Miller to make the call right then and there, she was mistaken. He said, "I'll let you know." And rose unsteadily. "If you'll excuse me." He moved around his desk in a beeline for the bathroom, one hand in touch with the furniture and the wall for balance.

Miller flung the door open and disappeared. The marine was waiting outside, hands behind his back, ramrod straight but relaxed and making eye contact with Keeler, who winked. No reaction.

Choi pulled at him. "Let's go."

He followed her through the door. The marine stood straight and tall, but looked at ease all the same.

Keeler turned to Choi. "Back there when I told you we should go, you almost cussed, right?"

She looked confused. "No. I didn't."

He nodded at her. "You came close though."

Choi breathed out through her nose, like a huff. "You're not taking this seriously."

"Oh, I'm taking it seriously enough. You do your thing. I sincerely hope it works, but I've got my doubts about the ability of people like that to get anything good done in the world. Seems to me a guy like Miller's just there to stand in the way." He gave Choi a chance to object, but she didn't take it. "The other thing, that guy's seriously ill. He needs treatment and he's not currently qualified to hold the post he's in. I observed palpitations, and he's short of breath." Keeler jerked a head toward the bathroom where Miller had fled. "Do you people have some kind of protocol for this?"

"I don't know."

Keeler addressed the marine. "You got a chow hall here, buddy?"

The marine cleared his throat. "I can take you to the cafeteria, sir."

He looked at Choi. "You hungry?"

She shook her head. "No. I'm going down to the office. Need to send a report up the chain."

He looked at the marine and shrugged. "Let's go."

THIRTY-THREE

THE MARINE TURNED to lead the way, but Keeler put a hand on his thick bicep, chin nodded to Choi, letting her get out of sight.

He turned to the marine. "I need to make a call to Azraq. Can you show me to a DSN phone?"

Azraq was the US military installation in Jordan where Calcutti and the other guys had been sent.

The marine's voice was low and smooth. "You need voice or data, sir?"

"Voice."

"No problem, sir. Follow me."

The marine led the way, down the hall and to the left. Another corridor with a patterned carpet and offices both left and right. At the end was a small room, just large enough for two or three people to squeeze into. The marine opened the door for Keeler. "Right in there, sir."

Two chairs and a desk with a phone on it, nothing too complicated about it. Keeler had never been inside an embassy before and didn't know the diplomatic protocols, or how to use their tools. Defense Switched Network was how US embassies and military installations communicate; there were codes and prefixes and special buttons to push. He had no idea how it worked.

But the marine did and was very helpful. He knew how to get in touch with the personnel officer at Azraq. From there it was a matter of waiting for that officer to figure out where on base the JSOC operators were hanging out.

While they waited, the small room started feeling a little tight, since the marine was a big man and so was Keeler. Both of them muscled like sacks full of walnuts, sharing space and breathing the same air. They looked at each other squarely, two sets of eyes calm and collected and about two feet apart. The marine looked like he had questions.

Keeler said, "Spit it out, marine."

"Are you Captain Keeler, sir?"

"I am. You don't need to *sir* me. What's your name, marine?"

"Thompson, sir." He said, "Sorry, just Thompson."

"What's your primary MOS Thompson?"

"3300."

"What's that when you're talking to a non-marine?"

"Food service."

Marine security guard's tours of duty are usually three twelve-month rotations. After that, they go back to a primary function. Thompson's primary job was a cook, or something.

Keeler said, "Getting some hoo-ha here in Ankara Thompson, is it worth it?"

"Hell, yes. I was deployed back at Pendleton for a year. They said going MSG might get me out of trouble, and I'm thinking maybe I could go for the augmentation unit and get back on track."

Which all meant that Thompson had gotten himself in some shit back home.

"What happened, you get knocked down?"

"You could say that again. Got cut down to the kitchen at Pendleton. I was with First Reconnaissance."

Keeler whistled. First Recon were a serious bunch of fighters. Thompson hadn't been a cook with them; he'd been a warrior. "Were you part of the deployment to Helmand, a couple years back?"

Thompson nodded. "Did Helmand, moved on to Trek Nawa, took some scalps."

Keeler inclined his head. "I kicked in many doors with First Recon back then. Don't recall that we met a Thompson. You guys did a hell of a job. What's the disciplinary charge, some bullshit?"

"I was with Charlie Company. Someone thought we were flying a Nazi flag, SS, but it wasn't a Nazi flag."

Thompson's skin was rich in melanin, but Keeler avoided the obvious question of why anybody would accuse a Black guy of being a Nazi, since it was irrelevant and anyway nobody was ever surprised by the level of bullshit that command could produce.

He recalled the incident a few years back. Someone published a photograph that was misinterpreted by the media. The soldiers weren't flying an SS flag; it was the US Marine Scout Snipers flag, almost identical to the infamous *Schutzstaffel* symbol.

"That was cleared up by the inquiry, if I recall."

"Correct, but the commander didn't like that I was getting with his wife back on base, so he used that as an excuse to send me down."

"Sorry to hear it."

The call came through from Azraq, but Calcutti wasn't there. Just an army corporal who sounded tired and said Calcutti's team had received orders and were currently en route to Al-

Tanf, the main US military base in Syria, almost smack dab on the triple border between Syria, Jordan, and Iraq.

En route and in other words, out of touch. The corporal was happy to take down the number from Keeler's burner phone and pass it to her counterpart at Al-Tanf. The stars would have to align for Calcutti to get the message. Keeler hung up the phone.

For a moment he thought about being there, with Calcutti, Cheevers, and Bratton. Maybe riding in the back of an MRAP, or more likely sitting in a helicopter, legs hanging out drinking a cold beer. Hot desert wind in your face. The good times.

He'd get back to that eventually.

He looked up at Thompson, liking the guy, even if it was because he'd been knocked down for getting with the commander's wife.

He said, "I guess I'll just get some food, then."

Thompson coughed. "No problem."

He led Keeler through the labyrinthian passages of the embassy. "My Detachment Commander says he knows you."

"Is that right?"

"It's what he says. Do you mind if I tell him you're coming down to the chow hall? I think he'd like to shake your hand."

"No problem."

* * *

THE CHOW HALL was half the size of a football field. Keeler and Thompson stood side by side looking at it.

Thompson said, "Impressive, right?"

Keeler recalled that the guy was a food service specialist. He said, "3300, what's that, the guy who peels the potatoes?"

"More like the guy who sweeps up the peels off the floor and takes out the trash."

"Someone's got to do it, right?"

Thompson shrugged. "True enough."

Keeler said, "What doesn't kill you just makes you stronger. You hungry?"

"Do I look like I'm ever not hungry?"

The two of them plunged into a multilayered buffet. Four basins deep with five distinct sections. There were many variations on breakfast, ranging from American classics like pancakes and scrambled eggs and bacon to more obscure options like oatmeal and granola. The lunch section featured specialties like meatloaf and lasagna and steak and even a good-looking gumbo.

It was hard to commit.

Thompson went straight for the salad bar, which was surprisingly colorful, resembling something you'd find in a picture of a Mediterranean country, which in a way made sense, given Turkey's location. Keeler followed.

Thompson said, "I never actually tasted vegetables before this posting, man."

In the end Keeler decided not to begin with salad, despite the deep color of the tomatoes. He started with breakfast and took a sample of as many things as possible, crowded onto two large plates and a bowl for the gumbo. He figured he could always come back for the salad, right before dessert.

Thompson dipped into his salad, looking on as Keeler got involved, his eyes widening as Keeler demolished both plates systematically, one item at a time, with relish and great enjoyment. What he realized, he'd eaten lunch at the clinic, but it hadn't been substantial enough. The portions small enough for patients on various pharmaceutical regimes. The last time he'd eaten properly had been back in that night market with Karim. He remembered the kebab and the coffee and the baklava. Most of all he remembered Karim, looking much better back then than in the picture Joe had shown him and Choi.

That image of Karim naked and cowed stayed in his mind, up there in front of everything else like a primary layer that he couldn't get rid of, like tinnitus or something. It was still there when Thompson's Detachment Commander came into the cafeteria, looking for Keeler and finding him and recognizing him. Keeler didn't know the man, but that didn't prevent him from being polite.

The man said, "Staff Sergeant Leonard. Pleased to shake your hand."

His hand was hard and calloused. Shaking it felt like holding on to a warm oak block wrapped in sandpaper.

"Likewise. I'm Keeler."

Leonard had a square jaw and a thick rectangular forehead. He nodded once, curtly. "I know that, sir. Uh, you might not remember me, but you saved my life."

Keeler stopped chewing. "I did?"

THIRTY-FOUR

LEONARD NODDED SEVERELY. He pounded a thigh.

"Al Anbar province, sir, 2007. Shooter with a Dragunov took my leg out. You know how it is. You don't feel a thing, just knocked on your ass. Forty-five seconds later, you're bleeding out and dying. So, one minute I'm confused and numb in the dust. The next, I'm looking at your face, yelling at me and dragging me into cover." He grinned broadly. "You planted your green boots on my ass man and I never got a chance to thank you."

Leonard's hand shot out for a grab, which Keeler took full-on, with vigor.

He sort of remembered the incident, among the many others, a particularly rough ambush situation, a marine unit with casualties. An enemy force more motivated and competent than usual. Him and his team, pulling out a bunch of screaming soldiers and plugging holes in their bodies as best they could. The medevac taking a while to get there and the haunted look of shock on the face of the wounded. The situation had been slightly sticky, a hot and humid day. Hot as in Middle Eastern hot, like a hundred and ten degrees in the shade.

In other words, the usual hell.

"Leg heal up okay?"

Leonard leaned forward in his seat, reached down and rolled up his left trouser break, revealing a prosthetic limb disappearing into a highly polished boot. "Bulletproof, sir."

Keeler had nothing to say.

Leonard turned to look at Thompson, sitting beside him. "Coffee."

Thompson went to get them coffee from a machine. Leonard leaned over the table, getting closer to Keeler. He spoke slowly and quietly. "They say the savages took one of our guys and nobody gives a damn, that true?"

"That's how it looks."

Leonard nodded. He had a hard stare. "I met your chief, Calcutti, before they exfiltrated him back to Jordan. Tell you what, when they quit the safe house downtown, they took out the combat operations pack you all had in there. It's still here at the embassy. We're in charge of that, sir, down in my armory."

"Is that right?" Keeler had assembled the combat operations kit himself. He knew what was in it, enough gear to cause a decently serious ruckus, if wielded by the right hands.

Leonard said, "Me and Thompson there, we're both off duty for the weekend."

Keeler didn't know what day it was. He said, "When's the weekend?"

Leonard looked at his watch. "Starts in about a half hour, sir."

"So what, you're suggesting that I take you two as tourists on some kind of cowboy exercise in ultra-violent hooligan behavior, marine?"

Leonard said, "That's exactly what I'm suggesting, sir."

"That's an outrageous suggestion."

"Yes, it is."

"What about your foot?"

"It's a good foot, sir, I like it."

The Detachment Commander's eyes remained level and looked to Keeler a little like an old recruitment poster he'd seen from back in the day. Above the face had been the word *HONOR*, large and up top. Below it read: *The United States Marine Corps Builds Men.*

Some guys had liked that poster back in 1966, some guys hadn't. That was life, complicated.

Thompson came back with the coffee. He shared a look with his boss, who gave a little nod. They'd already had a discussion. Keeler took the heavy-duty coffee mug approvingly. The brew was dark and hot and the cup was reassuringly substantial in the hand. He took a slow sip, thinking about these marines across the table from him.

Thompson and Leonard looked at him expectantly, like they were craving an adventure. He thought of his friend Karim Ahmadi lying bloody and beaten in some dirt hole. He thought, affirmative, whatever it took was what he was prepared to contemplate. It had to be fast, it could be reckless, but it shouldn't be panicked.

He said, "I appreciate what you're saying." And left it at that.

Thompson blinked and started to say something. Leonard put a hand out to Thompson's shoulder. He said, "I understand, sir. That's good enough for us." Nodded at his friend, who sat back and finished his coffee.

Keeler took another sip of coffee. It was good: strong but not heavy, black and smooth. "All right."

Keeler felt a surge flow through him, electric, traveling from head to toe and then back again and extending out to his extremities. He felt warm in the embrace of new comrades, like he could put his arms around these two guys and give them a big hug, but his arms wouldn't be wide enough, because it was pretty clear that the US embassy in Ankara had one hell of a gym.

Keeler used the three minutes and twenty-two seconds it took to get from the cafeteria down to the marine security guard armory to consider pros and cons. The first thing that was obvious to him: a rogue operation to get Karim back from those barbarians wasn't going to be controversial. The pencil necks might complain, but the military takes care of its own. If they were successful, the operation would be sanctioned retroactively. If they weren't successful, they'd be dead.

Not a tough choice, more of a no-brainer.

But then again, there were other options to exhaust first, Choi's way and Joe's way. Or maybe some combination of the two.

THIRTY-FIVE

JENSEN WATCHED TINA CHOI SPEAK. The woman was brilliant, young, and beautiful, as if two out of three wasn't enough. She'd put out feelers to people and gathered a few data points. Choi had multiple degrees in Middle Eastern languages and something very technical, plus she'd excelled in her clandestine service training courses. Consequently, the girl was on the career ladder at DIA, the posting to Ankara being a significant leg up. Field work, getting out there and putting your cards on the table. Either your team trusted you or they didn't. The hierarchy was a piece of shit, but at least in the clandestine world a turd is a turd.

If Choi came through like a diamond, she'd gleam.

At the moment the young lady was sitting on the edge of Jensen's desk holding a cardboard cup of coffee and telling Jensen that they needed to move hell and high water back in DC, invoking patriotism, reputation, and geo-political strategy in terse, complete sentences that, piled together, amounted to a great argument.

For example. "Getting our man back is one thing, but what if this girl ends up being a tool we can use against Nasrallah, or maybe some big shot in the Iranian Revolutionary Guards?" She opened her hands wide, as in, showing Jensen something large, with heft and breadth. "That's going to be hell-a valuable as an intelligence product that we can" —she ticked things off on her fingers— "trade, sell, threaten with, use as blackmail, run as an asset, you name it, Jensen. It's going to be hot. Think about the interested buyers."

Choi was right, of course, but that wasn't going to help the fact that this was a dicey angle.

There is a single hard belief, universal among intelligence people, held strongest by those with the most experience: you can't trust stuff that someone gives you for nothing.

She said, "I agree with you Choi, a hundred percent, but you know everyone hates a walk-in."

Choi's face fell. "Yeah." She looked tired.

Jensen said, "I've got a little pull with the Undersecretary of State for Politics." She opened her thumb and forefinger an inch. "Just a little." Jensen patted Choi's leg. "I'm going to use it, and I'll let you know how it shakes out." She made a shooing gesture. "Now go get some sleep and change your clothes and eat something healthy, like kale and chickpeas. Check back with me at around fourteen hundred hours."

* * *

BACK IN DC, Undersecretary of State for Politics Victoria Neuman was eating cake. Not just any cake, a great big fluffy thing with strawberries and whipped cream, white and red and pink, where the first two were bleeding together. The mouthful was incredible, a soft and sweet fluff with hits of tart fruit amid the gloss of thickening agents in the strawberry sauce.

Bob had taken an overly ambitious bite. She watched him actually push the piece into his mouth with a forefinger. Thankfully they were with friends, one of whom guffawed at the sight. *Guffaw* being a word that Victoria Neuman appreciated, and had resolved not to abuse, ever.

It was midnight and she'd had six martinis over the four-course menu at Pineapple and Pearls. For a main dish she'd chosen the lobster and octopus lasagna thing, with Bob going for the Shenandoah lamb, which was of course some demented version of what the name suggested, par for the course in a two-star Michelin restaurant. Her phone rang; it was the office.

"What?"

Her assistant sounded very relaxed. "It's a call from Kathy Jensen in Ankara. She says it's important."

"Tell her you couldn't get ahold of me. I'll call her back in the morning." The martinis had begun to kick in just before half time on the menu, after the roasted potato ice cream with caviar.

Her assistant said, "Yeah, well, Ms. Jensen had a message for you, in case you couldn't be reached."

"What is it?"

"She said to tell you she was wearing red socks."

"Oh." She glanced at Bob, who was noticing the turn in the conversation, from a quick *screw you* to something that needed dealing with. She said, "Hold on a second."

Neuman rose from the table, putting the fork into the cake plate, eyeing some part of the restaurant where she could have the conversation. Moving among the tables, still feeling good in the black dress from Alexander McQueen, the one Melania had worn at some MET gala, the same dress everyone in DC was now craving.

The flashback.

Third year in college, Jensen was her roommate in the house, Alpha Chi Omega. A mixer with Sigma Chi. They'd started at the sorority house with pre-drinks, of which she had a hazy memory, tequila and cheap margarita mix in a blender with cucumbers, crushed ice, and mint. The party had been at the frat house, a vaguely disgusting place that smelled like a football team's locker room. What Neuman really remembered, seared into the brain: being pushed into a bedroom by two frat boys that she already knew, shit-faced and ready to pass out but not harmless. She suddenly sobered up, terrified because the guys had turned mean on her.

Maybe it was the alcohol or they'd done too much blow, or maybe they were just evil; whatever it was, they'd pushed her down into the bed, pushed her face hard into the sheets. She remembered the feeling of a big guy's palm on the back of her head. Other fingers grasping at her, groping at flesh, pulling at her clothes. Kathy Jensen and another girl busted in. They'd gone nuts. Hitting and screaming, but also scared shitless, desperate to get out of there.

Jensen had taken her back to the room they shared, where Neuman sat on her bed shaking, her dress torn. Jensen fetched her a glass of water. She came back into the room, and Neuman remembered the dialogue verbatim, the first thing coming out of her own mouth as an involuntary blurt.

"I'm wearing red socks."

Meaning, it was her own fault, that what had driven good boys to transform into evil rapists wasn't their inherent evil, but her essential sluttiness. When she'd said it, she'd looked up at Jensen, seeing Kathy pause ever so slightly, the glass of water held delicately in her hand, threatening to spill. Jensen kneeled down and handed the water to her.

"Drink."

Neuman was still seeing double. She drank greedily, deeply, eyes watching Kathy's face. Seeing patience, her friend waiting for her to finish the water, hand outstretched to receive the empty glass. Taking the glass and placing it calmly on the bedside table. Jensen had turned back to her, now flushed with anger. She slapped Neuman hard, once on the cheek. The blow stinging and humiliating.

She pushed her face close in on Neuman, teeth bared, spitting out the words. "Bullshit, bitch. It's not your fault. They're a bunch of rapist pigs."

Nothing had happened to the would-be rapists. But from then on, the phrase had become a thing between Kathy Jensen and her, like a joke that's not funny. Something shared and unique. A code of defiance for when A, the women were in a sticky situation, and B, the world can burn.

She took the call out in the greenhouse, bumming a smoke off a busboy.

"So, you've got your red socks on, hey, Kath?"

* * *

LATER, Bob was giving her a foot massage back home. He listened to the whole thing, quiet and calm and thoughtful while she recounted what Jensen had said, and what she'd wanted. Neuman raised her eyebrows once she'd finished the tale.

"You see what I'm saying?"

Bob nodded gravely. His thumbs riding up the plantar fascia, doing wonderful things for the lateral plantar nerve. "Do you know what the JSOC guy is doing now?" he asked. "Are they going to exfiltrate him to Amman as well?"

"My guy in Ankara says he's fraternizing with the marine security guards."

"Your guy?"

"The political officer, I called him after speaking with Kathy." Bob nodded approvingly. "My guy said Miller's keeping everything fire walled, hasn't even called him in on it yet."

Bob said, "Miller's riding a fine line. Hmmm." The fingers

had grasped the outer parts of her foot. "What does she want you to do, Vick?"

"Kathy wants me to press for an immediate intervention, her words."

"Strong words. What do you think she means, drones and a JSOC raid, all that?"

Neuman said, "Yeah. Maybe get the Turks involved, make it a NATO problem. What do you think?"

Bob's thumbs had closed in on the nerve, digging in strongly, and it felt great. He hummed a few lines of a catchy tune from the restaurant. "Fraternizing with marines, you said."

"Yes. You want the details, he was last seen eating ice cream with them and they were having a good time. Now tell me what you think, Bob."

"Hmmm." His intelligent eyes came up, somewhat piggish. "Here's a thought experiment Vick. Imagine yourself in like, 1896: You're in London at the heart of the British Empire. A room with a good globe in it. The kind they have on a stand that you can spin and put your finger on a place you want to own. Same thing happens: there's a problem out there somewhere with a man on the ground. Maybe it's someplace in India, somewhere hot and dusty with a million people running around with animals and stuff. You've just come in from breakfast in Mayfair or whatever, so you're a universe away from what's going on. Still, your man on the ground's got serious problems, like maybe the locals are rioting, burning shit; maybe they're killing British officials, whatever. It's a bad situation and some version of common sense would tell you to get the damned cavalry down there in force. You know what they'd say, those guys who ran the empire?"

"No, Bob, what would they say?"

"They'd make a couple of stiff gin and tonics. They'd say this. Vicky." Now Bob put on his best upper-class English accent and opened his eyes real wide. "I suppose we'll just have to let our man *muddle through*."

"Muddle through, which means what, exactly?"

"It's the genius of the British Empire. Muddling through means the man on the ground is the best one to figure shit out, even if he doesn't know it." Bob's eyes glowed, his face turning a little red, the way she imagined him with his grad students. Bob the geek. She stifled a laugh and he stopped talking and looked at her weird. "What?"

"Nothing."

He said, "Muddling through is a strategy for dealing with a complex situation, Vick. One that you don't have a full grasp on. Instead of prescribing a top-down solution—like bringing in the cavalry—you let this guy down there figure it out. You *make* him figure it out. You trust his intuitions and his skills. I mean, that's what he's supposed to be good for, right? We chose him, we trained him, he's *there*."

"He went through a tough pipeline to get to where he is, right?" Neuman didn't feel Bob's thumbs anymore. She was focused on what he was implying, which was as usual, a little fiddly, but not a bad idea. "So we tell Jensen to go screw herself. I mean, gently."

"With a velvet glove. Let her know that you have full confidence in the Ankara mission."

Neuman liked it. "And then we'll just, like"—she waved her hands in the air like a magician— "see what happens!"

Bob smiled, the twinkle in his eye. "Exactly."

THIRTY-SIX

TINA CHOI CAME out of Jensen's office, closed the door and leaned back against it, looking at Keeler and shaking her head.

He said, "No dice?"

She ran a finger across her throat and then put it to her lips. They walked the corridor.

"That is one unhappy woman in there." Meaning Jensen.

He said, "Political train wreck."

"Completely." Choi looked at him and shook her head, like she couldn't even imagine something that bad. "Not only is nobody coming; they're exfiltrating you tomorrow morning to Amman. End of story."

Keeler looked at her. They'd come to the stairs. Choi's office was up, Keeler wasn't going up. He said, "You did what you could, Choi."

She breathed out a sigh. "I might get a response from the bosses back home." Crossed her fingers and held them up. "Fingers crossed, right?"

"Right."

Keeler pivoted and took the stairs to the lobby.

Outside the embassy, he walked up the hill for a couple of

minutes. They had a nice park up there with benches organized into a circle around a pond. He took a bench and dialed the number from the business card Ruth had given him. It was white with a pipe and a wrench and the rest in Turkish. Some guy answered and he did what she'd said, asked to speak to Ibrahim. The guy hung up without responding.

A minute later the burner phone buzzed in his hand. Not a call, a message with one word, *Anıtkabirm*.

* * *

Anıtkabirm, the mausoleum dedicated to worshiping Ataturk, father of the post–Ottoman-Turkish state. The place an enormous site of paving stones, long pathways, and gardens. A monumental building took the center, with pillars and a whole lot of Turkish flags blowing in the wind. Families scooted around, women protecting the integrity of their headscarves.

Neither Ruth nor Joe were in sight. Keeler was out in the open, considering the plan from their side. They would be running counter-surveillance on him now, making sure he wasn't with company, friendly or not. His role now was to be a tourist for a while.

Inside the mausoleum were exhibitions dedicated to the great man's life, like his custom-made Cadillac from the mid-1930s, restored and glossy in a tight room. There were paintings of the man on horseback, and walking out in front of his people, surrounded by mustachioed men in uniform. The great Ataturk himself had a good mustache at one point and a round Ottoman-style hat. They had his favorite weapons mounted behind Plexiglass.

He found Ruth in front of a diorama, something called the Battle of the Commander in Chief. Like she knew he was on his way there and had strategically relocated. Keeler liked that style, the aura of preparation and competence. She didn't look at him at first, so he watched her for a while as she read the plaque.

Ruth was wearing jeans and an Islamic headscarf, her auburn hair poking out from under the scarf, looking good.

The diorama showed soldiers in a trench using a radio, with the battle beyond, painted as a mural. She turned to him, no greeting, just immediately present. Ruth pointed to a portrait of Ataturk, this time before he had a mustache.

"This guy was supposed to guarantee a secular state for Turkey, which makes it hard to understand why they got so busy killing Christians so fast."

Keeler said, "Am I about to get a lecture?"

"Don't get me started." She touched his elbow and started walking, not speaking until they were out into the paved and windy courtyard. She stopped by a statue of Ataturk, mounted on a horse with a saber in hand. She said, "My people got in touch with your people back in Washington." She let the fingers of her hand spring apart. "Nothing doing, huh? Total chaos." She smiled at him like a sad clown.

"Pretty much."

She shrugged. "Which makes it the same on my side, like a mirror, pathetic. We won't touch it if you don't, kind of thing."

He said, "But here you are."

"Right. I was born with the *screw them all* gene. Got it from my grandmother." She watched him for a moment before speaking. "What I've also got is the last-known enemy position and access to low-orbit satellite imagery. Intelligence wise, that's it. I don't know how many there are, I don't know details about the place. You understand."

"When was the last flyover?"

"We're up on their signals in addition to the satellite imagery. Last flyover was yesterday. Unfortunately, we don't have any priority on the target now, but I've negotiated an updated image set for later today. We can stage tonight." They were on a pathway with roses on either side, now just tangles of gray-brown gnarls with thorns.

He said, "I do this with my own team."

Fake surprise. "Oh, so you have a team now?"

"I have a couple of guys."

She smiled and touched his arm again. "You don't need to insist. I don't have a team, my friend." The sad smile again. "It's either you get involved, or nothing."

"What happened to Joe and the others?"

She blew out through pursed lips, gave him a *'you wouldn't believe it'* laugh. "You think you've got it bad." Ruth was staring into his eyes, searching. She said, "Don't worry about Joe. I'll be there with a man or two. If you have a team, we'll split up. I can provide overwatch, vehicles, and some gear."

Overwatch in this context meant a shooter and a spotter who could both kill and communicate.

He said, "You're in it for a piece of the girl, is that right?"

"Correct. I've got the DNA kit. We only need a couple of hair follicles, blood, a finger, whatever. Fizza's a good name for a fake name, don't you think?"

Keeler did like the name, but he didn't say so. He said, "Fizza's a better name than Ruth, in my opinion. Ruth's a little old-fashioned."

She stood there and took it, smiling. "Yeah, so?"

He looked at her directly. "So, let's do it."

Ruth's eyes seemed to glimmer. She gave off surprisingly wise vibes, despite her age, maybe thirty-five.

She said, "Sababa."

THIRTY-SEVEN

THEY CAME AFTER DARK. Keeler's team in the Mercedes and Ruth's in the Lada, taking different routes to the same destination, an eight-hour drive southeast to the Syrian border region. Thompson drove and Leonard rode shotgun, the two of them dressed in civilian clothes, looking like dangerous hikers. Keeler sat in the back, studying the satellite images Ruth had furnished.

The target was a house in a village named Khirbat As-Sikkin. This was just west of the Euphrates river, a seemingly flat and featureless land that was actually cut by deep gullies. The terrain was stony and dry after the summer, rough country for buzzards and snakes.

Keeler liked this kind of country, it felt clean and hard.

Elevation was around five hundred meters, cold and barren. His window was open and the chilly air whipped in with a light spit of precipitation. He liked it, the cold and the hint of rain. Rain made noise and people tended to stay out of it, which made it the raider's friend. The country went by, a gray-scale landscape of rocks with a low-built structure whizzing past once in a while.

Keeler closed the window and adjusted the red LED head-light, examining the target in a high-altitude satellite shot.

The building was on the edge of town, literally the last structure before the landscape descended into a dry river gorge they called a *wadi*. The next house over caught his interest, this one a hundred meters from the target, but separated by the wadi. The differential in elevation gave it a slight height advantage, overlooking the target house.

Keeler liked it for that reason and because the satellite images of the target showed nothing except a farmhouse with a couple of outbuildings on the edge of town. From above it looked deserted. No vehicles in the yard, no movement, no laundry hanging on clotheslines. No chicken coop and no dogs walking around. Only high-resolution images of stones, dirt, roof tiles, and cement.

The marines had said they'd be up for some hooligan behavior; they just might get some.

The two vehicles were three kilometers from the town, pulling into the lee of huge boulders scattered across a high plateau, a location chosen by Keeler. Upon arriving there, he saw his intuition was rewarded. The place was an illegal-dumping site for construction waste. Trash lay everywhere, dumped and abandoned.

Leonard got out of the Mercedes and stretched, letting out a long groan, his spine audibly cracking like bubble wrap. Keeler spread a map over the hood of the first vehicle, which was hot from the engine and smelled like diesel. The Lada arrived with Ruth's team.

She stayed in the vehicle for a minute, conversing with her people, gesticulating, explaining something, or giving orders. Ruth stopped speaking and the two guys nodded in unison. She came out of the car and walked over, immediately focused and on point.

"Show me."

Keeler showed her the overlooking structure on the satellite image, compared it to the map position.

She nodded. "Okay."

He said, "I want to use this house as an observation and overwatch position. It's cut off from town by the topography and the elevation is higher than the target. My guess is it's a family home, maybe goat farmers or whatever. The folks living here would have seen our friends, but not necessarily interacted with them. Know what I mean?"

"You want to take over the house. I get it."

"My kit has enough morphine to chill them out, depending on how many generations are in there."

"The old people won't need tranquilizing, only the young."

"We'll see."

Ruth's people watched from the vehicle. There were two of them in there, one skinny guy Keeler hadn't seen before and the man from the clinic, whose head had been bandaged, now upgraded to a black wool hat.

Keeler said, "Are you making them wait in the car?"

"Yes."

He went around the back and opened the trunk. Inside was a large duffel bag made from beige Mil-Spec Cordura, the combat operations kit. He hauled it out and set it on the ground. The duffel had zippers and Velcro attachments to straps with side-release buckles. He squared the bag and unzipped the top-loading flap. He adjusted his headlamp to look inside.

The interior had multiple compartments and clever pockets. The last time Keeler had seen it was back in Brooklyn when Cheevers was handing him the plastic-wrapped Yavuz 9mm.

He loaded himself down with a couple of flash-bang grenades, each in its own pocket, and four dismantled Uzi Pro submachine guns with accessories, like sighting units and suppressors and enough 9mm ammunition for a decent gunfight. No connection to the Israelis present, just a convenient weapon for operating undercover in Turkey, since Turkish special tactics units used the platform. Other pockets held wireless communications gear for a tactical combat network. Plus, a bonus set of two black hornet drones.

Keeler removed one of the Uzi Pros and snarled at the marines. "Don't be shy."

The Uzi Pro was small, almost like a toy. One thing he loved about the platform is that as you began to assemble the accessories, the thing changed, transforming into some dream commando weapon with stock, suppressor, the micro sighting unit. It felt good in his hands, light and well-balanced with just enough heft to keep it real.

Leonard and Thompson dipped in and the clicking and snicking joined the wind's whisper. Keeler loved the sound of mechanical hardware being assembled. Ruth came over with three Kevlar vests.

"Put these on under your clothes." She examined Keeler critically. "They'll fit."

Thompson said, "Thank you, ma'am."

Ruth gave him a look. She pointed at the fourth Uzi Pro. "You mind?"

Keeler said, "Go for it."

He knew the weapon system back to front, using his hands without bothering to look. The marines weren't as familiar, but Ruth sure was, locking and clicking modular accessories into place, checking battery charge, testing spring tension in the magazines and dealing with the ammunition. They locked eyes, and he noticed with a little surprise that she looked happy.

The wind blew her hair around a little, hooting through

crevices in the boulders around them, making weird flute like sounds, in a minor key arpeggio. But for the howling wind and the snick and click of weapons being prepared, the night was calm, even beautiful. Maybe even perfect. Keeler found himself humming along with the wind.

Ruth activated the laser sight and got her weapon up. She aimed into the darkness and pulled. The suppressor muffled the shot and the only audible thing was a thick metallic click, like a gas cartridge being fired. Brass spun into dirt, only barely visible in its arc. Ruth adjusted the sight. She pulled another time and an empty two-liter bottle spun up out of the dirt.

She said, "Good enough for rock and roll."

Keeler knew that the sights were already zeroed, but an adjustment was always a good idea. The marines were watching Ruth, both of them turned to him. He nodded and they did the same, firing rounds and making adjustments to their sights.

Ruth called her team over and made introductions. The guy with the black wool hat smiled, which was a surprise, said to call him Roy. Roy would be on the long gun, while Ruth would be spotting. The third guy didn't speak and nobody introduced him.

Keeler said, "What about him?"

Ruth shrugged. "Don't worry about him. He's the geek, here for the DNA analysis. Once you get a piece of the girl, we'll process the sample on-site, before we leave."

Which implied that the Israelis wanted a rapid turnaround, like they'd approve a phase two or something, depending upon the DNA sample results. Which made Keeler suspicious. Maybe because he'd never expect the same from his own chain of command. Or maybe the Israelis were playing the game for higher stakes.

For the moment he decided not to care. He was there

primarily for Karim; the girl was a secondary consideration. The information and his feelings about it went into a corner at the back of his mind, next to the weird tune that he was still humming.

THIRTY-EIGHT

THEY LEFT the vehicles and humped the rest of the way. Cutting straight south until they hit the wadi. They dropped twenty-five yards into it and climbed gently northeast along a shepherd's path. They moved silently, spread out in single file, taking it easy. Keeler walked point, making the pace. Thinking, *Better quiet than fast*. He reflected that they hadn't seen a single person, only one solitary donkey tied to a tree, huffing at their approach.

Just after that thought passed through his consciousness, Keeler's sensory system kicked in. There was something out there, not a noise, not a smell, more like a feeling. He took a knee, signaled the team to a halt.

No sound came from anybody behind him, all operators quiet and alert and moving together.

The wadi smelled of rosemary and something wet, like moss on river stones. Something else came up from the depths, a scent that Keeler recognized immediately, musky, fermented, kind of like piss, and famously disgusting.

The smell of male wild boar in rutting season. He stood up

and continued walking. A minute later panicked hogs crashed through the underbrush.

Keeler stopped for a huddle, a half kilometer from the target. The team took a knee in an olive grove, taking measured sips from water bottles. He had four bone-conduction communication devices in the pack and distributed three to the marines and Ruth, keeping one for himself.

The Israelis had their own gear, but Keeler and Ruth agreed that Roy and the skinny guy would need to go through her. She pulled balaclava hoods out of her pack and handed them out. Keeler slipped his on; the black stretch material felt good against the night's chill.

The little team was now hooded and masked, wearing a combination of hiking clothes with tactical gear and high-end commando weapons smelling vaguely like oiled citrus from the scented gun oil. It looked to Keeler like the team had been transformed from a bunch of suspicious looking people to a gang of very scary-looking hooligans.

He was enjoying the moment before contact, thinking that his comrades might be having similar thoughts and reflections, some more or less philosophical. Keeler threw back the bolt-charging handle on his Uzi and stood up, feeling exuberant. He tested the comms system. "Let's do it."

Three voices came through in his ears, affirmative.

* * *

THE HOUSE on the hill had no security cameras, so they proceeded with plan A.

Keeler and the marines humped up to the plateau, on the left side of the wadi. They came into the yard from the cover of an olive orchard, ending up squatting behind an animal feed tank. The wet earth smelled mineral-like, a hint of freshness carried in from the fields higher up.

Neither Thompson nor Leonard were out of breath. They had the look, glazed eyes and easy breathing, like they were enjoying themselves, and why not? Two young, well-built US marines were wearing the high and tight on a clandestine operation with a bunch of Israeli special operations spooks. Was anything ever going to top that?

Keeler figured this was it, their peak, but it was exactly how he lived every day of his life.

The front door was conveniently located on the north side of the house, therefore hidden from view of the target property across the wadi to the south. Ruth and her men came up from the wadi a little later, taking a more direct approach. They paused behind an old Toyota Hilux truck parked under a carport, made line-of-sight contact with Keeler.

A wooden shed was on the other side of the carport. He noted it for later.

The house was dark and quiet. A light had been left on in the kitchen. Keeler scanned the windows with an IR spotting scope. Nothing moving, nothing doing, the whole place was speaking the language of sleep.

He said, "Clear."

Twenty yards away, Ruth heard him through the earpiece. She pulled on a fake Turkish Polis armband and removed her balaclava. Plan A involved establishing trust with the occupants of the house, try to keep them from panicking. Keeler moved across the yard, arriving at the left side of the front door. The marines took the right side. Ruth came straight in, rolling casually, flanked by the two men in balaclava hoods a couple steps behind her. She rang the doorbell and waited patiently. Ten seconds later she rang again, twice. A light blinked on upstairs. The sound of feet. A civilian descended a wood staircase, not wanting to wake the whole family.

No dog and even better, no geese.

The man said something from behind the door. Keeler didn't speak the language but knew it was definitely something of the *who are you* variety. Ruth said something in Turkish that included the word *police* and the man responded in a short syllable. You don't argue with cops after midnight in the Turkish–Syrian border region.

Locks were undone, the sound of metal on metal. The door opened and Keeler still couldn't see the homeowner. The man said something to Ruth. She spoke fast, in a harsh tone, saying something threatening with authority. The man was holding it together, keeping calm. Like a dad with nothing to hide.

He made another two-syllable response, and Ruth nodded in Keeler's direction, which meant that they had cooperation, game on.

She pointed into the house and said something to him. The man backed away and Ruth stepped through the doorway. Keeler followed first, as per the plan. The home owner was in his midforties, wearing white pajamas. He was bearded with a shock of gray inflected hair. More like a writer than a farmer. The man looked both surprised and unhappy. He gave a bug-eyed start when he noticed Keeler spin into the doorway, maybe not expecting more than the three men he'd already seen.

Ruth didn't give him a chance to second guess and hustled him up the stairs, literally pushing him. The man held up a hand and said something in a resigned voice. Meanwhile, the marines and Roy spread out, exploring the lower level of the house. Keeler went up the stairs with Ruth and the homeowner.

A woman called down, the voice echoing up the polished wood staircase. The sleepy wife, not exactly panicked, but concerned. The man responded in his best dad voice, trying for reassurance vibes, not an easy task under the circumstances. Even if the family were being marched to their death, Keeler thought this was the kind of guy who would still try to sound reassuring. Maybe that's just how the marriage contract worked.

He and Ruth had come up with the pitch: they were Turkish counter-terror police on an urgent mission. Something that might have sounded odd in Connecticut, but in Turkey sounded just fine. She hadn't divulged any further information, just demanded his instant cooperation.

Now the guy was up on the landing, looking a little shabby, his wife coming out of the master bedroom, tying the belt of her nightgown around herself, sleep blind and squinting in the harsh glare of Ruth's LED headlight. The guy reached for the light switch and Keeler took his wrist gently, guiding it away and shaking his head.

Neither husband nor wife were holding phones. Keeler slipped into the master bedroom, a large room with fireplace still giving off heat from embers. Two mobile phones sat charging on the mantlepiece. He returned to the corridor, both husband and wife looking at him, Ruth talking quietly, reassuringly. Keeler was holding up the phones to show, keeping things transparent. Both homeowners' mouths were agape, brains scrambled by the tension, like good civilians.

Ruth was doing a great job of keeping them focused, using a flat and neutral tone, at once official and authoritative, hopefully reassuring, the voice of a strong hand. Five minutes later, they'd herded the family into the downstairs living room, everything cool and under control. Two parents and two young boys, maybe ten to fourteen years old.

Keeler prepared morphine auto-injectors out of view of the family, coming back into the room and moving from one to the other, pushing product into muscle before they had any time to protest. The woman said something and Ruth said something back in a matter-of-fact tone. He gave mom twenty milligrams of morphine and she stopped verbalizing. The kids got ten mil a piece and they huddled with mom on the couch, sinking into the cushions and looking out of it.

He did the father last, firing the injection with a thumb on the black button. The man grunted and made eye contact. He spoke in English. "You're a good guy, I hope, like John Wayne."

For a second, Keeler wondered how the guy could have known he wasn't Turkish. He looked at the morphine injector he was holding. Printed in English on the tube, *Morphine Sulfate Injection, 20mg, CII*. The guy had made an educated guess. Keeler remembered military conscription in Turkey was mandatory for males. Maybe the guy had been a combat medic himself and knew something different about the Turkish military-issue injectors. He saw the man's face now that the morphine was kicking in, any anxieties he might have had were softening fast.

Leonard was in the doorway, beckoning to him. Keeler ducked out of the room. The marines had taken a position in the front room, facing over the wadi, the lights off. Thompson stood at the window with Keeler's spotting scope. He handed the scope over.

"Looks dead."

Keeler put up the scope and scanned slowly. True. The target house was gray, dark, and shuttered. It was exactly a hundred and thirty-two meters southwest. The scope read a twenty-meter elevation differential. The compound was fenced on the wadi side, built onto a triangular escarpment overlooking steep banks.

Keeler sensed Ruth next to him, the heat of her and her particular smell.

He said, "What's up?"

She said, "I don't think the guy's a shepherd."

"Which guy?"

"The one in the other room."

"What is he?"

"Says he's a professor of philosophy at Bilkent University."

Keeler smiled. "Figures. Did you look at his book collection?"

"It reminded me of my dad's."

"Maybe he's got ideas." Keeler handed her the spotting scope.

Ruth put up the scope and began to scan. "You've got some kind of feeling."

He hadn't thought about it very much, but once she said it, he couldn't deny it. The place did look empty. He said, "Yeah."

Ruth handed the scope back. She said, "Feelings are important, at least according to my sister's therapist. Let's go consult with the professor."

THIRTY-NINE

THE PROFESSOR WAS FEELING GOOD, that much was obvious. Reclining in his leather office chair, savoring a cigarette. Keeler sat on the desk looking down at the man. He wasn't having trouble speaking; he was having some issues articulating, spinning a drugged yarn, but the English was perfect.

"I think, already by my grandfather's time we weren't running the farm, you know, just managing the land with tenant farmers. It's mostly wheat and barley with some fruit for the household. I remember the smell of the river as a kid, in the winter. Now it's just the house. Our family moved out in the sixties, but we kept the house, not the land."

His eyes were shining and red.

Keeler said, "Tell me about the neighbors."

The guy inhaled and blew out, like this was an emotional subject. He pointed south toward Syria. "Look, since the war began everything's changed here. I need to protect my family's property, why I'm here now. I know exactly who you're interested in." He gesticulated in the direction of the target house. "Whatever they say they are, Peshmerga or Daesh, regime or whatever. You know it's just mafia. Everything here is clan mafia. They use the war you know, to do it."

Ruth said, "Just describe it. Who lives there, is it empty? It looks empty."

The professor nodded. "Nobody lives there, but people show up. I ran into them once in the village. Like I said, mafia people." His face became flushed. "What they say, the war, the politics. All bullshit. What's happening there is drug trafficking and human slaves, man, serious mafia shit, I'm telling you. They use politics and religion as excuses to make money, like everywhere, like Don Corleone."

Keeler said, "I thought Don Corleone was against drugs. Isn't that what the movie's about?"

The professor laughed gently, almost to himself and fixed Keeler with a doped intensity. "You do understand, of course, John Wayne, that if you don't get them all, they'll come here and kill my entire family, slowly, with big tortures. That's how it is here." He held his hand to his heart, as if pledging allegiance. "With great power comes great responsibility, John Wayne."

Ruth said, "Get to the point."

The professor said, "They come twice a week, Tuesdays and Sundays mostly. Once in a while people are around other days. Usually two guys. Toyota Land Cruiser, yeah? White. Nobody's living there."

Keeler said, "Any idea why they come to the house?"

"No." He straightened up in the chair. "I go to the village on market days." The professor pointed to the southwest. "Otherwise, there's a pretty good supermarket in Sivasa."

"How long have they been coming to the house?"

The professor said, "A year maybe. That house has always belonged to the Yilmaz family, from the Çepni clan, very traditional people. I guess they lease the property now, I don't know." He gave that little inward laugh again, the morphine acting.

"Another reason why I don't go into the village much, I don't have much patience for those traditional people." He got a professorial look on his face, addressing Keeler. "Like you guys now in the USA, country versus city, yes?" Pounded his chest. "I'm city now, used to be country but now I'm a city guy."

Keeler nodded to Ruth and she made a signal. Roy was leaning against the doorway behind them. He came and took the professor to join his family. Ruth was already moving out of the house to the front yard. She lit one of the professor's cigarettes with his lighter.

"So?"

"The house emits communications signals and from the outside it looks uninhabited. People come a couple times a week. Whatever's happening in there doesn't require constant management or supplies."

She dragged from the cigarette. "Could be a simple explanation, it's a place they hold prisoners, which accounts for the infrequent visits." She flicked ash. "But the signals intercept told a different story, indicating more than casual activity."

"Uh-huh. And the professor says the visits are only twice a week."

"Right. He's not seeing the full picture."

Keeler came back into the house and entered the front room, taking a position at the window. Thompson was with the woman and the kids. Leonard handed him the scope. He put it to his eye and tried to find things that remained unseen, overlooked details.

The compound's yard was wet from the weather. Still neither raining nor dry, but somewhere in between. What the British might call *spitting*. The windows were closed with wooden shutters, presumably heavy. It looked a lot like a summer house closed for the season. Within the walls was the main building and a stone barn. The barn door was open, the night vision incapable of penetrating, rendering a grainy dark-green interior.

Keeler took the scope away from his eye, getting the overview. The compound was situated at the edge of the village, but there were other houses beyond it. He began to scan slowly, dialing in on the periphery. The neighboring buildings were mostly dark. A few external lights bloomed in the night vision. One house had a light on inside. Directly to the east of the target house was a three-story building, cheaply constructed of poured concrete, presumably a multigenerational household.

Something about that building captured his interest, maybe because it would make a great tactical position, in relation to the target house. Nothing moved up there, the windows dark and impenetrable. He scanned back down to the house.

The questions populating Keeler's mind: Was this where Karim was being held, what about the girl? The girl hadn't looked happy in the photos taken at the clinic, but she hadn't looked like the kind of prisoner they'd toss into a dungeon. The other obvious thing: nose jobs were usually luxury purchases.

When he brought the scope down again, Ruth was standing beside him.

She said, "What do you want to do?"

He gave her the scope. "We're going in."

Roy came up behind her. She turned and said something to him quietly. Roy flipped his pack over and began to pull out hardware.

Keeler said, "What about the family?"

She said, "Contained."

Roy was putting together what looked like a Sako TRG sniper rifle. Keeler gave it a lingering glance, .308 Winchester, NATO rounds, made in Finland, used by a bunch of special operations units around the world—not the USA or Israel, as far as he knew, probably something the Turkish used, something deniable.

Staff Sergeant Leonard was looking at him, two intense eyes inside the rounded rectangle of the balaclava mask. Keeler checked his weapon, making sure the thing was cocked and locked, expecting the marines to do the same. From the side of the house they had a good view over the wadi to the target house, the compound lying flat in the new moon like a predatory plant.

The burner phone in Keeler's pocket buzzed. He pulled it out and looked at it. Tina Choi.

He denied the call and powered off the phone, letting it fall back into the pocket, then pushed a Velcro flap into place, getting his head ready for what was about to happen. Choi lived in the world of embassies and politics. Keeler had given that all a chance, but as usual the outcome had been disappointing.

FORTY

KEELER SCRAMBLED the last couple of yards up the wadi's edge and got behind the wall. He took a seat and put his back to the stone. The wind had risen some, whipping cold air up from the humidity of the valley. The two marines joined him. Something else, good and unexpected, a little waterfall ran through the village into the wadi. The sound was enough to mask any noise they made, including the mini drones.

Keeler removed the tactical case from his pack. The screen was built into the lid, with the controller single-hand operated. He flipped open one of the drone compartments. The thing looked exactly like a helicopter, small enough you could close a hand around it. One push on the controller and the rotors began to buzz softly. It lifted off, rising just over the wall and hovering.

Thompson was watching the screen. Keeler gave him a look, and the marine remembered the plan, scuttling over to the corner of the compound wall, taking up a defensive position with a good view of the wadi and the beginning of the village to the northeast. Leonard took the other side. Once the marines were in position, Keeler focused his attention on the screen.

The drone was fast, covering the distance from its base to

the stone barn in a couple of seconds. The camera penetrated gloom, infrared vision coming up grainy and showing farm tools and a wheelbarrow and a bunch of plastic buckets piled together. Piles of cardboard boxes and rusty bicycles stacked in a corner with a crumpled tarp and containers of what he guessed was fertilizer product.

Keeler piloted the device out of the barn and began a lateral sweep of the exterior of the main building. Shutters were closed, and the sensitive camera detected no electric light. The front door was locked from the outside with a padlock. It really didn't look like anyone was home. After clearing the other side of the building, Keeler turned the drone a hundred and eighty degrees, the wide-angle camera now aimed at the neighboring structure looming above.

Three stories, darkened windows facing him, something odd about it.

A three-story house in that part of the world usually corresponded to three generations of a family. Grandparents on the bottom, parents in the middle with the younger couple above, usually the eldest son's family, usually with young children. After the third generation they'd be building another house.

But not a single light was on in the house. Nothing forgotten, no bathroom light left on, no insomniac sitting in a living room grinding teeth.

Keeler moved the drone forward, rising to the third floor and trying to get close to the window. Nothing in there either, just the reflection made by the newly risen moon. Unhelpful in the circumstances because he couldn't see clear in through the glass. He canvassed another floor, moving the drone laterally across the building.

Not a single thing in there but reflection and darkness, grainy and a little green from the IR sensor.

He brought the drone back across the compound, flying it

low to the ground. He'd missed a stone outcrop with what looked like a basement entrance on the northeast side, something he hadn't seen before. Stairs descended into darkness. He drove the drone down, hovering it in front of what looked in the grainy gloom to be a steel door, closed and sealed from the outside by a regular barrel lock.

There was something strange about it that he didn't get at first. The lock looked new, the steel shining in the moonlight. New lock equals attention to maintenance and probably necessity, meaning the entrance was in use. Was it surveilled?

He tilted the drone up, rising to look over the door. A single camera eye looked back at him. Something was happening in that place. Keeler sent the drone over to the house again, pushing it into corners and awnings, paying more attention to the details. The place was set up with slick surveillance equipment, all of it micro sized and discreetly camouflaged, pushed back into recessed hollows. Three doors, each of them covered by a little black camera. Three more cameras covering the yard.

A new question, was someone actively watching the camera feeds, or might they rely on some kind of recognition algorithms to sense movement and sound an alert? Maybe there were pressure plates buried in the yard.

Keeler pushed a button on the controller and waited for the drone to return and settle in to its compartment, like an animal shutting in for the night. The compartment flipped back and he powered down the unit. The case went into his pack and he was ready, glancing at the marines, who were eager and watching him.

He waved Leonard and Thompson over to his position.

"The place has a security set up, cameras, and I don't know what else." Thompson and Leonard just looked at him. He said, "We have to cross the yard, get to the house. It's an open area and anything could happen. If they've got a real system, they'll pick us up then. If they've got a seriously real system, they've picked us up already."

Leonard said, "What are you asking us?"

"Either we go over the wall or we don't."

Leonard said, "What if we don't, do we go in another way?"

"No, we abort. We go back and rethink the approach."

"Like maybe going around the other side?"

Keeler said, "Wouldn't change anything. If they have an active defensive net, the front will be equally covered. Three of us wouldn't cut it, no matter how you slice it, Leonard."

"Uh-huh."

Thompson said, "But the man's inside, right? Our guy is in there?"

He said, "According to our friends, that's right."

Thompson nodded. "They won't see anything. Who watches surveillance camera feeds?"

Keeler said nothing, waiting for the other marine to speak his mind.

Leonard was watching his friend closely, an intense look to the eyes framed by the balaclava's slit. He nodded as well and growled, "Semper Fi."

High motivation. Keeler watched them for a second and then packed up the drone kit.

He said, "What's the worst that could happen, right?"

Thompson said, "We die."

Leonard said, "We die anyway, eventually."

Keeler got the pack on his back, straps clicked in and tight.

"Dying isn't the worst thing that could happen. Now shut up and boost me over the wall."

FORTY-ONE

HE DROPPED into the compound and moved toward the building, all joints and muscles firing off and working smoothly. For a crucial ten yards he was exposed to view from both the cameras and the position in the neighboring three-story house. Keeler pounded dirt and got his back to the wall, watching for the others. Leonard joined him five seconds later. Thompson dropped over the wall and twisted his ankle.

The marine crumpled to the ground and got up immediately, setting off at a halting jog, favoring the left foot. He was starting from the corner of the yard, a greater distance than Keeler or Leonard had covered. Thompson's trajectory, had a sense of inevitability, even tragedy about it. Keeler watched him, saw the marine's eyes narrow, concentrated on the goal.

He was about halfway across, when something moved in the air like a heat mirage. Keeler saw it before he heard it, the blurring distortion. Thompson got it in his face, the shape of it sucking inwards, as if a point on his cheek had been pushed by a powerful finger. Pushed with serious velocity, all the way through his face until the back of Thompson's head spewed bone and gore. The marine's body collapsed into the wet dirt like a discarded rag doll, instantly drained of life.

The sound came a millisecond later. The bullet's impact as it hit Thompson, a slap, cracking through bone and flesh, distorting, spinning off and expending its velocity on the stone wall with a click. They never even heard the initial shot. For a second after Thompson died, there was total silence; even the wind had stopped.

Given the angle of the shot, the shooter was in the three-story building, now out of sight. Keeler's eyes were drawn by a sharp flicker of light from the house across the wadi. It was Roy shooting back, the suppressed muzzle flash just a spark in the night, inaudible from that distance. The impact was glass tinkling on the other side of the compound.

Leonard's eyes were bugging, the visible skin immediately glossy and flushed. "Shit."

Keeler put a hand on the marine's muscled shoulder, feeling it hot and tense, Ruth's cool voice in his ear. "Shooter on the third floor of the building, other side of the house from your position. Neutralized."

He said, "Any other movement?"

"Negative."

Leonard was hyperventilating but getting it under control. He spit in the dirt. Keeler glanced at Thompson's body. There wasn't any time for regret or mourning; they had already committed.

He removed a set of bolt cutters from his pack. The shutter right by his head was heavy oak, recently painted dark green. He wedged the tool's blades in under the wood, wiggling against the tight fit and awkward angle. He found purchase and snapped the first bolt. The remaining three were easier. Leonard eased the shutter to the ground, leaning it against the house.

Keeler spoke into the bone-induction microphone. "I've breached. What are you seeing?"

Ruth said, "Nothing just now. I don't think you have much time."

"Right."

"Call it *more than a feeling.*"

Funny.

Leonard was kneeling, ready to give Keeler another boost. He stepped rudely onto the marine's knee, up onto his shoulder and broke the window glass with the Uzi. A foot on the ledge and he shouldered himself through the residual glass and wood and into the dark house. Keeler reached down, grasped the marine's hand and hauled him up.

He and Leonard were face to face when the industrial punch of a heavy machine gun broke the night open.

Keeler was already facing in the direction of the professor's house. Looking out the window, maybe a hundred yards away across the wadi, he saw the front of the house was receiving a pounding. Within a couple of seconds, the view was obscured by a cloud of obliterated glass, stone dust, and wood splinters from the long volley of heavy-caliber rounds.

Ruth was in his ear again as soon as the shooting stopped. "Well, there you go."

Keeler said, "MAG gun. You have the position?"

Another flicker of light came from the house. No sound of either the shot or impact.

Ruth said, "We're moving." Cool as a cucumber.

"Roger that."

Keeler flicked on his LED headlight and looked around for the first time. The room was without contents, the door open, the house dark. He moved out of the room, Leonard at his shoulder. They stood facing a bare living room with two trestle tables set up in a workmanlike way. The LED lights illuminated wireless internet routers lined up on the tables with connecting cables and rectangular boxes, maybe network routers and power, or something else. He didn't know.

Leonard made a low whistle and pointed. He'd found a steel-hatch door. What he was trying to communicate: the door looked like it went down into a cellar. When Keeler approached, he saw what Leonard had gotten all excited about. The house was completely dark, but electric light shone through the crack in the cellar door.

He walked away from the cellar door, into the other room, and spoke for Ruth's benefit. "The house is empty except for communications gear on a table, which accounts for the satellite intercepts. Cable is running into a cellar."

Ruth didn't need long to process the information. She said, "Roger that."

The implication: activity down in the cellar; people using the gear up top to communicate with the outside world. It was a lot of gear. It was hard to tell what that meant.

She said, "There's movement to the northeast of your position, village side of the house. I saw at least two individuals, unclear what they were doing. Either leaving or coming at you. I don't know."

"Roger that," Keeler said. "I'm going down into the cellar. We'll probably be out of contact."

The heavy MAG gun began to chug again. He could picture the rounds chewing through dirt and rock and cement and the trees, wherever they thought Ruth and Roy had moved to. After a while, she came on the line again, not sounding too anxious.

"I'm not sure it's wise, Keeler, going down there. We're going to have even more company soon. You don't want to be stuck underground."

Which was true—and why Keeler figured it would be better

to get in there sooner rather than later. He looked at Leonard, who was looking back at him. The cellar door was unlocked. Keeler got a flash grenade up and primed it.

He said, "Semper Fi."

Leonard opened one side of the door and Keeler dropped the grenade through. Leonard let the steel door fall and they turned away, covering their ears.

FORTY-TWO

KEELER BREACHED AS SOON as the flash bang went off.

He hurled himself down the stairs, using the surprise. Naked bulbs hung against a whitewashed stone wall. The vestibule was hazy from the grenade, chemicals burning his nasal passage.

Halfway down, a shape was moving straight ahead. He turned the gun and held it low, shooting three times in quick succession. The Uzi was made for close-quarters combat. A second later he was farther down and able to get the gun to eye level, crouching low and scanning for movement.

Off the stairs, he turned left and sought targets, moving and sighting simultaneously, both eyes open, the world a sensory synthesis of the scope and his organic vision. The adrenaline rush came strong and Keeler was ready for it, using it for the fearlessness it was good for.

He set the weapon on triple burst.

A flicker of movement to his left, a hazy silhouette rushing past, framed by an illuminated doorway. Someone shouting from another part of the cellar. The figure stopped moving for a fraction of a second. Keeler pulled the trigger once while moving closer, the shape coming into focus as three rounds pattered into the man's face, tearing it up and tossing him to the ground by the door.

The marine grunted something that sounded like words, maybe two syllables. Keeler turned, seeing more movement and the zip of rounds skipping by, pounding into the wall to his left. A fragment of stone sliced through the balaclava's thin material and stung his ear.

Leonard had taken a knee and was shooting controlled bursts through a door to the right. Keeler saw in there, the vague shape of a male figure in the haze. Hard to the right side, he caught movement in his peripheral vision. Time slowed as the enemy moving in close, a flash of determination and white-eyed fear in a bearded face.

Keeler was sidestepping, putting distance between himself and the oncoming man, moving out of the haze and into clarity. The guy was firing a pistol, maybe three shots so far, all of them missing. A big handgun kicking up, making thin wrists jump. Keeler adjusted the Uzi and put a burst into the man's chest. Full-metal-jacketed 9mm rounds slipped through a heavy flannel shirt and made a mess of flesh and bone and organs, stopping the man in his tracks.

Leonard was still focused on the other room. Keeler tapped his shoulder and moved left. By the door lay the fallen body of the first man he'd put down, limp and weird in its death position. Keeler snapped the selector to single again.

The smoke was clearing already. Another shape moved, someone running away, up a narrow passage. Keeler put a round down the hole, catching the man on his left calf and putting him to the floor. A second round clipped the top of the man's head, sending blood and bone shards slapping the wall behind the corpse.

The enemy was on the run, disoriented and resisting, but

not yet effective. He judged it condition orange, aware of a threat but not able to rally an effective defense. The element of surprise had worked, although that would fade off. Any advantage Keeler had was ephemeral and dissipating fast.

The body lay twisted at an elbow intersection. The dead man's mouth wide-open, revealing blackened and cracked teeth and an unhealthy tongue. The tunnel turned to the right, which was brightly lit with industrial bulbs evenly distributed along a thick black electrical cable. The low ceilings were just above head height, and moisture dripped from the rough-hewn stone. A cable duct ran the length of the corridor, a conduit for the communications lines going to the wireless network upstairs.

He spoke Leonard's name, the two syllables reverberating down the tight passage.

What he was realizing: the tunnel was extending beyond the house. This was a subterranean network burrowing under the village. Which made a whole lot of sense. They weren't in a temporary hideout; this was an established operational center of some kind. The corridor opened up to a bigger space, maybe fifty yards away.

Leonard didn't respond immediately. For a long moment, Keeler figured that he was dead, which would be a bummer. The marine's voice came in through the earpiece. "I'm coming up to your position." Leonard caught up to him. "The other room's a dead end."

"Did you search?"

"Affirmative."

Keeler said, "Did you search carefully?"

The marine paused. "Not carefully, no."

Keeler took a breath, calculating the probability of the enemy creeping up on his six, figuring it was possible. He pointed, speaking as calmly as he could. "I need you to put suppressing fire down the hole, keep the rounds to the right side of the corridor. I'll move down the left. Don't shoot me in the back."

The marine nodded. "Hooah."

Leonard didn't have a sense of humor, but that was okay.

Keeler gave him a love tap on the shoulder and sprinted down the corridor, hearing the methodical pop of Leonard's Uzi putting single rounds alongside him, the bullets hissing past, stupidly close to his head. He arrived at the end of the passage, no enemy. Keeler put up a fist and the firing stopped.

Leonard's irregular footsteps resounded down the corridor. They stood together, looking into an unlit foyer. To the left, a large workroom. Keeler got closer, using the LED headlight to see. He tried to figure out what he was looking at. Trestle tables like they'd had upstairs, six of them, a few loaded with cardboard candy boxes, assembled and in flat pack, others with industrial blue bins filled with pill-sized multicolored candies.

The marine put a hand into one of the bins, cupping a handful of candies and letting them run through his fingers. He picked up one of the flat-pack boxes. "A candy factory or something."

Keeler said, "It's Captagon."

Leonard said, "Capta-who?"

"Drugs. Dirty amphetamine stuff, like speed on steroids. What the ISIS people all take before battle. What helps them blow themselves up or decapitate prisoners. Now everyone in the Middle East is taking these and doing crazy shit. Most of it comes out of Syria; it's their biggest export. Funds Assad's regime, plus the Hezbollah in Lebanon." He swept a hand over the packing area. "They're packing it for transport as Turkish candy."

The other side of the room was set up as a sort of lounge. Sofas and a television and a glass teapot with glass teacups. A hookah on the floor by a chair with a red-velvet-covered pillow.

A walkie-talkie had been left on the coffee table alongside a bag of sunflower seeds and a pile of shells, spat out in a brass ashtray.

Keeler fingered the seed shells, still wet from somebody's spit.

He pictured the situation, people working on one side of the room, the other side a place to relax, or to oversee the workers. At the extreme end of the sitting room, two small cells had been carved into the stone. The barred door of one of them was open. Keeler felt the hairs rising at the back of his neck. The cell was empty of life, containing a red-and-green Christmas-themed blanket and dark stains on the pounded dirt floor. A thick chain was threaded through a ring embedded into the stone wall. The chain's ends were clipped into a pair of sweat-stained leather shackles with steel hardware.

Karim had been held here. They'd moved him in the last minute or two.

Keeler crouched, put a hand to the stain: blood, fresh enough to redden his finger. Ruth had given him four small specimen containers and a pair of tweezers. He dug into the pounded earth floor with the sharp end, shoveling the sample into one of the containers. Take nothing for granted; everything requires confirmation.

Leonard's voice came through the comms earpiece. "Check this out."

Keeler sealed the container and put it away. He stood up, moving out of the cell into the main room. Leonard was holding open a partition curtain, gesturing to a steel ladder bolted into stone. He was pointing up. Keeler could feel the breeze, this was the way out.

He climbed most of the way up the ladder and tossed another flash bang through the hole. The delay was a second and a half, enough time for him to have another thought and a half.

Thompson was dead, not a good thing, but the enemy was flushed from their comfort zone. So far, he figured the compromise was acceptable. No sign of the girl down here. What he was wondering was how they'd taken Karim up the ladder so quickly if he was badly injured. The answer was already obvious: they hadn't.

Leonard had failed to thoroughly check the other room, there must be a way out back there. The flash-bang grenade exploded, but he didn't follow it. He had to go back down, close off that potential loophole.

FORTY-THREE

KEELER CLIMBED DOWN THE LADDER. Leonard was forced to take a step back, a little off-balance.

"What's up?"

A police siren began its keening noise, maybe a half mile away. He punched the marine hard in the chest, pointing back the way they'd come.

"We need to finish clearing that area."

Ruth's voice was in his ear. "Is that you? The flash bang."

Leonard, also looped into the communications network, gave him a look.

"We're underground in some kind of tunnel network," Keeler said, aware his tone was different speaking to Ruth than to Leonard. He figured the communications were working now because her team was close, which was a good thing. "What's your position?"

"I can see the smoke from your grenade. I'm entering that house?"

Which meant that Ruth was upstairs.

"Copy that. The house connects to the tunnel network.

We're still down here, need to clear it first. You should find the ladder."

He turned, signaled for Leonard to follow him, speaking to Ruth meanwhile.

"Keep me posted. I've got three or four enemy KIA down in the tunnels. One of my guys is KIA outside." He looked up the passage to the corpse at the junction. "I'm moving away from your position, back toward the target house."

Ruth said, "Roy neutralized three up here, including the shooter. We intercepted a vehicle, three KIA in there. No people in sight up here, but there's serious interior design." She went into a singsong voice, counting off the luxuries. "Creme leather couches. Marble shelves. Ornate gold-framed mirrors. Oh, big tapestry on the wall. Looks like the Battle of Karbala. You know it?"

Keeler was by the corpse, checking the body for identification and finding none.

Leonard said, "Don't know it."

Keeler had been around long enough to know. A big symbolic thing for Shia Muslims. He said, "Where the Prophet Muhammad's grandson, Hussein, got killed. Now you know you're in the right place."

She said, "Okay, I'm looking at the open door to a fancy bedroom. Door has a biometric lock on the outside. Room inside is pink and red with flowered wallpaper and no windows. The sheets ruffled and flung off. I'm looking at the girl's bed, still warm. What's her name again?"

"Fizza Hamieh."

"Yeah, the stage name is good enough for now." Her voice cracked over the comms as the distance got greater. "All right, she left hair on the pillow and it looks like we've got saliva traces."

Keeler said, "So, they kept Fizza upstairs and Karim down

in the dungeon here. You should see what's going on down here."

"Roger that."

Keeler and Leonard had arrived at the room the marine *hadn't* cleared. Leonard was poking around, everything quiet. Nothing in the room except for two enemy corpses on the floor and a big oak wardrobe taking up the wall opposite the door.

Ruth said, "We've found the ladder, coming down now. Don't shoot at us. Copy?"

Keeler tapped twice on his earpiece. *Click, click,* acknowledging Ruth's request.

He had his weapon up, sighted on the wardrobe and ready to rock. Leonard was on one side of the big piece of furniture, extending a hand to release the catch. The door flung open and didn't reveal a rack of clothing. The interior was stacked high with junk. An old game of Monopoly, magazines, a bike pump—what you'd expect to find in someone's basement.

Leonard stepped back and shrugged, giving a *nothing to see* look.

Keeler shouldered him to the side and started pulling things off shelves. Once the junk was cleared, he was looking at the wardrobe's rear panel. He ran his fingers around the edges and found a discreet metal catch. A fingernail caught it and tested, sprung and ready to pop open. This was a false back.

He stepped clear, gave Leonard a significant nod. The Uzi Pro blurted rounds into the back panel, shredding plywood. Keeler kicked through it, revealing a dark tunnel on the other side. He activated the headlight and leapt in. A concrete stairwell was just ahead, marked with red LED light strips.

The short stairwell rose to an unlocked door. Keeler breached, sighting and ascending stone stairs leading to the ground level, the same stairwell he'd seen with the drone, where he'd discovered the surveillance cameras. The same camera watched him coming out now, dead-eyeing him, like a hard cop.

Deadeye, Keeler thought, looking into the camera, except maybe there was a living person watching him. He was liking nothing about the situation. Paving stones led out in a half spiral until he faced the exterior wall at the side of the house.

A narrow footpath ran to the exterior wall. It was dark outside, but a part of the wall was blacker than the rest. He sprinted across the yard, narrow at the side of the house, then found himself looking through a gap in the wall to another wadi, where a small and narrow spit forked off from the main channel. The footpath ran to the right, following the compound's wall at the wadi's edge.

The first police siren he'd heard had stopped earlier, now a second siren lit up from across the wadi somewhere. He could see the blue flashers, presumably the vehicle was headed their way.

Keeler got the scope out and used a boulder for stability, sighting down the length of the wadi's edge and watching the footpath curve down before returning to the other side. He made out a cluster of human shapes, five or six people hustling. They were far enough away, disappearing behind geographic features and then reappearing again as silhouettes. The enemy were five hundred yards down the path, according to the stadia lines in the scope's reticle.

He put the scope down; it was too far to go after them immediately.

Roy caught up to him, the Israeli understanding the situation, laying his long gun on the stone wall and sighting.

Keeler said, "They're gone."

Roy took his eye from the scope. "The wind is up now."

Keeler said, "Probably a road down there with a vehicle. Let's go inside."

Roy said, "One second."

He was looking at something down the path. Keeler moved out from the wall, seeing what the Israeli had noticed. A form was slumped against the backside of the stone wall, maybe twenty yards away, on the other side of a cluster of boulders and high grass.

Roy was already sprinting down the path. Keeler went after him, catching up ten yards away, seeing now that it was a human figure. The Israeli slowed, approaching carefully with a pistol drawn, long gun slung over his back. Handgun up, arms extended. It was Karim, and Keeler knew just from looking at his body's position that his buddy was dead.

Roy said, "Gunshot wound to the head, left temple."

Keeler got a bad feeling. He said, "Move back."

The Israeli operator looked at him for a second and understood. He took two steps back, but it was too late. The IED was a shaped charge, probably something intended for use against armored vehicles. They'd placed it under Karim's body, booby-trapping the corpse, aiming to get at Keeler and his team when they were the most emotionally vulnerable.

The detonation occurred in several phases, all kicking off at an ultra-high speed, while Keeler was experiencing it in a sort of dreamlike slow motion.

The initiation phase as the bomb was triggered, the radio wave hitting the detonator and opening a transistor gate for the electrical signal to fire off the first explosion. The main detonation phase as the shock waves began propagating through the device itself. By the time of fragmentation, both Keeler and Roy were clear, squirming into the dirt and trying to dig themselves deeper, ears plugged with fingers.

In real time it happened in a half second or less, ball bearings and metal fragments spraying in a semicircle, shredding Karim's corpse out of all shape and recognition.

Keeler was the farthest away, shaken but unscathed. Mostly, he was angry, which wasn't something that happened to him often. The Israeli wasn't doing as well, dazed and unable to walk on his own. Keeler got him into a fireman's lift and turned back to the compound, aware that they made good targets for a follow-up sniper, if one had been so positioned.

FORTY-FOUR

Leonard helped Keeler set the Israeli operator down. Roy was shaking it off, relatively unscathed. He didn't look great, but he wasn't dead and there were no immediate signs of internal injuries from the concussion. Roy nodded at him and made his way into the house, back to his team.

Thompson's corpse lay sprawled out where he'd fallen. Keeler used a two finger whistle to get Leonard's attention, pointing to their comrade's body. It needed to be moved.

The big marine grunted and huffed, getting his friend's corpse over his shoulder without hitting himself in the face with the slung Uzi Pro. Keeler gave him a hand with the hoist, and they moved the body closer to the house, settling the dead marine carefully to the dirt, trying to avoid stepping in the remnants of his head.

Looking at Leonard's face, Keeler could see the man was hurting, seeing his friend like that. The marine's face was glossed with sweat, and it wasn't just from physical exertion. Keeler wasn't enjoying the experience, but Leonard looked like he'd lived a hundred extra years. Keeler left him outside and moved into the house through the exterior stairs that Ezzedin's team had used to get away.

Either Roy or Leonard had smashed the surveillance camera. The dead-eyed device was now a scattering of plastic underfoot.

Upstairs, Ruth and the geek were moving around the trestle tables laden with the communications gear, thick cables snaking over the bare floor, feeding down to the subterranean Captagon drug-packaging operation. Ruth was finishing taking photographs of the gear with her phone. Roy was sitting and smoking a cigarette, the pack Ruth had found at the professor's house up on the trestle table.

He must have told them about Karim, because both Ruth and the geek stopped what they were doing when Keeler came in.

Ruth said, "I'm sorry to hear about your friend."

The geek said, "May his memory be a blessing."

Keeler looked at him, thinking it was pretty much the first thing the man had said. The geek held eye contact before going back to his job, dismantling the equipment that Ruth had been documenting.

Keeler said, "What's he doing?"

Ruth said, "Looking for the memory chips on each unit. They can contain buffer data from recent transfers. The goal is to scrape metadata or whatever we can get in the buffer, since the communications will have been end-to-end encrypted."

The geek had collected what he could find and was busy setting up a laptop with a DNA-sequencing device the size of a USB drive. He had a specimen container with the hair and dried saliva samples they'd found on the pillow upstairs. Keeler removed the specimen container with Karim's blood and dirt that he'd collected. Karim was no longer among the living, so there wasn't any point in sequencing his remains.

Keeler stepped out of the main area, to the small room where he and Leonard had entered initially. He unstopped the specimen container and looked at the contents, a pitifully small pile of sandy dirt, reddened with Karim's blood. He moved to the window and poured the contents out onto the ground below, a small ritual for a man whom he'd briefly known as a brother-in-arms.

"Rest in peace, brother."

When he returned, Leonard had just entered the room.

The marine was looking for him, eyes glaring and accusing. Angry and snarling like a competitive beast. "So what, we messed up and that's it? They're going to get away?"

Keeler moved directly into the marine's personal space. Put a hand on his shoulder and squeezed, looking him in the eye. "They won't get away, Leonard. Have faith. They'll get up the road a little, but we'll catch up to them and then we'll put them down."

"How?"

He didn't loosen his grip on Leonard's shoulder, only held him tighter. "Just because the optimal solution isn't looking you in the face doesn't mean it's not out there, marine."

The geek called from the larger room. "I'm sequencing right now. It'll take fifteen minutes and then I can upload." He said something to Roy in Arabic, handed the tall man a device about double the size of a smartphone. Roy tapped on buttons and flicked switches on the gadget, powering it on. He began to move around the room, holding the thing up and scanning walls and surfaces.

Ruth saw Keeler watching. She said, "Scanning for sensors and bugs. Sometimes the Iranians spy on their Syrian and Lebanese clients. Always good to know what the enemy's up to."

Keeler had no objections. The police siren was wailing now, louder and closer.

Leonard said, "What about the police?"

Roy laughed.

Ruth said, "They won't come here."

"Why not?"

Keeler said, "Because they're afraid of us, Leonard. For all they know, we could be a bunch of head choppers come over from Syria."

Ruth said, "There's worse things than getting your head chopped off."

The device in Roy's hand was making a soft electronic sound, subtle and nuanced, almost intelligent. The bleeps were closer together and Keeler realized that the Israeli operator was coming closer to him. They made eye contact. Ruth and the geek stopped what they were doing. All eyes swiveled in sockets, landing on Keeler as Roy approached him, nobody speaking.

Keeler felt a buzz descending, from the top of his skull to his abdomen. The Israeli was waving the device over him, the bleeps getting crazy now, nonstop as Roy centered the sensor at the back of Keeler's neck. Ruth approached, pulling down the rear collar of Keeler's shirt.

"Take it off."

He removed the shirt and handed it to the geek. The geek got out a jeweler's loupe from his kit and examined the shirt laid out on the trestle table. He got right up under the rear part of the collar, where the tag was sewn into cotton, and used a pair of tweezers, poking around. He looked up and nodded at watchful Ruth, who was running a hand through her auburn hair.

Keeler said, "What is it?"

The geek made a clucking sound. He said, "A sensor attached to the back of the tag. Not a regular surveillance device." He looked at Ruth again and said something in Arabic.

Ruth said, "Speak in English."

The geek said, "I think it's a particle sensor. We use them all the time, testing for nuclear materials. Should I remove it?"

Keeler said, "No."

Ruth said, "Why not?"

He registered that all eyes were on him, but the sensor didn't worry him; he had a suspicion about it, trusting the first thought that came into his mind. Which was a thought related to a very positive memory, soft and sweet and warm. A memory that was very recent, if at the same time distant. The scent that Tina Choi had been wearing when she had improbably kissed him. The way her fingers had felt, grazing around to the nape of his neck.

After all, her main job was working MASINT for the Defense Intelligence Agency, which involved deploying particle sensors for nonproliferation purposes.

He said, "Give me a second."

Keeler pulled out his phone and powered it on. Choi had called several times. He pushed buttons and got a tone. She answered after a couple of rings, her voice performing exasperation.

"Finally, I've been trying to get in touch with you."

"I've been a little busy." Keeler glanced up at the faces around him, raising a hand for patience. "One moment." He stepped into the room he and Leonard had initially busted into. He said, "There I was, thinking the kiss had been for real."

Silence on the line, wind coming out of the darkness. The broken window looked out over the wadi. He could see the professor's house up on the bluff, across the chasm. The house was dark now, looking suddenly abandoned, gutted by the raking it had taken from the MAG gun.

Choi said, "I needed to keep track of you, Keeler, in case you did anything wild."

"I'm always doing wild things, Choi." Down the wadi toward Syria, the horizon was nothing but a field of darkness. He said, "But you might have done something very smart, even though your intentions were a little controlling, which I don't normally appreciate so much."

"Okay, whatever. Smart how?"

"You used one of your MASINT particle sensors on me because it's got the tracking capabilities, correct?"

"Correct."

He felt relief and joy flooding through his system. The dopamine production suddenly moving into overdrive, flushing serious uplifting vibes through his system. In a word, euphoria. A Defense Intelligence Agency particle sensor testing positive for trace compounds, tracking south across the Syrian border was potentially something that could pull an undersecretary out of a hot tub.

The only issue was going to be tripping the sensor to test positive.

"So now you're going to tell me how I can trigger the sensor and get a positive reading."

Choi's next words came out slowly, each one spaced far apart as if she didn't really want to be saying them. "And, why would you want to do something like that, Keeler?"

"Because I'm curious about the political reaction you'd get if one of your MASINT chemical-weapons sensors triggered a positive read moving from Turkey across the border into Syria. What do you think, Choi, you figure that'd scare the shit out of some of those donut eaters back in DC?"

"Oh, my lord. I think that might scare a Washington, DC, whore, no question about it." He heard her stifle a shocked laugh, and knew he was onto something. She said, "You're a bad boy, Tom Keeler. Hold on a second."

Keeler put a foot up on the broken window sill, looking

down to where Thompson had been killed just a short while before. The remnants of the big marine's shattered head were still spread out in the dirt, some of it splashed on the wall behind where the corpse had fallen. He was feeling relatively patient, confident now that Karim and Thompson's deaths would be avenged.

More than relieved, he was itching for it, like a connoisseur looking forward to a fine-dining experience.

FORTY-FIVE

Choi went to the books, right there on the phone with him. She listed a bunch of ingredients and a set of procedures necessary for triggering a false positive in the particular microdot sensor she'd applied to his shirt.

While the Israelis finished up their work, Keeler looked through the available kitchens and bathrooms for the shopping list of stuff Choi wanted him to get together. Isopropyl alcohol and a box of matches and a pot to brew them in. He found a pot, but neither of the other two items. It seemed that lighters were all the rage among the available smokers, and nobody was using rubbing alcohol.

Meanwhile, the geek was finishing sequencing Fizza Hamieh's DNA samples. He needed to get that done before uploading the data to the network so that a team back home could get busy on a fast-track analysis.

Keeler and Leonard had fashioned a DIY stretcher out of curtains and rods from upstairs, put together using the roll of duct tape Keeler had in his pack. They'd managed to get Thompson's corpse onto the improvised stretcher and had it ready to go back to the professor's house, where an Israeli team would be meeting Leonard and Roy for extraction back to Ankara.

Karim's remains were too scattered to allow any collection effort.

Ruth and the geek were speaking furiously. She whispered something harsh, pushed him toward Keeler.

The geek came up to them, a little wired looking. He said, "May I ask you a question?"

"Sure."

"I understand that you were looking for Isopropyl alcohol. Is that correct? Ruth asked me if I had any."

"Correct."

"Because you're trying to trigger a false positive in the particle sensor."

"Right."

The man was watching him, the reflection of the moon in his eyeglasses. "Okay, so, your idea was to use material from the match heads and dissolve them into the alcohol, bring it to a high temperature?"

"That's what she said. Do you know how to do that?"

"Potassium chlorate, plus sulfur, plus phosphorus, raised to high temperature with the rubbing alcohol, sure. You'd have a chance of activating the sensor, equal to your chance of blowing us all to pieces."

Leonard said, "You only live once."

"May I suggest another solution?"

Keeler watched him. "Go ahead."

The geek said, "Gasoline vapor." He pointed back toward the house they'd come through. "We can open the gas tank of one of the vehicles up there and expose the sensor to the fumes. I bet you a million bucks it works within a couple of minutes."

"You have a million bucks?"

"No, but you get my drift."

Leonard said, "It's that easy?"

"I think it'll be that easy. Micro sensors get a lot of false positives that way. They kind of suck, and they always need to be verified."

Keeler removed his shirt and handed it to the man. "Do it."

The geek smiled, nodding. "Okay."

Leonard unslung his Uzi Pro. "I'll go up there with you."

Keeler watched them depart. He went outside again, over to the place where Karim's body had been exploded. The cool night air felt good against his exposed skin. Ruth came up, standing beside him. For a while they stood together, silent, looking out at the wadi.

He saw her glancing at him surreptitiously. Keeler said, "What?"

She said, "You're cut."

Keeler put a finger to his cheek and felt the wound scabbing, still wet with blood. He remembered being sprayed with rock debris back underground. The plain to the south was a field of darkness, maybe a thousand meters lower in elevation. It was as if some black hole were swallowing the light down there. Ruth pointed at the low lands.

"Look."

There were flashes far away, and the delayed reports of weapons fire.

She said, "That's where my family comes from."

"Syria?"

Ruth nodded. "Aleppo. My grandmother got my dad out through Turkey in sixty-two and the idea was for my grandfather to follow, but he didn't make it. He and several friends died on their way across the border. The two girls with them were raped before being killed. It could have happened really close to here." She faced him directly, tall with her auburn hair pulled into a fierce ponytail. Looking like a warrior. "The Syrian regime had the bodies dismembered, stuffed into sacks, and dumped on the doorstep of the main synagogue in Aleppo."

Keeler whistled. "Nice place."

She nodded. "Hasn't changed a bit."

They were both looking south then, down into the plain below. What struck him was the darkness, and he realized then that it wasn't just that he was looking into wilderness. There were people down there in towns and villages; they just didn't have any electricity. The lights were off. A sound came from the deep wadi in front of them, a thick cry, like an old man in pain. The cry turned to a moan, curling the fine hairs on the back of Keeler's arms.

The animal noise was terrible, like something dying.

Ruth whispered a word in Arabic.

He said, "What's that?"

"Hyena."

The hyena began to laugh, the high yips mocking the killing dark, black even under the moonlight. Keeler was already there in his mind, thinking about it, the enveloping badlands, a place without rules. He made eye contact with Ruth, who was similarly aroused, her mouth a grim line. The others would take care of the cleanup. She'd be going with him, across the border to meet the enemy.

FORTY-SIX

KATHY JENSEN WALKED into the situation room at the Ankara embassy. At present there was only Jim Miller, Acting Chief of Mission.

She said, "Hey, Jim."

And got no answer.

Jensen walked closer, taking a spot to the side but hesitating to sit down. Closer still, she had a better view of Miller. He had his head resting on the conference table, on his notebook, in fact. A pool of sweat had formed underneath him, and the notebook looked soaked through.

Jensen came around the table. Miller was panting like a dog.

"Jim, what's going on?"

She came around, now seeing his face. His eyes were open and staring into space, glossy, the pupils simply pinpricks, almost invisible.

A voice came out of one of the speakers on the audio-visual system. "Hello?"

Jensen leaned back and glanced up. The guy from the State Department had joined the meeting remotely, head and shoulders on screen number one. She ignored him, reached for the conference phone unit in the center of the table, and punched the button for the Chief of Mission's assistant.

The unit responded within three seconds. "Yes."

Jensen kept her voice calm and intelligible, slowing it down. "Can you please send the duty medical officer up as quick as you can, Jen?"

"What should I tell him?"

"Just to come up immediately. Also please check to see if the Regional Medical Officer is in town. If she's back from Istanbul, get her here as well. Do you have all that?"

"Yep."

"Thank you." Jensen ended the call.

A voice came from the guy from State, beaming in remotely. "Would you mind explaining what's going on?" He couldn't see Miller from the webcam view and had overheard the phone conversation. She ignored him.

Miller looked like he was dying. Jensen went to him and felt for a pulse. Not that she was a doctor, but his heart rate seemed to be going very fast, like a rabbit's. Miller was making a high-pitched whistling sound. The liquid pooled underneath him was sweat. He was basically leaking. The smell was weird.

Jensen stepped back so that the State Department guy could see her. She said, "It's an embassy situation. I'll get back to you as soon as possible."

The Langley legal liaison was up on screen two now. The CIA contractor guy hadn't made it yet. The duty medical officer entered the situation room, looked at her. She pointed to Miller and he rushed over.

The State Department man coughed for attention. He looked angry. "Obviously it's an embassy situation. You're in the embassy. What exactly is happening?"

Jensen watched the duty medical officer check Miller's vital signs and probe the man's neck with gloved forefingers. She needed to get rid of the State Department guy.

"I meant an embassy situation as in, right now this is an emergency that the embassy will take care of as a priority. I'll let you know when we can give you feedback."

"And you're making that call in what capacity, ma'am?"

"As Acting Chief of Station."

* * *

TWENTY MINUTES LATER, Jensen watched Choi come through the door, the younger woman's eyes immediately drawn to Miller, slumped in a chair at the head of the conference table.

Which was understandable, given the situation Miller was in. Now there were three medical officers gathered around the ex-Acting Chief of Mission, one of them the Regional Medical Officer, a forty-seven-year-old international expert on hygiene and public health. Jensen was in charge now, nobody disputing the fact that Miller was out for the count.

The Regional Medical Officer addressed her. "We're going to move him to the clinic downstairs. I've just called for a gurney, so it'll take a minute or two."

"Okay." She took a deep breath. "What is it, food poisoning?"

The Regional Medical Officer said, "Keep this under your hat but I don't think so. The way he's sweating, elevated heart rate, shallow breathing." He raised his eyebrows. "I think we need to do a sweep of his office."

"Checking for what?"

He shrugged. "I don't know. Some kind of toxin, maybe. If it's there, we'll find it."

Jensen caught Choi's eye and held it a second. She said, "We'll do that in ten minutes. I have an urgent meeting with the

Undersecretary that can't wait, and this is the only secure room in the embassy."

As if on cue, Undersecretary of State for Politics Victoria Neuman came up on screen one. Her eyes were already darting around, seeking immediate visual information, getting a handle on the room. Which meant she was in a panic. No doubt, the State Department guy had lit her fire. Jensen allowed her old friend to find her, eyes latching on and grabbing.

She said, "Good morning, Madame Undersecretary."

Neuman squinted, staring straight at Jensen. "What's going on over there?"

The medics were getting Miller onto a rolling stretcher. "Give us a minute, and we'll explain everything."

She made eye contact with Choi, who looked away. Choi would give the presentation, allowing Jensen to appear more neutral. The DIA specialist would explain how one of their particle sensors had detected traces of chemical weapons moving south across the border from Turkey into the Syrian badlands.

That would scare the shit out of Neuman, make her struggle not to cough up whatever fancy dessert she'd recently put into her face. The Undersecretary did look uneasy seeing the medical people milling around and moving Miller out of the situation room. It occurred to Jensen that she might add into the mix the suspicion that Jim Miller had been poisoned with some kind of neurotoxin—that would certainly put the fox among the chickens.

She called out to the Regional Medical Officer. "I need you to stick around for a couple of minutes."

The man nodded and gave instructions to his team. The gurney was rolled out and the door closed on a quiet and solemn situation room. Jensen felt in control, looking at Choi and the Regional Medical Officer, two competent people at the top of their game. Choi got going with her narrative. Jensen observed her old friend Vicky's expression and decided, Yes, Neuman was frightened. Once the RMO dug into it, she'd be scared shitless.

Choi was giving it all she had, speaking in the deadpan tone of a professional with no personal or emotional stakes in the game. Choi would be all right. She might even go far, having now learned how to scare whores.

3

BADLANDS

FORTY-SEVEN

KEELER PULLED the man's chin up and drew the blade across tautly stretched skin. The steel separated the skin unnaturally and painted the dirt with blood, spewing out in a thick arterial spray. He held the body away from him. The man had become warm with the futile struggle, shivering and shaking as he died. Ruth helped settle the corpse to the ground behind an abandoned police station.

The killing had taken a minute, the man's friend was still out front in a white Hyundai, waiting for the driver to take a piss.

Keeler went around the building, stealthily. Watching in the darkness from a thick grove of almond trees, Ruth got into position, resting her weapon on the sill of a charred window at the front of the police station. He tapped the earpiece twice to signal. She fired a suppressed burst of three from the Uzi Pro, making as much sound as someone typing a short word on an old-school typewriter, the image coming to Keeler's mind as he watched from the darkness.

A good shot. Ruth had managed to avoid hitting the car, all

three rounds going in through the open window. Two made contact with the man and the third went straight out the other side and exhausted itself in dirt somewhere out there in the North Syrian badlands.

Keeler pulled the dead man out of the vehicle and dragged him by the feet behind the old police station, setting him alongside his friend. Both dead men carried Hungarian Kalashnikov variants, presumably looted from the Syrian Army. More ammunition was found in the Hyundai, plus two twenty-liter jerry cans of gasoline in the back. Equally important were the ten liters of bottled water, two cans of beans, and a bag of rice with a butane tank and rudimentary stove that screwed to it.

A sandwich bag full of Captagon pills was in the glove compartment. Keeler had tried it a year before, with a couple of other guys from his team. The drug had been relatively new on the battlefield then. It felt like having your brain pushed through a spaghetti colander, or at least that's what one of his buddies had said.

Anyway, they didn't need it, since the US military gave them better drugs for combat, like Modafinil, which felt clean in comparison, as long as you weren't planning on sleeping.

The two ISIS men had been alone, just sitting in the Hyundai, chatting and smoking cigarettes, probably high as kites on the pills, grinding teeth and waffling endlessly. Ruth and Keeler had waited for one of them to take an inevitable leak. Now they had acquired local weapons and a vehicle and the men were dead.

Ruth sat in the driver's seat examining identity cards.

"ISIS. They're issuing their own identity cards now. These two are based out of Aleppo." Ruth pointed to the southwest. "Just down there." She read the names on the cards. "They're actually locals."

They went out back and buried the Uzi Pros, not bothering to do the same for the bodies. From now on they'd be living on the land, and this was the land of the Kalashnikov. The ammunition they looted was 7.62x39mm in full metal jacket.

Ruth stood off to the side while Keeler finished the job. She was concentrating on speaking in hushed Arabic, not to Keeler, or to herself, but to someone in Tel Aviv, if he had to guess. It looked as if Israeli operators behind enemy lines used the local language exclusively. Keeler figured Ruth had been chosen partly because of her family's background. She could probably pull off a convincing Syrian dialect, not that he would be able to tell.

Things had moved pretty fast since Choi had put the scare on the political people back in DC, that was for damned sure. She'd talked to him as he moved down the wadi and across the Turkish border into Syria, monitoring the particle sensor and letting him know when the border trespass had registered in the system.

Now their rogue mission had been transformed into a sanctioned combined operation with JSOC and Israeli Special Operations elements. The US and Israeli communications equipment was compatible, but they'd siloed off a multi-channel battle network. Keeler's old team, Calcutti, Cheevers, and Bratton, were apparently on their way from Al Tanf, a couple hundred kilometers away on the Jordanian border. The idea was to rendezvous south of Aleppo, north of a large salt lake.

One thing Keeler had to admit: when the suits got scared enough to wet their pants, at least they were able to get their asses in gear.

One consequence of the new situation was that he had a voice in his ear, some corporal out of Al Tanf tasked with maintaining a communications line. She was doing a decent job of keeping silent. Which was a blessing, given that Ruth had people in her own ear speaking a different language. The Israelis had tactical command on this one, at least until Keeler made the rendezvous with his team.

Nobody got to take tactical command over his team.

Choi's chemical-weapons ploy had also nabbed them a single Hermes drone rotation, courtesy of the Israel Air Force. The drone had already been in theater, on a different mission, and diverted briefly on its way back home to do a recon of their estimated route south. The drone had a bunch of sensors on it, able to detect human bodies as well as a wide spectrum of electronic signals.

The problem wasn't detecting the humans; it was detecting the hostile humans.

The Hermes had picked up the fleeing enemy formation crossing the border from Turkey. They'd identified two Toyota Land Cruisers, presumably trying to make it to safety in Damascus, where Assad's people had definitive control.

That would be Ezzedin with his team and the girl, Fizza Hamieh.

Northeastern Syria was a dynamic combat zone of intermittent control, much of it ISIS territory, but the situation was fluid, and influence on the ground fluctuated constantly.

Currently, the voice in Ruth's ear was telling her that Ezzedin's Land Cruisers had stopped short of Aleppo, not that far from their position. She was relaying the info as it came in, saying nobody knew exactly why Ezzedin had stopped but that there was speculation. Maybe they intended to sleep or tend to the wounded. Or maybe they needed to be careful and slow, traveling in hostile territory.

Both Keeler and Ruth figured the Hezbollah man would be looking to hook up with a Syrian regime or Hezbollah formation and beef up. Keeler hoped to get to them earlier than that, which is why having the vehicle was important. In normal conditions, they'd drive to the enemy's position in half an hour, but these weren't normal conditions. There were going to be roadblocks, the kind where if you're in the wrong tribe you get pulled out of your car and shot in the back of the neck while kneeling in the dirt.

Keeler and Ruth were in the wrong tribe, no matter who was manning the roadblock.

The Israeli drone had sent down a map of those roadblocks to Ruth's phone. She was busy pinching and tapping and widening fingers over the screen. Keeler was looking at the old police station. Imagining a cop there in more peaceful times, chewing nuts and drinking coffee, making phone calls and talking with friends and colleagues.

Keeler knew Syria by now, knew what it was, a hellscape of death and decapitation for combatants, starvation, political chaos, and enslavement for any civilian who hadn't been able to get out of there fast enough. Even though ISIS controlled much of the area, they were just as likely to run into an ISIS unit as they were to make contact with Syrian Army troops, or Russian mercenaries roaming around with a kill list.

But at least the situation provided some clarity. There weren't going to be many friends along the way, only enemies.

Their current position was at the outskirts of a destroyed village. As far as Keeler could tell, the place was uninhabited, the houses mostly bombed-out husks of concrete and steel-reinforcing rods bent awry. A pack of dogs had begun to howl and bark from down the road. They'd probably start eating the ISIS men's bodies once Keeler and Ruth were gone.

How did he feel about that? Was there some kind of moral issue here? Ruth made a sign to him, like she had the route all figured out or something and was ready to go.

How did he feel about the dogs eating the corpses? Not too bad, they had to eat something, and if those men hadn't taken any care of the dogs while alive, at least they'd be useful to them dead.

FORTY-EIGHT

THEY RAN THE VEHICLE DARK, no lights. Ruth driving, taking it easy, easing her way around the turns and potholes. He was feeling good with the Kalashnikov up and ready, eyes keen for detail and movement. The Hungarian AMD-65 variant, old and heavy but pretty nice, shorter barrel than the usual, with a folding stock.

Ruth said that the first roadblock was five kilometers down the road, relaying the information she was receiving in her earpiece.

"Concrete blocks across the road, which means either local village militia or the crazies." Referring to the drugged weirdos of ISIS. She gave him a look. "What I mean is it's not a tempo-rary roadblock."

Ruth turned the Hyundai off-road a half click short of the checkpoint. She navigated up a dirt track, climbing into low hills strewn with pine and tall grass, pushing the vehicle aggres-sively up the incline by the fading moonlight, the sky clouding over.

The road began to follow a low ridgeline. To Keeler's right was nothing but flat fields, now just a different shade of darkness. The track moved through a gate that had been blown open by explosives; its iron structure lay twisted in the gravel like something casually discarded. They entered what looked like a water-treatment facility.

Which turned out to be a disused fish farm.

Decals of trout were pasted on the office door. The logo on the concrete tanks was an illustrated jumping fish with text in Arabic. Ahead of them was a chain-link fence and a locked gate across the dirt road. Ruth stopped the vehicle. Keeler came out of the car with the bolt cutters. Long levers snipped through the steel padlock. Ruth drove through, and he walked to the car, enjoying the breeze, and tossed the bolt cutters into the back seat through the open window.

Ruth put her head out the driver's side. "This could get annoying," she said, her voice inadvertently echoing between the office building and the cement aquaculture tanks.

He'd learned that Ruth's statements sometimes required interpretation. This particular utterance referred to the four roadblocks the Israeli drone had identified on its pass over the area. Barriers that they'd need to go around, the idea being to avoid friction and hold off on starting World War III.

Keeler had met many aggressive operators, himself included. Ruth was up there with the best of them, in terms of general impatience and hell-raising spirit. He was pretty sure he'd beat her in a fight, but he wasn't going to volunteer for the experience. Keeler went around to get into the car and heard something that made him pause.

A cough.

Muffled but close, maybe just in front of the fish farm's small office. Keeler froze in place, listening.

Ruth said, "What?"

He didn't respond, his weapon up and scanning, moving rapidly back through the gate. Ruth killed the engine. The driver's door creaked open. Her figure slipped laterally into a small stand of pomegranate trees planted between the building and the fence. He heard another cough, again muffled, more obviously outside of the building and close.

Ruth moved in his peripheral vision, a soft shadow in the dark, covering the angles, improvising her position according to his path. He approached the building, keeping the fruit trees between himself and the building. The trunks were gnarled silhouettes against the cement wall.

Keeler started around the front. The breathing was pronounced now, rapid and shivering inhalations and exhalations, a nervous person. He came around the corner, one hand on the weapon, the other flicking on his headlight to blind whoever it was, the weapon sighting at chest height.

For a second he didn't register what he was looking at, and then the woman moved slightly. She was wearing a full black abaya and niqab, so that the only things visible were her eyes, peeking through the rectangular slit, and her hands, which were holding something out at him. She was gasping in fear. Ruth was up on his right shoulder, lowering her weapon. The woman was holding out a pomegranate.

Ruth pushed past him, said something in a quiet voice. The woman's response was barely audible, lacking energy. Ruth nodded, putting a hand on her shoulder, bidding to reassure. After a minute or two of intense whispering, Ruth turned to Keeler with a significant look. He let himself be led around the side of the building, waiting for an explanation.

"She's got a kid in there who needs medical attention. Wanted to offer pomegranates and dried figs they've been cultivating if we agreed to help." He was going to say something negative about that idea, but Ruth put a hand on his arm. "Hold on. They've got clothes. I asked her. Probably the clothes of people who are now dead, but look how *we're* dressed."

Keeler liked what they were wearing, good-quality civilian hiking gear, adapted to their military purposes, but she had a point. They looked a little out of place, like two people who'd walked into the wrong party. Sunrise wasn't far off, an initial trace of light tickled the hovering clouds over a flat horizon. Ruth's eyes gave off a muted green, a shade lighter than the enveloping darkness.

FORTY-NINE

THE WOMAN LED them down a narrow, confined staircase, the kind of passage that nobody feels comfortable with, a place you'd like to avoid. If he were to be shot in there, Keeler thought, Ruth would need help extracting the corpse. The cellar itself was freezing, several degrees colder than outside, like the walls sucked in the chill and held on to it. An oil lamp shone from the corner, where a half dozen human figures huddled together with whatever they had: cheap blankets and hats and gloves.

The wounded kid was set off to the side, half entombed already in a filthy military-issue sleeping bag. The man wasn't actually a kid but in his twenties and obviously a combatant who'd been on the wrong side of a firefight.

He was the only military-aged male in the room. The others were women and children slumped against the wall, silent, staring at the newcomers, the whites of their eyes yellow in the oil lamp glow. The women were wrapped in full-length abayas. The place smelled of human waste and rotten meat, making it tough to breathe.

Keeler got down to business while Ruth negotiated the

wardrobe. He had to peel back the sleeping bag carefully, trying to get at the source of discomfort. The man was in a dazed hallucination somewhere between a waking dream and death.

The initial wound was to the calf, but the bullet hadn't made a clean exit. The lead bullet had mushroomed and bounced around inside the leg, tearing it up and coming to lodge in his thigh. At least that was Keeler's best guess, after cutting the trouser leg up the seam, exposing the man's quadriceps in front of the thigh, and seeing the trauma and infection bulging like a double-sized softball.

The wound stank of rot and neglect. There wasn't going to be a happy ending to this one. At a minimum, he was going to lose his leg, and he'd need to make it to a medical facility within the next four hours, Keeler estimated, otherwise he would be dead by midday.

Ruth huddled with the women and children, speaking in whispers, asking questions and receiving responses in quiet undertones. He couldn't do anything for the guy, but Keeler cleaned the wound and applied a fresh dressing. He zipped up the sleeping bag and made eye contact with his patient for the first time. The dying man's gaze was weirdly intelligent and clear, as if for just a moment he'd been able to leave the haze of resignation.

The woman from earlier looked to the floor with hands raised in supplication, repeating the same phrase over and over again in a hushed mantra. *Allah ykhalik, allah ykhalik.* Some kind of blessing maybe. Ruth was looking at him, a significance in her posture. She turned and spoke in a whisper.

"In the corner, where the smell is coming from."

He saw it, a small shape in the dark. Keeler flicked on the LED headlight and realized exactly what he was looking at, the small figure of a deceased child, bundled into a Minions-themed fleece blanket. He caught Ruth's eye again and understood what she was saying, they needed to bury the body.

A woman began crying, held by two others and wailing softly.

Ruth said, "She asked that we bury her son under a pomegranate tree."

Which was the last thing that Keeler did in his old clothes, using a hoe he'd found in the old office building. It didn't take long digging a small hole and interring the bundled body. He did it as fast as he could, partly because he was angry at it all and partly because they needed to move.

The new wardrobe was a black abaya for Ruth and a pair of sweatpants for himself with an Adidas zip-up jacket and a light wool turtleneck sweater. Dawn was coming, the first light like a line of blue across the horizon. He was still wearing the shirt he'd had on when Choi did her little trick back in Ankara, adhering the particle sensor to the tag.

If he dumped the sensor now, the tracking would stop. Someone somewhere in some room filled with computers might have a minor heart attack. He figured the gimmick had worked. There were no chemical weapons to track, so all the thing was doing now was giving away his location.

They changed in the half light, afterwards throwing the old clothes into a pile that Keeler soaked with butane and burned in a fast and furious explosion. The fire was like a reset, both of them crouching around it and looking at each other in the new outfits. Ruth looked fine in the abaya. He said, "You look like a killer nun."

She laughed. "You look like someone's criminal younger brother." Using her teeth, she extracted a cigarette from the pack found in the Hyundai and lit it with a stick dipped into the burning fuel and clothing.

Keeler said, "A very bad nun."

Ruth grunted, flashing her eyes at him. "That woman said they escaped from a village south of here. A place called Qassen Shata. Maybe some place we're going to have to pass through."

"What does that mean, *escaped*? You make it across a road here and you've escaped something."

"Yeah, well, I'm not sure." She indicated the building. "Their situation is pitiful, all right, but that's the new normal, trying to stay alive. They're not from this Qassen Shata place originally; these people are trying to get across to Turkey. It wasn't quite clear what happened, but they ran into trouble, were imprisoned or held hostage." Ruth dragged on the cigarette. "She said, *Yad Al-Shaytan*, the devil's hand. Meaning, I think, to be trapped into the devil's hand. *Yumsik* was the word she used, caught or gripped."

Keeler had no idea what Ruth was talking about. Sure, there was a bad place. As far as he was concerned, it was all bad.

He was feeling good, almost reborn, watching the clothes burn, letting the embers curl into ashes and kick at the little smoldering pile spreading in the dirt. He was hungry, but also thinking more about what Ruth had said. They didn't need to get involved in any extra drama, that was for damned sure.

They came down the dirt road as the sun was rising over the featureless landscape to their left. The hill descended very slightly, and the Hyundai's shadow preceded them as they passed through a copse of olive trees on both sides of the track. A whitewashed one-story building was on a curve. For some reason, Keeler was distracted by the silhouette of a palm tree against the sky.

In the corner of his eye he spotted something very wrong. Ruth had already hit the brake and was shifting fast into reverse, getting the Hyundai back into cover behind the building.

In the remaining fragment of a second, Keeler saw the road-block clearly, where two Toyota Hilux trucks painted matte beige with mounted heavy machine guns were parked in a wedge shape on either side of the road. The Hermes drone hadn't spotted that.

They'd been exposed for maybe four seconds. The sun was behind them, making it a coin toss whether they'd been spotted.

FIFTY

Ruth flipped the Hyundai into a U-turn, and they headed back up the hill, the track curving southeast along the ridgeline. No sniper shots or RPG rounds came their way, which was a good thing. She stopped the vehicle in a copse of olive trees. Keeler got out and found a vantage point, steadying the scope against a low bough. The roadblock was five hundred meters away by the range finder's reticle, magnified and flat in telephoto. Two men wearing desert-beige tactical gear were smoking cigarettes, and at least one other guy was in one of the trucks. The long hair and beards said ISIS.

Keeler walked back and leaned in the window.

"It's a zombie checkpoint. But they don't seem agitated. Let's go find someplace to eat."

Ruth was sitting there in the black abaya, looking at him through the eye slit of her niqab. She arched an eyebrow, liking the casual suggestion of breakfast in the face of death. Which made him like her all the more for it, seeing her enjoyment matching his in a scary way.

He got into the vehicle, feeling a sense of something heightened, a light-headed feeling of tranquility, the buzz.

She said, "Is that what you guys call them, zombies?"

Keeler closed the door quietly. "I just made it up."

"Works for me."

Zombies because of the ideology, the weirdness of the ISIS death cult, Captagon addicts obsessed with social media, LARPing as religious fanatics, basically living out a snuff movie for real. What Keeler knew: the leadership wasn't like that, being originally ex-Baathist security officers from Saddam's regime next door in Iraq, weaponizing the poverty and ignorance of lost young men.

Turning them into zombies.

Ruth drove, thinking out loud about how they could improve the rice and canned beans. Not being much of a cook or a gourmand, Keeler appreciated food however it came. She turned the vehicle into a farm, parking behind a one-story house with broken windows. For some reason, he thought of chickens, what should be strutting around the yard. Chicken would have been fine with the rice and beans. But no chickens clucked freely in this ravaged land.

Keeler got started cooking the rice and Ruth took a walk. She came back with a lemon and a fistful of foraged herbs, adding them to the pot. The cans held Levantine-style broad beans in tomato sauce. Mixed into the rice, with the herbs and a squeeze of lemon, breakfast was working out just fine.

They used spoons, squatting close together, eating hungrily, hot steam rising from their mouths. The sky was clear and blue and empty. Keeler went in for another spoonful, thinking that a little Tabasco sauce would have made breakfast perfect.

Ruth was sitting back on her heels, spoon down, phone in hand.

"Found it. Qassen Shata." She showed him the screen. "It's really close."

Keeler finished a mouthful, scraping the pot for whatever he could find. "We're not going there, Ruth, it's not in the plan."

A rumbling noise stopped the conversation: approaching vehicles. Neither of them moved, listening intently but remaining calm as a small convoy of pickup trucks passed in front of the farmhouse. Keeler could make them out, roaring down the incline behind a screen of olive trees at the edge of the dirt track. He counted five vehicles, each with two in the cab plus the gunner standing on the bed of the truck with a heavy machine gun.

There had already been two trucks down at the roadblock, now seven total made this a pretty strong formation by ISIS standards. He was thinking about force protection, if they would have mobile squads on the perimeter. Maybe, maybe not. Either way it was time to move.

Ruth leaned forward to get at the pot. She scraped out a spoonful and gave Keeler a look.

He said, "You having fun yet?"

She gave a little snort, chewing with her mouth closed, nodding with a secret smile.

He said, "You married?"

Ruth finished her mouthful, flashing her light eyes at him. "Why, you want to marry me?"

"No, I was just wondering who did the dishes in your house."

"He does, obviously."

"Obviously."

They packed up the cooking gear and got back into the Hyundai. Keeler swigging from a liter bottle of water, settling himself into the driver's seat. Ruth adjusted her abaya, raising the niqab to cover her face, getting it straight so that the connecting thread was flush between her eyes, then she settled the folds of the gown around her for comfort, resting her short-ened Kalashnikov on her lap under the fabric.

Her phone made an interesting bleeping sound, like a robot. Ruth looked down at it, reading something from the screen.

"The DNA results came in from the girl." She read the screen for a moment. "Damn. The trace matches Hassan Nasrallah." She glanced at him. "That's insane. We think it's Nasrallah's secret daughter."

Keeler said, "Who's the mother?"

"They don't say. Maybe they don't know." She kissed her teeth. "But then again they wouldn't tell us even if they did." Ruth gave a short laugh. "They feed us just enough information to keep us motivated."

He said, "Nasrallah's daughter's a big deal." He was thinking about the pledge. It was going to be hard to keep this girl safe. The mission was now on to get her into custody. The Israelis would be sharing her with the CIA, most likely. Competing with other agencies. Everybody would be looking for a piece of Hassan Nasrallah's secret daughter, particularly if he cared about her. It would be the weak spot they'd all been seeking, a way of getting at the leader of the Hezbollah.

Ruth was still reading the message she'd received, or maybe a new message.

"Operational assumption is that Ezzedin's trying to get the girl out of Syria, back to Lebanon, where they'd be on home turf." She looked up at him.

Keeler said, "What I don't understand is why the girl was getting a nose job in Ankara. That seems reckless and stupid."

He caught Ruth rolling her eyes in his peripheral vision. "As if she's the first teenage girl to pressure her dad into agreeing to something reckless and stupid."

He grunted. Things always got strange with real life.

Keeler let the clutch go and brought the Hyundai around the house, got them back on the dirt road. Patches of farmland flanked either side of the vehicle, the breeze playing through the window dry and warm in the sun. Another abandoned farm came up on the rise, passenger side of the vehicle. The main house looked like it'd always been poor. Now it was a burned-out shell, the olive groves around it blackened.

He glanced across Ruth to the house, seeing a thin figure sitting under a scorched olive tree. The man wore a red-and-white kufiya wrapped around his head, his face a collection of sunken shadows in the sparse white beard.

Keeler turned to the road. Coming up to the top of the hill, the Hyundai mounted the rise and tilted down again. Ruth inhaled sharply, involuntary. Twenty yards away, two armored pickup trucks cut the road. Three bearded men leaning against the vehicles, watching them approach. One of them making a *slow down* gesture with his left hand while the right held the pistol grip of an AK-47.

Keeler said, "A surprise ISIS roadblock, isn't that great?" He looked at Ruth, seeing only her eyes within the niqab slit. He put his hands where they could be easily seen.

Two heavy machine guns were mounted above the cabs, each with a man behind it pointing the weapon directly at them. It was definitely too late to reverse course; there was only one direction, straight ahead.

Ruth said, "You should probably let me do the talking."

"I'm not so sure this is going to make it as far as the talking part. Your drone people sure did a shitty job."

She cursed under her breath, a word in a language he didn't know, but understood just the same. From under her abaya came the distinctive snap, crackle, and pop of a Kalashnikov bolt being racked back. Keeler's weapon was under the driver's seat, maybe three feet away from his hands, a couple seconds to get it up and ready.

Without a doubt, those would be some hot seconds.

FIFTY-ONE

Despite the rotor thwack, Tina Choi was enjoying riding in the Black Hawk, the physical sensation of movement and engine roar and vibration. The sound dull but all-encompassing, a body-shock bass. Looking at Calcutti, she saw the guy's face like a rocky landscape with thorns as he chewed a wad of tobacco, spitting the juice out into an empty Coke bottle. Eyes invisible behind a pair of Ray-Bans.

All the noise, the rock and roll of the chopper, and this was supposed to be stealthy. Calcutti had explained to her that the stealth part was about its being tough for radar to detect, not quiet to some guy on the ground. They were flying dangerously low, which was exciting, like being on a roller-coaster ride.

Cheevers, had chimed in. "By the time they hear you, it's too late."

Calcutti said, "It's too late anyway."

Contour hugging was the name for it. Avoid radar detection by flying so low that you blend with the ground. Choi had traveled by helicopter before, but not like this. They'd started off before dawn. Now the sun had come up and the light was orange, making long shadows of olive trees and buildings.

She was crammed into the screaming Black Hawk with three large men and all the gear necessary for a couple of days' heavy combat in the badlands. The third one's name was Bratton. She hadn't heard him speak yet, since he'd been mostly asleep. Bratton, the last to get into the helicopter, long spider legs striding, the body languid, like a rubber band. He'd come into the cabin, slumped into a chair, and immediately closed his eyes.

Choi looked at her watch: not even seven in the morning, and it already felt like the longest day of her life.

The night before, she'd led Keeler over the phone through his part in the chemical-weapons spoof, watching the digital representation of his particle sensor tracking south, over the border. For some odd reason, she wasn't too worried for his health. Something about Keeler and these men made her see them as not mortal, not because they possessed any special powers, but because they were already somewhat dead.

Potentially dead, with a daily imperative to get undead. All the same, Choi was feeling good. Riding in the chopper like one of the guys.

The move into Syria with a positive-testing particle sensor had dislodged all manner of inhibitions from the masters in Washington, coalescing resolve and focusing minds. Keeler had made a joke when she'd voiced concern about being like the boy who cried wolf.

"Take it easy, Choi, it's not like you're the first person who ever faked chemical weapons so you could invade a country."

Which wasn't that funny, if you thought too hard about it, unintended consequences and all that.

The good part was that she got to play along. If there was going to be a chemical-weapons scare in the north of Syria, a MASINT expert was required. Someone qualified to measure and verify, maybe even repeat the experiment and report.

Nobody was more qualified than her. So one minute she was a suit in the Ankara embassy, the next she was in the back of a Black Hawk, wearing brand-new combat fatigues a size too big and clutching a short-barreled version of the M4 assault rifle. Keeler's crew was sprawled out in the back, not bothering with seats, or seat belts, Calcutti, Cheevers, Bratton, looking a lot like their missing-link comrade.

This was her third air journey in the past ten hours. First the ride to Incirlik Air Base in the back of an MD 6 Little Man chopper, the big military cargo plane to Al-Tanf. Calcutti had been waiting for her on the tarmac, inscrutable behind the shades, but clearly overjoyed, in his way. It was like he'd won the lottery, or Christmas had come early. She'd never seen people so focused and organized and fast and efficient. People who packed their own gear and modified every single instruction that anyone else dared to give.

Doing it their way.

The pilot spoke over the comms. A half hour left in the ride. Choi tried to loosen herself up a little, feeling apprehensive, the elevated heart rate not helping.

The desert landscape brought to mind the word *featureless*, but that wasn't quite correct. There were features, just not that many of them: this rocky outcrop, that patch of sand. A scrub of something growing and single-story cement buildings, whipped by grit and wind into monotony.

The north of Syria was slightly less arid moving up toward the Euphrates. Bratton woke at some point, like an alarm clock had gone off. One moment he was slumped and snoring, the next he was up at the door gun looking like he'd just consumed a gallon of espresso, chewing gum like a ball player, spitting it out the open door into the onrushing wind.

The other guy, Cheevers, was at the opposite door. Same thing, serious and focused with the belt feeder all squared away and the bolt flung back. M134 Minigun, if she remembered correctly. The letters and numbers tumbling freely into her mind.

The immediate target was a cluster of houses just south of the enemy's current position. They had some cooperation there on the battlefield, local help sourced by the people up at JSOC. Keeler and the Israeli operator were approaching from the north, the rendezvous happening at some point in between.

Calcutti was giving her a nod, tapping his headset. Choi had turned hers off, trying to get some rest, wanting only silence. She depressed the switch and his voice came through, hoarse and hard.

"Get ready to dismount."

She looked out the door, the landscape streaking past, beige and brown with splotches of purple iron deposits. Choi leaned forward and looked toward their destination. A shimmer lay ahead of them, visible for miles in the flat landscape. A saline lake that supplied salt to most of Syria and Lebanon. Totally desolate, from what she could make out. Nothing really lived in there. No fish, no real plants, only single-celled organisms and bacteria, the occasional brine fly.

The kind of place you go, where if you don't make it back, nobody is going to be surprised; they'd figure it's your own damned fault.

FIFTY-TWO

COMING over an abandoned hamlet at the edge of a salt flat, the Black Hawk lifted sharply, jolting Choi out of her dream state, then hovered over a dust-beaten field with warped soccer goal posts.

Three small figures stood near a dilapidated one-story building blown clean of color. The men were slinging AK-47s and dressed in green Vertec camouflage, Italian Army donations, originally designed for European forests. One guy stepped out from the shade, holding something up in the air like a mystical charm. Calcutti was crouched at the door with a phone, pointing it down at the man and getting some kind of verification.

Confirmation. Authentication.

He put the gadget into a pocket, evidently satisfied with the result. Calcutti spoke into the mic and the pilot gave the thumbs up. They descended fast, guys at the doors looking extra alert, scanning the horizon, the old buildings. Choi guessed this was the vulnerable moment, when the Black Hawk wasn't moving fast.

The chopper didn't actually set down, just hovered a couple

feet up, kicking dust in billowing clouds, rotor chop scissoring air and sand. Calcutti shoved her out the door. Coming down into a crouch, she felt the gear heavy on her back. Cheevers was there looking at her calmly. Nudging her in the direction of that one-story building. Bratton was already there, dappled in shade, doing something with his pack. Calcutti was the last man out of the helicopter, turning to the pilot with a thumbs up.

The Black Hawk lifted, nose up, roaring as it tooled backward and spinning in a one-eighty. A minute later the chopper was gone. The surface of the salt lake mirrored the sky and cloud formations. Choi felt heat, the sunlight hard and direct out there. The other thing she noticed was the horrible honking sound.

Birds, she thought, some kind of bird. Flamingos rooted around in the saline sands thirty yards away. One of the locals strolled toward them, a tall man in his late thirties, one hand on his weapon, keeping it from swinging too much, the other hand up with a finger in his nose, digging around. Which was disgusting and way too casual.

These were men from the Syrian Democratic Forces, SDF, a militia partly trained and equipped by the US, supposedly the good guys. The tall guy, plus two other younger men, maybe in their late twenties or early thirties, although it was hard to tell because these people lived hard lives, bad nutrition, lots of sun exposure. You could look at a guy thinking he's sixty, when in fact he's forty.

Calcutti watched the tall nose picker approach, inscrutable behind the wraparound shades. The SDF man shouted in English, loud with a strong accent.

"Welcome to Free Syria. Come this way."

Choi noticed the bird shit on the ground, pretty much everywhere. The Flamingo cries thickened, the hoarse bellows crescendoing before dying down.

She jogged after Calcutti and the tall SDF guy, all the way to a dirt track, on the other side of a clutch of unfinished buildings. Two Hilux pickup trucks were parked nose out. Calcutti had a map on the hood of one vehicle and started pointing at things and gesticulating to the tall guy, who became agitated, trying to control himself, but very unhappy.

She got close enough to hear Calcutti. "I don't care what you think, bro."

Clearly there was a disagreement.

One thing Choi didn't want was for the SDF people to know that she was fluent in Arabic. At the moment it was the first guy speaking bad English to Calcutti. The other two had backed off several paces, looking tense. One of them glared at her, light eyes and a monobrow.

Cheevers leaned against the other side of the truck, watching the rear. Bratton was beside her and put a hand on her arm when she started moving closer.

"Stay here with me."

"What's going on?"

"We never give locals the plan in advance; we give them some bullshit and then change it up when we get on the ground." He glanced at her briefly before refocusing his attention on the perimeter, the buildings around them. Choi noticed that Cheevers was doing the same, keeping tabs on another angle.

Bratton said, "Don't worry about it. Nobody ever likes it. We get this all the time."

She said, "I guess we're not here to be liked."

"Damned straight."

Choi focused her attention on the three SDF soldiers. She said, "You've worked with these people before?"

"You betcha."

Calcutti was insisting. The man he was arguing with

stepped back a ways and spat in the sandy dirt, pulling a Motorola unit from a pocket of his tactical vest. He turned toward the lake and spoke vigorously. The reply came back swiftly, a blast of static hiss from Choi's distance, although the man seemed to understand it. He spoke again and then put the Motorola away. He nodded at Calcutti, who looked over at Bratton and Choi, lifting his chin subtly.

Bratton said, "Let's go."

They mounted the trucks, the tall SDF man driving the first, clearly the commander. Calcutti rode shotgun. The stocky monobrow man climbed into the driver's seat of the second truck. Cheevers got in with him. Bratton and Choi vaulted into the bed of Cheever's truck, each taking a seat on the wheel-well cover. The third SDF man went solo in the back of his commander's vehicle.

The drive was long and even less comfortable than the Black Hawk, certainly less exciting. The landscape was uniform and flat, punctuated only by ruined buildings or sometimes entire small villages that looked as if some giant hand had carelessly flattened the structures in a single blow. Once in a while, there were animal corpses on the side of the road, and once Choi saw a human corpse by an abandoned gas station, the place like something out of a post-apocalyptic horror movie.

An hour later, the lead truck pulled over into yet another abandoned hamlet. The roofs had all been blown off. "Barrel bombs," Bratton said, watching her.

The truck ahead stopped. Bratton was alert now, face covered in a film of fine dust. Choi wiped at her cheek, and her finger came off coated in grit. The SDF men were dismounting. Calcutti approached.

Bratton said, "What's up, boss?"

"They said it's prayer time."

"For real?"

"They've got an app for it. I guess it's legitimate."

Choi watched the SDF men lean their weapons up against the wall of a blown-out mosque. Devout Muslims pray five times per day. She knew the terms in Arabic: *Fajr* was the dawn prayer, *Zuhr* was at noon. *Asr* was the mid-afternoon prayer, *Maghrib* at sunset, and *Isha* in the evening.

The men opened their arms to the sides and began mumbling and bending and kneeling and standing, the three of them in a line facing toward Mecca. Bratton was alert up on the bed of the Hilux with his weapon laid on the cab roof, eyes squinting and scanning. Calcutti had walked over to one of the shelled-out buildings, urinating against the wall.

Cheevers leaned against the truck next to her. "Swahili time."

Choi grunted acknowledgement, knowing the phrase was used by American troops who had to work with Arab partners, whose sense of time, urgency, and punctuality were often very different than theirs. Obviously the saying came from the British and their own specific colonial experience among the Swahili of East Africa.

She felt weird; there was something wrong, and it wasn't just Swahili time. The momentum had been sucked out of the situation all of a sudden, and it didn't seem natural. They had zoomed over the country in the Black Hawk only to now be stuck here with the local men who suddenly required a prayer stop. What she wanted was to get up with Keeler and take care of business.

Watching them pray reminded her of church and what she was missing back home, so very different to this place, practically its opposite. The verse came to her, Philippians 4:13, Choi spoke softly to herself. "I can do all things through Christ, who strengthens me."

Cheevers was watching her. "Amen, sister."

FIFTY-THREE

THE ISIS MAN beckoned with a gesture, and Keeler inched the Hyundai forward until he was almost touching the vehicle ahead of him, an old beige Mercedes taxi with tasseled curtains pulled across the rear windshield. The men wore desert-beige camo uniforms and tan hoods with eye slits. One of the private units, the guys specializing in spectacular executions.

There were three men at the checkpoint from the private unit, plus two guys in green camo standing back by a house at the side of the road, regular ISIS frontline men.

Two of the execution squad guys were checking the Mercedes from either side, putting their faces against the dusty windows to cut out sun glare, focused, Kalashnikovs up and ready.

The checkpoint was well placed, nestled into a dip between hills. A position that a driver might come across all of a sudden, by which time it would be too late and he'd be trapped. For some weird reason Keeler smelled gun oil coming from Ruth, which was impossible, clearly some kind of hallucinatory effect of the high-pressure situation. Both of them were maybe minutes away from death—or worse.

His heart was beating a little fast and Keeler focused on settling it down. He said, "What kind of gun oil do you like to use Ruth, back home?"

She said, "G96."

"The smell?"

"Sure, that too."

The sweet smell of G96 gun oil, which Calcutti had been saying he wanted to switch to using instead of Ballistol. *The smell.*

The car in front of them trembled on its springs. The rear door opened, and a female foot emerged seconds before the woman herself, large and dressed in a head-to-toe abaya with niqab. She bustled out of the low seat with difficulty, clutching a baby encased in a multicolored fleece onesie. He couldn't hear the woman speaking, but she was holding up her child to the ISIS man in front of her, shaking the little girl like a doll.

The guy wasn't reacting, eyes steady inside the hood slit. It didn't look like he was interested in her problem. Maybe he didn't know things about kids, how diapers needed changing, how kids need to urinate. He made a brisk gesticulation to the side of the road to the house where the foot soldiers lounged. The woman moved in a waddle, with difficulty. She set the girl down to walk, glanced at the men, and led her daughter around the side of the house.

The ISIS guy on the right side of the Mercedes was crouching, feeling with a hand into the rear wheel well, his other hand holding the Kalashnikov against his body. He wore gloves and a pair of desert combat boots. Tactical vest with ammunition and a Motorola handset. These guys had decent gear.

Keeler was examining the disposition of enemy forces, thinking that this might be the moment. The guy crouched in a compromised position with his hand all up in the old car. The other guy hassled by the big woman. He ran it through in his head, the sequence of actions. Get out of the car like you're going to stretch, or piss. Bring the gun up from the floor, the weapon cocked and ready to go. He'd take out the guy standing off to the side first, and then the one feeling up the wheel well. That'd be done in a second or two, by which time Ruth would have taken out the third.

The foot soldiers in green would run away, terrified. Or they'd shoot and miss. Or they wouldn't have time to shoot because Keeler would get them as well. A win-win situation, as far as he was concerned. He looked at Ruth to see if she was thinking the same thing.

Ruth, reading his mind, said, "Look up to that building on the right."

Keeler glanced to his right, seeing what she was talking about, a sniper positioned on the roof of an older stone house. The shooter barely visible but his spotter now standing and stretching, the scope dangling in one hand while he smoked with the other.

She said, "See what the spotter's wearing?"

Black suit, ISIS commander or suicide bomber outfit. In this case it'd be the commander.

He said, "Looks like they're preparing for something."

"Yep. They're expecting something. This isn't just a routine stop. There's an operation going on or something, and we're right in the middle of it."

Farther to the right, a herd of goats tried to find grass to eat in a dirt patch, while a skinny shepherd in a white robe with red-and-white kufiya stood among his flock, holding a newborn lamb, the scene definitely biblical. Keeler glanced up, looking at the shooter on the roof, now saying something to his spotter, both of them laughing.

The woman with the child was waddling back to the Mercedes, the kid heavy in her arms. She caught her foot on a rock and almost tripped, recovering with difficulty. The child was jostled and got scared. She began to wail. The ISIS guy in the wheel well came up, looking over the car at the source of anxiety, everyone's hackles up with the kid's screaming.

The incoming mortar round came very fast, but its trajectory was broken down into a couple of discrete phases and accompanying noises. The first was a characteristic sucking sound, followed by a crack. By the time the thing landed, both Keeler and Ruth had their heads down, fingers plugging fast into ear cavities. The impact was a dull thud that rocked the body.

Keeler glanced up, seeing the stone house where the shooters were positioned. Smoke and dust billowed from its base, the round had penetrated the roof, exploding against the ground floor. The two men were still up there, now struggling to maintain their balance, eardrums possibly ruptured.

The second round followed close, the sucking sound, the crack. Keeler was already maneuvering the Hyundai around the Mercedes. The ISIS men had hit the ground, seeking cover. The round exploded with a booming thud, and the roof of the stone building collapsed, throwing up a cloud of dust and smoke.

Keeler hit the gas and wrenched the wheel, turning the vehicle in a sharp arc. The car rose up over a mound, and the woman was directly in its path, screaming. He couldn't hear her voice. The baby was in hysterics at her feet. He hit the brakes hard and narrowly avoided killing mother and child.

He backed up the vehicle a few yards, then spun the wheel again, pulling around. He mounted the incline and launched the vehicle into the backyard of the house, tires skidding out in the dirt. On the other side of that house, the road dropped down from a low retaining wall, and the Hyundai banged heavily onto the hard dirt road running through the village. Two more mortar shells sucked in, the cracking and thudding boom following. Smoke rose in the rearview.

No rounds came through the windshield, either front or back. The ISIS people had themselves to worry about. He hit the gas and sped down the village road, coming around a turn almost on two wheels, right into the main square.

Ruth cursed next to him. "Shit."

He looked.

To the right was a dirt courtyard. A dozen corpses were piled haphazardly under a palm tree, tossed together carelessly with limbs akimbo. Military netting was strung between a small building and the trees to avoid detection from the air. Men, women, and children. Maybe the entire population of this hamlet, massacred and thrown into the yard like garbage. An ISIS man in beige sat on a low stone wall smoking, cradling his AK-47. He looked up at them and froze, mouth open, smoke seeping out, maybe in shock because of the shelling, caught between wanting to do something and fear.

Ruth wasn't waiting for him to make a decision.

Her weapon came up and she pulled. The man's mouth closed a half second before a round caught him on the right cheek, making a red flower blossom. A second round caught him in the chest as he slumped. Keeler put his foot down and the Hyundai lurched, wheels spinning out in the loose gravel. The ground shook from three more shell impacts in close succession.

A minute later they were out of the village, speeding past an orange orchard. Keeler half expecting sniper rounds through the windshield, not getting any, thinking that each extra yard away from that nightmare was a small victory.

More low buildings were either side. The area was greener than what they'd previously been driving through, and he quickly saw why. The road descended in a series of curves toward a streambed, a tributary of the Euphrates. The surrounding hillsides were lush with vegetation. A hundred yards down, a small bridge forded the stream, a makeshift speed bump loomed just before it, dirt piled up across the road in a defensive mound.

Keeler hit the brakes, slowing the vehicle over the obstacle. The bottom of the car scraped stones and dirt, lumbering across. To the right were the desiccated remains of a cow, the head almost intact while the body was half skeleton and half sun-dried flesh.

It took Keeler a second to realize what he'd been looking at. The cow hadn't been hit by any artillery, it had stepped on a landmine. By that time it was too late to change course.

The first soldier emerged from the trees in front of him on the driver's side, weapon pointed through the open window at his head. The man was shouting words that he didn't under-stand, although the meaning of them was very clear. Men swarmed the vehicle on all sides, regime soldiers in the French lizard-patterned uniforms of the Syrian Commando forces, loyal to Assad.

Ruth was calm, her hands up on the dashboard. "Put your hands on the wheel."

Keeler had already done that, not wishing to become a statistic just yet, knowing they still had time to get undead. Clearly, they'd just crossed some kind of front line.

He didn't struggle when a couple of sweaty Syrian commandos dragged him out of the vehicle. He could see the desperation, fear, and fatigue in their glazed eyes and knew the score in that situation: combat stressed people out; you're always going to be a second or two away from getting a bullet in the head. One of the soldiers hit him with a rifle butt, a hard knock between the shoulder blades. Keeler shook it off, looking at Ruth in her abaya and niqab. The three commandoes on her side weren't even pretending to give a shit. Two of them ripped the gown off Ruth, exposing her half-naked body, clad only in underwear with the Hungarian Kalashnikov slung over her shoulder.

An officer stepped forward and removed the weapon, examining the action and clearing the chamber. He clicked the folding stock out and butted Ruth in the face, sending her tumbling to the dirt. Keeler jerked into action, moving to get at the man. He saw the first incoming blow as a flitting shadow, ducked and felt a heavy rifle butt whiffing air by his neck. The second one was invisible to him, coming at the back of the head from behind.

He felt no accompanying sensation, just a smooth ride into the black zone of nothingness.

FIFTY-FOUR

THE FIRST TIME Keeler regained consciousness he didn't open his eyes. The burlap hood smelled rank, like the fearful residue of men who had recently departed this mortal coil in poor style.

He did an inventory. Hands bound behind him but no sensation in the fingers, which meant the bindings were too tight and he'd lost circulation. He was seated not on dirt and rock but on a chair shoved directly into a hole in the ground, which was interesting and hinted at the possibility of something to come.

On the plus side, nobody was currently applying an electric drill to his knee, or beating at him with a stick, or attaching electrodes to sensitive areas. On the other hand, he was feeling a little nauseated and disoriented, his head spinning. The last few days had been pretty hectic, so here was an opportunity to sleep. He allowed himself to drift back into dream land.

The dream was a good one, falling freely out the back of some kind of big military airplane from the future. A full-on HALO jump with oxygen system and navigation plus communications package: the whole confusing shebang, including gear that didn't exist yet, but that he somehow knew all about in the dream.

More importantly, he appreciated the sensation of being out there in the stratosphere, hurtling through thin air, cold and blue. The sun coming up over the horizon, the curvature of the Earth distinct and alienating. Interestingly, he wasn't falling down; he was falling up. The atmosphere burned and roared as he passed through it, watching the sparks fly off of his gloves hurtling up into space. He could look down on the Earth and see it, like the guys from the Apollo 8 mission. The way they saw the world for the first time, gifting a planetary vision to humanity.

The next time he became conscious, the hood was being removed. A bright light was shining directly into his face and for a while he couldn't see a thing. A voice was saying something in Arabic, and the light was turned against a wall. After a few seconds, he got his vision back and saw a sparsely furnished room. A chair faced him, the light up on a tripod, a wooden table by a blacked-out window.

The chair was occupied by the bearded guy he'd seen in the photographs from the Ankara clinic, Zaros Aesthetica. Amal Nizar Ezzedin was maybe the second or third in command of Hezbollah. Ezzedin was smoking a cigarette, looking right at him, very relaxed, Keeler had to admit. Given the circumstances, there was something admirable about it, the man leading what must be a stressful existence.

Keeler cleared his throat before speaking. He said, "How do you deal with the stress?"

Ezzedin gave a little nod of surprise. He tugged on his cigarette. "The stress." A little smile. "Like everything, it's not only about you. The secret is to try not to put your own stress onto other people. You keep it between yourself and God, you know what I mean?"

His English was fluent, but with a heavy Lebanese accent.

Keeler said, "You're a dead man walking, Ezzedin. It's just a matter of time."

Ezzedin's sly grin faded and his mouth straightened out. "Your friend received injuries while resisting. Then he became a liability." He cracked knuckles. Opening his hands in a gesture at reasonableness. "After that he was an opportunity. Nothing personal."

Keeler grunted. "Whatever." He fixed Ezzedin with what he knew was a look of blank indifference. "There's no going back from here. We're going to get you one way or another. If you let my friend and I go without complications, I'll do my best to give you a clean death. Otherwise, you'll end up in a black site. You'll live the rest of your life in a hole." He examined Ezzedin: maybe thirty-five years old. "Forty more years in a hole, muzzled and kept on a drip of antibiotics and antidepressants. They'll feed you through a tube if they have to, just to keep you alive and suffering. We're like that. We'll keep you alone, in solitary confinement without light, without friends, without anything."

The man made a mock-surprised expression. "In other words, like living in a normal senior citizen facility, or suburban Ohio." Ezzedin laughed. He lit another cigarette off the butt of the first one. Held it up as an offer. "You want?" Keeler shook his head. Ezzedin said, "I'm a dead man walking, right, so what the hell, whatever doesn't kill you makes you stronger."

"I'm still breathing air, which means you think there's something I can do for you."

Ezzedin leaned forward casually and punched Keeler in the solar plexus. The impact was a solid bull's-eye, sending him over backward in his chair, convulsing and gasping for breath. The nausea came back, and he looked up at the Hezbollah man standing over him in jeans and a pair of hiking boots.

Keeler's mouth had filled with bile, which he spat out. "I killed a couple of your guys recently. It was good, I enjoyed that. I'll be putting you down as well."

The big man laughed. "They weren't my men you killed, they were my friend's. And because of that, he made me promise to give him some time alone with you." Ezzedin turned his head and barked something harsh in Arabic. He looked back at Keeler. "I'll let you two get reacquainted before we continue this conversation. I have all kinds of interesting things to say to you."

The door opened and he made room for a slim man to come through. Keeler was on his back, barely able to see past his boots. The slim man took a few slow steps and stood over him, looking down. Keeler recognized the eyes from the few times he'd run into the man in Ankara, translucent grey-green like a jackal's. His neck was bandaged and Keeler recalled the shot he'd fired back there. The way the pink mist had clouded up. Unfortunately it'd only been a graze.

The Jackal was swinging a weird contraption in one hand, something steel and heavy with leather straps. It took Keeler a moment to recognize the thing, an equine speculum, what horse dentists use to keep the animal's mouth open. The other hand was holding a small leather bag with a zipper. He walked over to the table and set the objects down, unzipping the case. Ezzedin lifted Keeler from the floor, putting the chair upright again with no real effort. A strong man.

He pointed at the thing in the Jackal's hand. "Apparently there used to be a horse ranch here, back before the war. You believe that?" Ezzedin put his face close, giving Keeler a better look at the worry lines around his eyes and the flecks of gray in his beard. "I won't lie to you. This is going to hurt. The worst thing about it is we don't actually want any information from you; it's just pure revenge for my friend here."

Keeler yawned. "Sadists aren't very reliable friends."

"Luckily we've got satanic imperialist oppressors like you to keep them distracted." He tilted his head toward the door. "Maybe you'll see what he did to that Zionist whore you brought us, if he leaves your eyeballs in place. I told him he should focus on removing your thumbs first."

Ezzedin closed the door behind him as he left. The Jackal turned and approached, singing softly to himself, the words incomprehensible to Keeler. His eyes were drawn to the objects in the Jackal's hands, the dental speculum, a set of tweezers, a surgical scalpel, and a ball-peen hammer.

FIFTY-FIVE

IT WAS NOTHING BUT PAIN.

The Jackal played it like a virtuoso. Maybe he'd studied torture in some Iranian Revolutionary Guards training course and knew the trigger points. He probably knew some other stuff, had spent some time in dental school, but right now he wasn't getting into that. Keeler's mouth was forced open by the speculum. The Jackal's face was close, the man humming to himself and manipulating his tools.

He'd made an incision with the scalpel into the gum just over Keeler's two front teeth. He was using the tweezer to get at the nerves deep inside, playing with them, occasionally hitting at it with the hammer for emphasis, watching Keeler sweat and howl involuntarily. The pain was intense. He didn't feel it only in the tooth or the mouth, or even the head. The waves of agony radiated out to strange places, making him spasm involuntarily, his whole body going taut.

Five minutes in, Keeler had detached himself from the experience. It wasn't fun, but it wasn't so bad either, just pain. What he already knew: pain is terrible when you're in it, but it's something you forget about after.

He'd learned that from his mother. She told him that giving birth was the worst pain she'd ever experienced, but she had no memory of it. She remembered the suffering, but nothing remained of the thing itself, the actual affliction. Some people said that women have a higher pain threshold than men. Keeler wasn't able to have an opinion on that. He'd been put through pain, a hell of a lot of it. He still didn't know how to measure it.

But pain is only a message, a warning to the brain. In other words, information that he could ignore, or at least try.

Which wasn't easy. The guy was good, pushing in there and playing his face like a stringed instrument. Keeler wasn't even trying to resist the pain, he was howling and hooting and hollering like a stuck pig. The Jackal pushed in deeper, opening a new area with the scalpel and finding a new nerve to fool with. That was getting a little too intense, and Keeler felt himself cross the line. The out-of-body experience had been going well, but the two parts of him converged, and he slid into the sick vertigo.

* * *

HE CAME to for the third time, again in a chair and hooded. Same hood, same smell of the burlap, but new smells were wafting in through the loosely knit fabric. His whole face was throbbing. This time his hands were bound in front of him, not behind, which was weird.

A conversation was ongoing, male voices in Arabic, speaking softly. He had no idea what they were saying. It felt like a bigger room, the way the sounds were bouncing around. He figured they'd moved him, unconscious, from the other room. He was sitting on the chair, head lolled onto his chest. The conversation stopped when he lifted his head from his chest. A hand grasped the hood and tore it off.

A large room, some kind of workshop. He was seated in the center of it, an area siloed off by transparent PVC sheeting, stained with white residue from whatever it is they were producing there. Three bearded men stood around an old wood desk with small ceramic coffee cups and an overflowing ashtray. Ezzedin and two others.

His eyes roamed, landing on Ruth, ten yards away, hanging unconscious from a wooden beam. Her wrists were bound with plastic zip ties, and her naked body was covered in blood and cigarette burns. Keeler felt cold fury mounting and feeding into his brain. He made the analysis that she had not yet been raped. It was impossible to forget the scene in Dr. Erkin's house, back in Ankara. The way the woman had been violated while Erkin was made to watch.

Keeler unstuck his eyes from Ruth, forcing them to move around, gathering data. To his right was one of the stained PVC tarps, behind which he could make out three rusty gas canisters in a row connected to a set of pipes. Each of the canisters was the height of an average man.

The floor was chaotic with hoses running from the canisters to large vats and cauldrons on the other side of the curtained-off area. Other hoses ran in other directions. Ezzedin was leaning back against the wood table, smoking, watching Keeler. He was rolling a thick orange hose with a booted foot, playing with it.

Another bearded man was sipping coffee right next to two open cauldrons raised off the ground. Keeler recognized him, the Syrian officer who'd captured him and Ruth earlier. The same guy who'd put the butt of a rifle into her face. Gas burners flamed below the cauldrons, where the chemical smell was coming from. The vapors were being sucked off by fume hoods. Plastic sacks and canisters were strewn around the place; it was essentially a total mess. Some kind of makeshift lab, given the tubes and hoses, tarps and pails.

It wasn't difficult to decipher. This was a Captagon production facility. The Hezbollah and Syrian regime forces were operating an end-to-end solution, production and distribution into Turkey and beyond.

The third man had removed Keeler's hood. He was close by, laughing now, holding the burlap hood as a display and saying something that he clearly thought was funny. The guy had a thick wedge of a head the size of a watermelon. He was stocky and wore a handgun back of his right hip, encased in a standard Russian Techincom holster.

Ezzedin was nodding, agreeing with whatever the guy was saying. He stood up, lifting a pistol from the table, not just any old pistol but a fancy CZ Shadow 2 with a blue grip. Keeler recalled what Joe had said back in Ankara. Ezzedin had been a target-shooting champ. Evidently he still enjoyed a quality piece. The hammer was back, but Keeler could see no red dot, which meant Ezzedin had the safety lock up. He knew, from the direction of the man's movement, what he was going to do. They'd been waiting for Keeler to regain consciousness just so that they could execute Ruth in front of him.

The PVC tarp behind her would collect the splatter. They'd wrap that up and throw her into some kind of mass grave.

The man's holster was a foot away from Keeler's knee. The butt of a standard Russian-issue Yarygina was poking out of it. Another weapon in 9mm, although far less luxurious. The hammer was back in cocked and locked mode, which meant there would only be the safety to worry about.

It was too obvious and tempting to be real. He was being set up.

Ezzedin was knocking Ruth's face with the CZ's barrel, playing with her and smiling, prodding her to wake up. Her eyes fluttered. Keeler figured that he'd shoot her as soon as he knew she was paying attention. She moaned incoherently, eyes opening and trying to focus.

The holster right in front of his face, tempting and maybe a setup, but what if it wasn't?

Keeler didn't think twice. He rocked forward, shifting his weight and reaching his bound hands to the holster. The chair tipping up on two legs. All eyes in the room were focused upon Ezzedin's little pantomime. A smile was etched onto the Hezbollah man's bearded face. Keeler focused on the task in front of him: balancing the chair on the two legs without falling over.

What he wanted was to get forward far enough to grab the weapon, fall back onto four legs and use it, avoid tipping over too far either way.

Ruth was close to waking. Her eyelids had fallen again, and she was moaning and shaking her head listlessly. Keeler tipped forward another two inches, some fingertips brushing the pistol butt, while others grazed at the Velcro fastening. Now was the time.

He let the chair fall back, pinched the Velcro, ripping the flap open. His other hand found purchase around the butt. The falling back action of the chair pulled the weapon out of the holster and it was free and ready.

Keeler got a bead on Ezzedin. His thumb flicked the safety off and he pulled. The hammer clicked onto an empty chamber, a dull snap of steel on steel. All three men turned to him, blank expressions on their faces. A hand gripped Keeler's shoulder, and the Jackal came from behind him. He took the pistol out of his hand and checked the action, smiling and giving Keeler a wink.

The other men broke into hysterical laughter, doubling over like it was the funniest thing in the world. The Jackal handed the pistol back to the guy with the holster. Ezzedin looked at Keeler, shaking his head in mirth.

"Gotcha."

The Jackal went to sit on a high barstool right behind his boss, taking a pack of cigarettes from a shirt pocket, his eyes unreadable and strange.

The other two turned Keeler around so that he was facing the wall. It had already been prepared with a PVC tarp to take the back splatter. A cold steel barrel brushed at the nape of his neck and was pressed more forcefully.

"You have anything to say?" Ezzedin asked.

"No."

Silence. He waited for it, wondering what it was going to be like, or if it was going to be like anything.

The pistol clicked and he felt a light thud at the nape of his neck as the hammer fell once more on an empty chamber.

The room was dead quiet. A half minute later the chair was turned around again. The four men were still looking at him. Bunch of jokers, playing games while the world burned around them.

He looked the Jackal in the eye, singling him out. "What?"

The Jackal held the eye contact for a moment, a little smile on his face. He looked away. The others seemed disappointed. Ezzedin cleared his throat. "Well, usually they piss themselves at least."

Keeler realized what they'd been after. It was sick. They'd been at war too long. This is what they required for entertainment now, the ritual humiliation of a defenseless enemy. He'd seen a video of a Syrian regime officer opening up the chest of a living captive and cutting out his heart, eating it on camera. Nobody on the teams thought the video was fake.

He turned his head and spat blood onto the floor. "You done now?"

Ezzedin shrugged, picking up a full magazine from the table and loading his pistol properly.

"Just about."

He raised the pistol and shot Ruth point-blank in the chest. Her body shuddered as the bullet entered just above her right breast.

FIFTY-SIX

Choi watched the tall Syrian Defense Forces man leading the prayer. Three of them in a line with their hands out at their sides, bending and murmuring. He uttered a final phrase and the men raised their hands up to their ears, then broke formation and started passing around a water bottle, carefully cleaning their fingers.

Choi stood off in the shade, something tickling her internal alert system, probably just impatience. Once they were closer to the rendezvous zone, she'd be in contact with Keeler over the tactical communications network. That'd make her feel a whole lot better.

Calcutti was squatting by one of the Hilux trucks. He rose. "All right, let's mount up."

Bratton had remained up on the bed of the truck, looking out over the cab, alert and exactly the opposite of the sleeping man she'd seen climb into the chopper back at Al Tanf.

He said, "Roger that."

Calcutti spat out his wad of tobacco and gurgled from a water bottle, spewing a long stream of liquid, making splat sounds in the dust. The tall SDF commander hoisted himself into the driver's seat, letting his feet hang out as he typed into a phone with a single finger.

Cheevers said, "They don't look like they're in much of a rush do they."

Not a question, just a comment.

Choi was standing by the second truck, watching the skinny SDF guy making a play for the passenger seat, where Cheevers had been riding shotgun. The SDF man's thin fingers extended to the door, hopeful that he'd get a good seat up front. Cheevers grabbed his arm with a gloved hand the size of a grapefruit and shook his head, like, *no way*. He pushed the guy to the side, indicating for him to get up in the bed of the truck. The local man's face suddenly looked older, even though he was young.

The monobrow guy climbed into the driver's seat, making eye contact with Choi, who nodded, but received no reply. Monobrow turned to look into the distance.

Cheevers stood with the passenger door open, looking back at Calcutti in the first Hilux truck, who was engaged in a conversation with the tall commander. Bratton shifted up on the truck bed, a couple yards away from her. The vehicle bounced on its springs. Which made her look at him, the operator suddenly even more alert than before, searching through the weapon's scope for something he was noticing.

She shouted up at him. "What's going on?"

Bratton spat, not dropping his gaze, slowly scanning the burned-out hamlet northwest of their position. "Something's raising dust in there."

She glanced at the skinny young guy, catching his eye, like he'd been observing her. Something maybe he wasn't expecting. The man's pupils were hazel against bloodshot whites, set into the prematurely weathered face. What she read there, in his permanent squint against the desert sunlight, was nervousness and anxiety, a furtive look. The guy went for an unconvincing smile, revealing a missing front tooth. He lit a cigarette, holding it in the place where the tooth should have been, like a party trick.

His hands shook lighting the smoke.

Calcutti and the tall man had fallen silent. The skinny guy in front of her dragged off his cigarette and made eye contact with her again. The moment slowed down for Choi, who was suddenly experiencing it as if underwater. The guy spoke under his breath. The language wasn't Arabic, but Farsi, a language that she'd spent two years working on way back when she was an undergrad and hung out every Thursday night at the Bird in Hand café with the Iranian crowd.

The man obviously didn't expect Choi to understand. The words came out as a slur, expelled along with the foul tobacco smoke. But Choi understood perfectly well. The man said, "I'm going to enjoy your dead body, whore."

For a fraction of a second she felt a kind of cold freeze coming over her. Had she understood him correctly? The man was little more than a kid. Dragging off his smoke and brazenly maintaining eye contact. She felt herself suddenly magnetized into the eyes, and everything that had been hanging around at the back of her mind suddenly came crashing into the front of it with no warning.

All that stuff that had been tickling her in a weird way, kicked off while she watched the SDF men praying. Now she got it. Syrian Defense Forces soldiers were seventy percent Sunni, twenty percent Christian, and some tiny percentage Alawite. There were no Shiites among them.

But Sunni Muslims pray with their arms crossed, while Shia pray with arms open.

And these guys had been praying with their arms open. Which meant what, exactly? It meant, like a hundred percent, that they weren't Syrian Defense Forces fighters; they couldn't be, speaking Farsi and praying like Shia.

The whole of it flooded into her brain in a hot flash, what the Japanese call a *satori*, a kick in the teeth.

These men were Iranian Revolutionary Guards Corps. They'd intercepted Syrian Defense Forces communications and lured the Americans into a trap. The argument earlier, where Calcutti had changed the plan, that had forced them to adjust and pivot. The prayer stop had been an excuse to buy time.

Time for what?

Bratton had seen a dust cloud out there. Maybe reinforcements had sped in from elsewhere, adjusting the location of a planned ambush. She realized all of that in a sudden rush, with zero chance of articulating it properly.

Choi shouted something incomprehensible, a warning for sure, but not exactly words. In any case, the utterance was interrupted by the sound of Bratton's MP5 thudding rounds out in short bursts over the pickup truck's cab.

"Contact!"

The entire thing happened in about thirty seconds, which seemed to Choi like a really long time. Enough time to make a couple of movements.

Bullets rained down on them from the other side of the shelled-out buildings. The atmosphere instantly a riot of weapons fire and the flat pinging of rounds impacting vehicles, dirt, and stone.

Bratton's hot brass hit Choi on the cheek, making her duck left. In doing so, she narrowly avoided a round fired by the skinny guy who'd wanted to violate her dead body. He was right in front of her, his eyes now beads. She felt a surge of anger and moved at him, kicking him square in the balls with a steel-toed combat boot. The guy bent over, cigarette ejected, a high-pitched squeak.

Choi pulled the bolt back on her M4 assault rifle, already set on triple burst, and stitched three into him at close range, sending him to the bed of the truck like a sack of dirt.

She turned in time to watch through the back window of the first Hilux. The tall man had a pistol up. Choi saw it kick and Calcutti took a round to the head, folding out of sight as he tumbled from the passenger seat.

She didn't hesitate, moving closer to the truck and getting the M4 up on the enemy commander. The guy leapt out of the truck, untangling his AK-47. She stopped moving and felt the nip of something tugging at her sleeve. She sighted on the commander's chest and squeezed off a burst. Rounds pinged into the vehicle between them, one maybe puncturing the door and getting through it into him. Choi moved laterally, getting clear of the truck. She stopped again, looking over her sights at him, now clearly hit and faltering. She put another burst into his head and saw it pulverize, pink mist clouding up and catching the rising dust particles.

She detected movement to her left. The monobrow was running for the buildings. Cheevers shot him once with his MP5. The round took the man in back of the head, collapsing muscle tension and delivering him to gravitational physics.

Bratton was down off the truck's bed, pulling her elbow.

She ran then, sprinting with him to the closest cover. A heavy machine gun had opened up and the second Toyota Hilux took a blizzard of heavy metal, the rounds shredding its carcass and tires, making the vehicle shudder, almost like the death throes of an animal.

Cheevers took the lead. He moved out around the building, using hand signals that Choi didn't understand. Bratton said, "Just stick with me."

Which she didn't need to hear because she'd already had practice doing that, with Keeler back at Dr. Erkin's house in

Ankara. She needed both hands for the M4, but stuck close behind Bratton, watching their six. Keeler's team wasn't messing around. They'd rather be storming the enemy than waiting for them.

Cheevers made a *go go go* sign and started sprinting across an open area. The heavy fire opened up again as they approached a destroyed gas station, exposing the gunner's position. Bratton took a knee in the middle of the open space and aimed upward with his MP5, squinting into the sun and firing off bursts.

"Big gun down."

Choi was huddling by one of the out of service pump units. Bratton sprinted past and she followed, coming around the corner of the building just in time to see Cheevers sprinting directly at two shocked men. They were trying to adjust to his velocity, but failed terribly. Cheevers put triple bursts into each of the enemies, one at a time, like a skilled artisan working on shoe leather or something, was the crazy image that sprang into her mind.

She saw it in fragments, her vision doing weird things because of the heightened brain chemistry.

Bratton, not even watching his buddy, was looking out in other directions and covering the rear. Cheevers moved quickly from one enemy to the other, putting a single round into each man's head, ensuring that they were out of the game.

FIFTY-SEVEN

CHOI FOUND a vehicle parked in the street behind the gas station. She moved to it, weapon up and scanning. It was a beat-up Skoda sedan in white, now stained by the sand and rock and dust of a long life in those parts. She moved laterally across the side of the vehicle.

"Clear!" she said, seeing it was empty.

Bratton caught up to her and went in the driver's side door, leaning in and pulling out a Motorola radio set and a tactical vest full of AK-47 magazines. This was the vehicle the enemy had arrived in, probably creeping up on their six while their teammates had pretended to pray.

Choi covered, her weapon up and scanning, alert to the possibility of new visitors, while Bratton continued to search the vehicle.

Bratton kicked the door shut. "Let's circle back."

Cheevers was coming down an external staircase at the side of the gas station office building, where they'd positioned the heavy machine gun. He was hauling the weapon and its tripod in one hand, a can of ammunition in the other. Choi relieved him of the ammunition, taking some of the load off.

Calcutti's body had fallen back, out of the pickup truck, landing in an ungainly way, left foot still up in the Hilux. Cheevers muttered a string of very bad curse words and set the machine gun down. Choi didn't need to be instructed. She grabbed Calcutti's feet while Bratton lifted the body from under the arms. They moved him into the bed of the first truck, which was relatively intact.

Cheevers seemed to have taken command, clearly the next in line, speaking to Bratton in terse words. "Suck the EPKs, then set up the MAG on the truck." He pointed at Choi. "You'll cover the rear when we move, you each get a one-eighty, capisce?"

Choi nodded. "Roger that."

Bratton said, "Move the gun up onto the truck."

Choi lifted the heavy gun and set it on the bed of the Hilux. She retrieved the ammunition can and set it up on the tailgate. Bratton was moving among the enemy corpses, taking pictures of their faces with a phone. He jogged back to the gas station for the rest of the EPKs.

Enemy personnel killed.

The photos would be uploaded to the Defense Intelligence Network, where the Defense Forensics and Biometrics Agency system would grab at them, pinging the images around the network to be fed upon by hungry algorithms seeking matches on known persons of interest. Then the databases would assign names and code words and cryptographic hashes for facial recognition purposes.

Eventually the automated search would go out to known contacts, friends and family of the enemy personnel killed, transmissions of communications would be siloed out of the Echelon archives, and networks established and registered. New persons of interest generated and hashed. The possibilities were mind-blowing and impossible to deal with. What Choi was aware of was the informational overload was real.

Which made her think of those Facebook pages of dead people for some reason.

Bratton had come back and was speaking to her. "You good, Choi?"

She broke out of her daze. "Good."

He leapt up onto the truck's bed and began setting up the MAG gun, fitting the tripod feet onto placements set into the roof of the cab and making sure the belt was feeding correctly from the ammunition can. She got up there with him and closed the gate. Bratton fired off a burst and thumped twice on the cab. The truck rumbled as Cheevers got it in gear.

They moved out, tires spitting gravel and sand, defiling the dead enemy combatants.

Choi set her feet wide apart, one hand on the edge of the pickup's bed, trying to maintain her balance. Cheevers was driving like a maniac. Her left shirtsleeve was frayed. A round must have caught the fabric and sliced right through it without touching her. Calcutti's corpse was right by her boots. His eyes wide-open, staring at nothing.

She reached down and closed his eyelids, saying a prayer in her head without actually voicing it.

We know that death is not the end, but rather a transition to a new state of being.

* * *

TEN MINUTES LATER, Cheevers pulled the vehicle into a vineyard, the grapes flushed and rotting on the vine. The harvest had never happened here. The buildings surrounding the agricultural settlement were half destroyed and wholly abandoned.

Cheevers killed the engine. He climbed into the truck bed with Choi and Bratton, squatting over Calcutti's corpse. Bratton left the gun and came by his side, putting a hand on Cheever's shoulder. Choi didn't know what to say or do. Cheevers looked up at her and put out his hand. She took it and reached for Bratton's, the three of them making a small circle around their fallen comrade.

They stayed like that for a good, long moment.

Cheevers shook his head. "You were a decent man, bud, saved my ass quite a few times and pulled me out of the shit many more. I'm going to miss you."

Bratton said, "Rest in peace, brother."

Neither of them seemed to expect her to say anything, given that she'd hardly known the man.

Choi was undeterred. She closed her eyes and said a short prayer. Both Cheevers and Bratton repeated *amen* in rough unison.

Bratton coughed and said, "He was a bad-assed sumbitch, but I think he became a Buddhist in the end. I'm sure his eternal spirit appreciates your misplaced sentiment, Choi."

She felt a flood of embarrassment come over her. "Oh."

Cheevers said, "He's kidding. Don't listen to this asshole." He punched Bratton in the arm. When he turned to her, Choi noticed that Cheevers's eyes were rimmed with tears. He looked at her hard. "You did good back there. First-rate fighting. I'm proud to be downrange with you."

She felt a lightness come over her, a deep feeling of weightlessness and a flush of well-being.

Cheevers took a seat on the wheel well, looking at a tablet device, using his fingers to navigate.

"We're twenty clicks from the RDV." He looked up at her. "Any idea of what that was all about back there? You're the one from DIA. I've got my own theory. Let's hear yours."

Choi said, "They were Iranian, speaking Farsi. IRGC must have infiltrated the Syrian Defense Force communications, or worse, the SDF people sold us out."

He nodded. "Yeah, that's about what I was thinking."

Cheevers was fooling with a Motorola set, part of the gear they'd brought with them on the Black Hawk. He was keying in a coded message and getting nothing back from it.

"Keeler's not responding."

Bratton said, "You sure we're in range?"

"Just about. This is pinging up to the satellite. Should be going through."

Choi was thinking about Keeler, thinking that maybe he was distracted, with his own set of problems to deal with. She remembered he wasn't that different in action to how she'd seen Cheevers operate with those IRGC operators out by the gas station: no thinking, just pure killer instinct. Putting the enemy down without compunction.

FIFTY-EIGHT

KATHY JENSEN HAD BEEN in and out of the situation room for hours, mostly in. The funk that had developed in there was beginning to overcome the air-conditioning. The conference table was rimmed by people and laptops, its interior clustered with coffee cups and cut sandwiches sent up from the canteen. Jensen was able to count half a dozen US agencies and departments represented.

That didn't include the guests. The Israeli embassy had sent over two people with institutional affiliations they didn't bother to announce: an older guy calling himself Joe and a younger woman who hadn't called herself anything.

Obvious spooks.

The two hadn't said a word to the group and were observing and whispering into each other's ear once in a while. The woman had a laptop, presumably connected to the embassy's network. Given that the situation room was a sensitive compartmented information facility, she and the Joe guy wouldn't be saying much.

The whole thing was slightly odd.

Because of the gag that Choi had pulled with the particle

sensor, they were all there waiting on confirmation of its positive reading, what Keeler and Ruth were supposed to be out there seeking.

The reason there were so many people around the table was because of the contingency plan that had been put in place, what the DC-based honchos in Defense and State planned on doing if a chemical weapon was confirmed.

The contingency plan involved cruise missiles and an experimental space-based laser thing that Defense was itching to try out. They'd be turning a significant portion of Syrian territory into a moonscape, regardless of who or what was living in there.

Choi'd done a superb job of scaring the whores up in DC. It had been a smart ploy, but maybe too sly. Jensen looked around at all those intense faces. She was trying to figure out how you'd go about calculating the odds of starting World War III.

The woman from the Israeli embassy stiffened, moved by something on her laptop screen. She glanced up, caught Jensen's eye, then looked away quickly. She tried to look relaxed and stood up with her phone in hand, moving out of the room. Joe was also playing it cool.

Jensen eased herself out of her chair and moseyed over to the door, all casual and calm. She went out into the foyer. An assistant was sitting at her desk looking into a computer screen as usual. Over to the left, down the corridor leading out to the elevator banks, the Israeli woman paced back and forth, phone glued to her ear.

The assistant was looking up at Jensen, expectant. Jensen used her for cover, waiting for the Israeli woman to finish whatever she was doing.

She said, "Hectic day, huh, Jen?"

Jen pulled her hair back into a ponytail. "Par for the course." She tied it off and straightened up. "We maintain."

"Amen."

She made small talk, asking Jen about her life back home, her family. When the Israeli was on her way back into the situation room Jensen gave Jen a little smile and laid a hand on the Israeli woman's arm in passing.

The woman looked at her like a cat looks at a mouse, but Jensen was no mouse.

"Tell me," Jensen said, face blank and calm, eyes still.

"Tell you what?"

"Whatever it is that just put a stick up your ass, I want to know. This is a joint venture."

The woman stared at her a moment. "Give me a second," she said.

A minute later the Israeli woman was back out in the corridor with the guy named Joe. Jensen led them down to the kitchen and made half-assed espressos on the capsule machine there. She handed over the drinks and took hers in hand. Leaning back against the counter, Jensen said, "Shoot."

Joe said, "We've lost contact. An hour and a half ago the communications went dark."

The woman was a little dismissive. "Your people know. They just haven't informed you."

Jensen just looked at her, trying to decode any hidden messages there but finding none. She knew the American operation was a couple of orders of magnitude larger than what Tel Aviv was able to muster, which made things complex. If the JSOC cowboys down in Al Tanf had any issues to work through, she'd probably be the last to hear about it.

She said, "What now?"

Joe said, "This isn't going to impact our cooperation. Nothing changes." He indicated the woman. "Tali and I just needed to talk about it is all. Shall we go back in?" Joe nodded to the situation room.

Bullshit, Jensen thought. The Israeli's were freaking out.

They had a reputation in the spook world, not only for ruthless-ness, but for their total aversion to abandoning a comrade in arms. She'd read reports about them literally bombing entire neighborhoods into dust just to retrieve a single captured soldier. Half of the reason they did so was because of the leverage their enemies would gain by taking a hostage.

They called it the Hannibal Doctrine, better to kill your own soldier than to have them taken captive.

She said, "Tell me they're not prepping for Hannibal."

The woman's face hardened, like she was going to have a fit. Joe put a hand on his colleague's arm.

He said, "No, no. You can forget about that. It's completely out of the question here. I understand why you asked, but in this case nobody's put that on the table. Okay?"

Jensen wasn't reassured, but she nodded at Joe. "All right, go on inside. I'll be there in a minute."

She watched them enter the situation room, the woman making eye contact with her as the door closed. Jensen sighed, pushing out some tension she'd been building in her shoulders. She got out her phone and swiped and thumbed at the screen until she had Vicky Neuman's contact, then tapped.

Neuman answered on the second ring. "Kathy."

"You need to check on the Israelis."

Neuman said nothing, meaning she wanted more informa-tion. Jensen said, "It's intuition, Vicky. I'm sure you've got a horse or two in Jerusalem and Tel Aviv. Make some calls. I've got a bad feeling."

"You've got a bad feeling now, huh?" Neuman laughed. "You pulled a good one with that chemical-weapons shit. Who set it up, your girl in DIA? Now you have a bad feeling."

Vicky Neuman had always been the smartest person in the room. Jensen wasn't too surprised that she'd cottoned on. She said, "We've lost communications with the people on the ground, Vicky. I trust our people to maintain composure, but Tel Aviv doesn't play by the rules."

Neuman took a deep breath. "Thanks for the update, Kathy."

The phone connection disconnected. Jensen looked at the thing in her hand, a slab of plastic and silicon and glass and whatever else went into that device. She was thinking about Tina Choi, a person she'd begun to grow attached to. She wanted Choi back here in Ankara, safe as houses. The other guy, Keeler, he was already deep into the business, immersed in it, a native combatant, gung-ho like the Israelis. He'd take his chances.

FIFTY-NINE

ABOUT TWO HUNDRED and fifty miles away as the crow flies, Keeler was having a moment.

Back on his first or second team assignment, after he'd made it through the pararescue apprentice course and won the maroon beret, he'd recognized that some kind of weird appendage had grown. It wasn't a new arm, or a sixth finger, or anything external. The new thing had grown inside of him.

When the shit hit the fan, he was capable of slipping into a kind of combat trance. One part of his mind went on hold, slipping back into one of the brain's folds and creases and getting out of the way. Another part of his mind moved in and took over, the section of gray matter that takes care of survival and domination.

He called it *Berserker*.

Things that he did while under the influence were sort of hard to break down after the fact, when the new part of him had once again slipped into its cave, back somewhere in Keeler's reptilian brain. He was aware of strange things, the speed he'd moved, the physical stuff he'd done. Aware also of the lack of fear, the absence of reflection. Life and death were becoming meaningless and abstract concepts.

The Berserker cut loose and got shit done, end of story.

They'd all gone through the same pipeline, training sequences for developing muscle memory and rapid aggressive action without reflection. All PJs had that, a requirement for making it through twenty-two weeks of the PAC and getting the beret and patch. But as far as he knew, not all of his buddies had gotten into that trance.

He'd never met another Berserker.

Originally, it'd made him feel a little embarrassed, the way the guys had looked at him after action, sneaking glances. But then again, nobody ever complained. They tended to stay close to him when the hard times came. Keeler had never spoken about it, and probably never would.

Because he was still figuring it out. As far as he could make out, the Berserker was triggered in a kinetic situation by a combination of the unfair, the unjust, and downright wrong added to the unnecessary. An intersection of extreme circumstances that doesn't often happen in life, until it does.

Watching Ezzedin fire a round into Ruth's naked and violated body at close range. Seeing the look of cool indifference on the bearded man's face as the other men in the room turned to the spectacle and replicated the Hezbollah leader's pose and casual attitude to killing a defenseless captive.

Wrong and unnecessary.

The way they'd set Keeler up with the fake execution and the empty pistol put out there just in reach, trying to ritually humiliate him before he died.

Wrong and unnecessary.

How the Jackal had tortured him, not for any information that he could disclose but simply for revenge, trying to exert as much pain and suffering as possible. Not to mention, the things that he must have done to Ruth before Ezzedin got last licks.

Wrong and completely unnecessary.

How they'd killed Karim and left his body booby-trapped out there in the cold, desecrating his body.

Unjust and totally unfair.

In the split second between Ezzedin's pistol firing and the bullet penetrating Ruth's defenseless body, Keeler had flipped. He lost all emotional attachment, becoming purely operational. These people had made a critical mistake.

The error was careless and simple, they'd unbound his hands after he'd passed out from the Jackal's administration of torture. His hands had been zip-tied again, but this time in front of him. They'd done it for shits and giggles, making it so he'd be lured into grabbing for the holstered weapon dangled before his eyes, knowing he'd go for it because he had no choice, and they'd get a laugh out of the useless and desperate act, trying to humiliate him.

But they'd up and forgotten about it, leaving his hands bound in front of him, legs free. Probably carried away by their excitement. Keeler didn't need a second invitation.

The holstered weapon was no longer directly in front of him like low-hanging fruit. Now it was in the wedge-headed man's hand, hung down by his side as he gazed stupidly, mesmerized by the summary execution on the other side of the room. Ruth's body twitching once from the impact of Ezzedin's bullet. The way her eyes trembled open a fraction with the hit. Her nudity and the blood, all of it serving as a point of fascination to these people.

Keeler didn't actually make a plan. One just seemed to form spontaneously, probably developed in the back of his mind while he wasn't paying attention. He was too far away from the enemy to be an obvious danger. They'd have crucial seconds to

put a bullet into him if he stood up and charged, which is probably what they hoped he'd do.

But there were other strings to pull. The floor was a riot of
hoses, from one vat to another, from gas canisters to cauldrons.
Everything there was connected, like a messy machine made of
available parts.

Keeler let gravity do the work, allowing his body to crumple
from the chair to the floor, grasping a large hose with his bound
hands. He rolled fast to the right, pulling the hose taut and
giving it a hard jerk. The cauldron on the left tipped off cheap
cinder blocks that raised it from the floor.

There was a split second where it hung in the air, tipping
but not yet over. Keeler didn't know what the contents of the
thing were, some concoction for cooking up Captagon tablets.
He was still rolling when a round pinged off the cement floor
inches away from where he'd been.

Then the hot liquid hit the concrete and instantly raised a
thick cloud of vapor, the liquid rippling out across the floor.

He got to his feet, his mind empty of thought, relaxed and
good, holding in the existing oxygen supply he'd sucked down
before moving. Unlike Keeler, the stocky man in front of him
hadn't spent weeks practicing breath control in a swimming
pool, and then out in the open ocean for another month. The
man wasn't relaxed, he was panicked, his wedge head swiveling
around in desperation.

The other thing was the chemical haze couldn't be good for
the eyes. Keeler let his lids close gently, keeping chill, knowing it
was sufficient. He'd already printed a three-dimensional image
of the situation in his brain.

He knew about the Yarygina 9mm, held loosely in the
wedge-headed man's hand. He could hear the man breathing,
even as he got closer to him. He could hear the guy pulling his
shirt up over his mouth and nose, desperately trying to get some

kind of filter over his respiratory apparatus. The chemical vapor would have engulfed him by now. The stuff was already burning Keeler's nasal passages without him breathing in. Powerful chemicals, probably deadly if inhaled for too long.

He clamped his zip-tied hands around the pistol in the man's hand. The guy jerked away, but Keeler held on and pulled, kicking him square in his chest, sending him flying into Ezzedin and using the force of propulsion to rip the weapon from his weakened grasp.

That all happened in the first second and a half.

The guy staggered, coughing. Keeler, sensed the confusion, the way the man's boots scraped and clumped on the floor as he tried to stop himself from colliding with Ezzedin, but failed. Keeler heard Ezzedin's grunt as they made contact. He tracked their position and recognized the multifaceted problem they faced.

Ezzedin had maneuvered back, coughing now, trying to raise the collar of his shirt over his beard. He'd be getting his fancy weapon up, trying to shoot at Keeler. He wouldn't be able to see however, he'd open his eyes and get stung by the chemicals. Keeler ducked anyway, still holding his breath, eyes clamped shut, moving in the other direction.

Ezzedin got a round off, the shot making a *tink* sound as it fired. The bullet wasn't far off its mark, whistling past Keeler's ear, the round pinging off something behind him. The wedge-headed man and Ezzedin were in a tangle for the next crucial seconds. Keeler had them located in his mental map, plus the Syrian officer. He doubted the Jackal was where he'd been on the bar stool.

The Syrian officer had been standing closest to the spilled cauldron, and the operational assumption was that he'd inhaled more than his share of the initial vapor spill.

Keeler was moving to him, listening to the man's desperate

breathing. The officer had seen him coming. Now he scrambled and slipped in the chemical liquid, a clear sound of boots sliding against wet concrete. The guy's knee thumped to the floor. Keeler was close now, hearing the man making weird guttural panicked sounds.

Eyes shut, relying only upon the model his brain had made of the place, Keeler thumbed off the hammer safety and put the weapon up in the direction of body mass. He shot the Syrian officer twice in the back. The rounds popped off like thuds, a different sound than Ezzedin's gun. Keeler heard the officer collapse onto the floor.

The wedge-headed man who'd collided with Ezzedin was still having issues, grappling at the PVC sheet, trying to figure out his balance, trying to clutch the plastic, scrabbling with fingernails until he found purchase and momentarily kept his footing. Keeler was tracking their position, moving around the dead Syrian officer.

A part of his brain was seeking data from the Jackal and not finding any.

He shifted laterally, to his right, making sure that Ruth was out of the field of fire, listening hard to the wedge-headed guy trying to stay balanced. He couldn't hear Ezzedin, which wasn't good. Keeler opened his eyes momentarily. He had the weapon up and steady with both hands, sighting for Ezzedin but not seeing him.

The PVC sheet came down under the wedge-headed man's weight, sending him sprawling into the growing pool of chemical brew. Ezzedin came into view, having ducked back and moved fast in the other direction. Keeler let the pistol lead him for a second and squeezed two rounds from the Yarygina, losing the man in the vapor cloud, unable to see if a shot had landed.

The chemicals stung at his eyes and in his nostrils, but he hadn't yet taken a breath. He closed his eyes again, letting the tear ducts do their repair work, knowing he'd need those things working properly.

He'd seen the wedge-headed guy's face where he'd fallen, teeth bared, lips drawn back. A low moan coming from him, the whites of his eyes flashing. The eyeballs bulged in their sockets, swiveling around in fear. Ezzedin had gone. He was out there somewhere and would be back with help. A minute or two max.

Keeler moved in a crouch, allowing the pistol to touch the wedge head's left temple. He caressed the trigger and put a round in. The man's brains and blood and bone slapped into the liquid mix on the floor.

The gunshot had been loud, but Keeler sensed movement and something scampering over to his left. He hopped laterally in that direction, opening his eyes, ignoring the sting. The Jackal was crouched at the Syrian officer. Keeler got the gun up in a flash, but the Jackal was already behind the second cauldron.

Keeler moved rapidly forward, weapon out in two hands, still bound by the zip ties. The cauldron was on the other side of the dirty PVC curtain. Keeler brushed through it, arcing around the bubbling vat and finding nothing there.

The attack came from his blind spot, over his shoulder to the left.

A blur in the corner of his eye, moving low to the ground. Keeler adjusted his feet, getting himself turned in time to see the Jackal thrusting a combat knife into his left thigh. The blade sank deep into muscle, the Jackal's eyes following the gesture. If Keeler hadn't moved it would have been the small of his back, what the Jackal had been going for, maybe a spot at the base of his spine to paralyze him.

Keeler ignored the steel that had entered his flesh. He focused on getting the pistol around. The Jackal rose up from his crouch and made a grab for his arm. Keeler knew it wasn't going to work, getting the pistol sighted. His hands were still bound together, putting him at a real disadvantage at close quarters. The Jackal had managed to take a hold of the zip tie, controlling Keeler's arms and hands, pushing the 9mm pistol off to the side.

Keeler watched the blade come out of his thigh, smelling something sweet on the enemy's breath, maybe a candy or pastry he'd eaten. The blade was a Smersh-5 combat knife. The Jackal had taken it from the dead Syrian officer, probably something he'd picked up on a Russian training course.

There was no pain yet, only a dull feeling of impending failure. The Jackal pulled Keeler toward him, while the knife hand began its upward drive for his gut, going in for the kill. Keeler stepped into the arc of his thrust, using a sudden burst of force to turn the Jackal off-balance. The move shifted the blade off target, slicing razor-like through Keeler's shirt and the shallow flesh over his rib cage.

Keeler watched the Jackal's eyes roam from the target of his attack, up to the eyes. He waited a moment, holding his movement so that the man was set back on his heels. There wouldn't be a second chance. A fraction of a second later, Keeler drove his forehead into the Jackal's face, slamming the hard part of his skull into the bridge of the enemy's nose, collapsing the cartilage and driving through to teeth.

The man staggered back, stunned. Keeler leapt for the knife, taking the weapon from the Jackal with both hands. The man fell and Keeler was instantly kneeling on his chest. He put the point of the knife at the soft part of the Jackal's throat and slammed the twelve-inch blade through his mouth, driving it to the hilt. The Smersh-5 combat knife snapped through the skull, only four inches away, putting eight inches of steel into the Jackal's brain.

Keeler pulled the knife out and held it in his teeth. He used the blade to slice through the zip ties, leaving them on the Jackal's corpse.

He rolled off the body and into a crouch, letting himself take a few good deep breaths as he rose and moved toward Ruth.

She was breathing, which was both good and bad. Good because it meant that she was alive, bad because she was breathing in the wrong stuff. He cut her down from the beam, settling her onto his shoulder. The wounded leg wasn't hurting or stiff yet, but that was going to happen soon.

Keeler noticed the PVC sheets were holding in the chemical vapor and pushed through the sheet. The air still reeked of chemicals but was way more breathable than before. He got Ruth over to a long table on the other side of the room.

The entry wound was between her breast and collarbone, and it wasn't large. Ezzedin's bullet had gone straight through, coming out the back. The exit wound was also smaller than usual for a combat injury. He recalled the sound that Ezzedin's CZ had made, the *tink* of a steel-cored bullet. Good for target shooting, bad for stopping power because the steel didn't mushroom.

Regardless, the bleeding had to be stopped immediately. The only thing immediately at hand was a Syrian flag hanging on the wall next to a framed portrait of Bashir Assad.

Keeler ripped the flag down and tore it into strips. He balled one of them and shoved it into the open wound at Ruth's back. The other strips were used to bind it in there. She was barely conscious but breathing.

SIXTY

THE WORKSHOP HAD ONLY one exit that Keeler could see, in the same direction Ezzedin had disappeared. He shouldered into double doors and was immediately blinded by sunlight.

Keeler staggered, squinting, scanning left and right and straight ahead. He looked back at the building where he'd been held, a low single story with a long peaked roof, like a battery chicken coop on some farm back home. On the other side of that was a pitiful excuse for a fence, caked in rust, and beyond that were more low concrete structures set into rocky soil with sand and hard shrubs and the occasional gnarled olive tree.

His ears were filled with a low rumble; rising dust made visibility difficult. That, and up and down and left and right were challenging concepts. Keeler was having a hard time keeping his footing, staggering like a drunk. He didn't understand why, not immediately. He thought he might be light-headed from the chemicals. Or maybe it wasn't the chemicals, because the ground was definitely shuddering, rocks and pebbles trembling.

In another instant everything got stable and quiet.

Now he was hearing small arms fire and shouting. Not only shouting, the real screams of fear and panic, combat. A stampeding sound made him turn. Five men sprinted out of the dust storm, breathing hard and sweating, wearing the French lizard-patterned camouflage he'd seen earlier.

He watched them go, Syrian regime commandos with high-quality weapons, young men capable of jogging twenty miles with fifty pounds of gear on their backs. They hadn't so much as looked at him, clearly occupied with something they considered more worthy of attention, but Keeler saw the panic in their eyes.

Like a zombie movie, he thought. You can have your issues with the Syrian regime, brutal as they are, but when the ISIS zombies come, you better put that aside for a moment. One of the soldiers was bleeding from a head wound, staggering after his buddies, trying to keep up. The dust was settling, visibility improving.

The telltale suck of a mortar round arced in, followed by a crack and the boom. The ground shook once more, but now Keeler understood it. The initial blast when he was going out the double doors made the earth tremble like an earthquake. Dollars to donuts it had come from underground. He was aware of ISIS tactics, how they liked to tunnel under the Syrian regime positions, blowing them up from below.

Things were a hundred percent out of control in Syria.

Keeler got oriented. He and Ruth had been brought into a Syrian camp that was currently under attack. Slightly messed up, but in every crisis lies opportunity.

These days ISIS was generally overrunning its less-motivated opposition, so it wasn't looking good for the soldiers here. He almost felt sorry for them. He was on a different mission, told himself: *Keep to the task*. Medical supplies for Ruth, plus the girl Fizza Hamieh.

Remember the pledge.

He moved out to his right, jogging along the warehouse wall, in the same direction the young commandos had sprinted. A mound of dust up ahead looked bizarre, until Keeler realized it wasn't dust, it was a human being, maybe thirty feet away and hunched on all fours. At first, Keeler thought it was the Syrian soldier with the head wound, bleeding out and left behind.

He had the Russian 9mm pistol up, approaching with arms outstretched, but it wasn't a young Syrian soldier. The dust-covered man was Ezzedin, who hadn't gotten very far. Now the big guy was down on hands and knees, spitting blood into the dirt. Keeler's bullet must have clipped him, maybe done worse. Worse wasn't going to be bad enough. The underground explosion might have brought him down.

Blood was pooling under Keeler's tongue, the damage done by the Jackal hadn't closed up yet. He spit it out in a long squirt, blood mingling with dirt.

Keeler stepped around and kicked Ezzedin hard in the face, the top of his boot making contact with the guy's nose and mouth and lips and teeth. The head jerked back. Ezzedin looked up, the whites of his eyes visible. He spit teeth and some of the flesh from his lower lip, where it'd been impaled by a dental fragment.

Keeler got right up in his face. "Where's the girl?"

The man's eyes rolled back, clocking him but glazing over and losing focus.

Keeler shoved the pistol hard into his forehead. "Where's the girl?"

Another massive explosion rocked them from close by. The shock waves broke glass in the nearby buildings, and the pressure change popped Keeler's ears. The air became thick with dust again. He figured the explosion for a car bomb, what the ISIS people used when they attacked. They sent in kamikaze vehicles armored up with welded steel plates, hoping they'd make it to the line of contact. They'd breach and hit the suicide button, blowing the frontline soldiers to kingdom come.

A wave of foot bombers would follow, overwhelming the forward edge of the battle area, immolating themselves against secondary defenses and making way for the executioners to mop up.

After that it'd be game over, whoever had survived would wish they hadn't. Screams came from the wounded, the panicked rattle of Kalashnikov fire, badly trained men shooting off entire magazines at nothing, simply hysterical.

He saw where Ezzedin was wounded, a wet spot spreading up his shirt from above his butt. One of Keeler's shots had nailed him, putting him down. Possibly the round had shattered the sacroiliac joint over the buttocks. The fact that he'd made it this far from the door was a miracle, if you ignored the likelihood that he was relying on Captagon pills for his courage, like everyone was here.

Ezzedin was done for if the ISIS fighters broke through.

Keeler crouched and put his face near Ezzedin's. "Where's the girl, buddy? I'll get her out of here before the enemy gets here."

The guy gasped in pain. He said, "I'd give the whore to them myself if I could."

A clarifying statement that Keeler didn't attempt to understand. He just wanted to get to Fizza Hamieh, like he'd pledged in the beginning. He'd help her out. Help her do whatever she wanted to do with the limited options available to her.

He kicked Ezzedin's gun away. Leaving the Hezbollah guy to ISIS was an idea; they'd certainly be more cruel than any CIA black site torture team.

Ezzedin said, "Hurry up and do me."

Keeler crouched down again and looked him in the eye. "What do they call you when you're home, Amal?"

"That's my name, yes."

"What your wife calls you?"

Ezzedin smiled. "I haven't seen my wife in a long time."

"Take me to the girl, and I'll get you out of here. I can't promise your wife, but you'll live."

The bearded man coughed. "How will you do that?"

Keeler was looking around, alert, registering the situation. He glanced at Ezzedin's seemingly peaceful face. He said, "I have a team coming. They'll get you out if I say so. You're an intelligence curiosity. If you cooperate, maybe the Israelis will let you make a phone call once in a while. You'll be an important prisoner, good conditions, toilet paper, toothpaste and an hour a week with the TV if you play your cards right."

Ezzedin smiled. "Satan promised them and made them promises, but all that he promised them was nothing but deception."

He rolled over onto his back and Keeler saw the thing in his hand. A Russian fragmentation grenade, what they called a *little lemon*, bright yellowish-green in color. The index finger of Ezzedin's other hand was threaded through the ring. Keeler saw this, registering what was happening without knowing precisely how long it had been since the Hezbollah man had pulled the pin.

There was zero time to reflect. The F-1 *little lemon* is a lethal package, delivering deadly fragments in an arc of thirty meters. There isn't any easy way of getting away from it. No jumping, rolling, or running. He wasn't going to dig a hole in the ground either. Keeler did the only thing possible, he grabbed Ezzedin by the shoulder and thigh and rolled him onto the grenade, pinning his arms underneath the body and using his own weight to keep the man down.

The grenade detonated its initial charge, sending an intense shock wave in all directions. The ground absorbed half of it, and the rest radiated up in a dome shape. Ezzedin's body took it.

Ezzedin's body lifted a foot off the ground. Keeler was

thrown, feeling a thud and a sting in his neck. He rolled off, looking at the sky, thinking that was it, he was just going to bleed out there and die. He let his hands and fingers move around, looking for wounds but not finding any—until he arrived at the neck. Fingers flew over the surface, finding the bump. Fingernails pulled a single steel ball bearing out of his flesh, the fragment having come through Ezzedin's body, losing the vast majority of its velocity before finding a temporary home in Keeler's neck.

A little more force and an inch in either direction, and Keeler would be either headless or bleeding out. He stood up, testing his legs and rolling the little bloody ball bearing around between two fingers. The leg wound from the Jackal's knife wasn't feeling great, stiff and beginning to be annoying, making a pulsing throb of pain a couple times every second.

You couldn't make it up. Keeler laughed at the sky, howled like a banshee.

SIXTY-ONE

ANOTHER UNDERGROUND BLAST FLOORED HIM, sending the deadly little steel bearing falling from his fingers into the dust. Keeler picked himself up, thinking about how long it must have taken the ISIS fighters to tunnel under the compound in preparation for this attack, months maybe.

All of those vehicles he and Ruth had seen gathering, that'd been the final preparation. Maybe the Captagon factory was worth it, a way to finance their war, or make their leaders rich. Maybe that was the same thing.

He was alive and in relatively decent fighting shape, that was the important thing. Keeler got back to the business at hand. Time was running out for Ruth, bleeding naked on a table in there. If this was a military camp, there would be medical supplies somewhere.

He moved carefully across a dirt alleyway to another low warehouse building, putting the pain out of his mind. Three Syrian regime men were slumped in a doorway. Two obviously dead, the third man mortally wounded, gasping, a bloody hand clawing at his throat, the other hand blown off at the wrist. His good hand was trying to close a gash in his neck, from which life fluid seeped onto his soaked chest.

Keeler looked at the dying man, making eye contact.

The ISIS zombies hadn't entered the compound yet, which meant these regime men had been hit by something else. If he were on *Jeopardy!* or something, Keeler would guess they'd been nailed by a grenade dropped from a cheap Chinese drone. Some toy that'd been hacked to carry anti-personnel ordnance that probably had a video camera on it. If he really was put on the spot, he'd bet the successful hit had already been uploaded to YouTube.

Welcome to the future.

He was scanning the pile of sorry-looking, mangled humanity, looking for anything useful he could scavenge. Medical supplies or weapons, he'd take either.

One of the dead men had managed to get his hands on a relatively modern AK-74M, a version of the Kalashnikov that wasn't fifty years old. Keeler pried the man's hands from the weapon, relieving the previous owner of three loaded magazines. These guys hadn't been wearing any body armor, something that would have come in handy at the time of their death.

Keeler jogged along the side of the second warehouse. Another shell crashed into an empty yard, on the other side of a destroyed building. Up ahead, a half dozen regime soldiers huddled at the corner, seeking cover from whatever was happening down the alley to the right.

Which was no mystery. The enemy was down that alley, a point made obvious by the two dead uniformed regime men sprawled out in unfashionable poses, exactly where they'd exposed themselves to an ISIS sniper. The surviving men were trying to get focused, speaking rapidly among themselves, arguing even, maybe trying to come up with a plan, clearly lacking leadership.

Keeler had worked often enough with allied Arabic-speaking soldiers to know the generic word for *medic*. For sure he pronounced it badly, but he'd learned to pronounce it effectively, that is, to be understood.

He kept the AK pointed down and approached, hands over his head in an X shape, screaming the word for medic, which also worked for medical facility. "*Ilajiyy!*"

He was ignored, and realized why. These guys were summoning up their courage to do stupid things. One man was already there, hyperventilating like he was preparing to go underwater. The Syrian leapt away from the building into the alley, exposing himself to enemy fire. The guy howled and screamed, letting loose with an AK-47, unloading the entire magazine from the hip in a sustained rattle before darting back into cover. He'd made it, most likely without hitting a single enemy soldier, or even seeing one. The guy slammed himself back against the warehouse wall, laughing hysterically now, eyes agape, completely breathless.

Keeler got up close and personal. He figured the guy was half deaf already from the weapons fire. He spoke loudly, trying to be clear in the foreign language. "*Ilajiyy.*" Holding his arms up in the X-shape for medical assistance.

The soldier looked at him dumbly, shivering with adrenaline, his pupils pinheads, high on Captagon.

Keeler said it again, using another word he knew that meant *hurry up.* "*Ilajiyy, asrae!*"

The guy blinked and pointed at the other side of the alley. Keeler didn't understand why these regime men were in that particular spot, what they hoped to accomplish, but then again, neither did they.

Whatever, that wasn't his mission. He waited for another regime soldier to jump out with his AK-47 blasting in hopeless optimism. Once the guy got shooting and howling Keeler sprinted behind him toward cover on the other side.

Another long warehouse building. Keeler jogged and scanned, trying to see what the guy had been pointing at. He found it, a door with a Red Crescent sign, the Muslim version of the Red Cross. The door was locked and he kicked it in. The clinic had already been ransacked, but it wasn't completely empty. He rifled the shelves, pulling out antiseptic solution, a sealed set of tongs, gauze packs and bandage rolls.

He sprinted back the way he'd come, leaping across the alley again, past the terrified soldiers, past the men who'd been fragged, past Ezzedin's corpse.

Ruth was still supine on the workshop table. The makeshift dressing had at least staunched the blood flow. He removed the shredded Syrian flag from her wound very carefully, happy to see that her system was working well and blood had begun to clot. The chemical stench in the Captagon workshop was worse than he'd realized, now that he'd been outside. He needed to get her to fresh air.

There were more rumbles from heavy explosives, maybe another suicide vehicle trying to get through. A relatively good sign because it meant that the zombies hadn't breached the line yet. He was dressing Ruth's wound, kind of laughing to himself about the situation they were in. Keeler had a good imagination, but being in a Syrian military position with a bunch of Hezbollah fighters while they tried to repel an ISIS attack, that was one he wouldn't have invented, and if he did, none of his friends would have believed it.

He cleaned Ruth's exit wound with antiseptic solution, folded the gauze square twice, and inserted it into the wound with the sterile tongs. He stuffed the ruptured flesh with as much as he could get in there, soaking it all again with the antiseptic. At least any kind of infection would be delayed until they could get into a proper facility.

Ruth was conscious, looking at him. Keeler winked at her. "You're gonna be fine."

She closed her eyes, weak from the loss of blood. He wrapped the bandage around her tight and fast, already mentally kicking himself because he'd forgotten to source clothing.

Not hard to come by, given the chaotic combat scene around them. He stepped outside and dragged one of the fragged men into the warehouse. Keeler unceremoniously stripped him of his uniform and dressed Ruth. They made eye contact, hers heavy lidded. He looked away, focusing on the task. She grunted with pain as she tried to move.

Keeler had experience with wounded soldiers and their clothing. "Don't try. I'll do it," he said.

She stopped trying. In the left cargo pocket of the dead man's trousers was a little bag of Captagon pills. Keeler dry swallowed three and pocketed the rest.

"All right, let's do it."

He got her into a fireman's lift. Made a left turn out the double doors, and found a hole in the fence. He squeezed through and headed down an alley bordered by a block of one-story apartments, probably what used to be worker housing.

Keeler kicked in a door at random to reveal a single room with two beds, maybe quarters shared by junior officers. He laid Ruth down onto a bed. She was still conscious, moaning and trying to speak. He got his ear right by her mouth and tried to understand what she was saying, but there wasn't a chance.

He said, "I'm going to find a way out of here. You just concentrate on breathing, you hear?"

Ruth's eyes blinked slowly. She mouthed the word *yes*.

He still had the Russian 9mm pistol tucked into the waistband behind his back. He dropped the magazine and checked the witness holes, five rounds left. He put the weapon back together and placed it in Ruth's hand, lying at her side.

"Safety's off. Anyone comes through that door without announcing himself, you use that. Five rounds remaining, make them count."

She nodded, her eyes holding his, filling him with confidence that she'd pull through. Her voice was weak. "Roger that."

SIXTY-TWO

THE SMALL ARMS fire had intensified. There was real fighting going on up there by the line. Keeler jogged the opposite way, scouting. Looking for vehicles or a way out, or maybe someone who could help. The residential block ended at a kind of plaza circled by what looked like a main office building.

A very thin man was sitting on a concrete block, improbably looking at his phone. He was around sixty years old, thin and grizzled with white stubble and a big mustache.

Keeler got the assault rifle up and approached. Nobody else was around, the camp personnel having either deserted or run up to the forward line to defend against the attack. This guy wasn't doing either. His skin was perfectly gray, like he hadn't seen sunlight for a very long time. What Keeler noticed most wasn't the features, but the sorrow and despair so clearly etched into the face.

The man looked up. He said something in Arabic, voice soft and barely audible.

Keeler said, "I don't understand that."

Something was adjusted in the man's gaze, maybe stoked by the realization that Keeler spoke English. Maybe the implications that sprang from this fact. He raised the phone he was holding, limp hand extended, speaking in accented English. "Look at this."

A video of a man playing the *oud*, a Middle Eastern stringed instrument like a fretless guitar. The musician in the video was sitting cross-legged under an almond tree, somewhere peaceful. Keeler wasn't any kind of an expert in Middle Eastern music, but the man was playing soulfully, the sound coming out thin from the small phone speakers.

The thin man was observing Keeler now, intently focused on his face. "Is beautiful, yes?"

The rumble of an explosion came from the north, maybe a hundred yards off. Rifle fire crackled out like popping bubble wrap.

Keeler nodded at the man, running through the practical implications. The phone was working, it was connected to some kind of communications network, maybe even the internet. This was good. He put a large hand over the phone, not yet simply taking it away.

He said, "I'm looking for a girl. A woman who was brought here recently." He put a hand to his nose. "She might have a bandage on her nose."

The man nodded, eyes wide, being helpful. But he didn't speak.

Keeler said, "You're nodding. Do you know what I'm talking about?"

The guy nodded some more. "I know, I know."

"Show me."

The man stood up, in addition to being thin he was tall and looked like his body weighed nothing. Keeler couldn't figure it out. He was too old to be a soldier. The guy wasn't even holding on to his phone; he'd let Keeler take it out of his hand. He was at the same time helpful and completely vacant, giving off the impression that he'd agree to anything.

Behind the square was yet another low concrete building, scarred by bullet impacts. The man led him around the side, down a narrow alley. More explosions rocked from behind them. The man started talking, periodically turning his head over his shoulder like some kind of tour guide. Keeler, following behind, was alert with the assault rifle.

The man said, "Very bad place here. Nobody knows what happens now. If Daesh comes will it be better? Will it be worse? Nobody knows. Very bad here."

A Syrian soldier with a bandaged head sat on the steps of a building, holding a cigarette. He looked disoriented, turning the cigarette backward into his mouth, then taking it out again and looking at it. The thin man squatted and put the cigarette into the soldier's mouth the right way. He gently took a lighter from the man's hand and coaxed a flame out. He stood up again, not a word exchanged between the two.

The man looked at Keeler with his mournful eyes. "They do not know what they do."

He pointed to another building.

Keeler said, "She's in there?"

The man nodded and walked toward it. He struggled to open the heavy door, putting all of his strength into the effort.

The interior was dark and hazy, with a strong stench of human body odor. It took Keeler a moment for his vision to adjust, but when it did he saw people crowded into a single large room. As many as a hundred people were crammed in there, sitting or lying on the floor, all of them looking at him. It was mostly women and children with a handful of older men well past fighting age.

The thin man was looking at Keeler, making sure he was following. He turned to the group and walked right into them, making a tut-tut sound, the crowd slowly parting, people shuffling out of the way, some with great effort. Keeler was processing the scene. These were civilians. His first thought was that they were here for protection from ISIS, that the Syrian regime soldiers were defending them.

But that wasn't very likely.

He put it together with the Captagon production facility. These people were work slaves. Now they were gathered here in this place seeking refuge from the fighting. The faces watching him were haggard and beyond frightened, beyond hope. Even in the gloom Keeler noticed evidence of malnutrition. People were suffering from wasting and the skin flaking you see in desperate populations. An older woman was clearly suffering hair loss. The crowd parted, revealing a ragged group in the middle, clustered around a bright-green blanket. Light from a window over the door shone down onto the spot.

The three women hovering over the blanket wore headscarves. The thin man gently touched a woman with his foot, and she moved aside, glancing up with a lined face. Keeler saw the girl then, Fizza Hamieh, her head cradled in another woman's lap. It was definitely her; he recognized her from the photographs.

Hamieh was maybe nineteen or twenty years old. Her eyes were open, staring straight up, intense somehow. The bandage that had been over her nose was gone. Keeler was looking at her in semi-profile, realizing that not only was there no bandage, but the nose had the same imposing hook they'd seen in the first images, before Dr. Erkin's procedure. He'd laughed with Choi at the time, both of them saying the words simultaneously, *nose job.*

But Fizza Hamieh hadn't had a nose job.

Keeler felt creeped out. The war was one thing, but these people were weirdly silent, like they had a secret and were waiting for him to do something about it. Hamieh's eyes shifted, looking at Keeler. Her eyes were literally dancing, pupils moving around.

He squatted over her. "I'm going to get you out of here."

She looked at him, her face devoid of expression. He glanced at the thin man, who understood.

He leaned forward and said something in Arabic, quietly. Hamieh looked at Keeler, eyes still crazy like before. She giggled and said something in her own language before letting herself relax back into the woman's lap. The woman stroked Hamieh's hair, looking at Keeler blankly.

He spoke to the thin man. "What did she say?"

The man said, "Nothing very nice, sir. I think her Arabic is not very good."

"Just tell me what she said."

The guy dropped his eyes, submissive. "This girl was brought here yesterday. She is not well, sir."

"She's sick?"

The man looked up. "She's not right in her head."

Hamieh was laughing now, gently and to herself. Keeler shook off the confusion he was feeling. There would be plenty of time to figure out what was wrong with Fizza Hamieh once they were safe. Getting safe was now the only priority.

The thin man's phone was locked with a password. He handed it to him.

"Open that up. I need to use it."

The man got his phone working and handed it back. Keeler saw the icon for a map application and tapped it. Spreading forefinger and thumb, tapping and sliding with fingers, he got oriented to their current location. The camp was south of the ISIS roadblock they'd escaped and the place where he and Ruth had been captured.

He couldn't read the Arabic in the map.

He said, "What's this place called?"

The man said, "This is Qassen Shata."

The thin guy was staring at him hard.

Keeler pointed his chin at the subdued crowd surrounding them. "You want to get out of here?"

The man shrugged. "You think we'll be safer somewhere else? At least here they need us."

Keeler gazed around at the indifferent and docile gray-faced crowd. He had to recognize the truth of what the guy was saying. It made sense in the twisted logic of Syrian civil war. These people were operating the Captagon production facility, which meant they could keep it running once the new people took over.

Maybe this guy had been a chemist back before the war. Now he was useful to anyone who got control of the facility. If ISIS broke through and captured the place, why would they kill the only people who could run it?

"Fine, but I need this" Keeler said, holding up the phone.

The man gazed at him, real sorrow in his eyes. He made a gesture like flinging crumbs from his fingers. "I can't help you."

The man stepped into the crowd and turned his back, maybe moving toward his family. Keeler was left in the middle of it, standing over Fizza Hamieh holding the phone. The people in there began speaking to each other, as if whatever novelty he'd had for them was gone.

Keeler blocked them out as a nonthreatening distraction. He located himself on the map and figured out which way was what. Two minutes later he was sending a message from the thin man's phone, addressed to a randomly chosen contact. The addressee didn't matter, the message was the important thing.

The message was in English and contained the last brevity code they'd had for Calcutti's team in Ankara, plus the GPS coordinates of a rendezvous site three hundred yards to their south. If he needed to break through an enemy line, it'd be good to have some help.

What Keeler knew: no electronic signals came out of Syria that were not immediately vacuumed up by multiple intelligence agencies, several of which were on his side. Based on what Choi had told him, their people had helpfully focused ears on this place in particular. The code would be picked up and the message conveyed, no doubt about it.

Along with the location, it also contained the information that Ruth was wounded and that he'd found Fizza Hamieh. He didn't exactly put it that way, leaving the message ambiguous. *Package secured* is how he'd put it, even though the reality wasn't so certain. The people up there could interpret that however they liked.

What he didn't know was how long it would take.

SIXTY-THREE

Tina Choi looked out over the flat landscape. The shelling was not only loud; the detonations shook the ground like something she'd only experienced at a heavy metal concert she'd accidentally attended in high school. Bratton was beside her, both of them sitting on a kind of dune made from crushed rocks. He was operating a reconnaissance drone, eyes glued to the little screen on his controller.

There was fighting half a kilometer to the northeast, an ISIS force hitting a light industrial zone they figured had been used by the Syrian regime as a military camp. At least that was the speculation they were getting over the battle net from the intelligence people. The regime camp was being blockaded from the south by another force.

Bratton's reconnaissance drone was checking that out, since the second force was directly to their north. At the moment they were looking at two dozen soldiers milling around a cluster of pickup trucks.

These people weren't ISIS, not exactly. Their flag, shown in the images from the drone, was black with white Arabic script. The ISIS flag had the same colors, but the text was different. In their case, *La 'ilaha 'illa-llah*, "There is no God but God." A white circle below that had *God Messenger Mohammed* written in black.

This group's name was Jund al-Aqsa, currently allied to ISIS and a couple other Salafist groups. Choi said the name to herself under her breath, *Jund al-Aqsa*, trying to pronounce it with a good accent. The words meant *garrison of al-Aqsa*, which is supposed to be the third holiest place in Islam, after Mecca and Medina.

She was wondering why they'd chosen to focus on the third-holiest site instead of the holiest, the absurdity of it occurring to her suddenly.

Groups like Jund al-Aqsa popped up in Syria with the regularity of Korean boy bands, marketing themselves with catchy looking flags and slogans. They competed with each other for funding, mostly from wealthy Arabs in the gulf, Qataris in particular. That's what all the YouTube videos were about.

It was also most likely the explanation for why they didn't attack: the deal they'd made with ISIS went only so far, and no further. Block the line of retreat, we'll take care of the rest. In the end, despite the rhetoric, everyone was averse to the possibility of getting killed.

Cheevers had positioned himself at the crest of the little dune, which wasn't any kind of natural formation. They were inside what had once been a quarry, lying on crushed quartz gravel that in another time might have been destined for a rich Damascene driveway. Cheevers was prone, scanning the horizon with a scope while speaking over the battle-net to command.

The combat was raging below them on either side of a hollow made by a small stream. They could see that much by eye.

Bratton whistled to Cheevers, who made a controlled slide

down the gravel pile. The drone hummed, beginning its descent to nestle into the launch pod, a very nifty piece of equipment embedded into a small pelican case that Bratton carried in his pack.

He had a tablet out now, fingering it and maneuvering around a topographical map. "We can go around on the west here if we need to," he said, showing them a winding road that didn't intersect with any main artery. Those would certainly be subject to roadblocks, or else vulnerable to ambush by one side or the other. At this point their objective was a few kilometers west and north of the current position.

Cheever held a hand up for quiet, he was getting something over the comms. Choi and Bratton weren't linked in to the command channel. It took a minute, the new commander staring into space, grinding teeth. He took off his wraparound sunglasses, looking at her with clear eyes.

"Keeler's made contact." He jerked a thumb behind him. "He's in there."

Choi said, "In there how?"

Cheever actually smiled. "He's in the middle of that shit is how, inside the regime camp getting hammered by the zombies. The Israeli operator's WIA."

Wounded in action.

Choi thought about the last time she saw Ruth, in that car dropping them off in Ankara when she gave Keeler a card, introducing herself. Wounded in action could be bad or it could be very bad.

"Did they tell you her status?" Choi asked.

Cheevers said, "She's not operational, that's what they said."

"Which means she can't walk, for one thing," Bratton said.

Choi said, "So we'll have to get her out."

"Yeah." Cheevers looked off into the distance and spat. "It might get a little complicated now."

She saw him and Bratton exchanging looks. "How could it get more complicated?"

Bratton said, "I guess you've never worked with the Israelis."

"They can be a little, uh, gung-ho," Cheevers said.

Bratton laughed. "Yup."

SIXTY-FOUR

HAMIEH WAS WALKING but needed to be directed. Keeler held on to her elbow and pulled her along gently, knowing that if he let go, she was liable to walk off in any old direction, eyes agog and wandering. She was either mentally unstable from the beginning, or suffering from shock. The central puzzles encroached into his thought processes, despite his wishes to keep them out.

Why had Ezzedin treated her this way, throwing Hamieh in with the work slaves?

Why was her original nose intact, given the images they'd seen of the bandaged face, plus the fact that she'd been Erkin's patient at Zaros Aesthetica?

The DNA match to Nasrallah was positive. The evidence was incontrovertible that Fizza Hamieh, or whatever her real name was, had a family connection to the head of Hezbollah. But here she was, dumped like garbage into a place you could objectively refer to as hell.

Very strange.

The explanation would have to wait. Keeler had pledged to help the girl, and that's what he was going to do.

Now he was looking for a vehicle. Ezzedin and his Hezbollah men had come in with a couple of Toyota Land Cruisers, according to the intelligence that Ruth had received. They'd be parked somewhere nearby. Moving through the alleys between buildings wasn't hard. The camp had been pretty much deserted, the regime fighters up on the line, engaging in intense combat, judging from the noise.

Keeler foresaw another issue he was going to face, even if he found a vehicle. He'd need to figure out the best way to get himself, Hamieh, and Ruth in there with the least fuss. This was like a puzzle he'd once tried to solve, where you need to figure out how the farmer gets a wolf, a chicken, and a sack of grain across the river in a little boat.

He felt a kind of chill travel up his spine, going up all the way to the top of his head. A thrilling feeling of something coming on. It made him want to stand tall and arch his back, cracking the spine. He wanted to open his mouth and crack his jaw. It was like some kind of alien energy was moving out from his middle to the extremities. It felt good but weird.

Captagon.

The thin man's phone vibrated in his pocket. He looked at the phone, a message from a 963 number, a Syrian country code.

The message read: *Give the phone to the American*, with unreadable Arabic script below that.

Keeler felt another electric spark up his spine. The phone rang.

He accepted the call. "Yeah."

The voice was male, gruff, speaking English with a slight accent. "This is your Sparrowhawk friend. I've got eyes in the sky now. Are you injured?"

Sparrowhawk, US military terminology for the Israelis.

Keeler said, "Exactly what I need. I'm okay. Do you have my position?"

"Roger that."

"I'm looking for a vehicle."

"Yes. I'm going to guide you. There is a vehicle depot fifty meters to the south. It's a small open area with an olive grove on the other side. You're clear to move there now."

Keeler started moving, glancing at Hamieh. She was looking at the top of a building, not resisting his direction.

The voice said, "I need to know the condition of our colleague so that we can prepare for extraction."

Referring to Ruth.

Keeler moved as fast as he could, speaking into the phone while maintaining an alert situational awareness. "Penetrating trauma to the right chest, through and through. Entry wound maybe ten or twelve millimeters, located two centimeters above the right nipple. Exit wound is slightly smaller, just below the right shoulder blade."

The man said, "Nine millimeter?"

"Yeah but a steel jacket."

"Understood. Associated injuries?"

"Shock and blood loss; she's stable."

"Thank you."

The man stopped talking. Keeler could hear the clacking of a computer keyboard in the background, kind of like talking to a customer service rep.

Keeler said, "What about car keys?"

The man said, "Hezbollah don't have three-point ignition systems on their fleet. Check under the visor."

Keeler put the phone away, then moved south between small buildings, coming downhill through an overgrown area of tall grass and shrubs and an abandoned tractor.

There it was: a circular vehicle depot surrounded by buildings on one side and an olive grove on the other. The center of the circle was occupied by a roughly sculpted statue of Hafez Al Assad beside a large tree, the dead dictator recognizable by the high forehead and prominent ears that the artist had faithfully rendered.

Keeler observed, screened from view behind a rusted-out tractor, a relic from when this place had been a civilian-use industrial zone.

Three Syrian soldiers sat under the statue, in the shade of a tree, smoking cigarettes and clutching AK-47s. Once in a while the ground shook, and they'd look to the north where the rattle and rumble of small arms fire hadn't let up.

The tree had probably screened them from the overhead drone's view.

Keeler picked up the phone, speaking softly. "You missed three guys under a tree by the Assad statue. I could take them out but that would give my position away."

The man said, "Give me a second."

Keeler waited, crouching and breathing. Fizza Hamieh sat down in the grass and picked a long stalk, playing with it in the light. She was wearing a white dress and he noticed blood stains near her groin, like she was having her period, but there was no time to help or investigate that now.

The man's voice returned on the phone. "We have eyes on the guards. Stay clear because they're not long for this world."

"Roger that."

The man said, "Where is Ruth?"

"I put her in some kind of officer's quarters. I need to go back and get her."

"How long will that take?"

"Hopefully not long. Five minutes?"

The man said, "A hundred meters to the south is a blocking force, positioned to ambush a regime retreat. Unfortunately, it's the only way out, so we'll need to deal with them. In five minutes you'll see them lit up. We're going to blow a corridor open for you. A team will meet you on the other side."

"Five minutes?"

"For the big one, correct. How much battery life is remaining in that phone?"

Keeler looked at it. He put it back to his ear. "About half."

"Outstanding. We've only got one chance at this, so go and get Ruth, please, and take care."

The man ended the call. Keeler looked to the sky. Nothing up there as far as he could see. The drones were out of sight, up in the stratosphere, making rotations around the battle space. Fixing targets and beaming images and data back to a command center in Tel Aviv. They'd be preparing a barrage.

A length of old blue rope was tied to the tractor's radiator grill. He undid the rope and bound Hamieh's wrists to the grill. She allowed him to manipulate her, letting him reposition her body. Hamieh was really acting weird, docile as if in a dream, looking at him with big googly eyes. Maybe drugged?

She didn't seem to understand English, but he still needed to say it. "Sorry about this, I'll be back for you."

She looked away and started humming.

A rushing sound came on, like wind rising, quiet at first but quickly becoming louder until it was a high-pitched scream. The low-hanging leaves shook violently. There were three heavy thuds and then only dust rising where the Syrians had been.

The feeling came on again, electricity vibrating up into his neck. The Captagon pills were really kicking in now, and it wasn't bad at all. The leg wound wasn't throbbing. Five minutes to go before the escape route opened up.

Time to retrieve Ruth and get the hell out of there.

SIXTY-FIVE

KEELER MADE his way back up toward the room where he'd stashed Ruth. The battle was getting closer, which meant the regime people were in retreat. He was hearing shouts, small arms fire, screams of wounded and the whoosh and dull thud of shoulder RPGs.

Coming around a corner to the block of residential quarters, he heard yelling up ahead. Regime fighters were screaming at each other in Arabic, suffering combat stress, and hurling hysterical commands that he couldn't understand.

The main issue was that their voices were coming from very close to the room where Ruth lay badly wounded on a bed. Keeler was around the side of the building opposite, thinking of the best way to approach. It was a tricky situation and there wasn't any time to work it out as safely as he'd have liked.

A window right above his head spoke to him, as did the feeling of invulnerability the Captagon pills had put into him. Keeler put the barrel of his assault rifle through the glass, clearing the shards, then vaulted easily into a room with a couple of beds: a mirror image of where he'd put Ruth. There was some kind of sensation from his left hand and he saw a gash had opened up from broken glass. Nothing that would kill him.

He moved to the door and listened. Shouts continued from outside as feet pounded into dirt. He turned the knob on the door and inched it open, standing back and looking through the crack. A couple of regime soldiers were having a heated conversation, while three of their comrades slumped wounded against the stairs of the residential block.

Five men, the more capable guys, were arguing. Keeler had no way of understanding what they were saying, no real motive either. These guys were exhausted; combat screwed with frayed nerves, and shouting over gunfire made voices hoarse. Keeler moved to the left, looked down the alley, and saw nothing moving. Same thing on the other side, nobody else, just the five.

There was a clock ticking on this thing; patience wasn't an option. He didn't have time to find out if these men had a life story, or wives or girlfriends or kids. None of that mattered now, just Ruth.

The AK-74M had a standard magazine that took thirty rounds. He dropped it out of the well, checking the witness hole. This one was halfway depleted, so he exchanged it with another, snapping it into the lower receiver. The lighter mag got slotted into his back pocket for later. The weapon was cocked and locked. He put it on single-shot mode.

He came out the front door, medium speed. The AK-74M up and sighting, steadily held with both hands, eyes scanning and keeping the front notch inside the groove. The men were directly across from him, still arguing. Keeler put the man closest to Ruth's door in his sights. He'd be most likely to duck into cover. The soldiers saw him pretty much at the same time as he fired the first round, heads swiveling to a new and unusual threat.

Keeler put a round into the back of the first man's leg,

putting him down. He didn't watch the man drop. His aim was already moving as his feet descended three cement steps to the ground. The adrenaline was up, coursing through his system. He squeezed the trigger twice, and bullets whipped and slapped into a second man as his weapon was coming up. The rounds nailed the man in the torso and neck, throwing him unceremoniously into the concrete platform that served as an outside corridor to the residential block.

The third man had his weapon up, firing on full automatic, holding the AK-47 in front of him without aiming. The rounds snapped past to the left, a couple feet away. Moving laterally in the other direction, Keeler carefully put three bullets into the shooter. Two in the groin and the third smacking him fully in the face, literally wiping it out.

Clear.

The two others were too badly wounded to pose a threat.

Keeler sprinted across the way, not even feeling the wounded leg anymore. Heart racing, but managing to contain it. The training was working out like it was supposed to. The man he'd shot in the thigh was wriggling around, reaching for the weapon he'd dropped. Keeler shot him in the back of the head.

He kicked the door open. Ruth was on the bed, Yarygina pistol in her hand and firing. Keeler launched himself to the right, crashing into a chest of drawers. She'd done exactly what he said, fire at anything coming in the door unannounced. When he got to her side she was shaking her head weakly.

"Idiot." She handed him the pistol.

Keeler said nothing, sliding the weapon into his waistband. He lifted Ruth carefully to his shoulders. She threaded her arms around his neck, fingers clasping on the other side. The best way to move fast in those conditions is what's called a *lope*, leaning forward and allowing the weight to help you stumble faster than walking upright.

Moving downhill to the vehicle area, he tried to keep Ruth from jostling too much. Her head was just behind his ear. He heard her voice again, weak but clear.

"You're a big idiot."

Which brought a smile to Keeler's face.

She said, "You got the girl with the funny name?"

"I've got her tied up like a goat. It's all very weird."

Ruth was in pain, obvious because of her labored breathing and the moans she was attempting to stifle.

Keeler said, "Hang in there, kid."

"I'm older than you."

"How can you tell?"

"I can tell."

A minute later he was at the clearing, looking for Hamieh. The blue rope that'd bound her to the tractor was loose and she was nowhere in sight.

SIXTY-SIX

THE PROMISED drone strike barrage hadn't yet materialized. The guy had said five minutes, and Keeler hadn't been counting. He could guess, maybe four and a half had gone by since he'd left Hamieh tied to the tractor.

He was putting Ruth into the Land Cruiser when the first missiles hit a hundred yards to the south. It wasn't just a single strike; it was maybe two dozen. The detonations were intense, shock waves bending the olive trees and sending dust and sand and rocks out in a wide arc, shaking the ground.

The Land Cruiser's keys were not under the visor. Nice.

Keeler used his fingernails to rip off the plastic hood covering the ignition chamber. It wasn't his first time hot-wiring a vehicle. The hard part wasn't finding the correct wires, it was stripping them with his teeth, since he'd had very recent dental intervention. The two front teeth were wobbling, unstable. He had to get in there with his face, straining his neck and using the canine tooth to strip off the insulation plastic.

He crossed the wires, hoping for the best, and the engine kicked over.

The vehicle had a manual gearbox. Keeler kicked the clutch

down and put it into reverse, then turned his head to look out the rear window. Fizza Hamieh's ghostly shape was moving across the dirt patch by the olive grove.

"Shit."

He heard the words said, back in Ankara, what seemed like a million years ago outside of the safe house in the Çankaya diplomatic district.

The woman had said, *You help the girl.* Her gaze had been direct and hard, wounded and vulnerable but still forceful. She'd said, *You pledge.*

Looking directly into her eyes, he'd said, *Sure, ma'am, I'll help the girl.*

That's what he'd said—and he meant it.

Keeler put the vehicle into neutral and exited. He looked at Ruth, reclined in the backseat, concentrating on breathing. "Give me a minute."

As he loped across the dusty circle, the sight was pure horror and gore. The Syrian guards had been sliced and minced into a pile of scattered blood, flesh, and shredded clothing. One AK-47 seemed to have spun into the Assad statue, chipping off a chunk. The weapon was almost bent in half. The missiles that had hit them hadn't been explosive ordnance; they'd been bladed weapons for targeted hits.

He recalled thinking the strike had been weird, the whipping scream and then the thud and the dust.

Keeler knew that behind a strike like that were at least three operators in an air-conditioned room, teenagers kicking back in office chairs sipping cold Cokes, kids who had shown an aptitude for video games. Behind each of them were a dozen more intelligence analysts and technicians focused on bringing death to the enemy.

Theirs was a world of office buildings and coffee machines, computer screens and keyboards. They got excited about a hit in the same way as you'd get excited about receiving an email. Not that he was knocking it; it was just a different world from the one he knew.

That was for damned sure.

Fizza Hamieh was singing to herself when Keeler put his hand on her shoulder. The lower part of her dress was now soaked in blood, but she didn't seem to notice.

"Come on," he said, pulling her back toward the Land Cruiser. She turned to look at him, her eyes focused suddenly, softening.

Hamieh spoke in English. "Relax, Max."

"So now you speak English."

She nodded, looking around at the destruction. "This is so bizarre." Her accent rhythmic and slightly nasal. Hamieh's eyes met his. "The world is a sad and beautiful place."

Maybe fifty yards behind her there was movement out of the alley. Keeler pushed past Hamieh and took a knee. He scanned the area, aiming over the sights. Two uniformed regime men had come into the vehicle-depot area and were currently looking around at the destruction; one of them carried a shoulder-fired rocket-propelled grenade launcher.

Keeler watched the other one notice him, a little too late. He registered the excited look on the guy's face, the way he suddenly twitched into alert a second before he died.

Keeler put two rounds into the man's chest, dropping him. The man with the RPG ducked behind a Hilux truck. Keeler had to decide, hunt him down or get safe quickly. Others might be coming down there now, attracted by the initial drone strike to the south. He turned, seeking Hamieh, then seeing her only a yard away, staring at him dreamily.

The Assad statue and the tree were a couple of yards away. That would provide at least some modicum of cover.

He had to admit, Fizza Hamieh was quite a liability. He

grabbed her by the shoulders, turned, and pushed her hard behind the statue. Keeler had time to see her falling forward onto hands and knees. She let out a little cry of pain but it was cut off by the tell-tale sound of an RPG launching. The thick whoosh and hiss as it fired.

Keeler twisted to the threat, barely registering the rocket's trail coming at him erratically. There was no time to get behind anything. The grenade detonated against the base of the statue, not more than fifteen yards from his position. There was a feeling of icy cold washing over his chest and shoulders. Everything went dark and blurry for maybe five seconds.

He found himself on his back, floored by the blast. The cheap Captagon coursing through his system was probably helping., the heightened combat feeling amplified by the drug. Glancing down at himself, he saw blood and shredded clothing and charred black flesh. The shirt had been literally blasted off his body.

There was an icy sting and tingle all over his body, which wasn't a bad thing. At least there was sensation.

He got himself up on a knee, then was sort of stuck there, unable to move. Hamieh loomed over him. Her hands tugged under Keeler's arms, helping him up.

She spoke in English again. "Don't you want to go? We'll be late for the movie."

Keeler laughed involuntarily, the sound coming out like a cough. He'd pledged to save a bat-shit crazy woman.

"Anything you say, ma'am."

He got his legs under him and shoved Hamieh toward the Land Cruiser. His weapon was no longer in his hands, or anywhere for that matter, literally blown out of his grasp. He remembered the RPG, and the possibility of another one occurred to him.

He took Hamieh's forearm and staggered as fast as he could. Ten seconds later she was in the passenger seat.

A second drone strike whizzed in, this one at least as intense as the first. He knew the drill, they'd evaluated the first strike and were now targeting whatever had made the mistake of moving. The olive grove on the other side of the circle had caught fire, the trees in the back burning high, sending up black smoke.

He pulled the vehicle around in a tight circle, past the remains of the Syrian soldiers. The guy who'd fired the RPG seemed to have backed off, probably running for his life after the fresh round of drone strikes. Keeler grinned to himself. There was no way out for those people: either a ninja missile or an ISIS sword, like Hamieh had said, a sad and beautiful world—until you got hit by a bladed Hellfire R9X, or whatever the Israelis had. Then the world wasn't anything anymore.

Keeler put his foot on the gas and drove like a demented robot, barely able to see but impelled by the hard amphetamines throbbing through his system. Something had gone seriously wrong with his vision, but he wasn't going to look in the rearview to check himself out. His eyes were basically working, which was all that counted for the moment, but his head wasn't feeling good, waves of dizziness coming and going.

A sandy road carved around the circle and led into the olive grove. Bumping over potholes and rocks, he focused on a single point in the middle of the road and just followed it like an arrow, not looking anywhere else. What the guy had said was the team would meet him on the other side.

Two minutes later the twisting road entered something resembling a quarry, where piles of gravel and massive stone slabs were stacked one on top of one another. A figure stood up on one of the slabs, waving him down and pointing him in the direction of a mound of sand.

He'd seen that profile before, many times. It was Cheevers.

Keeler piloted the Land Cruiser around the sand pile and there was Bratton standing alongside a smaller figure. They were leaning against a Hilux truck perforated with bullet holes. He recognized her, Tina Choi. Keeler stopped the vehicle and came down from the driver's seat, the leg with the knife wound didn't make it. He found himself hitting the ground hard, falling on his ass and seeing the sky. Bratton's face showed up looming over him.

Keeler said, "What's up, Brat, you missed a great party."

Bratton was already examining Keeler's body, searching with his fingers for wounds.

"Shut up and concentrate on your breathing, brother," he said, ripping open a medical pack.

Keeler took a deep breath, letting it out easy. Choi's face appeared beside Bratton's. She looked serious, concerned, and as pretty as ever. He had something witty to say, but couldn't get it out of his mouth. His ears were ringing, but he could still make out the sound of low-flying helicopters coming in fast from the south. Three of them, maybe, in combat formation. The thrumming of blade slap was getting louder.

Bratton was cutting off the remains of Keeler's shirt with a pair of scissors.

He said, "The Sparrowhawks, bro, we're getting a free ride."

An Apache loomed suddenly, veering over them, the transmission hum and the high engine whine adding to the thwapping regularity of the rotors. The chopper veered up and held position. The chin cannon swiveled to the left and started loosening off a deep rhythmic thump at six hundred and twenty-five rounds per minute. The chopper rose further, orienting slightly to the northeast. Two rockets whooshed out from under the stub wings, Hydra 70s. Someone was having a bad day.

He closed his eyes and wiped a palm across them. Opening

them again, he could see better. Bratton and Choi were turning him on his side, doing something to his back; he didn't know what.

A Black Hawk roared into sight, the view from Keeler's sideways perspective looking weird. The pilot tilted the chopper's nose up and dropped the bird into a clear area. Three operators came out and jogged over, MP5s tucked close to their bodies. The first one up addressed Bratton, shouting above the noise.

"Where is she?"

Bratton was putting weight on him, maybe leaning a hand on his shoulder. Keeler looked up, saw Bratton jerk a thumb to the Land Cruiser. Keeler tried to get to his feet but failed.

Bratton said, "Don't even try, brother."

Then he was being rolled onto a stretcher and carried into the Black Hawk. Bratton and an Israeli operator strapped him into a bucket seat. Two female medics were already working on Ruth, giving her oxygen and taking apart the improvised dressing that Keeler had applied. They were professional, swabbing the wound, then setting an intravenous line and hooking her up to a drip.

Cheevers vaulted into the cabin. His grinning face came right in front of him. He reached up above Keeler and put the aviation headset on him. The noise from outside died down. Cheevers put on his own.

The man's large hand slapped him gently on the face. "Man, you look great."

"Oh, yeah?"

"Like an expired burger patty that someone decided to barbecue anyway."

Funny guy. Keeler realized they'd taken off and he hadn't even noticed.

The world down below took on a surreal aspect as they flew low, contour hugging. He had enough mental energy left to scan and register the scene. Cheevers had taken the seat right across from him. Choi and Hamieh sat together over on the other side. Bratton was next to him. The Israeli operators were busy, the medics and door gunners taking care of business. The Americans were passengers.

A body bag lay between him and Cheevers.

The missing link. Keeler said, "Calcutti?"

Cheevers caught his eye and nodded acknowledgement. "We're a man down, brother."

One of the Israelis was tapping Choi on the shoulder, indicating his headset and showing her five fingers. She nodded acknowledgment. Keeler watched her switch her headset to channel five. She said something short. Her demeanor changed suddenly, and he saw her mouth a more complicated set of words.

He was no lip reader, but Choi had obviously said the words, *Yes, Madam Undersecretary.*

Fizza Hamieh was sitting beside her, looking out the open side of the Black Hawk. Keeler eased himself back and closed his eyes, something they'd injected into him was overriding the Captagon. It felt good, fuzzy and warm and perfect.

SIXTY-SEVEN

RAMBAM HOSPITAL, Haifa, Israel

THEY MADE him stay in bed for a week and a half, after which he was able to stagger around the hospital in a thin gown that barely covered his body. Which wasn't a problem because beneath the gown he had as many bandages as the invisible man.

Besides the important stuff, he'd lost a front tooth. The left central incisor had just dropped off one morning , landing onto his tongue before he promptly spit it out into his hand. Luckily the hospital in Haifa had a dental wing, which was in fact part of a graduate school for young dentists. Because he was classified as a military casualty, they got working on him right after the surgeons and doctors were done addressing the more significant items on their list.

The RPG fragments had penetrated deep into his chest, shoulders, and arms, plus the knife wound in his leg had been surprisingly deep. But the real damage had been done by the shock waves from multiple explosions.

The lower part of Keeler's body was screwed up. One of the detonations had blown his sacroiliac joint out of whack, which made it pretty hard to walk. The medical staff treated him as a curiosity. He wasn't supposed to have been able to run or even walk, given the injuries. They had a team of experts who'd come up with explanations, essentially putting it down to shock and the strange way that the body can operate in survival mode.

Of course, Keeler knew better. The Berserker did what it had to do.

There were positive aspects of the hospital stay. First, nobody expected him to do anything and there was a beach view out the window and a flat-screen television with all kinds of international channels. Ruth was in a different hospital, closer to where she lived. She was going to make a full recovery.

Her parents were under the impression that Keeler had saved their daughter's life. Consequently he had frequent visitations, which usually entailed home-cooked lunches and English language books from her father's library. Ruth's dad was some kind of philosopher, the books weren't stories; they were about life and how to live it, or at least that's how Keeler interpreted the complicated arguments.

Because, when you're stuck in a hospital bed for a week and a half, even television gets boring.

Four men and a woman came into Keeler's room about four days into his stay. From their clothing and general demeanor he understood pretty quickly who they were, suits from the embassy in Tel Aviv escorting visitors from the CIA in Langley.

These were people habituated to ergonomic furniture and modern bathrooms. Chairs were brought into his little room so that they could get comfortable in a semicircle around the bed.

Two of them spoke, the other two watched him carefully, as if he were a museum exhibit, or some kind of performance artist. The two who spoke had questions, phrased in calculated language. Keeler didn't hold back much. He told them what he could, only keeping quiet about the chemical weapons issue. Thing was, Keeler wasn't supposed to know anything about that, and he didn't want to get Tina Choi into trouble.

The suits went away satisfied. They said he might even get some kind of medal, depending upon how the brass was feeling. That would wait for when he returned to duty, after another couple of weeks' leave. At that point he didn't even know what day it was, Friday, Wednesday, Saturday, none of it meant much.

Choi hadn't called and he wasn't expecting her to. They'd had a little moment there in the heat of a strange kind of combat. Not that Keeler knew absolutely nothing, he'd received a call from Staff Sergeant Leonard, the Marine Detachment Commander.

The phone line wasn't secure, and Leonard had stuck to publicly available information. But Leonard liked to talk, Keeler had been able to read between the lines. The Acting Chief of Mission, Jim Miller, had died, the exact cause of death as yet undeclared. The embassy had been invaded by a technical spook army from back home.

What Leonard hadn't said and Keeler knew: the spooks were DIA, probably led by Choi. They had quite a job on their hands, ripping up the rotten security protocols and fire-walling the clandestine service's emergency systems.

Once he got his legs back he started being able to stalk the hospital corridors with a frame walker. A couple days later he could do it without the prop. Three days after that he asked Ruth's father for a set of clothes.

Keeler started taking long walks, aimlessly exploring the scrappy neighborhood near the hospital and the beachfront areas to the south. There was a weird concrete oceanography research institute built on massive stilts, jutting out into the water, about a half-hour walk from the hospital. Just behind the building was a juice bar. Keeler liked sitting on the red plastic chairs and enjoying the sunset, sipping on pomegranate and grapefruit juice and thinking about nothing much at all.

One late afternoon, an older guy eased himself into the chair next to him. Joe hadn't changed, still had the steel-gray hair and wire-framed glasses and the pale-blue eyes. He was holding a green drink with a straw.

Keeler said, "What do you have there, Joe?"

Joe looked at the thing in his hand. "Kale, ginger, spinach, and orange."

Keeler said nothing.

Joe cleared his throat. "I'm not going to apologize about military compartmentalization." He grinned. "I have the same problem as everyone else, nobody tells me much, either."

Keeler knew what he was talking about, Fizza Hamieh. And yes, he'd been wondering about that.

He said, "I figured either someone would tell me something or not. I guess you've got something to tell me."

Joe's glasses were the kind that become darker once the level of luminance rises. Now the sun was low on the horizon and hitting directly, and the glasses had turned a shade of orange. He took a long sip of his green drink.

"Halfway between disgusting and amazing. I can't tell." He looked at Keeler. "Okay, for one thing, she's not Hassan Nasrallah's daughter."

"The DNA match was a false positive?"

"No, it was correct. She's related to him, just not likely to be his daughter."

"How do they know?"

"Well, they don't know anything with a hundred percent accuracy because she's unreliable."

"Last I saw she was completely insane."

Joe said, "Not true. She's deeply traumatized by what happened, but she's doing much better now." He sipped again from the green drink. "And by the way. her name is not Fizza Hamieh; she's not Lebanese or Syrian or even an Arab. I don't know her real name, but I do know that she's an Iranian national."

"So what's the connection to Nasrallah?"

Joe slipped his glasses up on to his forehead, looked out to sea, and then lowered the glasses back over his eyes. "Looks like she was Nasrallah's mistress. Which surprised everyone a little because the guy projects nothing but religious piety."

Keeler said, "But he's human like anyone else, big surprise."

Joe shrugged. "It appears that he became involved with her on one of his trips to Tehran."

Keeler said, "Which wouldn't be tourism related."

"Precisely. Nasrallah's visits to Iran would be strictly regulated. He'd be there fundraising, or holding strategic meetings with IRGC people. He wouldn't be hanging around a place like this." Joe waved his hand around to capture the beachside setting.

Keeler said, "Which means he hooked up with someone with connections to the Iranian elite."

"Correct again. It's likely she's part of the upper class." He grinned. "Maybe the daughter or wife of a bigwig. That information is above my pay grade."

Keeler said, "Yeah, but how did his mistress get his DNA?"

"Well, she was pregnant from him." Joe's eyes widened in fascination, looking at Keeler. "We thought she was there for a nose job, right? Wrong."

Out in the sea the sun had touched the water. A man standing on a paddleboard was silhouetted, moving the long oar gracefully.

Keeler said, "So they went all the way to Turkey for an abortion?"

Joe said, "Abortion in Iran carries a ten-year mandatory sentence. Plus, from what I understand, Hamieh, or whatever her name is, wanted to keep the baby and have the paternity officially recognized."

Keeler said, "In other words she wasn't playing ball, and they disappeared her to Ankara."

"Right." Joe said, "For a forced termination of her pregnancy."

"Brutal."

Joe sucked the remainder of his juice through the straw. He said, "One of the central mysteries here is the complicity of the Iranian Revolutionary Guards Corps in this affair. Because, if Nasrallah kidnapped her without informing the Iranians, this could be an excellent wedge to stick between them."

Listening to Joe, it began to make sense to Keeler, the reason the woman had asked him to pledge his help. She'd been a fellow Iranian with the opposition, and working in the safe-house, she'd seen her compatriot in that coercive situation, forced into a secret abortion, far from home. He could understand the emotional ties that would have been built.

Keeler said, "Things don't change, do they? Political expediency trumps principles or values. The girl doesn't play ball so they get rid of the evidence and dump her in Syria as a slave laborer."

"Punishment. She wanted to keep the baby and go public." Joe said. "There is one thing I don't understand."

"What's that?"

"How they drew the DNA from Hamieh if she'd already had the abortion."

Keeler didn't know either.

He said, "So what happens to Fizza Hamieh now?"

Joe said, "Out of sight. She's the joint property of the CIA and our guys. They'll do their best to use her against the Iranians and the Hezbollah. Maybe they'll succeed in getting an official or two executed by the regime. Maybe they'll succeed in recruiting one of them as an asset."

"But the girl will stay in some kind of secure location," Keeler said. "She's not going to the mall to get her nails done anytime soon."

"One of the black sites, for sure."

They sat together in silence for a minute, looking out to the sun as it was devoured by the Mediterranean.

Joe said, "We can also be cruel, you know."

Keeler said, "I know."

"You think we're better than them?"

Keeler said, "Yeah, just about."

Joe nodded. "I guess that has to be just about good enough."

* * *

KEELER LOOKED it up on the internet, lying back in the hospital bed. It was called cell transfer. The fetus's cells cross out of the placenta into the mother's blood stream. Especially if the DNA sample is taken in the late stages of pregnancy. He liked it, the fact that genetic transfer wasn't a simple one-way street.

He heard a knock at the door.

Keeler was expecting Ruth's dad to bring him dinner. It'd become a routine that he looked forward to each day. The door opened, but it wasn't him. A young woman stood in the door. She was carrying the usual containers. He saw her eyes dart to the phone in his hand.

"Am I disturbing you?"

"Not at all."

She was in her early twenties with an impressive frizz of

dirty-blond hair. She sat down near the bed and leaned forward to him, her gaze direct and open. She was pretty with tanned skin and freckles and large green eyes. He couldn't get himself to look away and he got a funny feeling in his belly.

"I'm Hannah." She couldn't stop smiling. "You're the guy who saved my sister's life."

Ruth's sister.

Keeler said, "She was tough and got lucky."

"Yes, I know, but you got her out of there. Shut up and take the credit."

He said, "Sure."

Hannah's eyes were at least a whole shade lighter than Ruth's, the same color but more like green water at the edge of a reef.

She said, "I just got out of the army yesterday. Otherwise, I would have come earlier."

The two-year compulsory military service women did in Israel.

Keeler said, "Out like really out?"

"Finished and I'm gone." Hannah made a hand movement like an airplane swooping low and rising again. Her mouth made a whooshing sound. "Gone like out of there. Gone like, so gone."

"So what's next?"

Hannah hadn't stopped smiling and it wasn't simply a dumb grin; the smile held a challenge, like she was testing him. "You can walk, right?"

"Yeah."

"Are you planning on lying in that bed for the rest of your life?"

She was looking at him, very direct, smiling, a beautiful young woman at the prime of her life. Exactly what he wanted to be looking at.

He said, "No. What's the plan?"

"The plan involves the concept of freedom and personal liberty, but it starts with us going downstairs to the parking lot. We get into my car and we drive to the desert." She lifted the food containers. "I heard you're always hungry, so you can eat on the way." Her smile hadn't diminished. "That's all I've got, in terms of formal planning."

Keeler said, "Outstanding."

He was thinking how wonderful the world was, figuring that it was now his turn to get lucky.

ENJOY THIS BOOK?
YOU CAN MAKE A BIG DIFFERENCE

Reviews are the most powerful tools in my arsenal when it comes getting attention for my books. Much as I'd like to, I don't have the financial muscle of a New York publisher. I can't take out full page ads in the newspaper or put posters on the subway.

But I hope to have something much more powerful and effective than that, and it's something that those publishers would kill to get their hands on.

A committed and loyal bunch of readers.

Honest reviews of my books help bring them to the attention of other readers. If you've enjoyed this book I would be very grateful if you could spend just five minutes leaving a review (it can be as short as you like).

Thank you very much.
Jack Lively

ABOUT THE AUTHOR

Jack Lively was born in Sheffield, in the UK. He grew up in the United States of America. He has worked as a fisherman, an ice cream truck driver, underwater cinematographer, gas station attendant, and outboard engine repairman. The other thing about Jack is that since he grew up without a TV, before the internet, he was always reading. And later on, Jack started writing. All through those long years working odd jobs and traveling around, Jack wrote. He'd write in bars and cafes, on boats and trains and even on long haul bus trips.

Eventually Jack finished a book and figured he might as well see if anyone wanted to read it.

Tom Keeler is a veteran combat medic who served in a special tactics unit of United States Air Force. The series begins when Keeler receives his discharge from the military. Keeler just wants to roam free. But stuff happens, and Keeler's not the kind of guy who just walks away.

Jack Lively lives in London with his family.

Made in United States
Troutdale, OR
09/16/2023

12954775R00219